About the Author

Douglas Blackburn is British. He has lived and worked extensively throughout Europe and the Middle East. During his long career in the British Military, he trained as an Arab linguist. Also fluent in German, he holds an MSc in International Security.

Douglas Blackburn's writing represents a melding of his academic knowledge in International Security, coupled with real-life experiences, living and working amongst a wide variety of foreign cultures. The sequence of events in this, the first book of a series, whilst potentially possible, are, of course, tempered by a thin veil of fiction as well.

Dar Al Salaam

Douglas Blackburn

Dar Al Salaam

Olympia Publishers
London

www.olympiapublishers.com
OLYMPIA PAPERBACK EDITION

A CIP catalogue record for this title is
available from the British Library.

ISBN: 978-1-78830-228-9

This is a work of fiction.
Names, characters, places and incidents originate from the writer's
imagination. Any resemblance to actual persons, living or dead, is purely
coincidental.

First Published in 2019

Olympia Publishers
60 Cannon Street
London
EC4N 6NP

Printed in Great Britain

Dedication

This book is dedicated to my father, Geoff, and to my mother, Elaine.

Acknowledgments

To my wife, Cristina, for her love, patience, advice and encouragement.

Preface

This book tells the story of a diverse group of highly talented people from competing nations who are forced together, through political expediency, to create the core of a newly-formed Institute within the United Nations. This new team will have to quickly learn to put aside their own personal issues and national agendas if they are to stand any chance of averting a near-total collapse of the world order as we know it today.

Between May 2016 and September 2017, a series of orchestrated events unfolded that came close to bringing the global order, as we know it, to its knees. The world's superpowers, including China, Russia, the USA and Europe, were led to the point of all-out war. A malevolent plan began with a stunning series of two daring attacks on strategic oil reserves. As well as delivering a crippling economic blow to these great powers, these daring strategic attacks initiated a chain-reaction of retaliatory counterattacks, culminating in an attempted tactical nuclear strike on the United States of America.

You will be taken on a journey through history, beginning in the middle of the thirteenth century, at the time of the last great Arabic Caliphate, centred in Baghdad. As history unfolds, events that occurred during the Second World War will play a crucial role in helping an Iraqi scientist, working at the University of Baghdad, in her family's centuries old plan to reinstate itself once more as leaders of the Arabic Peoples.

The story will take you across many continents; despite its being a work of fiction, many of the historical points are accurate and all of the technology used is currently being developed around the world. Although no such United Nations Institute exists, I hope that, by the time you finished reading this book, you will agree, that just maybe, it is time that it was considered.

Chapter One

Latitude 53° 54' 5.421'', Longitude -166 ° 31' 40.854''.
Lliukliuk Bay, Amaknak Island, Unalaska – May 2016.
Gone Fishing

The wind cut across the sheet ice and whipped and stung at Matthias's face. Despite having sailed and built boats since he was a little boy, both with his father and with his grandfather before that, he had never before sat in a craft that seemed so unsuited to its task as the one in which he now found himself. The sun appeared, briefly, though a rare gap in the clouds. It was at its zenith, Matthias noticed. It was still several degrees below freezing, and he knew that in less than two hours the faint northern sun would begin to lose its power, and once more transform this barren stretch of Pacific coastline into a dark, freezing, inhospitable place. *What the bloody hell am I doing?* Matthias mumbled to himself, peering back over his shoulder from his seat in the front of the boat, to glance at the giant of a man standing on the sheet ice behind him. The boat, a baidarka, as the locals called it, was unlike anything he had ever seen before. The primitive kayak had taken almost six months to build, an activity which had involved every man and woman in the small Inuit community. The dried and cured sealskins, stretched taut over the wood and bone skeleton of the boat, seemed to glide effortlessly over the ice, as the slim hunting vessel was launched by the giant man standing behind the boat, into the freezing waters of the protected bay.

Philippe, a natural outdoorsman and a close friend of Matthias, looked relaxed in the stern of the boat. His full dark beard, broad back and hands that seemed as big as shovels had been formed through years of tough manual work and life in extreme environments. Using his powerful body to paddle the boat, he smoothly guided it away from the packed ice on the shoreline and into the open bay. He grinned to himself as he glanced forward at his new friend, the professor. Matthias was precariously balanced on the thin wooden rail that served as a seat at the front of the boat. His portly frame and bespectacled face somehow seemed to be out of place in this harsh, near-Arctic environment. Once their paddling began to synchronize and the boat started to glide forward in smooth rhythmic pulses, they both had time to look up and acknowledge the people in the other similarly fragile craft around them.

They knew that this was going to be no ordinary boating trip. For Matthias, the world renowned Danish professor of anthropology, it was a once in a life-time opportunity to participate in a traditional hunt with the Inuit of Unalaska. For Philippe, who was married to Elisapie, an Inuit woman from this very community, it was a rite of passage. Glancing over at the other boats bobbing around them, they could see the two brothers, Tulugaq and Tikaani, to their left, smiling back across at them. Despite being more heavily laden than the other boats the two brothers' boat seemed to be able to move effortlessly across the light swell which was being kicked up by the easterly breeze. In the distance, Taliriktug and Uki could just be seen as they rounded the headland into the open sea. The sun was high in the cloud-filled sky, but the relentless easterly wind maintained a menacing presence, cutting and slashing mercilessly at any exposed areas of skin. As the small flotilla of boats left the harbour, it made an odd sight, juxtaposed as it was with the fleet of monstrous industrial trawlers currently disgorging their cargo into towering row upon row of plastic ice-filled containers. The wind still just carried the faint sound of the forklift trucks, scurrying back and forth, between the huge iron trawlers, groaning and straining at their anchors, to the stark tin-walled edifice which was the fish processing plant. Back in the late eighteenth century, before the Russian fur traders had come to the Islands and 'discovered' the Aleutian Inuit, hundreds of boats, such as the ones that now carried Matthias and Philippe out into the open sea, could have been observed leaving the once pristine shoreline, from the many tens of communities which relied for their livelihood on fishing and hunting, all along the archipelago.

The two-man crews sat hunched against the wind in their long fur parkas and strange wooden hats, peering into the open bay, as their sleek, delicate craft bobbed and weaved their way silently through the waves. The small hunting party had been paddling for almost an hour. Mathias was beginning to reassess the merits of conducting applied field research. In January, when the invitation had first come through to his warm, book-lined office at the University of Copenhagen, the idea had sounded like a good one. Right now however, he thought, *What the hell possessed me?* With the wind and salt water slashing viciously at his burnt and chapped face, he was straining every fibre of his being, in a vain attempt to maintain pace with Philippe's unwavering deep paddle strokes.

Suddenly, from the front of the lead boat, Uki, the hunting party's leader, stopped paddling and began to wave his short, blade-like paddle in the air. The two scouts had spotted a large family group of walrus swimming together near a kelp bed.

Philippe whispered to Matthias, "Look, my old friend. It's started. The hunt is on." Unable to speak, Matthias nodded vigorously, and thought that his heart was going to burst out of his chest with the effort, as they both picked up the pace and tried to steer the boat into its blocking position.

Matthias replied with a grunt, "Yes! At last it's happening. Let's hope we both survive, so that I can tell my students all about it."

The trio of fragile boats had now fully encircled the walrus herd, and it was Tikaani who was preparing his harpoon and the bladder-like float that would be used for the kill. His brother tapped him on his left shoulder, and silently indicated their target with a subtle head gesture. The old cow was on the outside of the group with another younger cow and her calf. Matthias and Philippe were now only a few yards away from the group. Matthias noted how the other boats had formed an open box shape around the Walrus, which gave the animals only one opportunity to escape through the open side. Tikaani was ready, harpoon in hand; his powerful frame was coiled tightly, like a baseball pitcher ready to hurl the ball, the harpoon held high above his head, ready to stab and strike the animal as it swam past.

At that moment, Matthias' boat was caught by a strong swell and perched precariously as he was on the thin wooden strut; he started to lose his balance. He feverishly slapped the water with his paddle to try to remain upright. The sound and energy waves from his panicked paddle slaps pulsed through the water, shocking the senses of the grazing walrus, and spreading fear and panic throughout the family group. The large bull, recognizing the need to protect his group, charged the nearest baidarka, which held the two foreigners. As the giant creature struck the delicate kayak, the thin boat, made from bone and seal skin, was driven high into the air, before crashing down on to frothy, heaving water. By now, the boat was listing precariously on its side, "Paddle, man, paddle!" screamed Philippe. Unable to gain any purchase on the foamy water with his paddle, Matthias tumbled from the boat into the icy water. Matthias's attempt to scream as he hit the ice cold water was immediately cut short, as the air was viciously sucked out of his lungs, seeming to draw the very life force out of him, as the cold frothing water began to engulf him. Noticing the two Westerners in danger, Taliriktug and Uki deftly turned their sleek long boat, and paddled quickly to the rescue.

Meanwhile, Tikaani had speared the cow, and after a brave fight, despite her efforts, the old cow could not drag the float that was attached to the harpoon under the water. The harpoon had dug deep into the animal. Tikaani tugged at the spear, and it twisted, ripping deeper into the flesh and embedding itself further into the animal's back. In a well-practiced and rehearsed manner, his brother, Tulugaq began to paddle the boat backwards, whilst Tikaani secured the harpoon rope to the bow of the boat.

The female had been selected by the Inuit hunting party because she was old. Sensing that she had only minutes to live – the deep cut was draining her of blood and oxygen – she tried one more dive, but by now she was too weak, and, although the float briefly disappeared under the surface, it quickly bounced back up to the surface, with the now still and lifeless body of the female walrus firmly attached to it. Tulugaq looked to his brother, Tikaani, and they both whispered a prayer for the female walrus as they secured her to the side of the boat.

"Hold on to the boat, Matthias," shouted Philippe.

"It's cold, I can't breathe," spluttered Matthias, as his numb hands began to lose their grip on the side of the boat. Just then, Taliriktug and Uki pushed their boat up beside the other boat trapping the professor between the two craft.

"Grab my paddle," shouted Uki, placing it along the rails of both boats; as he did so, both Philippe and Uki grabbed the professor's fur skin parka, and hauled him out of the water and back into his boat.

The house, half built into the side of the bluff, had a timber frame and sods of earth on its sloping roof. It was small, dry and very cosy. Towards the back, close to the granite wall of the cliff face, that served as the main supporting wall for the building, stood a fireplace. It was essentially a large pocket that had been hewn out of the granite wall; a chimney had been fashioned using a dry stone wall technique, and it rose up the granite wall until it disappeared between the wooden beams and sods of earth which formed the house's roof. Looking up at the disappearing chimney, Matthias was fascinated by how they had managed to create a weather-proof seal between the granite cliff wall and the timber frame. It was his nose, rather than his eyes, which drew his attention back down the chimney breast, to focus on the huge metal tripod under which hung a heavy iron cauldron. A rich meaty stew was steaming inside the cauldron. Stirring the blackened cooking pot stood, Tapeesa, the Inuit wife of the man who only two hours earlier, balanced precariously in a fragile canoe, had thrust a wooden and bone harpoon into the flesh of a walrus weighing nearly a thousand pounds.

With a scowl, Tapeesa interrupted her stirring, and turned to her husband, Tikaani. "What were you doing taking the professor out in the baidarka in this weather?"

"He's a grown man; he is big enough to make his own decisions, and you know how long he has been pestering us to go out in the boats," answered Tikaani, handing Matthias some spare clothes and a hot bowl of stew.

Still a little hoarse from his involuntary immersion in the chilling waters of the North Pacific, Matthias murmured in his lilting Danish accent, "You know, when that bull charged our boat, I thought that I would drown."

Philippe, who was sitting by the fire, looked up from his steaming bowl of meaty broth. "I guess you need a little more practice, old man."

"I'll have you know that I'm a perfectly capable seaman. I won best in my class in the Helsingborg to Kobenhavn yacht Regatta," retorted Matthias, indignantly.

"I bet," interrupted Tikaani, "Tell me, how many deranged bull walruses did you have to sail past in that race?"

The group laughed heartily, and Philippe raised his glass in a toast. "Here's to many more years of hunting."

Nodding and smiling, Matthias raised his glass, and said to Philippe, "Let's hope the electricity project works."

Tapeesa looked at her husband and said, "*Dux suxtasaq?*"

"No," he replied. "Not *wind* power, but *suxtasaq miduq.*"

She raised a quizzical eyebrow at the assembled group, reiterating, this time in English, "Energy from the air!"

Philippe stood; as he did so, his head nearly touched the pine beams supporting the roof of the house. "Yes," he explained, "there is a team at the professor's university in Copenhagen who have developed a way of filtering the charged ion particles in the air to remove the static electricity. This is then stored in large capacitors until it is needed."

Tapeesa still looked puzzled. Tikaani turned to her and said, "It is fishing for electricity. With this technology, we can not only continue to live here, but also you can have enough power to use a computer and telephone here in our house. It means you can Skype our daughters in Anchorage whenever you like, without needing to go all the way into town. Maybe *they* will be the generation that decide to return to us and help keep our traditions and customs alive."

After the meal, Philippe stood up. "My friends, I fear I must go; my wife, Elisapie, will wonder whatever happened to me, and I only have three more days before I fly back to Quebec, to the oil fields."

"I thought you had given that up," said Matthias.

"I take early retirement this October. Then I will be back here for good, and Elisapie and I can start building our own Aleut Inuit house. Maybe we will even be neighbours, Tikaani," he said, with a huge grin on his face.

"Hey!" cried Tikaani, "if you do come to live here, you'd better not speak any of that Quebec French. It's Unangax or, at a push, English only here!"

Philippe was still laughing as he trudged down the path to his jeep. Matthias, who, as usual, had drunk a little more than his share of the red wine, made to stand as well. "I suppose I should go as well. Although, I can't wait to try some of Taliriktug and Uki's cured walrus meat, the next time I visit."

With a slight grin beginning to play at the corner of her mouth, Tapeesa placed one hand on Matthias's arm. "Not so fast, professor. We have a little memento for you to show your students." Tikaani emerged from the gloom of the rear of the house, holding a long, pointy wooden hat. It was a *qayaatx ux*, an Aleutian hunting hat only bestowed upon the bravest hunters or village chiefs. Trembling slightly, Matthias accepted the hat from his friends, and, with a trace of a tear in his eye, he held it to the light of the fire, taking in the elegant craftsmanship. The hat was decorated with bright wave-like patterns, which appeared to swirl around its base and reach, tentacle-like, towards its pointed tip. It was crowned with long dark walrus whiskers. He knew with certainty that the hat had once belonged to Tapeesa's father, and maybe even to his father before him, and that it meant a lot to them.

Nodding reverently to his hosts in acknowledgement, he turned, wiped a tear from his eye, and said, "That is so kind, I really don't know how to thank you."

"Professor," Taliriktug said, "you have already done so much for the future of our community and way of life. This is a small token of our thanks." Mathias was smiling as he left the house; setting the hat on his head, he began softly whistling to himself, as he headed on down the path to his car.

Chapter Two

Latitude 40° 44' 54.8658'', Longitude -73° 58' 4.674''.
760 United Nations Plaza, Manhattan Island, New York –
January 2017.
Eternal Compromise

Guilherme Oliveira was sixty years old. A tall, handsome man, with a well-groomed beard, and large bushy eyebrows, he was acutely aware that he had not been selected as the Secretary-General of the United Nations by the Council of the Permanent Five because he was the most experienced diplomat on the shortlist, and certainly not even because his country was seen as one of the new world emerging powerhouses. As long as Guilherme could remember, his country had been cited as the 'next big thing'; it was known as a nation with a bright future, and to be on the cusp of achieving its potential.

Smiling cynically to himself, as he looked out his office window across the Manhattan skyline, he muttered to himself, *"Ordem e Progresso."* These words that were written on his country's flag pretty much summed up his own frustration. With order, progress would come, he knew. The problem was, how the hell was a country like Brazil, which had only experienced thirty years of real democracy since the harsh military Junta had collapsed, going to achieve order? Whatever the political parties proclaimed, he knew that his country had gone from being run by a cruel and inept dictatorship, to one which was controlled by huge multinational corporations and corrupt bureaucrats and politicians. No, Guilherme knew very well that his nomination for the top job at the UN was because of the fact that he was seen as a safe and neutral nominee. Unless mandated to do so by the UN, Brazil interfered very little in the foreign affairs of other nation states. It was located far enough away from the US and China not to be perceived as a threat or particular ally to either, and it carried none of the historic colonial baggage that most European nations had.

As he descended in the elevator down to one of the more discreet meeting rooms in the UN Headquarters building, he thought about the people he was going to be addressing today. His audience comprised of a representative of each of the Permanent Five members of the UN Security Council, as well as representatives from the World Health Organisation (WHO), World Bank and Interpol. They stood as he entered and he smiled whilst taking his time to greet them all individually. He was good with names. In fact, it was his remarkable memory and ability to never forget a face that had allowed him to rise so quickly through the ranks of the Brazilian Diplomatic Corps or *Itamaraty*, as it was known inside Brazil.

"Ladies and Gentlemen," he said, in his rich, earthy baritone voice. "The P5 members know why we are assembled today, and knowing, as I do, how difficult it is to keep anything secret in this building, I am sure that our colleagues from the WHO, World Bank and Interpol also, by now, have a fair idea about this meeting's agenda." A hushed chuckle rippled around the room.

OK, I've broken the ice, Guilherme thought, now it's time to deliver the news.

It had taken Guilherme weeks of wrangling and negotiating to get these people sitting around this table for this meeting. As with all things the UN did, it had been a compromise. *Everything has a price*, Guilherme thought to himself, as he shuffled his notes. "Dear colleagues and friends, today I announce the inauguration of a new UN affiliated body." He scanned the room for reactions as he spoke. Chuck Henderson, the US ambassador was glancing absent-mindedly at his watch, probably wondering when the meeting would end, so that he could get on with dealing with some of the more pressing 'real world' issues. Yes, thought Guilherme, those had been his exact words when he had first spoken with the ambassador about setting up the new agency.

After an intensive period of lobbying and bargaining, Guilherme knew that he already had everyone's agreement in principle, even if he didn't have their full support. So, the Secretary-General of the UN started to speak.

"The nation state system, despite first having been conceived of at the Treaty of Westphalia in 1648, was only truly policed and properly enforced after the tremendous destruction and carnage of World Wars One and Two, in an attempt to reorder and restructure the world following the dismemberment of various European and Asian Imperial orders. It was a way of establishing a new unit of 'currency', an identifiable entity, with discrete borders and a functioning government. Its intention was to allow for greater political control for each member country, without any country being subject to external interference by other nation states or external actors.

This organisation, the United Nations, which I now have the privilege to head, was established as a greater World Council, where each member state could be represented and have an equal voice. Ladies and gentlemen, I contend that in our haste to develop a system that would prevent future world wars, this system was established too quickly. As old Empires crumbled and dissolved, defined borders delineating new states were, in some cases, hurriedly drawn on maps after World War One and Two, and no consideration was given to the cultural identity of the populations living within the borders of these states."

He noticed that the French and British Ambassadors had both raised more than an eyebrow at his mention of how their governments, in particular, had been responsible for carving up large swathes of Africa and Asia by the end of World War Two.

Now comes the difficult part, he thought. How do I tell them that they are a bunch of dysfunctional neo-imperialists whilst securing their agreement to fund and support this new agency, that would, on the surface, at least, seem to act against their own national interests?

"This system has succeeded in preventing the world from spiralling into another world war. However, in a more important way, it is failing! Instead of great wars between nations, conflict has shifted to dozens of smaller wars within nation states. Since 1945, depending on your interpretation of the definition, there have been over eighty-two civil wars or cases of intrastate conflict, with at least seventeen conflicts currently on-going. But even this statistic does not fully explain the problems we are facing today, with a system whereby members of a religious sect or ethnic group or caste have merely taken over the role of the old imperial masters and continued to subjugate members of their own state; and whereby they continue to disproportionately apportion the state's wealth and resources to their own kin. Indeed! This very organisation, the UN, which was established to protect these people, has become its own nemesis. I would remind you all of our overarching commandment here at the UN: 'Non-intervention in the affairs of a sovereign nation state.'"

Now that he had their attention, it was time to soften the rhetoric a little, and engage the other members from the WHO, World Bank and Interpol who were sitting around the table.

"Dr Kim," Guilherme said, looking for support over to the older Korean, the Head of the World Bank. "What figures does the World Bank have to quantify the negative effect of the Arab Spring on the World economy?"

"Well," began Kim, in his soft voice. "In terms of industrial output, we calculate a global decrease of around fifteen per cent; most of this is due to uncertainty in the markets."

"OK," said Guilherme. "Any other effects?"

"Well," Kim continued. "Of course, you have to factor in the additional costs of security relating to all of the refugees, social and welfare payments made by other governments, not to mention the increased burden on the health systems of the mainly EU member States."

Helen Woo, Head of the WHO, raised a hand, and Kim stopped speaking to allow his old colleague and protégé to speak. She said, "You know, Kim is only speaking about the economic cost of this instability. At the WHO we have been overwhelmed with requests for support in combatting serious outbreaks of diseases that have long been eradicated in Europe, but which have been brought back into the EU with the influx of refugees. The EU health systems do not have the knowledge, capacity or experience to mount a coordinated campaign to prevent these diseases from spreading."

"Thank you, Helen," said Guilherme. "You know, this problem does not limit itself to what we like to term the developing world. This problem, with the current nation-state structure, exists in the developed world too. The most recent member of the UN was South Sudan, born out of bitter war and rivalry with the North. The Balkans remain fractured after the conflict that ripped apart Yugoslavia. Both Iraq and Libya have effectively been split into three political entities through internal conflict. Ukraine remains divided and is still volatile since the Russian-sponsored war. Spain, Britain, Belgium, France, Italy, Russia and China all have elements and regions within their current borders who are pushing for devolution through political means."

Stijn Mertens, the Belgian-born head of Interpol, interjected. "Mr Secretary-General, are you not painting a rather bleak picture? Interpol monitors all of these groups, and we have come a long way since the Chechen wars, the heyday of the IRA or the bombings and executions of ETA in Spain."

"Maybe you are right, Stijn," replied Guilherme. "But if history teaches us anything, it is that whenever we try to resolve one issue, we create the conditions for a new one. Looking around the room, Guilherme realised that he wasn't going to convince the representatives of the world's most powerful countries and international organisations that their view of the world was flawed; however, he did sense that, because everyone represented had a stake in trying to resolve wars within their own national borders, he would be able to seal the deal, and gain their tacit support for the new agency.

"So, down to business; I hereby announce the formation of the United Nations Centre for Technology and Culture, the CTC for short. This agency, which begins its preparatory organisation and training phase next month has the following mission statement." Guilherme clicked the mouse, and the screen was filled with a simple statement outlining the purpose of the new organisation. *"To develop stable conditions for coexistence and development between different cultures, and to support the development of autonomous regions not subservient to a nation state through the supply and use of pertinent technologies."* Not sure whether the lack of reaction from the assembled group was a sign of their indifference or their apathy, Guilherme pressed on.

"And, of course, every organisation needs a leader. I am proud to introduce Mr Li Qiang Wu." Subdued applause stuttered, rather than rippled, around the room. Most notably, observed the UN Chief, the Russian and US ambassadors were not clapping. Guilherme knew that both men had voiced strong opposition to having a Chinese head of this new organisation. It had taken some considerable time, patience and much convincing to persuade the two ambassadors to support the new agency. The Americans had been given the nominee for Head of Operations, effectively the CTC's second-in-command, and the Russians had been happy to be able to nominate their man for the lead agent position. Effectively, this meant that both countries would have their 'own' people high up in the CTC, and that they would receive full disclosure of any future operations undertaken by the organisation.

Li Qiang Wu was a pencil-thin man with stooped shoulders; he was unusually tall for a Han Chinese and spoke in clipped but fluent English. His years of study on his Chinese government sponsored Ph.D. programme at Cambridge University had allowed him to develop a very cultured English accent. Li rose to the stuttering applause and took in the assembled group. His face betrayed no emotion. He knew very well how much opposition there had been to his appointment. Standing erect and proud, he affected a humble tone. "I am most honoured to have been given the opportunity to lead this prestigious organisation. It is encouraging for an Asian nation to be given such responsibility and reflects the changing geopolitical focus in today's world."

Guilherme winced inwardly at these words; he knew that Li would use the opportunity to stick it to the Americans, but thought that he could have been subtler about it. As the meeting drew to a close, and Guilherme was saying farewell to the attendees, Sir Richard Belmarsh, the British Ambassador, squeezed Guilherme's hand tightly and whispered, "You do know what happened the last time an Asian had the opportunity to exercise some power? His name was Genghis Khan, and he conquered most of the known world and subjugated many of its peoples!"

Guilherme raised one of his bushy eyebrows, as he tried to extricate his hand from the Ambassador's firm grip. He whispered in reply, "I am aware, Sir Richard. Are you aware that today one in two hundred men are directly related to him? Have you checked your family tree recently?" Guilherme asked, with a wry smile.

Chapter Three

Latitude 40° 44' 54.8658'', Longitude -73° 58' 4.674''.
760 United Nations Plaza, Manhattan Island, New York
January 2017.
The American

As the meeting's attendees left the room, and began filtering back along the labyrinthine corridors to their respective offices, Guilherme turned to look at Li, and, with some resignation in his deep voice said, "Do you think they are on board?"

Li nodded sagely. With his head cocked to one side, and a wry smile, he replied, "I think we have their support for now, if only because they too see the problems the world is facing. The problem is that they are still clinging to the opinion that their system may still be capable of dealing with the challenges we face."

Li continued, addressing the UN Secretary-General. "You know, an old school master of mine in Beijing used to have a Confucian quotation hanging over the chalkboard. 'If we don't change the direction we are going, we are likely to end up where we are heading.' I believe that we have the support of the P5 and the WHO, Interpol and the World Bank, because, between them, they possess sufficient doubt about their capability to change the direction the world is heading in."

"You know," said Guilherme, a grim smile on his face. "I hope you are right. So, what do you need to get the Centre up and running?"

"Only your permission to contact the key team members and formally invite them to join us. After that, I will relocate the key personnel and support staff to the Headquarters in Singapore, and begin our capability development programme."

Guilherme nodded, as he bent over the table to collect his speech notes. "How is the work going on the Technology Transfer Centres?" Li held the door to the office open for Guilherme as they both left.

"It's pretty much on track; I have personally been supervising the local contractors." It had come to Guilherme's attention that although Li was using local labourers, he had appointed Chinese project managers from Beijing to manage each build. He hadn't said anything to Li about this but had surmised that this meant that the Chinese government would already have the blueprints and specifications of each of the Centres. Li continued talking. "The Centres in Windhoek and Muscat are complete, and the first staff have already moved in to set up the IT systems.

"The Namibians seemed particularly keen to get the project going and producing some results. No problems at the site in Girona. The local council was a little concerned that a shiny new centre might detract from the appeal of one of Europe's most resplendent medieval towns, but we have managed to convert an old farm estate about five kilometres outside the old city in Sant Gregori. Apart from a secure gated access to the site, no obvious exterior differences can be seen.

"We hit a couple of problems in Canada, at the site in Gander. We had to stop work for a couple of months, because of the high snowfall; however, the men are back on site now, and the project manager informs me that they are only four weeks off schedule, as they took the time during the snow to install all of the laboratory equipment and server rooms." Guilherme could hear the barely perceptible pride in Li's voice as he spoke about the professionalism of the Chinese project managers.

"And what about Sao Paulo?" Guilherme asked, resignedly.

"Actually, good news there too. It seems that your phone call to your old university friend, the Mayor, helped. They have allowed us to build an adjunct facility at the University of Sao Paulo. They have given us some room between the Applied Physics labs and the Nuclear Energy Research Centre. It also means that we will be able to collaborate and use some of their existing infrastructure."

"Excellent," Guilherme replied, as they reached his office door. "I trust I can leave you to deal personally with coaxing the final appointees into accepting our offer of employment?" Guilherme knew how Li had felt about not being able to make his own selection of personnel to fill the top posts at the CTC, Guilherme looked Li in the eyes and said, "You do know how everyone around that meeting table felt today about your being appointed as the Head of CTC? The only way we have managed to get this thing up and running in the first place was through compromise. Every member state represented in that room wanted their pound of flesh, or to be more accurate their own personnel to be working in the Centre.

"Your biggest job, initially, will be to get a group of people, some of whom don't have the specific skill set, and have no great desire to be there in the first place, to work together as an effective team. I just want you to know that you have my full backing in this endeavor." Li thanked the United Nations Secretary-General and turned to walk away; as he did so, he instinctively reached for his cigarettes. Li had starting smoking at fourteen, and, in China, Li had only ever had the opportunity to smoke counterfeit Marlborough cigarettes; however, here in New York, he had access to the original cigarettes, and, right now, it was just what he needed. He would return to his office, open the window, and draw heavily on the 'real taste of America'. He didn't know what it was about smoking that he liked so much; it might have been the nicotine hit that cleared his tired brain and allowed him to think more clearly; or was it being able to watch the cigarette slowly burning and to see the smoke drift upwards in mesmerizing spirals that allowed him to lapse into that daydream-like state where most of his most profound thinking was done?

An hour later, he had sent the last of the six emails, and had called his secretary to book the flight tickets. Tomorrow was going to be the start of a long series of flights and meetings, as he made his way around the world on his recruitment campaign. He had a midday flight booked with Delta airlines to Quebec City, leaving JFK at two in the afternoon on Monday. He would meet with the American agent, Maria, tomorrow morning, before taking the train up to Boston to the MIT campus to meet up with the Indian girl. If it all went smoothly, he would be back in New

York by ten p.m. and be able to get a good night's sleep before heading off on his global journey of persuasion.

Dressed in an immaculate pin-striped suit, Li stood up from behind his desk as Special Officer Maria Reyes and her boss, Inspector Dylan Flaherty of the US Secret Service were escorted into his office by the uniformed security guard. "Maria, Inspector Flaherty, thanks for coming up to New York to see me, especially on a Sunday morning."

Maria turned to her boss before taking Li's proffered hand, and, with a slight roll of her eyes, she muttered, "Did I have a choice?"

"Would you like some tea?" asked Li. Maria had already noticed the very old-looking steaming Chinese pot of tea and tea cups that were sitting on Li's desk.

"I'm more of a coffee person," she replied curtly. "Black, no sugar and as strong as you got it."

A little ruffled, Li affected a polite smile, and buzzed for his secretary to bring in some American coffee, as he poured tea for himself and the Inspector.

Maria was wearing her standard Secret Service trouser suit, with the jacket cut just tight enough to reveal the slender shape of her long neck and tight waist, whilst still being able to discretely hide her shoulder holster, containing the Glock 9 mm issued pistol. Before he began to talk, Li examined her at length, she was attractive for a *laowai*, or foreigner. Of course, for Li's taste she was far too tall and she had bigger shoulders than Li himself. He knew that she was a widower, and that her husband had only recently been killed on a joint Russian/American counter-narcotics operation in Florida; he also knew that she was a very good secret service agent indeed, with a commendation for bravery whilst protecting the US Secretary of State during a working trip to Indonesia.

"So, Maria, tell me a little about yourself."

Maria stared Li directly in the eyes and, in an openly hostile tone, said, "I'm tired, I just pulled a thirty-six-hour straight detail, and, thanks to this meeting, I have missed my regular slot at the rifle target range."

Inspector Flaherty gave Maria a sideways glance, and a slight smirk flashed across his lips. He then turned to address Li. "Sir, if I may be so bold, I would like to state for the record that I was against Maria's being given this post. She is an excellent agent, and our Chief Staff Psychologist at the James J Rowley Centre said that her ability to read the micro-facial expressions of suspected targets is nothing short of genius. In short, sir, the Secret Service is losing a good agent; but, as the call was made by the President himself, there is darned little I can do about it."

Li watched with some pleasure as Flaherty – unlike Li, who was composure personified – fought to contain his famous Irish temper. These Laowai, he thought. They understand nothing about keeping face.

Pouring himself another cup of steaming Jasmine tea, Li rose from his chair and came around to sit on the edge of his desk. He didn't want to start off on the wrong foot with Maria, but he also knew that both Maria and her Irish boss knew that they were cornered and had no choice but to accept the offer to join the CTC.

"Thank you, Inspector, for your candid words. I understand there is very little that either of us can do about Maria's selection.

Maria, have you had time to read through the contract proposal and the terms of service? You will of course be on probation for the first six months, as all members of staff will be. If you decide to stay with the CTC after that point, you will no longer have the opportunity to return to the US Secret Service. Is that clear?"

"Crystal clear, sir," Maria replied.

"Well," said Li, straightening himself up to his full height and once more proffering his hand, first to the Inspector then to Maria. "If you are in agreement, please stop by my secretary outside and sign the relevant paperwork, and I will see you in Singapore in one month's time."

As they left the office Li went to the open window, as he drew in sharply on his Marlborough and sighed. Why couldn't the member states that had insisted on having their people in the top appointments at the CTC have selected people for the job who had relevant skill sets? The way things looked at the moment, the CTC would eventually look like an international spy agency. Oh well, he thought, at least he had a nomination for each of the top posts. Inhaling deeply once more on his Marlborough cigarette, he thought: one down, one to go; not a bad start to a day's fishing.

Chapter Four

Latitude 42° 21' 25.3584'', Longitude -71° 5' 34.296''.
Massachusetts Institute of Technology, Boston, United
States - January 2017.
The Indian

It was raining heavily as Li alighted from the large white Boston cab with its distinctive green flash across the rear door and side panel. The train had taken a little over four hours. Of course, he could have flown in less than half the time, but Li enjoyed train travel; it reminded him of the many journeys he had taken with his father across his native China. The gentle rhythmic motion of the train helped him to think, although the principal advantage of travelling by train over flying was that, if you were careful, you could get away with smoking on a train; you certainly couldn't do that on an airplane. The meeting with Dr Charu Usmani, Ph.D., was to be held in Pat Lowenstein's office. Pat had a ground floor office and the nameplate on her door described her as Professor of Astronautics and Engineering Systems. Li wasn't quite sure exactly what Astronautics was, and certainly couldn't begin to imagine what type of person would become a Professor of Astronautics.

Li knew he had to tread carefully in this meeting. The Indian government had put a lot of pressure on Guilherme to have Charu involved in the project, mainly as a sign of their annoyance at the selection of a Chinese head of the CTC. Connected by the ancient Silk Road, and with both countries being amongst the most ancient civilizations in the world, India and China shared a long and uneasy history.

India had lost the month-long Sino-Indian war of 1962, and with this defeat came the loss of a large section of the Himalayas. During the brief conflict nearly fourteen hundred Indians and over seven hundred Chinese were killed. The root of the war was the predictable colonial interference that had been, and still is, the cause of many border disputes today. It was called the McMahon Line of 1914, named after Sir Henry McMahon. It separated India, then Britain's possession, and Tibet. After the Chinese annexation of Tibet, this line, drawn on a map by an Englishman, had become the *de facto* border between China and India.

Of course, Charu had had nothing to do with the conflict, or with the on-going Maoist insurgency affecting a lot of northern India, but Li knew that she would have been taught all about India's aggressive northern neighbour in her school history lessons, and, without doubt, this would have coloured how Charu now viewed China.

Opening the door to receive Li stood a kindly-looking woman, around fifty years of age, wearing a cream blouse and chequered patterned skirt, with intelligent-looking emerald green eyes. She greeted Li with a smile and a nod and welcomed him into her office. Behind Professor Pat Lowenstein, Li could see Dr Charu Usmani sitting awkwardly on a low brown stool, cradling a large mug of steaming tea. Neither woman appeared to Li as he had imagined them. Dr Usmani was young and beautiful; her high cheekbones were framed by long straight jet-black hair, which reached almost to the floor. But it wasn't her hair or her peculiar clothes – a large baggy cashmere cardigan, tied tightly over a simple white T-shirt and jeans – it was her deep black eyes. They were like two deep pools of dark water, reflecting her innermost thoughts. Li could read pain and fear in those eyes, and it was obvious that she had recently been crying from the swollen red skin that lay in puffy circles around her deep black eyes.

Charu eyed Li cautiously, looking up at him as she took another sip of her steaming hot tea. She didn't stand, just sat hunched on the stool, hugging the mug of tea. "Mr Wu," began Pat Lowenstein, "welcome, and thank you for coming all the way up to a very cold and rainy Boston to see Charu." She sat on her chair, and beckoned for Li to sit on the only free chair in the room whilst pouring him some tea. "I know," Pat continued. "That Charu was meant to come down to Washington, but with the invitation coming so soon after the, err, incident, we really thought it would be better for all concerned if the meeting were held here."

"Thank you, Dr Lowenstein, please call me Li," he said, sipping on his tea. Hmm, herbal he thought, definitely Indian; he could smell traces of cardamom and liquorice and, if he wasn't mistaken, just a hint of pepper. Although he wouldn't ever admit it, the Indians certainly made very fine tea indeed, but, more importantly, they appreciated how and when to drink tea. Unlike their former colonial masters, the British, who drank gallons of the same insipid black tea all day every day. To add insult to injury, they insisted on ruining any hint of fragrance by adding cold milk to the delicate leaves.

Before he could speak again, Charu rose from her chair and went to stand by the rain-soaked window. "This Centre of yours, Mr Wu, what is it for, and why do you need me?"

When she spoke, her voice was quiet and polite, yet seemed somehow detached and distant. "It's not my centre, rather it's a UN centre," he began. He had read Charu's file and had already prepared an answer to this question; he knew that she was an intensely intelligent person with a strong empathetic nature, and would need to be convinced of the purpose behind the centre before committing herself. Cautiously, glancing over at Pat, as if to seek permission, Li continued. "The aim is to try and create greater harmony or peace amongst the different cultures that act as natural divisions in our planet. I believe it is called *Shanti* in Sanskrit?" Li knew that, as well as being amongst the top few people in the world in the exciting new scientific field of Complex Systems Modelling, Charu was also very well read in Indian logic or *tarka*, as it was known in Sanskrit. Indian logic, which superseded all other forms of logical thought, was closely connected to the different, yet linked, Indian schools of philosophy.

"Will it stop people from being attacked and raped just because they have a different skin colour?" Charu almost spat the words at Li; the visceral hatred in her voice echoed off the walls of the small office. As soon as the words had left her mouth, Charu shrank back towards the windowpane and continued to gaze blankly out of the window into the windy, rain-soaked park area below.

Li, a little shaken by Charu's response, suddenly felt like an intruder in the small cluttered office. He toyed nervously with the rim of the tea mug, whilst trying to find the right words to reply. Eventually, in a resigned and quiet tone, he said, "In time, my hope is that our work may be able to break down some of the barriers that lead to acts of ignorance between different cultures."

Charu returned to her seat, and, placing the cup that she had been nursing on the edge of Pat Lowenstein's desk, she looked searchingly into Li's eyes, and said, "I am ready. I will sign the contract, and if I can help just one woman or child to forego the crime that was enacted upon me, then my efforts and energy will have been justified."

As the train rhythmically rocked its way back to New York, Li reflected on the meeting. He felt a great deal of sympathy for Charu, but also, knowing that she would be an integral part of his command group, he made a mental note to key a close eye on her performance when the team started work in Singapore. He was alone in the travelling compartment, and, although it was technically against the railway rules, he slid down the window and withdrew a crumpled packet of Marlborough cigarettes; as he withdrew the cigarette he made a mental note to himself to buy some more from the vendor outside Central Station. He had a long series of overseas travels ahead of him and was unsure whether he could buy these cigarettes in Canada, Denmark or Russia.

Chapter Five

Latitude 46° 51' 41.6016'', Longitude -71° 11' 19.2366''.
Beauport, Quebec City, Canada - January 2017.
The French Canadian

As the midday Delta airlines flight left JFK and started to reach cruising altitude, and the fasten seatbelts sign had been turned off, Li knew that they barely had twenty minutes before the airplane would begin its arcing descent into Jean Lesage International Airport. The airport was quite large, as regional airports go, but with a capacity to handle only 1.4 million passengers it was dwarfed by airports such as JFK in New York, which dealt with nearly fifty million passengers per year.

Li was determined to put the twenty minutes he had before landing to good use. Withdrawing Philippe Gagnon's file from his carry-on bag, he settled back in his business-class seat and began to read the file. In Li's mind, Philippe was one of the most interesting characters. Philippe had been born in Eastern Canada, where he had spent his spare time fishing and hunting in nearby Alaska. It was on one of these trips that he had met his wife Elisapie. Li noted that she was three-quarters Aleutian Inuit, and that despite Philippe's working in the oil fields of Quebec, Elisapie had already begun the planned relocation with their two sons to a small settlement called Unalaska, on one of the Aleutian

Islands. There was a note on the page explaining that what was left of the once wide-ranging Aleutian Inuit community were now concentrated around the Unalaska area.

Philippe himself was an enigma. A great outdoorsman, with hunting and fishing skills, but with an undergraduate degree in petroleum engineering and a master's degree in robotics. Li was building a picture of Philippe as a very capable and adaptable person. He had obviously recognized that the oil industry was changing and that new robotic technologies for the exploration of oil were emerging. Instead of being resigned to his fate, he had gone back to college, aged forty, and had put himself through a master's programme. This was a tough enough proposition on its own, but to achieve all this whilst holding down a full time job and with a wife and two young children spoke volumes, Li thought, for the man's persistence and innate intellectual ability.

Thirty-five minutes after touch down, Li was in a taxi pulling up outside number 216 Rue Charles Bernier. It was a large, mainly wooden construction, with a pleasant front lawn that swept down to the pavement and a long drive that wound round to the back of the house, where a large round swimming pool and barbeque area sat nestled in front of a neatly trimmed lawn.

Li had barely had time to clear the last step up to the house when the door was flung open, and he was met by a small woman with bright sparkling blue eyes and tightly plaited long black hair. "Mrs Gagnon," Li spluttered.

"Oh, call me Elisapie!" she said, as she stepped backwards in to the house to allow Li to enter. Li entered the house and was immediately struck by the warmth that it exuded. The walls in the hallway were covered in large, neatly-woven tapestries depicting Inuit life.

As Li entered the lounge, and saw Philippe standing next to Elisapie, he was immediately struck by the almost comical difference in size. It wasn't just that Elisapie was small, Philippe was a bear of a man. He towered above Li, as he took his hand to welcome him. "Welcome, Mr Wu, we have been expecting you; how was the flight?" The French accent was very distinct in Philippe's voice, and the cultured way in which he spoke seemed an odd juxtaposition to his physical presence.

"The flight was fine, thank you," Li said, already feeling slightly uncomfortable and beginning to fidget with the cigarette-packet-shaped bulge in his suit trouser pocket. "May we discuss this business outside, Philippe?"

Philippe glanced at Li's trouser pocket, and back up to Li's face. "We may talk in my study if you wish."

Subconsciously moving his hand, which had been squeezing the cigarette packet in his pocket, Li tried not to show his frustration at not being allowed to go outside.

On entering Philippe's study, Philippe beckoned Li to a comfortable chair, and, as Li sat, he pushed an ash tray over to him. Lighting his briar pipe, Philippe sucked in hard, and, with a playful smile curling on his lips, he said, "My Den, my rules. It's the only place in the house Elisapie lets me smoke."

He slowly exhaled, allowing the polished leather- and cherry-scented smoke to drift upwards into the high vaulted room. Li's eyes revealed his appreciation as he took one of his Marlborough's into his mouth and inhaled the sharp taste of tobacco and nicotine. "Shall we attend to our business?" said Li, briefly putting down his cigarette, and retrieving the file from his briefcase. "You are a very capable and successful man, Mr Gagnon, a successful petro-chemical engineer and a pioneer in Canada in robotic drilling techniques; you speak, French, English, Portuguese and Eskaleut. Did I pronounce the name of the last language correctly?" Li asked, looking up at Philippe.

"If I may stop you right there, Mr Qiang. Now, I don't want to appear ungrateful at being offered this position; however I made a promise to my wife a long time ago that, once I quit the oil industry, we would relocate to Unalaska and set up home there."

Li was busy stubbing out his cigarette as he looked over at Philippe. "I understand entirely your desire to settle in Unalaska. Indeed, I realise that you want to achieve more than that. You want to help reinstitute the Inuit society there, and create conditions for them to grow their own communities."

Philippe placed his pipe on his lap. This man has done his research, he thought. Tapping the remains of the burnt tobacco out into the small bin, and then picking up a short metal tool, he began scraping the burnt remains from the pipe's bowl. Li was already beginning to warm to Philippe. This man was cultured and intelligent.

"In short," uttered Li, "we, er, I mean the United Nations Centre for Technology and Culture, would like to support you in your endeavours. We are aware of your energy project and would like to help fund it."

"The CTC was established for exactly this reason: to help develop ethnic communities, and allow them to thrive in the twenty-first century world. If you choose to accept the position, you will have the time and resources to complete your project. Indeed, it was your good friend Professor Matthias Peterson who suggested that you might be a suitable candidate for this position."

"That sly old dog," muttered Philippe, as he tamped more tobacco down hard into his pipe bowl. "Well, I will give it my consideration; and, of course, you understand that I would have to have Elisapie's blessing before I say yes?"

Li nodded. "If you decide to accept the position, then just contact this number," he said, handing Philippe his CTC business card. Both men instinctively knew that the business talk had concluded, and Philippe rose.

Turning to Li, he said, "I believe you are booked on the six p.m. flight to London? Of course you will be our guest and join us in an early dinner."

Smiling as he stood, Li was ushered into the dining room where Elisapie and the two boys, Arnaud, aged fifteen, and Thierry, aged seventeen, were sitting at the table. "Tonight, I believe we will be eating á la Québécois. Elisapie is an excellent chef, and she has prepared some of our typical cuisine. I hope you like *ragoût de pattes de porc*?"

"Pig trotter stew," Thierry translated, "and, for dessert, if my taste buds don't deceive me, we have *pouding chômeur*. We call it Poor Man's Pudding, but it's to die for," exclaimed Thierry, with a broad smile on his face.

Chapter Six

After bidding farewell to Philippe, who had insisted on taking him personally to the airport, Li had around twenty minutes to wait until he boarded the six p.m. Air Canada flight from Jean Lesage International Airport to London Heathrow. The plane was scheduled to land at half past seven, UK time, which meant that he should be able to fully recline his business class seat and grab a good five hours' sleep. Eschewing the Business Class Lounge, Li headed straight to the smoking terrace, where he joined the small group of nicotine junkies who were huddled together against the wind and drizzle, enjoying their last few gasps of tar, nicotine and sulphur before their enforced abstinence, cocooned inside the Boeing 777 as it cruised over the Atlantic.

Before reclining his seat into the flat sleeping position, Li called the flight attendant. "Do you have a good, single malt whisky?" he asked the flight assistant.

"We have several," the assistant replied. "I would recommend the fifteen-year-old Dalwhinnie; or, if you prefer, I can show you the drinks menu?"

"Dalwhinnie will do just fine, thank you," replied Li. Li knew Dalwhinnie well. Whisky drinking was an affectation he had picked up during his time at University in England; after many a long and drunken sampling session, he had decided that his preference lay with the Scottish Highland whiskies. Before coming to study in England, Li had not appreciated that, in certain company, knowledge of which whisky to drink and how to take the drink were as important as the old school tie you wore or the name of your club. He took the Dalwhinnie whisky from the smiling attendant and sat back in his chair to contemplate how he would approach his next candidate. Convincing Penny Aldrich of MI6, or, as it was more correctly known, the British Secret Intelligence Service, was going to be a whole order of magnitude more difficult than it had been with the previous candidates.

First of all, despite Sir Richard, the British Ambassador to the UN, insisting that Britain had 'one of its own' occupying one of the top posts, the only position available was that of Chief Liaison Officer. This role would see the incumbent liaising on a regular basis with Interpol, other national police forces, intelligence agencies and a selection of some of the world's more specialised military organisations. As the only organisation with this expertise belonging to the Foreign and Commonwealth Office in the UK was MI6, the candidate would have to come from within these ranks. Li knew from the email exchanges that he had already had with Sir David Simmingford-Bell, Head of

MI6, that he was, as any Intelligence chief would be, very reluctant indeed to release one of his own agents into an organisation such as the CTC. To make Li's negotiating position worse, he knew that the presence of an active Chinese government diplomat inside Vauxhall Cross, the building at the very heart of the British Secret Intelligence Service, could be perceived at best as an unnecessary interference in the inner workings of one of the world's leading intelligence services, and, at worst, as attempted espionage.

Li knew from his own sources that the British Government spent almost as much today monitoring the movements of Chinese nationals, Chinese government organisations and known agents, as it had spent monitoring KGB agents at the height of the Cold War. The British were tenacious like that. It was one thing that Li admired about them. Despite all of their weaknesses, and the humiliation many of them felt at their lack of real influence in global issues in the twenty-first century, they very rarely took their eye off the ball.

"Urgh," Penny gasped, as she was kicked in the stomach. The savage leg sweep knocked Penny to the floor. The blow to the back of her head as she hit the floor dazed her, and she was left struggling to focus. Come on then, finish me, she thought; the attacker started to straddle Penny's body and began to push his thick forearm down hard on to her throat. She was struggling to remain conscious now; the kick had forced all of her oxygen reserves out of her lungs, and his arm was preventing her from drawing in air. Her attacker leant forward now, pressing more weight onto her throat and breathing his foul smelling breath straight into her mouth and nose. Now I have you, she thought, as she deftly wrapped her legs from the outside to the inside of her attacker's thighs and hooked her toes behind the attackers Achilles heels; with her last remaining reserves of strength she violently forced her legs to straighten. The effect was immediate. Penny felt the attackers groin muscles tighten, then snap, as his legs were forced outwards with such a great force and well beyond his normal range of movement. She rolled the attacker off her and stood up. The attacker remained on the floor on his side in a fetal position.

"I think that's about it for today's session, don't you John? Oh, and by the way, I would invest in some mouthwash if I were you."

John muttered a hoarse acknowledgement but didn't move. Penny Aldrich went to leave the martial arts training centre in the basement of the Vauxhall Cross building. Bugger, she thought, I am going to be late for the interview. She took a quick shower, and, whilst sliding into her plain grey skirt and floral patterned blouse, she thought about the fight with John Blackmore, her section head for the last three years, to whom she had taken an instant dislike, the moment she had met him. She felt no remorse; he had it coming to him. His sexist jokes or innuendo-ridden speech were the least of the problems. She knew it was he who had conveniently delayed her application for the new position that had just opened up in the Counter-Intelligence Division, leading to Michael Braithwaite, of all people, getting the position. She also knew he would try and dominate her in the gym; she knew he would try to assert his masculinity over her. Well, that just made it easier for her to beat him. All she had done was allow him to gain his position of perceived advantage, then struck hard and fast.

Still a little flushed from the exertion, Penny sat erect in the meeting room chair in front of the Director of MI6, Sir David and the Chinese visitor. The venue wasn't Sir David's plush upper-floor office, instead it was 'the cube': the term that all those inside Vauxhall Cross used for the rather odd-looking stand-alone room that was not only completely detached from any telephone or internet systems, but was swept for listening devices on a daily basis. The walls were intermeshed with actively charged metal filaments, which prevented any electronic signals from leaving the room.

The Director glowered at Penny. Since joining MI6, she had spoken to him only once, and that had been during a departmental budget meeting.

"Ms Aldrich," began Li. "I believe you have read my proposal to come and work at the CTC?"

She had read the proposal; in fact she had many spent many hours reading it and agonising over the decision.

"Yes, Mr Wu; I have read your proposal, and I have made my decision."

The Director's gaze was now boring a hole straight through Penny and into the wall behind her. "Ms Aldwich, may I remind you that if you decide to accept this offer, you will become persona non grata here at Vauxhall Cross? You can kiss any hope you had of a career in the Foreign Office goodbye."

"It's Aldrich," Penny said firmly, glaring back at the Director and rolling the letter R in such an exaggerated manner that it left no doubt how her name was spelt. "I completely understand my position here at MI6; and, as such, I would be delighted to accept your offer, Mr Wu."

Penny accepted the invitation to accompany Li to Heathrow. They both sat in the back of the Foreign Office car and talked quietly. "You are a very impressive woman, Ms Aldrich," he said, stressing the R. Your file shows that you majored in languages at the School of Oriental and African Studies."

Taking the hint, Penny switched to Mandarin and continued her conversation with Li, much to the frustration of the MI6 escort sitting in the front of the car, who would now not be able to report back on their conversation to the Head of Counter-Intelligence. They continued speaking in Mandarin. "I studied Urdu, Farsi and Arabic at SOAS. I was approached by MI6 whilst doing my studies, and they funded me through an extra year at SOAS, this time studying Mandarin. I took quite naturally to languages," Penny continued, in Mandarin. Li was impressed; of course, he could tell that she was a foreigner. It would take several more years of immersion for her to be able to sound like a native, but her command of the language and its tonal system was, nevertheless, impressive.

"May I call you Penny?" Li asked, as the car pulled up at terminal three departures, ready for his flight to Copenhagen.

"Of course!"

"I sense I have rather, what is your English expression, 'set the cat amongst the pigeons' back at Vauxhall Cross, and I realise that you will need a little time to complete the handover of any cases you may be working on and to be debriefed..."

Penny held up her hand to interrupt Li. "Honestly, you were doing me a favour. I am a grown woman who expects to be treated like one. If I am not appreciated in MI6, then it's about time I moved somewhere where I will be appreciated."

Li smiled and bowed slightly. Fumbling in his jacket pocket for one of his business cards, he withdrew a card and his cigarettes. "Please get in touch with my secretary on this number to confirm the contractual arrangements," he said, proffering her the card. "And I look forward to our next discussion in Mandarin when I next see you in Singapore."

He walked briskly towards the airport terminal, but instead of entering immediately, he opened the packet of cigarettes he had been clutching in his hand, withdrew one, and lit it.

Chapter Seven

Latitude 55° 40' 48.828'', Longitude 12° 34' 20.6754''.
Copenhagen University, Copenhagen, Denmark – January
2017.
The Dane

"I am truly sorry, Matthias, we have known each other for, what is it, fifteen years now? And you have been a loyal colleague and a superb head of Faculty. Your work on the Inuit project has not only increased the number of foreign students electing to study with us, but it has also attracted some serious research grant money to the university. You do understand why I am having to take this action, though, don't you? The Board of Trustees feel that it is no longer tenable for someone in your position of responsibility to remain at the University after this..." Henrik Samuelson, the Rektor of the University of Copenhagen, struggled to find the right words to express himself. "This, er, incident."

Matthias looked up at Henrik, his old friend, and gave a barely perceptible nod. He had barely slept since the accident, and now, sitting in the Rektor's office, he looked a rather dishevelled sight. His hair was unkempt; his clothes, which he had worn for three consecutive days, were creased and dirty; and the rings around his eyes evidenced his lack of sleep. Henrik sat down next to his old friend. "I've known for some time that you were struggling with your drinking problem, but I assumed you had it under control; you were always punctual at the lectures and attended all of the departmental meetings."

"That is exactly the problem," replied Matthias. "You become so enslaved to the need to drink that you learn to cope; indeed you may often seem more lucid whilst drunk than when sober. It is the inescapable urge to feel the first drops of alcohol hitting your stomach that drives you to believe that you can manage, that you can lead an ordinary life as well as a shadow life, subservient to the overarching desire to drink."

"In Exstrabladet, they reported that you were five times over the limit when the car hit the tree, and that you were lucky not to have hit any pedestrians as you left the Skovshoved Sailing Club.

Matthias jumped up and glared directly into Henrik's eyes. "Lucky? Lucky?" screamed Matthias, with spittle spraying from his mouth. "Do you call killing my daughter and putting my wife in a wheelchair lucky?" He slumped back down into the chair, and sat breathing heavily, whilst staring blankly at the clock on the wall behind the Rektor's desk.

Two weeks had passed since the accident, and not one minute had gone by that Matthias didn't wish that he could have swapped places with his daughter, Stina. He had held his wife whilst she cried at their daughter's funeral, and once they had finally lowered Stina into the ground, and the rest of the congregation had left, she had looked up at Matthias from the confines of her wheelchair, with dead eyes, and said, "You bastard!" striking him hard across his cheek as she spoke. This was the last time he had seen or spoken to his wife. The university had since suspended him, pending the Board's decision.

"Listen, Matthias, as your friend, can I give you some advice? I know you can't think of the future right now, not so soon after the funeral; however, I would like to introduce you to somebody whom you may find interesting." Matthias gave no acknowledgement; he just sat in the chair with his gaze fixed on the clock on the wall. "You don't need to give me an answer immediately," said Henrik, as he slipped his arm into the sleeve of his jacket. "I have invited the gentleman to a meeting next Tuesday at three p.m., and I really think you would like to hear his proposal."

Of course, Henrik hadn't needed to help his old friend, and he wasn't doing it solely for altruistic reasons. The Anthropology faculty would lose a considerable amount of its funding with Matthias' dismissal, and if the meeting went as planned on Tuesday, the CTC had promised to fund the shortfall in grant money at the Anthropology department for the next five years, as long as the university released Matthias without a blemish on his character, and allowed the CTC a 'reachback' capability to the Anthropology department's considerable wealth of knowledge and resources.

Henrik paused as his hand touched the door handle. "I will expect your resignation letter on my desk by tomorrow, Matthias. You will need to say that you have decided to leave the Faculty to spend more time on your field research, etc, etc. Oh, and don't be late on Tuesday. Three p.m. on the dot," he said, as he left his office. Gradually, Matthias's focus expanded away from the clock on Hendrik's wall, and he began to take in the sounds of the traffic in Krystalgade below him. He rose from the chair and shuffled to the door, opened it, and leaving the door ajar he walked straight out past the receptionist in the anteroom and down the stairs into the street below.

Li had been sitting in Henrik's office for fifteen minutes. They had exchanged pleasantries, and Li had been offered a hot black acrid tasting drink that passed for tea in Denmark. After a longer than natural pause in the conversation, Li asked whether Henrik minded if he popped out for five minutes to have a cigarette. Henrik was more than happy to oblige and took the opportunity to ring Matthias. "Matthias, it's me, Henrik, where the bloody hell are you?"

There was a pause on the line and then Matthias spoke, "I'm, er, on my way." Just then, Henrik heard laughter in the background and the sound of the old cash register being rung.

"You're in the bloody Midtown Bar, aren't you?"

"I may have popped in for a drink or two," replied Matthias.

The truth was that he had been in the bar since they had opened at ten in the morning and had been drinking beer since then. Like most Danes, he preferred beer and was one of the Carlsberg company's most loyal customers. His preference was for Tuborg Fine Festival, and with an alcohol content of over seven per cent, this simply meant that he could satiate his demons a little faster than with other beers that typically had an alcohol content of around four or five per cent.

"I'm on my way," he said, putting his mobile back in his pocket as he stood to leave the bar.

Li was just about to re-enter the Rektor's office when he saw an older, slightly portly, unkempt man in a dirty raincoat and scuffed leather shoes enter the office before him. Surely this couldn't be the man he had travelled halfway around the world to see. Was this man really the leading authority in the world on the application of technology to remote cultures? Li had read Matthias' ground breaking paper entitled 'The impact of technologies on remote communities: a cultural perspective'. And had immediately realised that the author was the person he wanted to be directing the anthropological element of the CTC's mandate.

Li readjusted his tie knot and placed his cigarettes back in his pocket before re-entering the room. "Aah, Mr Peterson, we meet at last. I have read your journal article on the appropriate use of technologies within different cultural settings and I must say that I found it fascinating." Li tried to mask his disappointment at Matthias's demeanour, and wasn't sure if he was being successful.

Matthias was swaying slightly as he stood in the centre of the room observing the older Chinese man. "I am guessing at Han Chinese, although I see a hint of something else in your physiology that I can't quite place. Your height and white teeth bear witness to your privileged upbringing. Your proximity to Henrik and to me, coupled with the way your hands are crossed in front of you low down near your groin area, and the arch in your eyebrows as they try to meet in the centre of your forehead, tell me that you feel disdain for me and you recognise Henrik's humiliation."

Matthias enunciated every word with perfect diction. Li's face could not hide his shock at Matthias' description of him. "Well, Mr Peterson, I guess I let my mask slip a little. You were correct on all counts except one. I am one hundred per cent Han Chinese."

"Sit down, man, before you fall down," bellowed Henrik. "I am so sorry for Matthias's little parlour trick; he has a habit of demonstrating his extensive knowledge of micro-gestures whenever he has imbibed too much alcohol."

All three men sat down, and Li began to speak. "My name is Li. May I call you Matthias?" he asked, offering his outstretched hand to Matthias. Matthias took the hand and gave it a firm yet friendly shake.

"Henrik has made me aware of your situation here at the University of Copenhagen, and I would like to point out that I was sincere about my opinion of your work, although I do admit to being a trifle taken aback at your rather dishevelled state. I am here to make you an offer, Matthias. I would like you to join my international team and me at the newly formed United Nations Centre for Technology and Culture. I am aware of your particular problem, Matthias, and conditional to your joining our team would be that you underwent therapy for alcoholism."

"What makes you think I would be interested in working with you, Li?" His voice was even, not threatening, more curious.

"Well," Li began. "Our Centre has been developed to work across and between all of the world's different cultural groups, with the aim of giving them greater economic opportunities through the application of appropriate technologies. I thought an opportunity to work on a project like that might have been right up your street, Matthias?" Li could see that Matthias was tempted, and that he would only need a little more persuasion. I don't know if you are aware of this, but a certain Philippe Gagnon is currently deciding if he would like to join us, and I did give him my word that the CTC would fund his, or should I say your, Inuit energy project."

Li noted that Matthias had registered genuine surprise at the mention of his old friend's name. Also, he knew that the alternative was for him to drift into academic obscurity and become a pariah within the academic community.

"If I were to say yes to this offer, how quickly would it happen?"

Henrik jumped in at this point. "Li and I are quite advanced in our discussions, and I would be prepared to accept the resignation letter you wrote forthwith; but you would have to begin your alcohol therapy here in Denmark for one month and demonstrate signs of improvement before you moved to Singapore."

"Singapore?" asked Mathias. "Why Singapore? Why not here?"

"It is only the Headquarters that is located in Singapore and despite its offering all of the amenities that we would require, I am afraid it was a political choice, as this location offends fewer people than the other options that were presented. We have also developed Technology Transfer Centres, as we like to call them, in the following locations: Gander in Canada, Sao Paulo in Brazil, Windhoek in Namibia, Girona in northern Spain, and Muscat in Oman."

Matthias immediately saw the logic in the locations: they were distributed around the globe close to major airports and the infrastructure required to run such a centre, yet also within a reasonable distance to be able to affect the different cultural groups which the centre was targeting with its research.

"It is certainly a very seductive offer, Li," Matthias said, as he stood to signify that the meeting was over. Reaching forwards, a little unsteady on his feet, he took Li's hand. "I will give it my utmost consideration." Then, leaning a little closer, with his mouth so close to Li's ear that it almost touched, he whispered, "You know, I am very rarely wrong when it comes to reading people. Are you sure you don't have a distant relative from Korea or further east?"

Li looked Matthias straight back in the eye; a little flushed, he said, "Quite sure, Matthias. I expect to receive your response by the end of this week."

Matthias stumbled out of the room, down the stairs and out into the bright street below. He had walked this route countless times before, in less than two blocks' time he had re-entered the Café Midtown Bar on Nørre Voldgade, and, without even needing to look across at the barman, he found his way to his regular table; on it was a freshly poured cold glass of Tuborg Fine Festival.

Chapter Eight

Latitude 55° 45' 35.3514'', Longitude 37° 37' 33.888''.
Federal Security Service of the Russian Federation (FSB)
Headquarters, Lubyanka Square, Moscow – January
2017.
The Russian

Leaving the Rektor's office at the University, Li took out his cigarettes. He could still feel that he was a little flushed from his encounter with Matthias. He knew Matthias would accept the offer; what other options did he have, after all? The question was not whether he would be able to stay sober, but whether Li could have a man working for him that seemed to show so little respect for him. Li turned right along Nørregade and walked the few blocks up to Nørre Voldgade, and from here he could already see the Nørreport Metro station, from where he would take the M2 metro, which, in a mere fifteen minutes, would whisk him directly to the airport.

He still had nearly three hours before his 11.40 p.m. flight to Moscow's Sheremetyevo airport, and took the opportunity to buy some more cigarettes from the airport's Tax Free Store. The airport was small by international standards, but it was clean and efficient, without being overly polished. He thought it a good metaphor for the Danes themselves. He had heard it said that a country's architecture was a reflection of its inner soul. If that were true, then he was not looking forward to his next destination, the Lubyanka building, a neo-Baroque yellow-brick building that dominated Lubyanka Square, was the former home of the KGB and the current home to the KGB's successor, the Federal Security Service (FSB). Lavrentiy Beria, whose cruelty had even gained notoriety during the shocking era of Stalin's purges, and who had been the main person responsible for the Second World War's Katyn Forest massacre, where twenty-five thousand Polish officers and intellectuals were shot to death in the forests near Katyn, had once used this building as his Soviet wartime intelligence service headquarters, which were then referred to as the NKVD. Ever since then it had been synonymous with brutal interrogations and executions.

The officer moved with a fluidity of purpose; his contact with the ground, although fleeting, was sufficient to propel him forwards in long effortless bounds. He appeared to be flowing over the ground in a determined wave of energy. His decrease in speed was barely perceptible as the gradient kicked up.

The run had begun close to the border between Russia and Georgia in the Caucasus mountains, about ten kilometres north of Mount Elbrus, Europe's highest peak. The MI8T helicopter, known to NATO as the Hip, was carrying its full complement of twenty-four border guards as it touched down on the icy ridge ten kilometres due north of mount Elbrus. Each of the Guards was wearing non-issue trail running boots, the latest Russian military cold weather thermal base layers, and a light vapour wicking jacket. Cocooning their upper bodies, each man wore an identical ultra-endurance running vest with a tracking beacon, water, food and emergency gear. The vest weighed no more than six kilograms and fitted snugly around the runner's body.

The only additional weight that each man carried was the MP-443 Grach 9 mm handgun, and a spare magazine. This was carried in an inside pocket of the vest, which kept the gun from freezing in the bitter mountain environment. These men were known as the волф пакк or Wolf Pack. They were part of a secret Russian military physiological research programme. It had learned its lessons from the wars in the Caucasus, where, on many occasions, the lightly-armed insurgents would flee into the mountains, leaving behind them the Russian soldiers who were either too unfit or carrying too much equipment to be able to keep pace with the insurgents.

The realisation that the problems with separatists would continue to threaten Russia's interests for the foreseeable future had spurred the Russian FSB into developing a research programme to try to enhance the human endurance capabilities of its military forces. The aim was simple: unencumbered by heavy packs and equipment like most military units, this new group would have one purpose. They were a pack of hunters, working in groups like wolves, able to run extremely long distances on a minimal calorie intake and over the most arduous of terrains, with the skills to be able to eliminate their target once caught.

In the open, boulder-strewn terrain, the team was running in a diamond formation, with about ten metres between each man. Their leader, Andrei Semynov, had taken point position. Under normal circumstances he would be in second or third position, but the aim of today was to test his men. Andrei was the benchmark against which the other men would be tested. Today's exercise was being monitored by live feed from the FSB Headquarters at Lubyanka Square in Moscow.

The large screen in the Op Centre was subdivided into four sections, one for each man. In each section, there was a high-definition live camera feed, and a selection of live biometric data. Heart rate, blood sugar level, oxygen consumption and lipid absorption were all displayed on the screen. Each of the border guard troopers had electronic sensors surgically attached to their bodies. The objective was to reach the Priyut 11 (hut number eleven) at 4160 metres, without stopping either to rest or to acclimatise, and to do so using as little carbohydrate fuel as possible.

They had been given just three and a half hours to cover the thirty-six-kilometre-long route. This would have been challenging on a flat route for most competent marathon runners, but to be able to achieve this over the rough terrain in temperatures approaching zero Celsius and up to an altitude of 4160 metres was nothing short of miraculous.

After the exercise was over, the elite Russian Wolf Pack were transported back to Moscow for a debrief. The scientists were buzzing with excitement as they analysed the bio-data that had been obtained from the soldiers. "You see here the deflection in Trooper number four's blood sugar level," said Dr Sergei Aziminov, tapping the monitor with his finger to show his colleague.

"I see," said his colleague. "But this man was at three thousand five hundred metres when it occurred; I would normally expect to see that happen at around fifteen hundred metres." The review room was stuffy and claustrophobic. Andrei and his team had reached the hut on time and had been flown back to Moscow for the debrief.

All four men sat rigidly to attention as their General Officer Commanding entered the room to conclude the debrief. He was a tall man in his early fifties, still with a thick head of hair and intelligent piercing blue eyes.

"Gentlemen, I have spoken to Dr Aziminov, and he assures me that Project Ultra has exceeded even his expectations. The combination of severe endurance training in a state of near-starvation, coupled with the enhanced oxygen-carrying capabilities each of you has, thanks to Dr Aziminov's ground-breaking work on developing an enhanced haemoglobin-carrying molecule, means that the FSB now has the capability to hunt out these separatist scum in the Caucasus, and pursue them over any terrain for days at a time, using only four men." The general banged his fist on the table to emphasize the point. Looking each of the four men directly in the eyes, he said, "You are the genesis. We will now expand this project and train more people. In one year from now, I expect to have a full Squadron of Ultras."

After the debrief was concluded, the men began filing out of the stuffy briefing room. "Captain Semynov, can you stay behind for a moment, please?" said the general.

"Certainly, sir," shouted Andrei. He knew by the tone of the general's voice that this was an order and not a request.

"Captain Semynov, I have been following your progress keenly." The general spoke in a clipped voice, which made it clear that he was not to be interrupted. "I also note from your record that you served with distinction in Volgograd in the operation that stopped those Chechen scum from blowing up the hospital. However, I have been informed that your sister is married to a certain, Sasha Yiranek, a Ukrainian from Luhansk." The general's voice didn't waver, as he slowly turned his head to face Andrei who was standing to attention in front of the large monitors at the front of the room. "We believe that this Yiranek is responsible for interdicting some of our *special aid convoys*." The general used the hand gesture for inverted commas and bared his teeth in a sarcastic gesture as he said the words 'aid convoys'. "So far as we know, this dog, Yiranek, has the blood of seven Russians on his hands, and has managed to intercept several tons of weaponry, including anti-aircraft missiles."

Andrei, eyes looking at a point straight above the general's head could feel his face suffusing with colour. His hands were balled into tight fists and he was beginning to sweat. "You do understand what a difficult position this places me in, don't you?" asked the general, in his clipped monotone. "You may stay with the programme if you wish; however, from this point forward you will no longer have access to any operational planning, nor be able to participate in any operations, as you pose too much of a security risk to the Ultra programme."

Andrei felt the emotion welling up within him. It had taken three years of blood, sweat and tears to get him to where he was today. He had spent countless hours in a near-starved state, running and swimming until he became almost unconscious. What for, he thought. Just to be told that because your stupid little sister had run off to Ukraine and married some idiot idealist, that all of your hard work was in vain?

"Look at me, Andrei," said the general, in a softer tone. "I know how you must be feeling right now, and, believe me, it is a blow to the programme that you can no longer become fully operational. I have given it some thought and spoken with the Russian Foreign Minister personally on the matter. After some consideration, you have been nominated to be Russia's main representative in the newly formed United Nations Centre for Technology and Culture."

Andrei looked at the general with a look of incredulity. "The UN what, sir?"

"The CTC." The general repeated the phrase again, annoyed at being made to repeat himself.

"I am not a tech geek, sir. I do my best work out in the field."

"I know, I know," said the general, in a more conciliatory tone. "Actually, that is why I want you there. We need to know what is going on in this new organisation, and you will be our eyes and ears on the inside. Now, I will meet you at eleven hundred hours tomorrow morning in my office. There you will meet your new boss, a Chinese man called Li Qiang Wu." The general almost spat the words out; the thought of a Russian being commanded by a Chinese man was unthinkable to him.

"Yes, sir!" Andrei shouted, as he saluted the general.

Once the general had disappeared, Andrei sat a moment and thought about what had just been said. Andrei knew what his options were. His career in the FSB was effectively over, and all because of his stupid sister. He could go back to St Petersburg, but with his skills, knew he only had one real option, which meant working for one of the crime syndicates, and, after his recent joint mission with the FBI to take out a Russian Mafia drugs cartel in Florida, he knew that it would only be a matter of time before he would be recognised. With this thought in his head, he strode out of the room and back to his quarters.

Li had been made to wait for forty minutes in the colonel's office before he could get in to see the general. He knew it was a game they were playing, trying to intimidate him and show their Slavic superiority. This did not faze him, because he knew that, strategically, the battle had already been decided. He was ostensibly here to brief Captain Andrei Semynov on his new role at the CTC, and knew he needed no coercion. The only bonus about his being left with the Colonel for so long was that the Colonel was a chain smoker. During the entire time Li had been sitting in the office, neither man had spent more than a minute without a lit cigarette in his mouth.

"Mr Wu," the general said, standing in the doorway of his office and nearly filling the frame. The action was meant to intimidate Li. However, Li's lean body stood over six feet tall in bare feet, and, as he rose from his chair in the colonel's office, he could see the general's demeanour change as he shrank back into his own office. The general was seated behind his desk as Li finally entered the office. In one of the two chairs opposite his desk, a tall fair haired and extremely fit looking captain sat bolt upright.

It was almost like observing a statue, Li thought to himself. "Mr Wu, I am General Kiryokov, the Commander of Border Guard Operations for the Caucasus Region." Li knew from his briefings that this meant that the officer in front of him was responsible for the repression of mainly Islamist separatists in Chechnya, Dagestan, Ingushetia and North Ossetia. For the

69

Russians, this was seen as their 'War on Terror'. However, amongst many nations in the UN, it was seen as the Russians trying to retake control over the region, in an attempt to reform something like the old Soviet Union.

"General," said Li, with perfect English diction and with no hint of impatience in his voice. "An absolute pleasure to meet you. This must be Captain Andrei Semynov, whom I have travelled so far to meet?"

The statue turned to face Li; his piercing blue eyes gave no clue as to his inner thoughts, his carved face cracking imperceptibly, as he uttered, "Yes, Mr Wu, I am Captain Andrei Semynov of the FSB."

Determined not to be shaken by the Russian officer's other-worldly behaviour, Li reached out a hand to Andrei and said, in a calm voice, "Please call me Li. We will be working a lot together in the future, and I am glad to have been given this opportunity to come to brief you in person." After nearly an hour of briefing, and with the general showing growing signs of impatience at the protracted time it was taking Li to conduct the briefing, Li left the office and returned once more to the colonel's ante-office, where he found the middle-aged officer sitting at his desk reading a report, cigarette in mouth.

"Ah, Mr Wu," said the colonel. "Please won't you join me for a cigarette? I am ordering your transport now. The driver should be here in ten minutes. You want to go directly to Sheremetyevo airport, is that correct?" Taking one of the colonel's proffered cigarettes, Li sat in the chair opposite him and nodded his head. After inhaling deeply on his cigarette, Li gazed over at the colonel who had just finished speaking on the phone.

"May I ask you a question, Colonel?"

"Of course."

"Captain Semynov: he is a very intense person. I mean that he is almost without emotion."

"Ahh," sighed the colonel. "Yes, they can come across like that, before you get to know them. I believe it is a side effect of some of the blood enhancement treatment they have had."

Li shot a glance over at the colonel, "'They'? You said 'they', Colonel; I was speaking about Captain Semynov."

"Er, yes; sorry, Mr Wu, I meant 'he'. I have probably said more than I should." Just then the door opened and a young Border Guard Non-Commissioned Officer entered the room and stood to attention. "I believe this is your transport, Mr Wu. Have a pleasant journey back to America, won't you?"

Li rose and shook the colonel's hand. "Thank you, Colonel; if I hurry, I may catch an earlier flight."

Li followed the driver as he walked him through the labyrinthine corridors and to the waiting car. It would take them around forty minutes to reach the airport. Li sat back in his seat and breathed a deep sigh of relief. He was glad to be out of there. Out of the cramped warren of offices, away from the Russian officers, who all peered at him as if he was an insect. Glancing at his watch, Li was relieved to see that he would make the two thirty p.m. Aeroflot flight to New York.

Li had been surprised by Aeroflot. Prior to his flight to Moscow, he had laboured under the common belief that they were a backwards airline with a poor safety record and poor on-board service. Nothing could have been further from the truth. The airline operated a brand new fleet of the very latest Boeing and Airbus planes. As for the service, well, somebody within the company management obviously had a penchant for tall, thin, blonde-haired, high-cheek-boned girls. Li felt that every single stewardess on board his Boeing 777 flight would have easily felt just as at home at the Milan or London fashion shows, strutting up and down the catwalk.

His recruitment work, for now, was over; and Li was looking forward to a long weekend back in New York, before he began preparing to move himself and his family to Singapore. What was it that his American colleagues had said? Yes, that was it, *"Time to kick back and relax,"* Li thought, taking the single malt whisky from the beautiful flight attendant, and settling back in his chair.

Chapter Nine

Latitude 33° 16' 6.7008'', Longitude 44° 23' 20.1408''.
The Al Abbasin Household, Baghdad, Iraq, former
Mesopotamia – October 2016.
Death by Remote Control

Despite her being seventy years old, Fatima Al Abbasin, had an elegance about her that was almost regal. She still walked with a tall erect posture, and even though, nowadays, she felt exhausted after a full day's work in her laboratory, situated in the Al Kwarizmi College of Engineering of Baghdad University, she remained a formidable woman indeed. One look into her deep brown almond-shaped eyes allowed the observer to peer into the mind of a person who possessed not only a reassuring and calming wisdom, but also a tenacious grip on life itself. "Ali, Hamed, Ana Mawjooda," she said, as she let herself into the large and ornately decorated house that sat nestled inside the large loop on the banks of the River Tigris, barely two kilometres from the university.

In winter, Fatima would walk the two kilometres along the bend in the Tigris to the university. She enjoyed the walk, not only because she used to take the walk with her husband, who had been a professor at the physics laboratory, but also because, as a little girl, she had often walked the same stretch along the palm-lined riverside to visit her grandpa in the very same building where she now worked. She took delight in bringing him his favourite lunch of falafel and salad, or kibbah, the aromatic minced meat, mixed with bulgur flour, rice and his grandma's special mixture of spices, and, of course, a fresh flask of hot sweet mint tea.

The house, which had been in the family for several generations, was well located, close both to Iraq's centre of political power and to its intellectual centre, Baghdad University, which, in the far distant past, had once been known as the House of Wisdom (*Bayt al Hikma*, or 'centre of knowledge') for one of the largest empires the planet had ever known. Between the ninth and thirteenth centuries, Baghdad University, which was founded in the eleventh century, was the pre-eminent place of learning in the world. As well as generating new knowledge in almost every conceivable scientific and artistic discipline, they also imported texts and ideas from around the known civilized world, which at that time lay principally to the east of Baghdad in Persia, India and China, and exported some of this knowledge to the less developed western world, sowing the seeds of knowledge in subjects such as maths, astronomy, literature, chemistry and physics, upon which western thinkers would later build their own systems of study and invention.

"Boys, where are you?" Fatima shouted again. She still referred to them as her 'boys', although the eldest, Ali, who was married to Miriam and had two daughters himself, was forty years old, and lived in a separate wing of the house with his family. Hamed, the youngest, was thirty-five years old, and lived in a few rooms at the back of the house which Fatima had allowed him to convert into a mini-apartment. Hamed was not yet married; it was probably due to his shyness, which was something that troubled Fatima, although, since her husband had died, No, been killed! she corrected herself) she had been glad of Hamed's company, particularly as he was a very bright and talented physicist. In many ways, he was very similar to his father.

Hamed slouched into the main hallway to meet his mother. He was barefoot and wearing jeans, and a Simpsons T-shirt. His round glasses fitted his round face, and his medium-length black hair was held in place by a baseball cap. "Hi, Mum, how was work?" he asked in his quiet voice.

"It was fine," she sighed. "The department had yet another meeting to discuss how it can be downsized and which of the eight remaining research projects should be cut. It really is getting beyond a joke; I speak daily with colleagues and friends all around the Gulf and in Egypt and they all say the same. There is no money available for research, lab time is being monopolized for government programmes, and they cannot attract any bright talented students any more." She continued speaking, whilst removing her headscarf and turning to hug her son.

"Do you know that some of the equipment in our chemistry lab is the same equipment that your grandfather was using in his petro-bacterial experiments?"

"Wow, that's real old, Mum; I mean that must be what, 1950s technology?"

"Earlier," Fatima replied. "Your grandfather was working in that lab as a post-graduate student at the very start of the 1940s."

"Well, Dad is always saying that—" Hamed paused, and, with a slight tremulous quiver to his voice, corrected himself. "Dad always SAID…" Hamed began to sob, and his mother leant forward to hold him.

It had only been a month since Hamed's father, Hassan, had been killed in the explosion that had vapourised the Mercedes car he was being driven in, whilst making his way to day two of a nuclear physics conference in Lahore, Pakistan. His father had been presenting some of his theoretical work on the role that gravity plays in Particle Field Theory. His work was genuinely ground-breaking, and one of Pakistan's leading nuclear physicists had been eager to discuss Hassan's work in private. Sitting in the back of the old green Mercedes Benz, on their way to the conference at Lahore University, Irfan Qureshi, known to the American CIA by his codename 'Manhattan 1', was deep in discussion with Hassan about the potential practical applications of his work.

Hassan had never met Irfan in person, although they had exchanged emails prior to the conference. He found him to be pleasant enough, but always so serious. It was obvious that he was an ultra-conservative Muslim. He was heavily bearded, and always dressed in a Shalwar Kameez, the traditional Pakistani menswear, effectively a pair of long cotton trousers and a very long plain shirt that hung down to the knees. Hassan could not recall ever having seen Irfan without his prayer beads clutched tightly in one hand.

"Mike Two Zero Bravo, this is Charlie Alpha Sierra. The target is live. I am illuminating it now. I repeat, the target is live," crackled a voice into a hand-held encrypted satellite phone. The

CIA agent was standing only forty feet away from the Mercedes under the shades of a nearby teashop; he was pointing an ultra-high frequency laser target designator directly on to the vehicle's bonnet.

"This is Mike Two Zero Bravo," a voice replied, from a temporary US Air Base just over four hundred kilometres away, in Mosul, Northern Iraq.

Ever since the US had been helping the Kurdish fighters, known as the Peshmerga, whose name, when translated from Kurdish, literally means 'the one who confronts death', to fight President Assad's forces in Syria, the Kurds had allowed the US Air Force to fly its fighter-bombers and drones out of the air base near Mosul, in the autonomous Kurdish region of Northern Iraq.

Piloting the MQ-9 Reaper Drone was a twenty-six-year-old US Air Force pilot. "I see the target," screeched the young Air Force pilot into his microphone; his voice was louder than normal and a little tremulous. Some of his colleagues sat at nearby computer terminals in the dimly lit, air-conditioned, purpose-built operations room turned to stare at the young lieutenant. Most of them had been in this situation themselves: the thrill of the kill, holding the tiny joystick, which controlled the drone, whilst staring at thousands of pixels on an LCD monitor. They had the power to extinguish life remotely, with no knowledge whatsoever of the target.

The target was simply another coded identifier, which arrived at the beginning of each shift on a targeting list. "Standby, Charlie Alpha Sierra, I am locked-on and beginning missile launch confirmation procedure." The young pilot looked over his shoulder, and, perspiring slightly, with a dry throat, requested verbal confirmation from his supervisor to go ahead with the strike. "Missiles released," he said into his microphone, "Charlie Alpha Sierra, I repeat, missiles released."

"There, there, Habeebee," whispered Fatima into Hamed's ear. As she was kissing him on the top of his head, the door opened with a bang, and Ali, Hamed's elder brother, walked in. He was dressed more conservatively, in a white ankle-length cotton thawb, and sporting a dark straggly beard. Ali took in the scene.

Watching how his mother held his younger brother he said, "How do you expect him to grow up, if you continue to wrap him in cotton wool and smother him, Mother? My God, don't you think we aren't all upset about father's death?" This time his rage was directed at Hamed.

Hamed turned to peer at his older brother, whilst still clinging to his mother. "We cannot allow what happened to our father to go unpunished. We know it was those cowardly American infidels using their drones that killed our father. We need to take revenge on these Kufar."

Fatima turned to stare at her eldest son. In a calm and measured tone, she began to speak. "Ali, you think too narrowly. You need to broaden your thinking. This is not just a religious struggle that we are engaged in. Indeed, in my opinion our chosen religions are merely a way to identify both sides in this struggle. This is a cultural struggle. These Kufar, as you call them, are trying to destroy Arab dignity and unity." Releasing Hamed, she became more animated, and began to pace around the room. "Look across the Arab world! Everywhere you see fragmented states, tribes set against tribes, and corrupt leaders lining their own pockets with their people's mineral wealth."

If her plan was to succeed, Fatima knew that it was about time that her two sons understood the larger global picture. "The

West wants us to be beholden to their superiority, they want to bring us to our knees and accept that we are inferior. These dogs were living in filth and squalor in the period they quite justifiably call the 'Dark Ages', at which time we were forming our first universities, inventing Algebra, developing advanced surgical techniques and making the finest optics the world would see for five hundred years. In fact, what we now call the USA was a simply a vast patchwork of territories populated by less than forty native Indian tribes." Fatima was now in full flow; she marched around the large hallway gesticulating wildly with her arms. "Mark my words," she shouted. "When the Americans start to lose their grip on global power, they will be replaced by other older nations such as Russia or China. Each of these nations has its own nationalist agenda, seeing themselves as superior to other nations. They aim to subjugate not just Muslims, but Arabs; they want us to remain divided and weak so that they can steal our land and our resources." The diatribe finally over, she breathed out heavily, and went to sit down.

"Hamed, fetch me some tea, please. Ali, I understand that you are hurt, as am I; we all are. You must learn to temper your anger and direct your energy where it will do most harm. You must promise me that you will not do anything rash to try and avenge your father's death." Ali had calmed down a little by now, but Fatima could still see the anger, glowing like an ember in his eyes.

"I promise, Mother," he mumbled, non-committedly, as he turned to go back up the stairs to his wife and family.

Chapter Ten

Fatima was sitting down, clutching her cup of tea and feeling very tired. "Hamed, where is Zainab?" Fatima asked, without looking up. Zainab was Fatima's daughter. Both Fatima and her husband had been surprised when, at the late age of forty-seven, Fatima had found herself pregnant. But they both wanted to keep the child. Now twenty-three years old, Zainab was in the third year of her university studies.

"She is out visiting her aunt. She went there directly after school. I said I would pick her up later on."

"You need to get her right now," said Fatima, firmly but calmly.

"Why now, Mother? I am in the middle of marking my students' work."

"You need to get her right now and tell her to go to her room and prepare herself."

"What do you mean prepare herself?" stammered Hamed.

"She knows full well what to do; just go and fetch her. We have a very important visitor arriving in exactly two hours. I will be meeting him in your father's study, and, when I call, I would like you to bring Zainab in to us."

Hamed, never one to argue with his mother, gave a resigned shrug of his shoulders, and left the house to pick up his younger sister. He knew that his mother had invited prospective husbands into the house before, so that they could be vetted, and so that Zainab would have the chance to form an opinion herself. Fatima went to her bedroom to get changed for the meeting. She bathed, and spent more time than was customary applying her make-up and dressing in her finest clothes. This was a very important visitor, and he had to be persuaded.

Less than two hours later, Fatima opened the front door to the house as she heard the car rolling up the drive. She had knots in her stomach, and, becoming slightly dizzy, she felt the need to steady herself against the door-frame. "Oh my! Allah preserve me! What am I doing?" She was beginning to panic, as the short stocky man who had grey tinges to his closely cropped black hair and very high cheekbones strode towards her. She closed her eyes, uttered a silent prayer, then opened them again, and, with a big smile, strode out to meet the man.

"*As Salaam Alaykum Ismee Ganzorig*," he said, in halting Arabic. He was a barrel-chested, muscular man, probably around fifty years old, Fatima guessed. Although she made no attempt to offer her hand, he took it anyway and shook it firmly. Despite his being a Muslim himself, in his culture the relationship between men and women was different to that between men and women in the Middle East, where a stranger would not dare to take the hand of a female he was neither married or related to.

"*W Alaykum Asalaam ya Ganzorig, Ahlan w Sahlan.*"
Seeing a lack of comprehension on his face, Fatima reiterated in
English. "Welcome, Ganzorig. Please come in. Let us go to my
husband's study."

"It is a great pleasure to meet you, Fatima Al Udayn," he
said, as he entered the house. He had switched to English now,
and although heavily accented, he was far more fluent in it than
he was in Arabic. As they walked through to the study, Hamed
peered gingerly around the corner of his door. Who is this man,
he wondered to himself. He's certainly no Arab. He looks
Chinese. But wait a minute; surely he is too big to be Chinese.
He ducked quickly behind his door as his mother and the large
man approached his room.

Once in the study, Fatima sat behind her husband's old
wooden desk; she fidgeted with the inlaid leather writing pad, as
her guest took his seat on the other side of the table. "Would you
like some coffee, Ganzorig?" she said quietly, as she poured a
cup of hot cardamom coffee.

Staring directly at her, he replied, "Yes, please; thank you,
Fatima. I fear I don't have too much time. I have much work to
do before the 'Collective' are called to council in just over three
months."

"Well, let's get down to business, then, Ganzorig. My eldest
boy, Ali, will be informed about his role in this affair in the
coming weeks."

"Good, good," said Ganzorig, as he slurped his hot coffee.
They talked for another half an hour; then, looking at his watch
Ganzorig said, "And now to the other matter. The price for my
assistance remains as discussed?"

"I remember," replied Fatima; her heart was beating so powerfully in her chest that she thought it would explode. "Hamed!" she shouted her younger son's name. "Hamed, bring Zainab in here please."

Hamed entered the room with his sister, and, without daring to look the strange man in the eye, he left.

"Zainab, this is Ganzorig." Zainab was wearing a long flowing gown made from silk; its light blue edges were delicately embroided with tiny golden flowers. Around her head she wore a light muslin shawl, which was also adorned with the same delicate golden flowers. Her long flowing black hair cascaded down her back beneath the shawl. She wore no other jewellery and wore only a hint of lipstick. For a moment, Ganzorig was dumbfounded; utterly speechless, he was transfixed by the beauty of this girl in front of him.

"I see that you approve, Ganzorig," Fatima said calmly. "Zainab, pour some more coffee for our guest, please." Fatima turned back to Ganzorig and stood up from behind the desk. "I believe our business here is concluded, Ganzorig," Fatima said, a little too icily. "You mentioned that you were busy with preparations prior to the big meeting of the Collective in Öndörkhaan." The city, which lay about two hundred kilometres north of the Mongolian capital of Ulaan Baatar, was to be the host venue for the next meeting of the representatives of three specially selected families from around the Arabic and Muslim world.

The big man stood up; smiling, he turned to Zainab. "I look forward to getting to know you better when you accompany your mother to my country." Zainab, still a little shocked, and feeling very nervous, looked up from her seat with large watery eyes at the big man, and simply nodded.

Fatima walked the Mongolian to the door and wished him well until their next meeting. As soon as she had closed the door, she fell back against the inside of the door and began to sob. It took her a minute to compose herself. It was a great sacrifice indeed that she was making. "At least he is a Muslim," Fatima thought to herself. It wasn't always so. When his kind had travelled on horseback over the great Asian Steppe lands and swept down into Arabia a little under eight hundred years ago, to destroy Baghdad they had entered as Kufar, but, over a period of several generations, some of them had assimilated Islam into their culture, and adopted it as their religion. This Arabic-born religion had travelled back to the steppe land with them. It was for this reason that Fatima had chosen these people to help her.

Once his mother had retired to bed, Ali came down the stairs and walked straight into Hamed's room. "Hamed, have you seen these?" Ali demanded. Hamed looked up from his computer monitor. He had been in the middle of marking one of his undergraduate physics students' essays. The question he had set, a reasonably straightforward one, Hamed thought, was: *The antisymmetric eigenfunction of the helium atom can be written in the form UA - C(uab-uba), where uab and uba are orthonormal. Show that the normalization constant $C - 1/root(2)$*. He had even given them a hint, explaining that their first step was to prove that *(uab-uba) (uab-uba)* * = 2. Anyway, that would have to wait. What did his idiot bullying older brother want from him now?

"I found these papers in father's study. They were hidden away behind a panel in the wall. I only discovered the panel when

I removed a picture of him and his students at the university. Do you know what Father was writing about? And why they would be hidden away like that? It looks like gibberish to me." Hamed carefully took the deep red leather-bound dossier from his older brother and held it reverently in his hands. Rubbing a layer of dirt and grime from the front cover, he gasped and sat bolt upright in his chair.

"These aren't father's papers, Ali. These papers belong to Mum's father, our grandfather!"

"How do you know that?" hissed Ali, embarrassed that once more his little brother had made him look foolish.

"Look carefully at the front cover of the leather folder. Do you see that emblem?" Ali peered closer at the folder, and, in the light of Hamed's computer monitor, he could just make out the black imprint of an eagle rising above a swastika.

"But that's German, isn't it?" Ali asked. "Yes; more precisely, it is a Nazi symbol. Mum told me today that father was working in the laboratory at the university from 1940. Don't you see the connection?" Hamed asked. Looking up at his brother, he saw the realisation slowly dawning on his brother's face.

An expression of incredulity started to spread across Ali's face. "We have to talk to mother about this straight away."

"No," replied Hamed. He paused, waiting for his brother's reaction. Normally his brother got angry when he contradicted him. "No, er, I mean, these have been in father's study for decades, and mother is sleeping. Surely it can wait until morning?" Eyeing his brother warily, Ali nodded his agreement and walked out of the room, leaving Hamed still clutching the documents.

Chapter Eleven

Latitude 33° 16' 6.7008'', Longitude 44° 23' 20.1408''.
The Al Abbasin Household, Baghdad, Iraq, former
Mesopotamia – October 2016
Nazis, Bacteria and Oil

Fatima was picking through a basket of dates in the kitchen. The sun was just rising over the river Tigris casting an intense orange glow, which filtered through the date palm fronds of the trees that lined the riverbank. She had already been up for over an hour. After the encounter last night with the Mongolian, she had slept fitfully. She didn't mind being awake at this time, she loved the warmth of the morning sun, and did most of her best thinking sitting here in the kitchen with a cup of tea, watching the sunrise. At around seven thirty a.m., she heard Hamed waking up. She had already heard Ali get up for the *fajr*, or dawn prayer, but then presumed that he must have gone back to sleep.

Fatima turned with a start, as both boys strode purposefully into the kitchen. As always, Ali was leading, but Hamed was close behind, and, unusually Fatima sensed a unity of purpose in her two sons. Hamed moved forward and embraced his mother. "Good morning, Mother, Ali and I wanted…"

Ali cut in, speaking over his younger brother. "I found these papers in Father's study, Mother. We want to know what they were doing there. Hamed says they are Nazi documents. Is this true? Was Grandpa a Nazi?" Fatima had grown used to Ali's impetuousness and his arrogance; she sighed inwardly.

"Sit down, boys; there are a couple of things I need to explain to you both. I will explain about the documents today and give you time for the ramifications of what I have to say to sink in. No doubt what I have to say will generate many more questions. I will try and answer these questions as time unfolds.

"First of all, let me set the scene. You have to remember that the world looked very different in 1941. The German Nazi party had already approached several Muslim leaders, not only in Iraq, but in Syria, Egypt and Palestine, with the aim of entering into a quid pro quo agreement. Both the Arabs and the Nazis shared common enemies. They both had an intolerance of the Jews, and both parties had a desire to see the demise of the British and French Imperial systems."

"Just like we want to see the end of this neo-American imperialism that has oppressed us for so many years," said Ali, with more than a hint of bitterness in his voice.

Fatima nodded agreement to her eldest son, and continued speaking, "It was to be a relationship with mutual benefits. The Nazis would encourage Arab nationalism and help us to rid our lands of the British and French." Fatima sipped at her coffee and eyed the two young men. She could see that she had their attention. Ali had sat down next to his brother Hamed, and they were both sitting transfixed.

She continued, "You have to remember that many influential people in Iraq really believed in National Socialism and saw it as the way in which they could regain control of their land. Your great grandfather's colleague, Saib Shawkat, who was the Minister for Education at the time, was the leader of the Iraqi youth movement called the Futuwwa. This group was modelled on the Hitler Youth, you know. Were you taught in school about the Farhud? Do you know that in the aftermath of the failed uprising against the British, the Grand Mufti encouraged the organised killing of Jews and the destruction of their property? I was just a baby, but your grandfather told me that the programme of killing, killed over eight hundred Jews."

Fatima's dark eyes began to betray her emotions as she started to recount the story as told to her by her father. "It was 1950; I was barely ten years old, and your grandfather, my father, was already showing the early signs of dementia. It happened right here in this very kitchen. He sat me on his knee, and said he had something important to share with me. Of course I doted on my father, and hung on every word he said. So let me explain in the words of your grandfather how that dossier comes to be hidden away in our study."

Fatima's father, who had been one of Iraq's best young pre-war scientists, had begun to unburden himself, revealing the immense importance behind his life's research work to his daughter. "Fatima, my daughter; let me first tell you about the Iraq in which I grew up. I grew up in an Iraq that had just witnessed the end of the Ottoman Empire. The Ottomans had held sway over Mesopotamia for nearly three hundred years, ever since the Treaty of Zuhab between the Persians and the Ottomans in 1639."

Fatima was ten years old, and only vaguely aware of who the Ottomans were. "Of course, as you know, my dear, nature abhors a vacuum, and, with the Ottomans gone, it was the British who came to rule over us and plunder our soon to be discovered oil wealth. The British struggled to rule Iraq and instead of allowing us to rule ourselves, they used our land as a prize to give to their lapdog, King Faisel, as a thank you for his support to the British Empire during World War One. Faisel was a threat to our family's plans, as he also descended from a competing family, the Hashemites, who also declared themselves related to the Prophet Mohamed, and therefore eligible to use the title Caliph." Fatima, who was sitting on the floor at her father's feet, asked her father to tell her more about the Caliphate, but her father told her that that story would have to wait for another day.

"My father, like many men of science at the time, was both inspired and impressed by the scientific advances the Nazis had been making, and he saw the opportunity in 1936 to gain favour with the National Socialists in Germany. He offered the Nazis support from our Baghdad University for their scientific missions in Iraq, and also secretly helped to coordinate a series of radio broadcasts on behalf of the Nazi party.

"I was just finishing off my studies as one of the first 'home grown' petro-chemical engineers in Iraq, and for my dissertation I had been given access to German research and had even been allowed to travel to Freiburg, Germany in 1940, to study under Professor George Wittig. It was here that I made my breakthrough. This is what I am so keen to share with you." Staring up into the face of her father, Fatima had seen the intensity of excitement emanating from her father's eyes. "Whilst experimenting in Germany, I had stumbled upon a bacterium that could be used to break down certain elements in petroleum oil, and cause this normally smooth viscous liquid to turn into a thick hard gum and become worthless as a fuel."

Looking down at his daughter, Fatima's father stared hard into her eyes to try to establish whether this ten-year-old girl had fully comprehended the enormity of his last statement. "My work was of great interest to the Nazis, because, if the tide were to turn against them in the war, the Nazis were desperately keen not to let the huge oil reserves in Iraq fall into Allied hands. I was forced to swear an oath of silence about my research before leaving Germany. The country I had returned to was very different indeed to the one I had left. In early April 1941, the Iraqi Army led by Rashid Ali had seized power by crushing the British in their bases."

Fatima had been taught about this act of Iraqi rebellion against the British in her school history classes. She also knew that Rashid Ali's victories were short-lived. "The rebels, under Rashid Ali, were poorly equipped and extremely disorganised, and one month later, after some heavy fighting, the British took back control of the government. In late May 1941, as the British tanks and infantry were advancing into the suburbs of Baghdad to recapture the city, the German Luftwaffe had been ordered to bomb our university, and German agents from the Gestapo were sent to destroy any evidence of my work. They also wanted to retrieve any remaining samples of the cultivated bacteria to be taken back to Germany."

By this point in the story, the ten-year-old Fatima could clearly see that her old father was becoming emotional. "During the night I escaped the city with my notes in a red leather dossier. Your grandfather, I am afraid, was less fortunate. He was killed by the Nazis, because he would not tell them where I was hiding. Until this day, I have carried the burden of this secret. My health is failing now, and I fear I am beginning to lose my mind."

Struggling to retain his composure, Fatima's father finished his story. "Now that you are old enough to begin to understand, I believe I can entrust this legacy to you. Because, you see, Fatima, this simple elegant bacterium which I discovered, quite by accident, will be the weapon by which we will once more regain our dignity. So promise me two things, my daughter. Firstly, that you will study hard at school so that you can understand the power of my discovery; and secondly, that you marry wisely and have strong healthy boys to carry on our family line."

Fatima finished recounting the story, exactly as her father had told it to her. She looked across the heavy wooden table to her two sons. Both Ali and Hamed were shocked and saddened by the story they had just heard. Mouths agape, they just sat and stared uncomprehendingly at their mother. "I have spent the better part of my working life studying your grandfather's bacteria, learning how they function, what they need to perform their work, and, most importantly, how they can be improved."

Hamed, by far the more intellectual of the two boys, managed to speak first. "That's an amazing story, Mother, but I still don't understand the relevance of grandfather's discovery today in the twenty-first century. I mean, we are no longer under threat of invasion, and we have our own government and country."

Fatima placed her hands on Hamed's and Ali's shoulders. "Ever since oil was discovered in the mid 1920s, it has been used by the great powers to build industry and create advanced military weapons. It's quite simple; In the twenty-first century, without oil, our industrial and military complexes would collapse..."

Abruptly, Ali stood up, and paced towards the kitchen window. He didn't possess his mother's or brother's academic brilliance; however, he did possess an innate cunning. He had used this ruthless cunning to his advantage, countless times before, during business negotiations. Looking for weaknesses in his counterpart's position, he would unearth personal or financial issues or secrets, and then use them as levers to help him get the biggest margin possible in a deal. "It's about power!" he said triumphantly. "Power and control. We have created a world that simply cannot function without oil, and Mother holds the key in her hand to destroying that oil."

"Wait a minute," interrupted Hamed. "If we truly do possess the ability to destroy oil, there are still so many unanswered questions and variables that need explaining. I still don't get why we should do it, now of all times, if this capability has existed all these years and not been used. I also don't see how or even why our family should take action. Indeed, I am more puzzled about who we would take action against. Are you really considering destroying Iraq's oil supply? That would be economic madness, Mother!"

"I told you at the beginning that I had two things to share with you. First, I must give you time to let the ramifications of what I have just told you sink in. Ali, you are correct in recognising that it is about power and control; and, Hamed, your questions are valid questions. I will hopefully be able to answer all of those questions as time unfolds."

Fatima placed her coffee cup in the sink, and, with her back to her two sons, to signify that the conversation was over, she said, "Hamed, I thought you had some of your students' work to mark. Ali, is that Miriam I hear calling you from upstairs? Now off you go, you two, otherwise if you keep me here much longer I will be late for work." She picked a couple of juicy ripe Medjool dates that she would take for her lunch, grabbed her leather briefcase, and, looping the shoulder strap over one arm, she strolled out of the house. The two boys left the kitchen in silence, both deep in thought, and headed back to their respective apartments.

Chapter Twelve

Latitude 1° 17' 28.8348'', Longitude 103° 47' 13.3296''.
United Nations Centre for Technology and Culture
Headquarters, Heng Mui Keng Terrace, Singapore –
March 2017.
Introductions

It could never be considered a beautiful building. The CTC HQ was a tall, shiny glass and steel construction, much in keeping with the buildings clustered around it. Despite its being built on the University of Singapore's campus, it was surrounded on three sides by lush tropical vegetation. The front of the building looked directly across at the University's Institute of Micro-Electronics and Systems Science.

In actual fact, the site had been chosen with considerable care. It wasn't that the Centre wanted to hide its presence, but it certainly did not want to advertise it too widely either. The University infrastructure meant that the HQ had access to a secure high-speed Internet and enough data storage space to allow for the centre's expansion, should it be necessary. The synergies that could be achieved in terms of access to technical knowhow and hi-tech laboratories were second to none, thanks to the Centre's close proximity to both the Systems Science and Micro-Electronics Institutes.

Living in Singapore was certainly not going to be a hardship, either. Admittedly, Singapore was small, but that only added to the charm of the place; and the team would be travelling internationally so often that it would be nice to be able to come back to this neat and ordered little city-state. One of the problems arising from Singapore's diminutive size was the exorbitant cost of vehicle ownership.

In a bid to keep congestion under control, the government had introduced some very harsh tax disincentives. To buy a car, you had to pay the government a whopping forty-one per cent tax, based on the value of the car, plus a whole raft of road and licensing taxes that could soon mount up to six to seven thousand dollars. This was, of course, if you were one of the lucky ones who managed to secure a Certificate of Entitlement in the monthly lottery. Luckily, working for the UN had its perks. The UN had been given sixteen Certificates of Entitlement, and the CTC had purchased several Toyota Land Cruisers and Toyota Hiluxes as team vehicles. In addition, each team member lived rent-free, and paid no taxes, as each member was outside their own tax jurisdiction and was legally classed as an expatriate worker.

It had taken just over a month from the first arrivals until the last team member was in place. Charu Usmani had been one of the first to arrive; she had been keen to leave MIT and put everything that had happened there behind her. Andrei had arrived soon afterwards and had already begun to moan at the limited space available, and the almost complete lack of hills for him to pursue his passion for ultra-distance running. Penny had needed just over three weeks from being recruited to her arrival at the Centre in Singapore. In that time, she had undergone a very thorough debrief procedure, and had spent what seemed like countless hours completing the mundane bureaucracy required to hand over her active case files to her colleagues. She wasn't sad to leave some of her colleagues behind; however, there were some people at MI6 that she would miss. Of course, she didn't mind, at all, leaving rainy cold London behind for steamy Singapore.

Maria and Philippe had been the next to arrive. They arrived within hours of each other, and, to the other team members, it seemed as if they couldn't be more different. Philippe, the congenial giant of a man, almost permanently seemed to maintain a half smile on his lips and had an endless supply of encouragement and kind words to say to his colleagues. Maria, the first team member to be recruited, seemed distant, even imperious, during the first couple of weeks at the centre.

The last person to arrive was Matthias. He had completed just over a month of his alcohol dependency treatment and had very quickly moved through the different levels that an addict needs to negotiate on their way to being able to, at least, live effectively with their addiction, if not be able to cure themselves of it. Of course, the remorse he felt for being responsible for the death of his daughter and the disability he had caused his wife had been strong motivators. Waking each day in an empty house, knowing he would never hear his daughter's laughter, was the main catalyst behind his determination to beat his demons.

Li sat at the head of the briefing room table. With such a full room for the first time, the air conditioners had to work at nearly full capacity. The annual north-easterly monsoon period had almost finished for the year, and Singapore found itself in that more pleasant time of year between the two rainy seasons. Of course, they still received regular afternoon thunderstorms, which cleared the hot moisture-laden air and gave the local inhabitants a much-needed release from the stifling humidity. The outside temperatures were beginning to climb. The mercury in the thermometer was already creeping up past thirty degrees Celsius.

Looking across the table at the people assembled in front of him, Li knew that if the CTC was to have any chance of surviving its first year and becoming an effective agency, then his first task would be to create a team out of this group of highly talented individuals. He had already picked up on the fact that Maria was still railing against being here; Charu, despite being relieved to be away from MIT, was still very introverted, and kept her distance from the other team members.

Andrei was different; he was very sure of himself, yet remained strangely distanced from the group. Li thought that probably came from his superb physical conditioning and finely-honed military skills. Li recalled his first exposure to the men of the Chinese Special Forces. In China, the units were divided by district. The Shengyang unit was called the Siberian Tigers. The members of this unit were the specialists in survival in extreme conditions, as well as sabotage operations by land, sea and air. Having only been formed in the early 1990s, they were still relatively unknown outside of China. Li had witnessed these men in action during a display that was put on for high-ranking Chinese Communist Party officials. Whilst talking to these men after the display, Li had noticed the same self-assurance and detachment, which at times bordered on arrogance, that he noticed when he observed Andrei. Then, as now, he found this lack of respect for superiors both annoying and a little disquieting.

Li had requested a round table for the briefing room. Just as with King Arthur's court at Camelot, he wanted each person around the table to feel equally important. Obviously, no perfect system existed, and it could still appear that those who sat closest to Li were of greater importance. To his left sat the statue-like form of Andrei, with his ubiquitous sports drinks bottle, filled with his homemade fruit and vegetable juice. To Li's right sat Maria; her eyes never stopped moving. She was constantly scanning the other members in the room, looking for imperceptible changes in their demeanour. Li didn't mind this; he knew she would soften up in time. What he did mind was the huge silver New York Giants thermal coffee mug that she seemed to have with her permanently. The steam from the strong acrid liquid was percolating into his nose and making him feel nauseous.

Looking studiously at each team member in turn, Li addressed the meeting. "First of all, I would like officially to welcome everyone to the CTC. I know some of you have been here for over a month now. But today marks the day when the whole team is assembled for the first time." Matthias, who had been the last to arrive, had not even had time to unpack, and sat sweating in his chair, still wearing the same clothes that he had travelled in from Copenhagen.

Li looked over at Matthias who was sitting opposite him, and wondered if he was doing his little trick again, analysing those present around the table. "In this meeting, I would like to achieve three things: firstly, for us all to get to know each other; secondly, to understand better what our purpose is, the Mission Statement if you like; and, finally, I will outline what the programme holds over the next few months." Li continued talking in his clipped British accent, whilst trying to work out how much confidence these people had in his leadership.

"I am reminded of an aphorism attributed to Sun Tzu. 'Know your enemy and know yourself and you can fight a hundred battles without disaster'. The very essence of our work here at the CTC is to try to understand as much as we can about each individual culture that we encounter, so that we are able to engage with that culture in an effective manner, to support it as an individual entity, regardless of its position in the society of the country to whom its members belong. Sun Tzu's aphorism is as true today as it was two thousand five hundred years ago, when it was first recorded. Therefore, I suggest that, after a brief introduction by me, we should take some time to get to know each other."

Li began to introduce the members of the team to the group as a whole by reading out a short biography of their career and particular skill set. After he had finished, he invited Matthias, first, to stand up and speak a little more about himself. "Lonely, remorseful and bitter! Marginally overweight, and nearly every waking hour is spent trying to curb my desire to drink alcohol." There was stunned silence in the room. Matthias looked around the table and absorbed their astonishment.

"You see, the biographies that have been read out only give us the impression of each other that our countries, our respective organisations or ourselves as individuals, wish to portray. Actually, knowing yourself, isn't that straightforward. Understanding your weaknesses and desires, as well as recognising how you are perceived by others, is a difficult trick to master." Li began to speak, but Matthias continued; he was in full flow, and it felt good to talk; it reminded him of his days lecturing at the university. "When a group is first formed, a hierarchical battle for dominance ensues. Each group member is attempting to gain a dominant place in the hierarchy; to achieve this, they 'self-present.' That is to say, they project an impression of themselves that they believe will most likely serve their purposes."

The room was still silent and Li, whose mildly flushed face was the only sign of his annoyance at losing control of the meeting, looked on at Matthias. "So," continued Matthias, "we can either waste the next three months lying to each other and presenting a false image of ourselves, or we can get right down to it here and now." Matthias wasn't trying to be aggressive or confrontational; he was simply being pragmatic.

"Charu, you live inside your own world, burdened with an intellect that most of us can't even conceive of. This causes you to become sexually frustrated, lack confidence in personal encounters with your colleagues, and lack the ability to communicate your thoughts to us mere mortals, because your thinking is quite simply on another plane." Charu's face began to suffuse with blood; her head slowly dropped in embarrassment as Matthias spoke, and tiny teardrops began to form in the corners of her eyes.

Matthias continued addressing each of the team members around the room; getting to Maria, he said, "You provoke people to get attention, you want to be recognised as an independent and capable person. In doing so you come across as androgynous, or even robotic. But actually, in your subconscious, you are a deeply caring person who has recently undergone a deep personal tragedy, and you are struggling to come to terms with your life." Maria's eyes briefly flashed an icy stare at Matthias, but then she returned her gaze once more to her large aluminium thermos of coffee.

"I am truly sorry if I have offended any of you with my insights, or my candid opinion of your personalities; however, as a career anthropologist, and someone who has recently had to ask these questions about himself whilst facing up to an alcohol addiction, I believe it is necessary to get things out in the open early on."

Li was relieved that he had not been forced to lose face in front of his team, and that Matthias had stopped his little parlour trick before he had begun to dissect his character. Adjusting the knot in his tie, Li stood up to continue speaking. "Well, er, thank you, Matthias, for your rather candid appraisal of the group. Moving on, I will explain a little more about the centre and its proposed role."

Li spoke for over an hour about the envisaged purpose of the CTC, emphasising the very real threat of a fracturing world order, where many ethnic groups and cultures would be caught up in the maelstrom of violence, as nation states collapsed and new groups or political parties battled to seize control in the power vacuum that would inevitably exist in these regions.

Chapter Thirteen

Latitude 1° 17' 28.8348'', Longitude 103° 47' 13.3296''.
United Nations Centre for Technology and Culture
Headquarters, Heng Mui Keng Terrace, Singapore –
March 2017.
Human Terrain Mapping

After the introductions were over with, Li changed the discussion at the table to begin to explain how the CTC would go about achieving its mandate. "Our mandate is deliberately broad, and how we are meant to achieve our effect is still uncertain. It has been decided that in the first year of our existence we should be used to develop pertinent technologies and investigate the application of these technologies in an equitable way amongst some of the world's more disenfranchised ethnic groups." There was a general nod of agreement around the table. "We will begin our mandated work with a Human Terrain Mapping exercise in the autonomous Kurdish region of Northern Iraq; and, if we get the relevant government permissions, we will continue this work over the border in Turkey."

Andrei raised a hand. "You said 'Human Terrain Mapping'; I am not familiar with this term. Please expand." Much to Li's relief, Matthias offered to explain.

"It is very much similar to what all of you are trained for in different ways. Penny and Andrei are used to gathering intelligence about their enemies' intentions and behaviours. You, Maria, spend each day conducting threat analyses, observing people, and trying to distinguish whether they pose a threat to the person you are trying to protect. Charu, your day is taken up with trying to understand how different elements in a system interact with each other, and how this causes the system to behave. My good friend, Philippe, here has had some first-hand experience of Human Terrain Mapping with me, up in the Aleutian Islands on the Inuit Power Project. In essence, it is the way anthropologists go about discovering all they can about communities of people and their relationship within the group, between different groups and with the environment. The only key difference between this sort of intelligence gathering and the type that Andrei, Maria and Penny are used to is that, at the end, we don't have to decide if we are going to kill the people we are observing." There was a ripple of soft laughter around the room as Matthias spoke these last words. "In fact, believe it or not, many Western military organisations already use this methodology when they are fighting their 'hearts and minds' campaigns. They have specially trained soldiers that speak the native languages and have had a degree of anthropology training. It is their job to make sure that their commander becomes effective at winning over hearts and minds."

Charu raised her hand tentatively. "Please, Charu, do you have something to add?" asked Matthias, with a warm smile.

"I was involved in producing some fractal maps for the US Department of Defence once."

"Fractal what?" said Andrei. "I'm getting more confused by the minute!"

"Oh, it's quite simple really," said Charu. "A fractal is simply where the whole has been broken into a large number of irregular pieces, and these pieces are represented as one object when viewed from a certain level of granularity."

Matthias gazed around the room gauging the team's reaction to Charu's extraordinary intellect. "The best metaphor is a map. If you look at a map of the solar system, our planet earth is represented as a sphere, and is sized in relation to the other planets. Now, if you look at a specific region of our planet, using what we refer to as the map of the world, you see the Alps as a grey feature with rough contours. If you bought a local one to fifty thousand scale relief map of an area of the Alps such as Mont Blanc, you would see far more irregular shapes, as each mountain and valley would be expressed in greater detail."

Even Andrei had to agree that Charu could take a complex idea and manage to make it comprehensible in terms that even he could understand. "What the DoD wanted from me was to be able to display Human Terrain Data at different levels of granularity, depending on who used it. One map showed the particular tribes in Helmand Province. I used the same data to create individual maps of the relationships and sub-groups within these tribes; it displayed their hierarchies and interconnectedness. Obviously, the map is only as good as the data, and, for that, we had constantly to send patrols out to the villages, to gather the information."

"Thank you, Charu," Li said, as he stood up, eager to regain control of the meeting. "That, in essence, is what we will be doing on our first exercise. We will deploy into the field of study, in this case to Northern Iraq, and we will gather intelligence and map that intelligence with the purpose of understanding how we can best support these communities with the technology that we are developing."

"We will need to conduct some preparatory planning and elementary training before conducting this exercise, which is as much about getting to understand the 'customer' a little better, as it is for us to be able to develop slick working practices and be able efficiently to carry out our mission statement."

Penny, Maria and Andrei were all nodding in approval; as security-focused individuals they understood the approach Li was taking. Philippe also nodded his approval; from his time working on oil projects he realised the efficacy of developing a well-thought-through project plan before starting work.

Only Charu looked a little less convinced. Her razor-quick mind had already reviewed Li's methodology, and found it to be too linear, and therefore lacking the creativity that went into her own very non-linear and extremely dynamical thought processes. She kept her thoughts to herself, and made a mental note to review the methodology the centre used in more detail, and then to try to model alternative solutions that might yield better results.

Li was relieved that his outline and planning had been well received by the group. "Finally, I just want to outline the Five Technology Translation Centres that are set up to support us. Philippe, would you mind talking us through them please?" Philippe had been the natural choice as the focus for these technology centres. He had spent the last three weeks reviewing the research at each site and trying to understand the applicability of each project. He stood up, and, with a click on the mouse, brought up the first of five slides he had prepared for the meeting.

"This will be a very brief overview, because, first of all I have to make it in English and not French, and, secondly, I have arranged for us to visit all five sites very soon, to get a first-hand look at the tech." His heavily French accented words actually served to make Philippe sound genuinely enthused about his subject and gave the listener the impression that he had a deep understanding about what he was talking about. "First off, what we are doing is taking already existing technologies, developing their capability further, and looking at ways of making them either more rugged or reliable to withstand use outside of the lab environment."

Clicking on the remote control for the PowerPoint presentation, Philippe continued to deliver his briefing. "So, very briefly, our tour will start in Muscat, Oman; here the team is developing self-healing materials. Imagine, if you can, a road that gets cracked and potholed in the winter. Well, this team are working on concrete and other materials that contain bacteria that, when exposed to water via a crack in its surface, begin to produce a substance that acts like a cement and repairs the crack." Philippe spoke rapidly and confidently. "Next, we travel to Windhoek in Namibia. This site is doing some incredible work, developing ways of generating electricity through movement using Piezo-electric crystals. You will get a demo and a better explanation when we visit, but, put simply, these crystals can be embedded in a road surface, a mat or even a tyre or tank track, and, as pressure is applied to them, they generate a low electric current. This current is captured and stored, then used as a battery to power other devices."

The team hung on every word that Philippe said. What they were hearing sounded more like science fiction than science fact. "Moving on, to Girona, northern Spain, the facility is working on another, yet very distinct power project. This one aims to couple hydro-power produced from wave action with traditional hydro-electric power which uses a reservoir high up on a mountain, and relies on gravity to turn the turbines. In this case, we have managed to harness wave energy to generate sufficient power to be able to pump the water that comes down the mountain to the hydro-electric plant, back up the mountain and back into the reservoir. The beauty of this scheme is that none of the generated electricity is being used to run the generating plant, and only a finite amount of water is needed, so the plant can work in all seasons around the clock. With over forty-four per cent of the world's population living on or near the coast, I guess you can already begin to see the impact this technology could have?"

Charu seemed particularly interested in this scheme. Her home country of India had seemed to suffer from continual power brown-outs and blackouts. It was her belief that this lack of sufficient power supply was one of the key factors that held back the development of her country's economy.

"Next, we will visit Sao Paulo in Brazil. This group has teamed up with researchers from MIT, and is developing self-controlling drone swarms, which act very much like a flock of birds or insects would. Equipped with an array of monitoring devices and sensors, they are capable of autonomously monitoring large areas of a country and providing live data via satellite up links. They are being trialled as we speak, in a project to monitor the Brazilian rainforest, looking for cross-border incursions, and for other illegal activity such as drug factories, illegal airplane runways and deforestation. Finally, we end our journey in my country, Canada. We will go to the site in Gander Newfoundland. This, for me at least, is the most amazing tech that we are currently working on. We have helped design Ion scrubbers. These devices basically take in positively charged ions from the air, and remove the positive electrical charge, then release the ion back into the atmosphere. It works best in stormy or very dusty environments, but, essentially, is capable of providing free energy from the air."

Penny looked up at this last comment. "OK: I was with you on the crystals, and even the self-healing concrete, but energy from the air? Really?"

"I know, I know," said Matthias, in a defensive manner. "I too could not believe my eyes when I first read the project report. That is why we are going to visit."

Li rose from his seat with a wry smile on his face. As expected, the revelations about the tech that was being worked on had been as surprising to them as it had been to Li when it had first been disclosed to him. "So now, I think we are all a little better informed. You understand the priorities. Firstly, we will tour the other facilities. This should help to inform our planning for the exercise in Iraq. In conjunction with the exercise in Iraq. Matthias and Philippe will also be preparing some more work on their Inuit Power Project. I would like you all to provide assistance to them, should they require it."

With that, Li stood up and left the room. Maria was sitting idly circling a note she had made on the corner of her pad during the meeting. It was a note to check out Li's past. Somehow, she didn't trust him; and, although it was just a hunch, she was concerned that everything they were doing and saying was somehow being monitored. After the meeting, Li and Philippe had been joined by Matthias in the glass cube designed for smokers, which Li had insisted be installed inside the building. Matthias only smoked occasionally, normally to distract himself from wanting to have a drink.

The cube's design meant that those on the inside could be seen by all around them. This could have created the feeling of being a goldfish trapped in a bowl. However, Li had installed a couple of comfy chairs in the cube, and enjoyed sitting there, slowly drawing on his cigarettes and observing his employees. "Are you seeing what I am seeing?" asked Matthias, calmly. Both Philippe and Li followed his gaze.

Outside the cube, over in a darker corner of the main operations room, by a bank of large LCD screens, they could see Maria and Andrei arguing. They were standing facing up to each other. By the light of the monitors, it was possible to see Maria's contorted face, as she whispered something sharply into Andrei's ear. His reaction was a quizzical look, and, with his head half-cocked, his face distorted into a sarcastic smile. Then Maria raised her arms in the air in utter frustration and turned to storm away.

"That is a manifestation of the hierarchical battles that go on when a group forms," said Matthias.

"I know," said Li. "I have witnessed several incidents over the last week alone."

Withdrawing his pipe from his mouth, Philippe cut in, "Sure, sure, *mes amis*, but they will work it out eventually. If this Maria is as good as her file says, then once we start to operate, she will have the chance to earn Andrei's respect."

Matthias had already seen it in Andrei's posture. "I am not too sure; you know, these Special Forces units do not have many women attached to them, and they do not like taking orders from anyone who has not had their level of training, man or woman."

"That is true," said Li, remembering his encounter with the Shenyang Special Forces unit.

Chapter Fourteen

Latitude 33° 16' 6.7008'', Longitude 44° 23' 20.1408''.
The Al Abbasin Household, Baghdad, Iraq, former
Mesopotamia – November 2016.
Al Mustansim Billah

Just under a month had passed in the Al Abbasin household. An air of expectation was ever-present. Both Hamed and Ali had read their grandfather's documents, and the true potential of the discovery was still only just beginning to sink in. Ali had been more secretive than usual and had been away for a week on a carpet-buying trip to Irbil in Northern Iraq. The carpets actually came from Iran, but Ali had a well-connected contact in Irbil that imported the carpets and distributed them all over Iraq. Most evenings, dinner was an occasion that just Hamed and Fatima enjoyed together; however, tonight was different. Ali was back, and Fatima was keen to divulge the rest of her secret to Ali and Hamed. The clock was ticking, and so much work remained, if she wanted to implement her plan by wintertime.

"Ali, would you like more lamb?" Fatima was serving the boys' favourite dish; it was chopped lamb shank that had been stewed in a pot with eggplant and onions. The meat had been cooking on a low heat for several hours, and the smell of the spiced lamb had percolated throughout the entire ground floor of the house. Ali nodded eagerly to his mother; it was delicious, and it just seemed to melt in your mouth.

"I wish Miriam could cook meat like this," he thought. Miriam, his wife, had gone with the children to spend some time with her family. They were from Basra, further south in Iraq on the Shatt al Arab waterway. Ali didn't like visiting Miriam's family. He knew that her father, who was a Lieutenant General in the Iraqi army, had always thought that Ali wasn't good enough for her. Placing another warm pitta bread into the bottom of Ali's bowl, Fatima generously ladled the thick stew on top of the soft bread.

"Now, boys, I have something of the highest importance to tell you. In the summer of 1980, just as your grandfather was succumbing to his dementia, and in one of his last lucid moments, he revealed his most closely guarded secret to me. You, Ali, were a young boy of five, and I was pregnant with you, Hamed. I had remained at the university after finishing my Ph.D. in chemistry. Opportunities for female scientists in those days were limited indeed. But through his connections, your grandfather had secured me a place in the Chemical Engineering faculty."

The boys continued to devour their delicious stew, whilst listening to their mother speak. As young children, both of them only had distant memories of their grandfather, and these were of a frail man who had trembled slightly when he held a cup and seemed to have a perpetual vacant stare on his face.

"I knew my father wouldn't have many more lucid moments in his life to share his thoughts with us, so I decided to record our conversation." Fatima stood up slowly from the table and walked over to the old stereo system in the house. She first placed a small cassette tape into the old music centre, then pressed down the big hard black button to start the recording. There was a loud hissing sound, and Fatima reduced the volume slightly. As the hissing faded away, a quiet, yet clear voice began to speak.

"My daughter, I would like to reveal to you a story so incredible that it will appear unbelievable. It is the story of the destruction of the greatest ever Arabic Caliphate, and our family's role in it." Fatima heard her own voice on the scratchy tape recording, as she asked her father to sit a little closer to the microphone.

"The apogee of Arabic cultural and linguistic achievement was between 1242 and 1258 AD: a Caliphate which stretched from the furthest corner of Persia in the east, to what today is known as Algeria in the West. In the north, it encompassed all those living as far away as the Caucasus Mountains, and its southernmost tip looked into the Straits of Hormuz, from what today is called Yemen. At its centre sat Baghdad. The Caliphate was ruled by the last true Arabic Caliph, Al Mustansim Billah. Under this Caliph, government, religion and science all coexisted in a harmonious relationship. Baghdad was the very epicentre of mankind's cultural and scientific achievement. Through his emissaries, and through visiting ambassadors from other countries, the foundations of science, as we know it today, were spread throughout the known world. It is true that not all of the knowledge was generated within the Caliphate, but under the Caliph's guidance, it was the recording of this knowledge and translation from other great eastern empires that allowed this knowledge, for the first time, to be codified and disseminated. As you will now hear, this grand period of cultural enlightenment was to change irrevocably."

Although the recording was old, and sometimes difficult to understand, both boys sat in complete silence, hanging on every word their grandfather had to say.

"We often think today that the Nazis invented the concept of Blitzkrieg or lightning war; however, over one millennium before their existence, it was the nomadic horsemen of the Asian steppe lands, whom we today call Mongols, who had first developed this devastating military tactic. An Army of some hundred thousand soldiers swarmed towards Baghdad from the East, after first conquering Persia. On January 29th, in the year 1258, with Hulagu Khan at their head, this vast Mongol army had Baghdad surrounded. After watching his twenty-thousand-strong force of cavalry be destroyed by the Mongols, the Caliph surrendered. Expecting to pay a heavy price for his surrender, the Caliph met with Hulagu Khan to discuss terms. The Khan refused the Caliph's vast wealth and ordered the city to be sacked." Of course, the boys had been taught about the sack of their city by their teachers at school, but somehow hearing it in their grandfather's voice on this old recording gave the whole story a greater significance.

"In a period of less than forty days, up to one million people were butchered by the Mongol horde. The Caliph himself suffered the indignity of being rolled in a carpet and trampled to death by the Khan's cavalrymen. If this wholesale massacre of Baghdad were not horrific enough, the Khan went on to destroy the great library. It is said that the waters of the Tigris ran black with the ink of the destroyed books." Fatima paused the tape recording and addressed the two boys. "This next part is the most relevant part for you."

"After the attack, one of the Caliph's daughters was spared and enslaved as a concubine in the Khan's Harem. What is less well known is that the Khan ordered one of the Caliph's sons to be sent back to Mongolia. This son, Walid Ibn Mustansim, who was twelve at the time was brought up in a Mongolian household and, in time, at the age of fifteen, he married and had children with a Mongolian woman. As their son was growing up, the Mongols who were returning from Arabia to resettle in Mongolia had converted to Islam. They brought Islam to Mongolia, and although there were many convertees, the majority of Mongols did not convert. This partial conversion allowed their son to observe the five main pillars of faith, and openly be a Muslim. He could publicly recite the *shahada*, the Muslim profession of faith and belief in God and Muhammed (Peace be upon Him) as his messenger. He prayed. He gave *zakat*, a portion of his wealth, annually, to those needier than himself; he could also practice *sawm*, or the observance of fasting, during Ramadan; and, to complete the five pillars of his faith, crucially, Walid was now permitted to travel to Mecca, to conduct *hajj*. Despite this tolerance of his religion, he realised that he could never reveal his true lineage, as to do so could pose a threat to the Mongol Khanate, and he knew that that would cost him and his family their lives."

Ever impatient, Ali interrupted the recording, saying, "Mum, I don't see how this history lesson is important to us."

"Be patient, and let your grandfather finish explaining," said Fatima, with just a hint of exasperation in her voice.

"The Mongols bought many Arabic women back from their conquests to Mongolia as concubines. Some managed to escape their bondage, or earn their freedom, and soon sought the protection of this growing Muslim Arab diaspora, which had settled in Mongolia. Over the centuries since Baghdad was sacked, from Walid Ibn Mustansim to me, there have been fifty-four successors to the last Caliph, Al Mustansim Billah. I am the fifty-fifth." Both Ali and Hamed looked to their mother for confirmation of what they had both just heard. Fatima just signalled that they should continue listening.

"Although the Arabic Muslim population thrived in Mongolia, they were never truly accepted, and never given the same rights as the Mongols; they were tolerated due to their ability at maths and geometry, which helped the Mongols to build greater buildings, and develop their agriculture. However, they were often persecuted, and it was the great grandson of Walid Ibn Mustansim, the third successor to Walid, who, seeing an increase in this persecution, eventually left Mongolia with his wife and children. He escaped whilst travelling to Mecca on *hajj*. Over several years, he and his family made their way back to Baghdad." Understanding began to dawn on Ali and Hamed's faces.

"The Arabs who remained in Mongolia were, over many years, eventually killed off, through successive purges, first by the Mongolian Khans, then, later, by the Russian Imperial Czars, and, finally, by the Chinese Communists and Soviets, either by enslaving them in forced labour in the gulags, or in huge relocation pogroms. Walid's grandson, now well established in Baghdad, began to renew the study of science; he taught astrology. As his sons grew up, one fathered no children; the other had two girls and a boy. Due to the patronage they received from the Ottomans, it is this hereditary line that has continued unbroken in Baghdad since the early fourteenth century." Switching off the old tape deck, Fatima turned to face the two boys.

"Do you now see, my sons? Our family are the last remaining custodians of the Al Abbasid Caliphate. It is our right and our sole purpose in life to reform a new Caliphate."

Fatima switched the tape recorder back on. "Our family's status gradually grew, as the Ottoman Empire, forced ever more into wars on their western borders, relied upon the educated council of families like the Al Abbasids to raise taxes, supply soldiers and govern Iraq by proxy on behalf of the Empire. Each successive generation has been involved at the highest level in either politics or science. They have all guarded this great secret of their birth lineage with an untempered zeal."

"This next part will help you to understand why I am letting you into our family's secret now, and why we must not lose this unique opportunity to act." Fatima's father continued to outline why the Caliphate had not been re-established before now. "This story, and the secret of the heir to the Caliphate, have been safely passed down through all these generations. And so it was the fiftieth successor, a man called Ibn Walid bin Mohammed, during the reign of Mahmud II from 1808-1839, who, on realising that the Ottoman grip on power was weakening, established a secret society with his two sisters and cousins, with the express aim of seizing power and regaining their rightful position once the Ottomans left. This was, unfortunately, not to be; the Ottoman Empire collapsed far too quickly, and, in the ensuing void, the British entered to claim their prize. They were quick to seize the opportunity to control Iraq. The British were in a desperate search for a replacement to steam which could power their great warships, and thus help them maintain the global dominance of their huge navy. They knew that with control over the next source of power, oil, they would remain the dominant nation in the world.

"You see, my daughter, my era was plagued by war and colonial power struggles; and, with my deteriorating health, soon your eldest son Ali will be the rightful heir to the Caliphate. Now that we are no longer a vassal state ruled by Emperors in far distant lands, the time has come for us to unite the different Arabic tribes under the true banner of the last Caliph and seize back what is rightfully ours. We can once more unite the Arabic peoples, and create a harmonious House of Peace where Government, Religion and science can coexist."

Fatima's father gripped her hand, and she let out a brief shout. "You know what to do, don't you? Use the formula to destroy the oil, which fuels our enemies' very existence. The secret society remains, and in my papers I have a list of twelve families, spread throughout the old Caliphate who will support you in your task. You must also go to the land of our destroyers and seek help there."

Fatima was weeping, as the large black button on the tape recorder clicked off. Both Hamed and Ali were sitting spellbound in their chairs. A skin had begun to form on their mother's delicious stew, which now lay cold and thick in the bottom of their bowls. They were completely entranced at hearing their grandfather's frail voice, whose final words were still resonating around the dining room. No longer bent over sobbing, but now standing tall and erect, belying her seventy years of life, Fatima leant forward to address the two boys.

"My boys, I have spent my entire life preparing for this opportunity. My research, my marriage, your births were all parts of this plan. Ali, as my first-born son, I am aware that I have placed this great burden of responsibility and expectation upon your shoulders, and I have only revealed your true destiny today because I wanted you to have a normal life and be able to do the things you wanted to. Your life in the future will change beyond belief. I have contact with the twelve members of the Society and a meeting has been called for the beginning of next year, just under a month from now, in a town a little way north of Ulaan Baatu in Mongolia. If our plan is successful, then, in one year from now, you will be the new Arabic Caliph, governing a benign and beneficent Caliphate, even greater in size than Al Mustansim Billah."

Chapter Fifteen

*Latitude 1° 17' 28.8348'', Longitude 103° 47' 13.3296''.
United Nations Centre for Technology and Culture
Headquarters, Heng Mui Keng Terrace, Singapore – May
2017.
Jet Lag*

"Five countries in ten days is ambitious, however you look at it," said Penny to Philippe.

"Yeah, I guess it is; but I got Charu to do the planning, and as we have our own CTC Gulfstream G550 jet, and can travel at whatever time we want, she said it could easily be done with the minimum amount of jet lag."

"Oh, really?" said Penny, and how does she propose to travel halfway around the world without getting jet lag?"

"Well," said Philippe, scratching his beard. "It's all about the route really. We kind of zig-zag."

"Come again, Philippe; zig-zag?"

"Yeah; you see, you only suffer from jet lag when your body travels too far west or east in one go. The evidence is that it takes about one day to recover from each hour of time difference. Our doctors have come up with a sleep management plan for us. Firstly, we fly at night, when our body clocks want us to sleep anyway; there will be strict rules on light usage within the plane, and the ambient temperature will be set to seventeen degrees

Celsius, the low light levels and reduced temperature will encourage our body's natural mammalian instinct to sleep. Secondly, we induce or augment the hormone melatonin, and inhibit the hormone serotonin on take-off, this enables us to sleep, and helps to reregulate our bodies."

Philippe used his thick index finger to point at the world map on Penny's computer terminal. "We fly from Singapore to Oman; then, instead of continuing on to Girona, which would only exacerbate the jet lag, we zig down to Windhoek in Namibia. From here we zag back up to Girona. Admittedly, Girona to Sao Paulo will be a long haul in terms of actual hours in the sky; but not as long as you think, in terms of time difference. Finally, we go straight north to Gander. After that, we fly directly home, and have three days' leave to get over any jet lag accumulated on the journey. Plus, of course, our serotonin and melatonin therapy."

"Wow!" declared Penny. She had heard of the melatonin/serotonin therapy before; some of her colleagues in the Secret Intelligence Service (MI6) had tried it during its experimental stages, when they had been required to travel large distances overseas at no notice.

Latitude 23° 35' 15.8784'', Longitude 58° 10' 11.8092''. Technology Translation Centre, Sultan Qaboos University, Muscat, Oman. – May 2017.

Indestructible

The sleek fuselage of the Gulfstream GS 550 shimmered in the heat of Singapore Changi International Airport. The jet could easily be reconfigured to carry from fourteen to nineteen passengers in complete luxury. With an extended flight capability of just over twelve thousand kilometres, it had by far the best range of any plane in its class. It could cruise efficiently at just over nine hundred kilometres per hour and reach a maximum speed of 941 kilometres per hour. Most importantly, it only required a short runway, which meant it could be used to fly into smaller regional airports and avoid the congested main international hubs.

"Have you ever seen anything like this before?" exclaimed Maria. "It's like a miniature Air Force One; you know, the US President's plane."

"It is certainly a lot more luxurious than anything I have ever flown in," said Charu, placing her carry-on bag in her personal kit storage area. Matthias and Philippe were already aboard, sitting opposite each other, just in front of the Galley, which gave the whole team access to a wide selection of hot and cold food throughout the flight.

The seats were configured in pairs opposing each other, with one pair on either side of the fuselage. There were four pairs of soft beige leather chairs, capable of fully reclining into a flat bed. The crew consisted of two pilots: Guenther Kramer, a former German Air Force fighter pilot, and Fabio Cancerelli, a former Italian Air Force pilot. Both men had accrued hundreds of flying hours in this exact aircraft, as they were routinely used by both the German and Italian militaries for a host of specialised roles. The third crew member was Lieutenant Christi Gudmanson. She was 'on loan' from the Norwegian Air Force, and, as well as acting as the in-flight attendant, she was also there to deal with

Immigration issues, refueling and restocking the plane, as well as dealing with any medical emergencies.

Li had decided not to join the team on this flight; he hoped they would begin to bond as a group, and, anyway he had already visited the sites with Guilherme. The last pair to arrive on board were Andrei and Penny; they had found it easy to get along with each other, as they both had come from a similar background. The plane's engines roared into life, as it began accelerating down the Changi runway. Andrei looked at his watch. It was eight a.m. local time.

"What time do we arrive?" said Andrei to Christi, who was sitting in one of the pair of chairs on the opposite side of the plane.

"Well," said Christi. "The flight time is just about seven and a half hours, and there is a four-hour time difference. So we should be touching down at Royal Air Force Base Seeb in Muscat at midday, local time."

All of the team had taken their melatonin inhibitor shots, which should delay the production of melatonin for at least a couple of hours. This way, when it got to eight p.m. Muscat time, and their bodies thought it was twelve p.m. Singapore time, they wouldn't feel as tired.

None of the team needed to sleep immediately, so, after take-off, they all moved to the back of the plane and sat around the briefing table. The table, which could seat eight people, had a plasma touchscreen panel built into its surface. It was an adaptation of the type of touch screen seen on many tablet computers; it allowed anyone sitting at the table to log in using a discreet finger print ID check, then, as the meeting took place, using hand gestures such as swiping and pinching, the participants could pass documents to each other, and display maps or data, and access the CTC Servers in Singapore wirelessly.

The technology was so impressive that, as the team assembled around the table for the first time, nobody knew what they should do with their hot drinks cups. Everyone was reluctant to be the first to place them on the shiny plasma surface. "If you feel the side of the table, just to the left of your seat, you will be able to pull out the folding drinks table," said Charu with a smile.

Once settled, the team began to review the upcoming tour. In the middle of a discussion about which piece of tech could offer the most opportunities for translation into real world applications, an audible tone began to sound. It was emanating from the table. It was almost like receiving an electric shock. In unison the team pulled their hands away from the table's surface. Then, with a broad smile on his face Philippe clicked the top corner of the table's surface to receive the video call. "Good morning, team; I trust the flight is going well, and you are looking forward to your grand tour?" Li's face occupied the whole of the top half of the table. From Li's workstation in the CTC HQ, he could also see each one of the team members sitting around the table, using the mini-cameras that were embedded in the plane's fuselage. "This is just a social call to wish you well, and to remind you that you need to remain focused on the technology and its applications, and not to get too carried away with enjoying yourselves at the various locations you will be visiting!" The team laughed in unison and promised that they would behave.

The plane began to lose altitude on its final approach to the British Royal Air Force Base Seeb in the North of Muscat, Oman. The azure blue sea shimmered up at them as the plane approached the Omani coastline. In the distance behind the airport, the Jebel Akhdar or Green Mountains, could be seen standing sentinel over Oman's capital. Muscat was a long thin city stretched out along the coast, bordered on one side by the mountains, and, on the other, by the Gulf of Arabia. The flight of just over seven and a half hours passed without incident, and the team had already eaten lunch before they got off the plane and were ready to travel straight to the Technology Translation Centre, or simply TTC, as it was referred to by the team. As they left the plane, a British Royal Air Force Warrant Officer greeted them.

It seemed slightly incongruous to be met by a member of the British Royal Air Force in Oman, but the air base at Seeb was part of the British Military Loan Service contingent that was still based in the Sultanate. The British had helped Sultan Qaboos win the civil war, known as the Dhofar Rebellion, which had ended in 1976; and, ever since, they had maintained close military links with the Omani Armed Forces. Indeed, many Omani Officers still went to the United Kingdom to undergo language training, prior to attending military specialism courses at various military establishments in the UK, including the prestigious Royal Military Academy, Sandhurst.

Penny had made the travel arrangements with Muhammed Al Abdali, who was the Muscat TTC's local administrator. Muhammed's family was originally from Seeb, where the airport was located, and he knew the area very well. The Centre had been built by kind permission of the Sultan, just inland from the coast, on the site of the University of Oman's campus. It lay only a few kilometres south of the military airport. After leaving the airport, they turned right at the Burj al Sahwah roundabout, and headed along the large dual-lane Highway 15; after barely five kilometres, they crossed the bridge over the large stretch of water known locally as the Wadi Mansah. Just as the team were climbing out of the 4 x 4 vehicles to enter the TTC, they all stopped.

As one, they looked skyward, inclining their heads to listen to the 'Dhur' midday call to prayer. It was a truly poetic sound; the words sounded like an incantation beckoning, almost luring the people to come and pray. The melody rose and fell in pitch and seemed almost soothing to listen to. The prayer call was emanating from the Sultan Qaboos Masjid, or mosque. This ornately decorated mosque was built on an unimaginable scale, and housed the largest carpet ever made in the world.

Chapter Sixteen

Building Bridges

They entered the TTC and were met by the team of scientists that worked there. Some, but not all of the scientists were observing prayers. Oman was like that; it seemed to offer a compromise between the Western world and the Muslim world. You were not whipped or chastised if you didn't attend prayers, as was the custom in other Arabic countries, and men and women could be seen wearing a whole array of different clothes. Oman truly was a moderate and very accommodating society.

Led by Mohammed, the team were taken down a long corridor into a large environment-controlled hangar. In it, they saw miniature structures. They saw tiny houses, bridges, roads and domes. Elena Yurnayev from Moscow University and Renata van Buskirk of the University of Delft, in the Netherlands, were the senior scientists in charge of this project. Elena was a microbiologist, and Renata was a structural and materials specialist. Handing the team safety helmets and goggles, they entered the large hangar. Renata began. "As you can see, we are testing the materials on various structures. We expose the structures to a whole range of stresses, such as high temperatures, flooding, fire and earthquakes." It was obvious that the two scientists had rehearsed this demonstration and appeared very excited at what they had to demonstrate.

Elena took over the presentation. "Please observe the tower in the far corner. I will vibrate the platform that it is built on, to simulate a level six magnitude earthquake." Twisting a dial on her control panel, then depressing and holding down a small button, the scientist caused the tower to shake. "Note that the tower sways considerably in the earthquake; this is due to the unique junctions that have been used in the steel girder construction." She released the small button, and the platform and tower stopped vibrating.

"Come with us!" Renata shouted, as the whine of the electric motors began to die down. The group walked through the hangar, past a miniature house. It was so small that Andrei could peer into the upper-floor windows. As they approached the tower, they could see a myriad of tiny fissures that seemed to cover the outside of the tower like an intricate spider's web. Philippe's curious engineer's mind caused him to speak first. "I am guessing that you are encouraging this type of splintering of the material as a way of dissipating the energy?"

"Exactly," said Elena. "So far, you have seen only half of the demonstration."

"Half?" interrupted Charu. "I mean, it is impressive enough that you have managed to design a tower that can withstand such a force." The two scientists looked at each other, then gave each other a knowing smile.

"If you don't mind," said Renata. "We will return to the hangar in about four hours. Before that, can I suggest we grab something to drink and have a chat in the briefing room, where we can talk in more depth about the technology?"

Leaving the miniature world behind, the team left the hangar, and returned to the briefing room. Mohammed was waiting to welcome them. On a table in the corner of the room, he had prepared some refreshments. Freshly brewed mint tea, and rich black coffee, that had been delicately spiced with cardamom, ginger and saffron sat steaming in pots. Next to this stood a large glass bowl of freshly squeezed orange juice and a selection of juicy medjool dates.

The two female scientists sat down with the team and began to explain what was so special about their work. "First of all, this is no ordinary concrete. It has two ingredients that make it quite unique." Elena was animated and appeared genuinely excited and proud of 'her concrete'.

Philippe interjected. "Yes, I read the research report. You have mixed live bacteria and calcium lactate into the concrete, is that correct?"

"Yes," said Renata. "You see, the bacteria which can only be found naturally in a few places in the world, exist in geological formations in Egypt, as well as here in the Wadis, just west of this centre near the Jabal Shams mountains."

Almost seamlessly, Elena took over. "Bacteria, being living organisms, require a food source. This is the calcium lactate that we also mix into the concrete. The whole process is triggered by moisture, which enters the fissures of the concrete once it cracks under load. Once triggered, the dormant bacteria 'wake up'." Elena used the inverted fingers symbol to stress her figurative speech. "They 'wake up' and begin to eat the calcium lactate.

They secrete limestone as a by-product, and it is this limestone that fills the cracks."

"Truly unbelievable!" said Maria, as she sipped on her strong black coffee.

"Of course, there are technical limitations, and this is where we have been focusing our efforts," said Renata.

Charu interrupted. "Philippe showed me the report; you are limited to a maximum crack width of less than 0.8 mm, and you have to wait up to three weeks for the repairs to be effective?"

"Yes," replied Elena. With a broad grin, and turning to Renata, she said, "But that is where we have made our biggest advances."

"You see, by stimulating the bacteria with an electrical charge, we have managed to speed up the process exponentially. We apply a weak electrical current through the reinforcing bars inside the concrete, and it stimulates the bacteria inside the concrete. The moisture in the cracks ensures that the current is transferred over the entire healing surface."

"You said you have speeded up the process exponentially. What does that mean in real terms?" asked Maria.

"Well,", said Elena, the grin broadening on her face, "We are still in the early phases of the trials, but we have the time down to less than twenty-four hours for large cracks, and much less for small cracks.

"Crikey," said Penny, "that's incredible."

"Sorry," interrupted Philippe. "You said there were two variables that were limiting factors. What about the crack size limitation?"

Renata stood up. "Yes, that is still troubling us. We have managed to increase the size of crack that we can heal considerably, from 0.8 mm to 5 mm. This has been achieved by developing a method to bundle more tightly packed clusters of bacteria into the material. We call this nano-clustering. There are limitations; if we include too many bacteria, then the concrete becomes too weak."

"Truly impressive," said Andrei to Elena, surprising himself by his reaction. He mused to himself, that less than two months previously, he could never have conceived of becoming even remotely excited about watching bacteria replicate inside concrete. "When can we see the results?"

"Right about, er, now," she said, glancing at her wristwatch. The team once more donned their protective headgear and glasses and walked through the Lilliputian landscape to inspect the tower, that, only four hours ago, had been struck by the equivalent of a magnitude six earthquake.

Philippe stopped in his tracks. "I don't believe it!" He walked up to the tower, and tentatively poked the smooth outer surface. Less than four hours ago the whole outer surface had been a web of fine cracks; now it was a smooth, contiguous surface. The rest of the team stepped forward one by one to marvel at the tower's healed walls.

Having left the hangar, and once more seated back in the briefing room, the team was buzzing with excited chatter. Charu and Philippe were busy discussing the processes, and how the electrical current was applied, with Renata. Both Andrei and Maria were busy trying to understand a little better from Elena how the bacteria worked. Over in one corner, Matthias and Penny were standing talking to Mohammed.

"Guys," shouted Matthias. "I have a suggestion. Mohammed has kindly offered to show us around the Sultan Qaboos Grand Mosque. It is only about fifteen kilometres west of here, and we get there straight down the highway. It really is worth a visit, and we should be able to get in and out before the *maghrib*, or dusk call to prayer." The team nodded enthusiastically. "After that, we have been invited to eat at the Royal Oman Army Officers' Club, down on the Coast."

Out of respect, the female team members covered their heads with a plain silk headscarf, before entering the grounds of the Sultan Qaboos Grand Mosque. Dismounting from their four-wheel drive vehicles in the mosque's car park, they could hear the honking of car horns and revving of engines from the nearby freeway. However, once inside the grounds of the mosque, everything changed. Charu and Matthias were the first to arrive at the entrance with Mohammed. "It is unbelievable!" whispered Charu to Matthias. "It is like I have stepped out of the real world and arrived in an oasis of peace and tranquility."

Matthias held his breath at the sight before him. Shimmering white marble adorned every surface on the exterior of the mosque's grounds. The marble gave the building a seamless and never-ending appearance. Philippe was the first to comment on the architecture. "This is incredible!" he said. "Look at the use of geometry, the repeating patterns of triangles and arches, mirrored on every surface."

Mohammed said, "You know that we Muslims must not produce images or idols. This does not mean we do not possess the ability to be decorative." Charu had noticed the fractal-like patterning on a long colonnade, which supported a covered archway. The slightly pointed arches were scaled at exact ratios to each other, to deliver a stunning display of scale and grandeur. In the smaller cornices and window frames, the intricately-adorned dome shapes were repeated with incredible geometric precision. The overall effect was truly one of perfection.

Removing their shoes as they entered the main mosque, Andrei commented to Penny that the guys who fitted the carpet must have had a hard time getting it through the door.

"Actually, it was built inside the mosque, and is the largest of its kind in the world," commented Mohammed; he could not mask the pride in his voice as he continued to speak about the mosque. The ornate decoration on the inside of the mosque was incredible; the large flourishes and swirls of paint made intricate patterns, which, in themselves, constituted works of art. It was Penny this time who spoke.

"You know, these pictures are actually *surahs*, or chapters of the Quran that have been elegantly stylized to create works of art, as well as to display the text. It took me three years of Arabic study at SOAS before I could even begin to decipher the individual letters and words; however, each one contains the exact script, as it is written in the Quran."

After about twenty minutes, Mohammed looked to Matthias, and indicated that they should leave. It was ten minutes before the dusk prayer, and Mohammed was keen to get the team on their way before the mosque began filling up, and also so that he would have time to conduct his ritual washing before praying himself. As the team settled into their vehicles to head to the

Officers' club, the muezzin once more began his slow sonorous call to prayer.

The meal at the Officers' club, which was taken at an especially reserved balcony table that overlooked the sea, was simply sublime. The whole team were heavily engaged in animated conversation discussing the Mosque visit as the main course of *mashual*, a delightful Omani delicacy of spit-roasted kingfish on a bed of lemon scented rice, arrived.

As the team began to eat, the conversation turned to the programme for the following day. The morning would be spent back in the lab with the two female scientists, where Matthias and Charu wanted to learn more about the bacteria, and ways in which they could be harvested and stored. The remaining team members were going to spend the morning getting their hands dirty, constructing miniature buildings using the new materials, so that they could understand how the materials were used, and consider how they could be put to good use in the various locations around the world, where so many different variables were in play. For example, could the structure be built in cold climates? Did the type of sand in the concrete mixture make a difference? Was the material suitable for use in hot tropical conditions? How could they supply power to the reinforcing bars to activate or supercharge the bacteria?

The final course of the dinner was served with the traditional rich, strong Omani coffee. The dessert was also typically Omani: *halwa*, a very sweet dessert made of tapioca flour and eggs, with many different seasonings, such as dried fruits and nuts, as well as rosewater and saffron. The effect was sublime; there was silence around the table, as the team devoured the differently-flavoured Halwa dishes. Slurping down his final dash of coffee, Matthias stood.

"Team, I am sure you will all join me in thanking Mohammed for his excellent hospitality today. I am sure if I ate just one more piece of that delicious Halwa I would burst." There were nods of agreement around the table. The team stepped out into the warm Omani night air, and could feel the gentle sea breeze, which stirred the palm trees surrounding the entrance to the club.

The following morning the team got straight to work in the lab at around two p.m. After a short break for midday prayers, they said their goodbyes to the team at the TTC; and, as they still had several hours before they needed to leave for the airport, Mohammed once more surprised them by offering to take them on a shopping trip to the main Souq, which was located just near the main port near the southern end of Muscat.

Reluctant to leave Oman, the team arrived back at the Gulfstream plane at RAF Seeb by eight p.m. Although they were not scheduled to fly before eleven p.m., they had been told to be on board so that they could receive their melatonin-inhibiting medicine. Also, Charu and Philippe used the on-board communications suite to make a video blog of the visit to the lab and upload it to Li at the HQ in Singapore. Once this administration was done, Lieutenant Christi Gudmanson, who had finished administering the melatonin medicine, cleared the table and set it for dinner. Using the on-board galley, she had prepared a supper of swordfish steak and salad for the team, before they climbed into their reclining chairs for the onwards flight to Windhoek.

Chapter Seventeen

Latitude 22° 36' 44.3052'', Longitude 17° 3' 28.7676''.
Technology Translation Centre, University of Namibia,
Windhoek, Namibia. – May 2017.
African Crystals

The local time was eleven p.m., and, despite having a nine-hour flight ahead of them, their bodies would only suffer a two-hour time difference. The flight to Windhoek was nearly six thousand eight hundred kilometres, well within the Gulfstream's nearly twelve-thousand-kilometre range, so they wouldn't need to land until they arrived in Windhoek. The route took them south over the Indian Ocean, down the East Coast of Africa, and, just as Madagascar was in sight, the plane turned to the West and headed over Mozambique and Zambia. It started to descend as it crossed into Namibia, heading for the Atlantic coast.

The touch down happened just as the sun was rising over the South Atlantic coastline. The shimmering hues of gold and blue were incredible to behold, as the light reflected up to the plane from the golden rolling dunes that seemed to pour down towards the deep green sea. Long before they reached the coast, the plane began to descend into Eros Airport. It was the smaller of the two main airports in the Namibian Capital, Windhoek. This suited the team perfectly; it lay just four kilometres from the University where the TTC was collocated with the University's Faculty of Engineering and Technology. The main Jose Eduardo Dos Santos Technical campus lay about seven hundred and fifty kilometres to the North, in the town of Ongwediva, but there was also a small engineering and technology faculty in the Windhoek campus. The runway was damp with the remnants of the morning's shower. The wet season was coming to an end, and the area around the airport was lush with green vegetation.

The team was met by Petrus Hambuda, who was the lead scientist on the Piezo Crystal Project. He was a jovial man from the Owambu tribe, aged about thirty-five, Matthias guessed.

"Welcome, welcome to Namibia!" Petrus said, in a bright, high-pitched voice which seemed incongruous with his heavy build. "We have a tightly-packed visit planned for you all. I hope you don't mind? We will start with an overview of the project in the briefing room; I have some hot coffee in there for you, to help you recover from the flight. Then we will go into the applied sciences section and see the crystals in action. Tomorrow we fly north up near Mount Brandberg, where we will see an application of the technology in the field."

"Great!" said Matthias and Philippe in unison. Both of the men had been discussing the use of the crystal technology for their Inuit Power project.

Once inside the centre, they were led into a large briefing room; the walls were decorated with images of the Piezo Crystal technology. Starting on the left, with a close-up of an individual crystal moving around the room, the images got more complex, as arrays of crystals, then images of the crystals embedded in different materials, showed how the project was developing.

Whilst drinking their coffee, Maria leant over to Petrus, and said, "I can't help noticing, and I hope you don't mind, but you have a very un-African name: Petrus."

"Oh, that!" he said. "Yeah, in Namibia it is quite common. You see, when my people, the Owambu, were converted to Christianity, the missionaries came from Finland, and it became very popular to name your child after one of the first missionaries. That's how I got my name. It could be worse, you know. Nowadays, there are many children from the North called Barack, after Barack Obama!" Maria grinned; she was warming to Petrus. He had an infectious positive air about him that seemed to rub off on you.

"I hope you are all rested after the long flight. I want to give you a summary of where we are with our research, then let you take a look at the working prototypes." Petrus was a good speaker. His tribe fell loosely under the Bantu group of peoples, and despite his excellent English, his first language was Oshimbalanhu. Namibia itself was a real melting pot of cultures. On the street, it was not uncommon to hear Afrikaans, German, English and even a smattering of Portuguese being spoken alongside the seven or eight different Owambu dialects.

"The use of piezo-crystals in the generation of energy is not a new phenomenon," Petrus continued. "As early as 1880, this effect was first demonstrated by the brothers Pierre and Jacques Curie. Since then, it has been put to many uses. Early World War One sonar used it; modern-day microphones, fuel injection systems, electronic cigarette lighters, even inkjet printers rely to some degree or another on piezo-electric electricity. Only in the last ten years, have we turned our attention to generating energy through human movement and storing that energy." Philippe and Matthias, who stood at the back of the group, had already begun to discuss how this technology could be used with the Inuit community.

"Various projects exist around the world. An Israeli team from Haifa University are trialling a road surface made with piezo-crystals embedded within its surface. Haifa, by the way, is my alma mater; it is also where I undertook my first post-doctoral position. The Japanese are also very active in the field; they are currently evaluating its usefulness at turnstile gates in two of their subway stations."

At this point a smaller man with a neat beard and bald head entered the room. "I would like to introduce my colleague, Dr Benjamin Livni," said Petrus.

"Thank you, Petrus, and welcome to you all. I am here to show you how we are getting on with the application of the technologies."

"Does this mean we are going to be working as builders again?" said Andrei. There was a ripple of laughter around the room.

"No, not here, although we may ask you," he pointed with his index finger directly at Andrei, "to do something a little more strenuous tomorrow," replied the diminutive Israeli with a wry smile.

As the team walked down the corridor to the TTC's testing and evaluation centre, the hallway lighting illuminated only the area immediately in front and behind them. "What you are currently witnessing is the piezo-crystal phenomenon," said Benjamin. "Your weight transfer through the floor initiates the micro-deformation of the piezo-crystals set beneath the floor's surface. This energy charges tiny capacitors, which then serve to power the hallway lighting."

"You mean we are supplying the power for the hallway lights?" Matthias said.

"Yes," interrupted Petrus. "There are certain limitations, though. Here, let me demonstrate. If we could all stand perfectly still for a moment?" The group halted and looked at Petrus; after about ten seconds, the hallway started to darken. "There, you see; without movement, unless we actually store the energy in batteries first, we lose power."

The team began moving again, and soon arrived at a large hangar. The TTC's testing and evaluation facility was similar to the one in Oman. The large hall contained a whole series of working prototypes. One by one, Benjamin and Petrus demonstrated the different prototypes. Sections of road, moving walkways, railway lines and vehicle tracks could all be seen in the large hall. Each section of seemingly inanimate material was wired up to a series of sensors and power meters. Some devices were being tested by human traffic; others were being tested by wheeled vehicle traffic, or by robots designed to impersonate the cadence and pressure of different types of human and vehicular traffic.

At the end of the demonstration, Benjamin turned to the group, and said, "Of course, one of the fundamental laws of physics is the conservation of energy. We know that energy is never lost; it is only transferred to a different form. So we don't exactly get free energy with these devices. You see, a human being has to eat to generate energy. This energy is very poorly converted into mechanical energy when we exercise. I say poorly, because we expend about eighty per cent of the energy in heat whilst exercising. It is this remaining twenty per cent of the energy that is being converted through our movement into electricity by the crystals.

"Tomorrow, we are going to conduct a live field test; and we would like one of you in particular to be part of that experiment." The team looked at one another, trying to figure out who was going to be selected. Philippe already knew what was planned and had already discussed it with Andrei. He said, "We are going to the Brandberg Mountain area, north of here, in the Namib desert, to test the endurance of one of our machines against Andrei. It not so much a competition as a live trial. We want to see if our machine can keep pace with human movement over rough ground for extended periods of time."

Chapter Eighteen

Latitude 21° 13'7.1688'', Longitude 14° 52' 2.4708''. Uis, Namib Desert, Namibia. – May 2017.
Run Like the Wind

The helicopter touched down in the tiny village of Uis, which lay around two hundred and eighty kilometres north west of the capital, Windhoek. The flight had taken just over two and a half hours. In Uis, the team disembarked and the helicopter was refuelled.

"OK," began Benjamin, who was already beginning to sweat, as the temperature in the Namib desert began to climb towards thirty degrees Celsius. "First, let me introduce you to 'Snappy'." The name had been given to the small buggy by Charu, who had been instantly reminded of a snapper turtle when she had seen the device. It was a considerable improvement on P-C track 2-18, which was what it had been referred to as by the team in Windhoek.

The device was a squat vehicle, with very wide tracks to give it propulsion, and had what looked like a turtle shell on its back. The shell had large rounded cones, which undulated across its entire surface. It looked a very expensive oversized egg-carton.

Petrus began to describe the vehicle to the team. "The outer shell is covered in photovoltaic cells; we have used elevated surfaces, the egg box pattern you see, to increase surface area and allow for maximum contact with the sun's rays. The tracks have a piezo-crystal lining, and, as the machine moves, its own weight provides the stimulus for the electricity generation. You may notice that on the front and rear drive wheels there are what look like laterally mounted spinning tops with vents in them. These are wind generators, and the forward movement of the vehicle or normal winds cause these to spin; this generates electricity electromagnetically and provides extra power to these wheels, to assist with turning the machine. According to our trials at the TTC, the buggy is basically able to power itself, during the day, at least, and should be able to run on a fully charged battery at night, using its piezo technology for between four and five hours."

The team were genuinely impressed. Charu cut in, "I helped out with an algorithm. Basically, Snappy is autonomous; he uses GPS to guide himself. My algorithm simply tells him he must stay within five hundred metres of Andrei at all times, whilst still having the autonomy to select its own route." Andrei, who had been missing from the group, appeared from a building just behind the helicopter. He was dressed in desert endurance running gear; a lightweight vest with pockets held his water, map and medical kit. He was wearing fell-running shoes with a studded grip on the sole, and short athletics-style running shorts. Maria eyed Andrei with some interest from the back of the group and had to admit that he had a damned fine pair of legs. Andrei joined the group, and Benjamin went to him to check that his bio-sensors were functioning correctly.

"OK, guys," said Philippe, in his booming voice. The aim is for Andrei to run approximately forty kilometres through the desert and bushland, up to an altitude of just over a thousand metres, to a point just past the famous White Lady Paintings. We will be monitoring his oxygen, lipid and glycogen consumption, and measuring his calorific expenditure which we will correlate with the expenditure of our little friend Snappy here. The aim is for Snappy to try and keep pace with Andrei. On an operation, Snappy would be used to carry heavy loads, such as communications equipment, food, water or medical supplies. However, when fully loaded, Snappy is limited to a top speed of ten kilometres per hour. We will monitor their progress from the helicopter to the base of the mountain; however, from there we will walk the final hour up to the White Lady Paintings, as there is nowhere for the helicopter to land up there."

As the team bundled into the helicopter, Charu and Petrus had a final tinker with Snappy, and Andrei drank his final sip of his isotonic drink. The sun was high in the sky as the helicopter took off. Andrei consulted his map one last time, then stowed it in his vest and began his journey towards the large monolith that was Brandberg Mountain. Its internal GPS sensors detecting movement, Snappy woke up, turned to face the direction that Andrei had run in and began to follow. The first four to five kilometres were fairly easy going, for both Andrei and Snappy. The terrain was low scrubland with a hard-baked floor and loose brush and stones. From experience, Andrei kept to the dry river and streambeds as he made his way north west out of Uis. He had learned that dry riverbeds offered some limited shade from the by now harsh sun, as well as the best natural navigational tools in open country; and he also knew that ultimately, they would lead him to gain altitude as the river neared its source.

He covered the first five kilometres in just over twenty minutes, and this put the little turtle-shaped robot a good ten minutes behind him. His breathing was relaxed, and his light footfall barely disturbed the ground as he picked his way through the debris of the riverbed. "Look!" shouted Matthias from the helicopter, as he passed the binoculars to Maria. "Can you see how our little friend Snappy is altering his route, and has come out of the riverbed?"

"Yes," said Maria over the helicopter's intercom system.

Charu tapped Maria on the shoulder, showing her a tablet computer screen, on which a red dotted line plotted Snappy's current course, speed, power level and predicted course. Maria looked at the screen and winked a thanks to Charu. Penny, who sat next to Maria, had a handheld tracking device that displayed both Andrei's course, speed and ETA, as well as that of Snappy.

"It looks like Snappy is able to recalculate its route to be able to stay as close as possible to Andrei, despite currently being much slower than him."

"Exactly," said Charu. "She is now heading for the softer sand areas that Andrei is avoiding. With her deep tracks, she can move very efficiently over the sand, and also take a more direct route."

Both Matthias and Penny had picked up on Charu's use of the word 'she' to describe the robot, and exchanged a knowing glance. "All right guys, give me a break. When you spend as much time as I do working on these devices, you really develop a bond with them." Temporarily forgetting that her headset broadcast her voice to everyone in the helicopter, Charu's face reddened as laughter broke out inside the helicopter.

Down on the ground, nearly two hours had passed. Despite the intense sun, Andrei was running as efficiently as ever; his arms and shoulders were relaxed, and his feet barely skimmed above the surface of the ground. He breathed gently through his nose and stopped only occasionally to check his map. He knew that sooner or later he would have to lift himself up out of the dry riverbed and cut across the thicker sand to the base of the mountain.

Stopping once more, he took a long drink of water in the shade of a medium sized umbrella thorn tree, before scrambling out over the side of the river bank and on to the sandy plane. Like a soldier climbing bravely out of the safety of his trench to face the oncoming machine-gun fire, Andrei scrambled up out of the protected shade of the river bed and straight into the scorching winds, which carried with them thousands of tiny abrasive sand particles. The sandy undulating plane rose, gradually at first, but then more steeply, as it neared the base of the rocky mountain, which was reflecting the vibrant hues of red and yellow from the sun's rays. Snappy had been travelling over the softer sand for over an hour and had managed to maintain a solid ten kilometres an hour, despite the strong side wind that hummed and whined as it blew over Snappy's angular conical shell. The time gap had closed a little, and Snappy was now only seven minutes behind Andrei.

The helicopter was being buffeted by the strong winds outside, and the team were forced to sit back in their seats and buckle up their safety belts. In a calm voice, the pilot announced that they would have to gain height to stop the fine sand particles from entering the engine, until they got to the leeward side of the mountain. Back on the ground, Andrei was finding this new terrain tougher going. Whatever he tried, he just couldn't seem to gain an efficient purchase on the soft sand that seemed to dissipate under his feet.

The wind was also beginning to annoy him. The fine sand particles in the air acted like sandpaper, stinging and abrading, as they made contact with his skin. He looked at his map, and realised that it was going to get worse for at least another forty-five minutes, until he too got into the lee side of the mountain. After another thirty minutes of hard running, he spotted something reflective over to his right. About five hundred metres away, on a tangential path, he could just make out the outer shell of Snappy, smoothly making its way over the soft sand. "Bloody robots!" he cursed under his breath, as he laboured on.

The helicopter touched down by the Park Guides' hut at the base of the path that led up to the White Lady Paintings. Before the group set off on their hike up the mountain, Charu checked the GPS positioning of Andrei and the buggy. They were approximately fifteen minutes away, and on a convergent path, set to meet each other around five hundred metres from their current position. The team set off at a brisk pace up the path. After nearly thirty minutes of hard walking, Maria, who had been walking at the back of the group talking to Petrus, turned around.

"Shhh, did you hear that?"

"Hear what?" Petrus asked in a low voice.

"That noise."

Maria had sensed for the last few minutes that they were being followed but hadn't spotted anyone. "There, again." Petrus heard it this time: a faint tinkling noise, as small pebbles slid softly down the path. Then, from around the corner the lithe athletic frame of Andrei appeared. He barely seemed to be out of breath, and his face showed no sign of stress.

"Last one to the top buys the beers," he shouted, as he skipped nimbly past the group. Right on his heels, Snappy was skidding and rotating wildly, trying to keep pace with Andrei in a vain effort to maintain traction on the ever-increasing gradient.

The team made it to the top and arrived several minutes behind Snappy and Andrei. The two ultra-endurance machines made for a sorry sight indeed. Andrei had tiny cuts across much of his exposed arm and leg skin surfaces, and his face and shoulders were coated in a fine reddish-brown coating of Namibian desert sand. Snappy hadn't fared much better, either. The solar panels on some of his westerly-facing surfaces had taken the brunt of the wind's force and had been badly scored and abraded. Also, the tiny vehicle's tracks were shredded, and considerable damage had been done to the piezo-crystal matting on the inside surface of the tracks.

"Before we start our descent back to the helicopter, I would like to show you our beautiful White Lady," Petrus said, in his sing-song voice. If you look just under this overhanging piece of rock, you will see a fine example of the rock art that is prevalent in the Brandberg Mountains. There are over forty-five thousand individual paintings of animals and humans in this area, but this one is the most perplexing."

"Yes," said Matthias. "I remember my old anthropology professor telling me about this: it was found in 1917 by two German cartographers who had spent the night sheltering under this overhang. One of the men made a copy of the picture, and, well, I guess you can say the rest is history. You see, the picture is unlike the other art from the area and seems to be painted in an Egyptian or Mediterranean style, depicting this athletic and obviously white female figure, which still, to this day, has not been properly explained. Some theories postulate that it is Phoenician in origin and was painted by Phoenician explorers. Others say that some non-Africans settled in what we now called Zimbabwe; and others simply maintain that it is simple bush art, as the local bushmen sometimes used colours in an indiscriminate manner. Personally, although the paints and dyes used are locally sourced, I believe another Mediterranean civilization came here and painted it."

After spending another ten minutes examining the paintings, the team made their way back down the path to the waiting helicopter. The helicopter stopped only once, in Uis, to allow Andrei to take a shower, before continuing on its journey back to Windhoek. Once back at the TTC, Benjamin and Petrus thanked the team for taking part in the field trials and acknowledged that they still had more work to do to make the little buggy more robust, as they all moved back into the briefing room to review the day's data.

"I realise that time is escaping us, and you need to be on your way. I will upload the data from today to the main servers, for you to look at later," said Benjamin.

At the airport, Petrus hugged each one of them in turn as they left the vehicles and headed back on board the waiting plane. The team had enjoyed their short stay in Namibia, the vast, rugged, sun-scorched land was a stark contrast to Muscat, which was encased by the high Green Mountains on one side, and the ocean on the other. Christi Gudmanson was waiting on board to greet the team, and, as was the usual protocol before take-off, they all took their melatonin shots and sat down to supper.

Christi was smiling, as she brought the food from the galley. After speaking to some of the locals at the airport, she had managed to get hold of springbok ribs and ostrich steak. These had been grilled on a glowing barbeque in a small hut just outside the airport, and then kept warm on the plane's galley. With the meat, she served spinach and pap, which was a local maize-based dish, similar to mashed potatoes. The team barely spoke as they hungrily devoured the food. Maria, observant as ever, noticed that despite Andrei's extreme running feat through the desert, he didn't appear to be eating any more than the others sitting around the table. She made a mental note to ask him about this later. Strapping themselves into their seats once more, they prepared for take-off.

Chapter Nineteen

Flying directly north over continental Africa to Girona is a little more complicated than one would assume. Due to numerous on-going civil wars, a private plane can't travel up the eastern part of the continent, as it has to avoid overflying the Congo, Somalia and South Sudan. To the west, it is unadvisable to fly over the Ivory Coast, Mali or Nigeria; and Libya remains a dysfunctional series of fiefdoms ever since Gadhafi was removed from power. Instead, Guenther Kramer and Fabio Cancerelli flew the Gulfstream up to Guinea, making a brief refuelling stop-off at a friendly air force base in Sierra Leone; they then steered the plane west, avoiding Mali and the Gambia, and only once they were approaching Morocco did they change their flight path, setting a direct course to Barcelona International airport.

The stay in Girona was going to be brief, just one day in fact. Despite having travelled the entire length of the African continent, and crossing the Mediterranean, the team had only lost one hour in time difference. They climbed out into the cooler

April air of Barcelona and looked expectantly for their local contact.

Lieutenant Christi Gudmanson was a little flustered as she came into the main compartment to brief the team. "I'm sorry, guys, it seems that Pau, our local guy from the TTC in Girona, will be a little late. All of Central Barcelona is in lockdown. There are demonstrations in all of the main squares, and many articulated lorries are blocking the motorways." Charu flicked on the tabletop display and linked to the BBC World News website.

"It seems that the locals are not happy with the government in Madrid's response to the recent Catalan parliament's vote on whether they should devolve from the Republic of Spain," she said, reading the text in front of her. "The Catalonians voted fifty-two to forty-eight per cent for devolution. The government in Madrid say that the vote was unconstitutional and refuse to accept the outcome. They have ordered that the President of the Catalan government step down, as he has acted unconstitutionally, under Spanish law. They demand that new elections should take place, to elect a new President for the Catalan parliament."

Ever the pragmatist, Christi interrupted Charu's in-depth analysis. "This isn't going to get fixed in a hurry, guys. I think I have a work-around plan, guys. Pau is going to meet us outside the airport perimeter down by the sea. I have spoken to immigration, and it seems that our UN Diplomatic passports pull some weight after all. They are sending an escort of Frontier Guards to take us down a service road to the coast."

As the three Frontier Guard vehicles approached the sea, a large, rigid inflatable boat could be seen pulling up to an old

Police jetty. A young man in his late twenties, with a full head of brown hair and olive skin was waving to the group. "That's our man, Pau; get aboard, everyone. I need to get back to the plane and make sure it is ready for us to leave tonight," said Christi, as she helped the last team member into the boat.

"Hola!" said Pau, once the whole group was aboard. Pau's full title was actually Dr Pau Garriga; he held a Ph.D. in fluid dynamics from the University of California, Berkeley. His English was fluent but heavily accented.

"Sorry about the change of plans. Actually, most of the technology is right down here on the coast anyway. We had already planned to show you the tidal energy converters today, so we have simply switched the day around. We will go directly to the offshore site first. It is about four kilometres off the coast, adjacent to a little village called Tossa De Mar."

The boat was just over nine metres in length and was what is known as a Rigid Inflatable Boat, or RIB for short. It was the type of boat that many military and rescue organisations used. Its rigid hull gave it excellent handling capabilities, and the inflatable gunwale meant that it was practicably unsinkable. This version had a soft canopy covering the pilot and crew area, and seating for twelve people. The front of the boat had a small deck area, suitable for carrying stores or tools. The exceptional part about this boat was its twin two hundred and fifty horse power engines, which allowed the boat to cruise comfortably at fifty kilometres per hour. This meant that they would easily reach their destination in less than an hour.

As the boat's engines slowly began to growl and rumble, its black pointed bow bucked upwards out of the water. Charu and

Matthias were caught by surprise, and both of them nearly toppled backwards over their seats as, following its own nose, the boat's hull lifted out of the water, and began planing smoothly across the sea.

There's something about fast acceleration which is thrilling, almost addictive, Matthias thought to himself, as he looked around the boat. Without exception, every member of the team had a broad grin on the face. There was a slow swell, and Pau piloted the boat expertly, managing to keep the boat in tune with the frequency of the waves, and making the whole journey much more relaxed for everyone on board.

Despite the exhilaration of the boat's speed, some of the team were holding onto their harnesses as if their lives depended on it. There were three obvious exceptions, Matthias thought: Maria, Andrei and Philippe. Maria and Andrei had no doubt used this sort of craft before, during their training or on operations. Philippe had spent a lifetime in every type of river craft imaginable, hunting and fishing in the Canadian wilderness as such; this quick sprint up the picturesque Spanish coastline in the bright May sunshine would not worry him in the slightest. It was a far cry from racing headlong down a rapidly flowing river in a fully-packed Canadian canoe with only one paddle, as Philippe had experienced many times before. After just over an hour, Pau cut the throttle, and the boat lowered itself from its high-planing position and settled into a rolling, slow approach.

The beautiful aquamarine water sparkled as the sunshine bounced off it. In the near distance, Penny could make out a series of floating bell towers, with lights placed high up on their masts. There must have been about twelve in all. As the sun steadily rose higher in the clear blue sky, it was becoming increasingly difficult to see because of the reflection from the water. Pau passed around sets of sunglasses to each team member.

"These bell towers demarcate the area that we are using for the sea turbine generating plant," Pau said, sweeping his hand from left to right in front of him.

Penny was a little disappointed; she had expected to see vast machines floating on the water's surface. "I don't see the generators; are they not being used at the moment?" said Penny.

Pau grinned, and said, "Let me get a little closer, and I will show one to you."

"Wow!" gasped Maria, as the boat approached an orange buoy. "Look, guys, on this side."

The team turned and stared over the port side of the boat. What they saw beneath the surface could only be described as a giant Leviathan. The beast was shackled around its neck by a thick iron chain to an orange buoy, and its body appeared to snake away into the distance, probably about twenty metres in length. It writhed rhythmically with the swell of the water. It was eerie to look at; it was like a giant sea snake. Its neck was the size of a bus wheel, and it appeared to swell at the mouth, then send this swelling down its body, as if it were devouring its prey.

"What the...?" whispered Penny to Charu.

"I presume the turbine is at the tail end of this device?" Charu said to Pau.

"Exactly," he replied. Wave theory had been something Charu had been interested in during her undergraduate days. Pau looked over at Charu, and, sensing her keen intellect, said

"Would you like to try to explain to the rest of the team how it works?"

"Er, yeah; I guess so. OK, remember that energy is never lost, simply converted," she began. "Well, in this case, the energy is kinetic, stored in the waves. The wave action squeezes the tube head, a bit like you would squeeze a toothpaste tube. This sends that bulge of pressurised water that you can see travelling down the length of the tube to the generators that are fitted to the tail of this beast. The next part is exactly the same in almost all power generation. In this case, it is simply the water, which provides the mechanical power to turn the turbine's generators."

Pau was impressed; this girl was smart. He would enjoy discussing the project with her, and also the difficulties they were having on the land side of the operation. "If I may, I would like to add to your explanation," Philippe said. He was a natural engineer, and what he lacked in formal qualifications, he easily made up for in intuitive reasoning. "If you look around you, you can see that there are more orange buoys, around fifteen to twenty, I guess. These are designed to work as system. The thick chain that you see tethering the beasts to the orange buoys are there to allow them to change direction, so, a bit like a weather vane they are always at the optimal angle to the sea swell.

"Secondly, I noticed back there," Philippe pointed to a spot on the shore side of the boat, about a hundred metres away. "That there is a hub connection. The power cables from each generator all combine there, and then the generated power is carried back to the shore in one bundle."

"Very impressive," Pau said, with a broad grin. "If I am not careful, I will soon be out of a job!"

They all laughed. Matthias joined in the laughter, but also stood slightly apart from the group. He hadn't paid much attention to the explanation of the power generators; he had been watching the group dynamics. He was relieved to see that the team was starting to relax and coalesce. The physical cues were abundantly clear, if you could spot them. Each team member tolerated their personal space being imposed upon far more easily. There were fewer aggressive arm movements and body posturing, and far more submissive, open facial expressions. Even Maria and Andrei seemed to be more comfortable with each other.

"We will now head directly towards the shore, to see how this system works in synchronization with our hydro-electric plant. Just a couple of points to round off what Charu and Philippe correctly said about how we generate power here. In total, we have twenty of these generators tethered at this site. They generate one megawatt each, so in total that's twenty megawatts; if my maths is correct, and depending on the time of day, it is enough power to provide electricity to around eighteen thousand homes." Pau left the team with that thought as he powered up the twin two hundred and fifty horse power engines, nudged the boat into gear, and powered off towards the coast. As they approached the coast, Philippe's keen eyes spotted the two shiny silver pipes that travelled down the mountain side from the peak, some eight hundred metres above the beach, all the way down to a small building on a raised section of land just above the beach. Pau throttled back the boat and allowed it to drift some five hundred metres from the shore.

"This is probably the best place to be to give you an overview of the whole project," Pau said. "What you see is known as a pumped storage plant. Now before I go any further, what you are about to see isn't exactly revolutionary technology. Indeed, part of it even dates back to ancient Greece. But what is important about this project is that, according to our own UN statistics, two thirds of Africa's entire population live without electricity, and over seventy-nine per cent of the people living in the fifty poorest countries in the world have no access to electricity. The top-down approach of the government, building huge electricity-generating and distribution infrastructures, will not work in these countries, because the governments are already highly burdened with debt, and do not have the economic resources to build such networks. In fact, the cost of maintaining and improving our own networks in the developed countries is becoming prohibitively expensive." There were nods of agreement from the group, as Pau continued to explain the project.

"What we are aiming to achieve here is to generate cheaper local alternatives to these energy issues, by allowing local groups to build puddles of power generation which serve their communities. Built and financed by them, using microloans, which allows them to be part owners in the project and therefore receive revenues from the surplus electricity that is sold on to neighbours or into any existing networks."

"I see what you are trying to achieve," said Philippe, "but not everyone lives by the coast with a bloody great mountain next to them."

"Sure," said Pau. "What we are working on here is twofold. Firstly, demonstrating how these systems can be coupled together to be mutually supportive and provide twenty-four-hour electricity at very little cost. Secondly we are looking at ways to make the manufacture and construction cheaper and easier to achieve."

"You mean like an IKEA pack," said Andrei. They all laughed, and he reddened slightly.

"Actually, you are not too far wrong. We intend to be able to provide the blueprint, generators and technical knowhow for free from the UN. The communities would be expected to provide the construction labour, and source the materials required for the pipes, cables, etc.

"OK, then, let me briefly explain what you can see in front of you," said Pau. "At the top of the mountain, you have a naturally occurring reservoir; no dam has been built. Into the rock we have drilled a large hole which slopes steeply downwards and exits the mountain where you can see the metal pipe up on the hillside." Pau pointed to the glistening steel pipe that cut through the trees."

"It's not very subtle, is it?" said Penny.

"No, but it is deliberate; we want to be able clearly to see it, so that, as we are doing today, we can demonstrate the system to people. In the future, communities will have the option to bury or camouflage the pipe, or, in fact, our feedback tells us that some groups want to keep it like this one here, because, believe it or not, they are proud to show off their technological capability."

"OK, got it," said Penny, feeling a little foolish for asking the question.

"So, in this system, the easy part is the first part. The water falls down the hill in the pipes, and this gravity-fed water acts to turn the turbine blades at the bottom of the hill. The water is caught in a reservoir at the bottom. This reservoir is much smaller than the one on top, because we return to the water directly back to the top."

"OK," said Charu. "So far so good, but how do you get the water back to the top without using a lot of energy?"

"That is the tricky part that we are experimenting with. On the right of the down pipe you will see another metal pipe that is the 'up pipe'; this is how the water is returned. We use several techniques in combination to try and limit the power needed to get the water back up to the top."

"Let me guess," said Philippe. "You mentioned ancient Greeks a minute ago. Are those fatter sections of pipe screws?"

"Exactly," said Pau. He was clearly happy to be discussing his project with these quick-thinking engineers. "Yes, the Archimedes Screw is how we help to draw the water up the mountain at discrete stages. To prevent the water from building up too much pressure, we have divided the pipes into sections, and fitted one-way valves into the pipes. This allows the water to pass through on the way up, but stops it from falling back down past that point."

"Rather like our own venal return system in our legs stops our legs from filling with blood and swelling, right?" Philippe interjected, more as a question than a statement.

"Exactly. Finally, we power the Archimedes screws using impellor pumps that are driven by the downward force of the water in the down tubes. You see where the pipes are joined at intervals. Yes! that's it, the bits that look like fat ladder rungs. On the left you have an impeller pump, and, on the right, an Archimedes screw is linked to it by a rotating shaft."

"How close to being energy-neutral have you got?" said Philippe.

"We are not there yet. We are currently ninety-seven per cent energy-free, and we supply the remaining three per cent of energy into the system from the wave generators that we saw a while ago."

"This is impressive stuff," Andrei said, regarding Pau carefully. "But how is it different to what we already do in my country and many others around the world?"

"Yes, good point," said Pau, shifting slightly as he spoke. "As I said before, the tech isn't that new, we have been innovative in coupling the systems and achieving a high level of energy efficiency. The main benefits lay in what I said earlier about central governments' inability to supply the power. In countries like Afghanistan and Pakistan, they do have power generation, and they produce electricity. Obviously they can't afford the infrastructure costs to develop a countrywide network, but, more importantly, currently these governments can be selective about who they distribute the power to. This is one factor that helps to foment and maintain inequalities within a country, and leads to disgruntled members of the population migrating on mass to other parts of the country. This, can then, lead to frictions between ethnic groups, as these different parties struggle for resources such as housing, jobs and water. Ultimately, it can be one of the causes for civil unrest or civil war."

Andrei's face relaxed a little as he comprehended the benefits that such a system would bring to the many countries which, like the Russian Federation, had many diverse ethnic groups living within its borders.

"OK, that's about all from me," said Pau. "Are there any more questions before we dock at the shore?" There was a general murmur of satisfaction from the group, so Pau turned the key and fired up the boat's powerful engines, pointed the craft towards the shore, and began to move towards the small harbour.

"Hey," said Charu, nudging Penny. "Can you see that?" As the boat neared the harbour in Tossa de Mar, the old castle which stood out on its high rock came into sight.

Chapter Twenty

Latitude 41° 43' 20.9964'', Longitude 2° 55' 49.3212''.
Tossa de Mar, Spain. – May 2017.
A Day on the Beach

"Stunning, absolutely stunning," said Penny.

As the boat docked, Pau received a call on his mobile phone. "*Si, si, vale.* Well, guys, it seems that we have to make further amendments to our plans. I was going to take you back to Girona to visit the centre and get to meet some of the team; however, it seems that most of the roads around Girona are blocked with the protests as well. So," he said, with a slight twinkle in his eye. "If there are no major objections, and you don't mind, we will have to spend the afternoon here by the beach in Tossa de Mar. We can have lunch. I know an excellent fish restaurant, if you like, and then maybe we can sit near the beach and discuss the project in more detail?"

The team looked from one to another. It didn't take long to come to a consensus. In fact, after the last couple of days, some time outdoors in the sun wouldn't do any of them any harm. As they stepped ashore with their backpacks, Maria and Penny were already looking for somewhere to get changed into their beachwear.

After a brief walk of only two hundred metres, the team settled into a small seated area in one of the many beachside restaurants. The setting was truly idyllic. Looking out to sea, there was no sign at all of the wave-powered electricity plant. On the right, the noble old castle dominated the bay's edge, its silhouette describing one fluid form, anchoring the castle to the very rock on which it had been built. The beach was a shallow crescent which led around to a marina.

"Who wants coffee?" Pau asked the group.

"One moment, we are still waiting for Penny and Maria," Charu said. At that moment, both of the girls emerged from a beachside changing room several feet away. Pau's jaw dropped; these girls weren't like the other bikini-clad beachgoers. It was obvious that these girls were athletes. Both, however, had different physiques: Maria was slightly heavier set, and had a rippling set of abdominal muscles; Penny had a lithe, toned figure and much paler skin. Both girls had great definition on their thighs and upper body, and, as they approached the group, they both moved with precision and poise.

Matthias noticed that it wasn't only Pau that had been struck by the impression the girls had made. He noticed Andrei clinically regarding the two girls. It was obvious from watching him that he liked what he saw. Matthias thought he caught Andrei lingering slightly longer over Maria than Penny.

"Right, er, sorry, as I was saying, coffee anybody?" There was a slight chuckle in the group as Pau ordered coffee. "*Siete tallats por favor, si llet llet.*"

Maria looked at Pau with a quizzical look. "I got the bit about 'seven', but *tallat* means 'cut' or 'cropped', doesn't it? And what is *llet llet*?"

"You speak Catalan?" said Pau, in a surprised voice.

"Not really, I just understand a little," replied Maria.

"*Llet llet* is *leche, leche* in Spanish, and means 'double milk'. We put condensed milk at the bottom of the cup and whipped milk at the top. The two stay separate, with the black coffee in between."

"Sounds dreamy," said Maria. "But I don't know what it will do for my figure."

"I don't think you are in any danger of ruining that figure," said Pau, with a twinkle in his eye.

The coffee arrived, and the team ordered a mixture of different tapas, including grilled sardines and dorado baked in garlic, rosemary and olive oil. The fish came with small pots of new potatoes, also lightly coated in olive oil, and a leafy salad with vinaigrette dressing.

Charu turned to Pau, and said, "You were telling us about the problems you were facing trying to be energy-neutral in the power plant, and how you still needed to find the extra three per cent of savings."

"Yes, that's right," said Pau. Philippe leaned in to listen to the conversation. After devouring another sardine, Charu continued.

"Well, I was inspired by your snake-like monsters that use the wave-energy out there." Charu pointed with her fork out to see to where the wave power plant lay. "Remember the bulge of pressure that forces the water down the length of the snake?" Pau nodded, and Philippe leaned a little closer. "I also recall Philippe's talking about the human venous system, and the one-way valves that prevent the blood from pooling in our feet. Well, you know how most of the blood is ultimately returned to the heart, don't you?" It was a rhetorical question, and the pair allowed Charu to continue. "Muscular action, you contract your leg muscles by walking or running, and this contraction squeezes the pipe. In this case, the vein and the blood is shunted back up to the heart against gravity."

"Brilliant," said Pau, already beginning to see where Charu was going with this.

"We can use your same impellor pump system driven by the falling water in the down tube to drive a collar that winds its way up the pipe and squeezes the pipe slightly as it does so."

Philippe had caught up by now and continued what Charu was implying. "Yeah, right, and the one-way valve leaves the water only one direction to go! Straight back up?"

"Exactly," said Charu. Pau was nodding enthusiastically. I will have a look into this when I get back to the TTC and run some models, to see how the system will affect the flow rates and try to calculate the energy costs and savings."

"Great! Can you let me have access to the models, so I can see how you are getting on?"

"Sure, I'll put them on the CTC's servers."

The team stayed on the beach discussing the power project with Pau until the late afternoon. It was good to be outside in the sun and fresh air. They had another long flight ahead of them that night, heading to Sao Paulo in Brazil, and they would be losing another three hours in time difference.

"Pau, this trouble today in Catalonia, how bad is it?" Matthias asked.

"You know, Matthias, Catalonia has always strongly defended its independence and its language and culture." Pau looked serious for the first time that day and put down his glass. "Historically, only through marriage did we ever voluntarily form any alliances with the Castilians, and, even then, we kept our own courts and systems of governance. I am talking as far back as the twelfth century now, you realise. At many stages throughout history, the Castilians have continually tried to make us carry an unfair burden of taxes or levies." He was becoming more animated now, not aggressive, but clearly passionate. The rest of the team had stopped chatting to each other and were listening intently to what Pau had to say.

"We, by which I mean the Catalan people, have successfully rebelled several times, during the Napoleonic wars, and even before that, in 1635, during the Franco-Spanish wars. But it was the Spanish Civil War and the rise to power of General Franco that ultimately sealed our fate. He systematically tried to destroy everything Catalan, including banning the language. Today, we are again a very prosperous part of Spain, and, yet again, we feel that our masters in Madrid are increasingly asking us to pay too high a price in supporting the Spanish economy. That is why we are trying to achieve complete autonomy using the democratic process." He glanced briefly towards Penny. "But as the British realised, when Scotland wanted to devolve from their union, there is very little clarity in international law on what passes for legal or illegal action when a new state wants to be created by popular demand, and without the use of force."

Matthias nodded, "I know, Pau; I have a friend at Cranfield University in the UK. He is probably the foremost expert on the subject in Europe, maybe in the world. He has spent his whole academic career studying referendums, and even he admits that there is very little legal precedence for such actions. Imagine if you will that Catalonia secedes from Spain. It would then have to apply for membership of the European Union, and for it to be admitted, all of the countries in the EU must agree. I believe hell would freeze over before that happens! You know many of these countries, such as Belgium, France, Italy and the UK, to name but a few, have their own independence issues, and don't want to set that precedent."

Pau nodded in agreement. The sun was beginning to approach the horizon, as Pau rallied the group and said that they would have to start to make a move soon because he needed to get them to Barcelona and then return to Tossa de Mar before nightfall. The team members were more than a little reluctant to be leaving the beach; however, every cloud had a silver lining. The next stop was Sao Paulo, Brazil. Penny and Maria quickly got changed. Again, Matthias noticed both Pau and Andrei following the girls with their gaze. The boat roared away from the jetty with the team aboard, the noise was deafening as Pau opened up the big engines, and the boat's bow lifted and began to plane smoothly over the gently rolling waves of the Mediterranean Sea.

Some of the crew glanced out to sea, to where the wave power generators lay eerily snaking through the water, like giant sea snakes. Others looked landside at the gleaming metal pipes that neatly covered the hill and cliff face. They were the only evidence of a power generating system that could potentially power many thousands of houses. They had no real CO_2 footprint, and, if you discounted the build costs, they produced practically free energy, minus the three per cent inefficiency that Pau and his team were working on.

Pau had called ahead, and, as the team approached the Police jetty just outside the airport fence, the Frontier Guards were once more waiting to escort the team back to the plane. Christi was with them, and, smiling as ever, reported that the plane was refuelled and ready for take-off. The schedule had changed a little. They would eat on board, then have a short meeting to try to consolidate the trip so far, before arriving in Sao Paulo.

The Gulfstream would be nearly at the limit of its flying endurance on this trip, as such the two ex-military pilots had decided to reduce the cruising speed to the plane's sweet spot to conserve fuel. Once in the air, the team reconvened at the back of the plane around the shiny touch-screen table. Philippe led the meeting, reviewing in turn the different technologies they had experienced so far, and leading the discussion on the pros and cons of how they could be used in different regions of the world. Most of the discussions focused on the limitations that without knowing the 'customer', i.e. the different cultures, they were in no place to decide what would be best for these communities. As the discussion drew to a close, Matthias asked if they could all stay for a while longer and carry out a quick cultural mapping exercise.

"It's quite simple," he said. "Use the stylus pen I have given you and draw a small circle on the table's screen." A little hesitantly, they each had a go at drawing a small circle on the screen below them.

"That's really cool," said Penny, as she continued to draw ever increasing concentric circles around the first circle she had drawn, as Matthias had asked them to.

"OK, now write your name in the smallest circle. I want you to define yourself in each circle. For example, my circles look like this." With a sweep of his hand, he pushed his circle into the middle of the table for them all to see.

"I am a white European male, I had a wife, I also have an extended family, parents, nieces, nephews, etc. I am Danish, I am a Protestant Christian. I am European. OK, you get the idea," he said. "Now, my point is this, you can comfortably navigate amongst and identify with all of these groups when you are not stressed. By stress I don't mean at work. I mean your physical security is under threat. You are unemployed, moved off your land or not allowed to work because you are not tolerated by those around you. Now the big question. What would make you fight, take a life or even go to war?"

They all turned and stared at Matthias. Had he secretly been drinking again? Or had he completely lost his marbles this time? "OK, bear with me. Philippe, if your family was threatened would you use force to protect them?"

"If the government didn't provide protection, I guess, yes."

"Maria, if, in your community, Hispanics were being refused work, based on their race or being burdened with onerously high taxes by the rest of the community, just because they were Hispanic and you had no government help, would you support the use of force as a group to assert your rights?"

"Maybe, I guess, if we couldn't feed ourselves."

"Andrei, if the Russian Federation was attacked by Islamists or even by NATO, God forbid. Would you defend the Federation?"

"*Da,*" he immediately replied, with no hint of emotion. "Immediately."

"OK; without wanting to take this to extremes, do you all understand that when the environment changes then we can *all,*" – Matthias stressed the word – "*All* feel obliged to use force, and we simply form groups and alliances based on who we identify with. In the Cold War, it was East versus West, and God only knows, both sides spent enough money making us all feel part of one side or the other. In other cases, it is an ethnic group such as the Tibetans or Uighurs in China, The Kosovar Albanians in the Balkans, the Kurds in the North of Iraq, Turkey and Syria, and, to a lesser extent, the Catalonians here in Spain, who feel passionately enough to take action."

"Yes, but," interrupted Charu. "Surely the Catalonians are not considering using force, are they?"

"Probably not, at least not at the moment. But it does seem that they are willing to face down Madrid and defy the central government by going ahead with devolution." Heads slowly began to nod around the table. They all slowly realised the object of Matthias's lesson. If you feel unfairly done by, then you will act to change if you think you have the means or the leverage to do so, especially if you have a shared history with the oppressor.

On that note, the team rose from the table and made their way back to their seats. The time was nearing ten p.m. in Girona, and they had been in the air for two hours. They would touch down in Sao Paulo at around seven a.m. The cabin lights were dimmed, and the melatonin injections were already starting to take effect. As the team drifted into sleep, the Gulfstream glided smoothly onwards across the Atlantic to the shores of Brazil.

Chapter Twenty-One

Latitude 23° 33' 24.5160'', Longitude 46° 44' 4.2432''.
Technology Translation Centre, University of Sao Paulo, Sao
Paulo, Brazil.
– May 2017.
Miniature Swarms

The Gulfstream G550 touched down at Congonhas airport to the south of the sprawling metropolis of Sao Paulo, at three minutes past seven in the morning. The flight had been uneventful, although strong headwinds had added an extra forty minutes to the journey. Congonhas was one of three large airports serving Sao Paulo, although an annual passenger through-put of over eighteen million passengers didn't make it a small airport. Its larger neighbour, Guarulhos International Airport, which lay to the North-East of the city, enjoyed over double the annual passenger through-put. Of all the places they had visited so far, Penny and Maria were keenest to see Sao Paulo. The city itself was the twelfth-largest in the world, and typically displayed the full spectrum of society that such large cities attract. As the team entered the main airport terminal, they were hit by a cacophony of noise. The airport had been chosen because it was far easier to get landing slots for smaller private planes like the Gulfstream, and because it was situated just thirteen kilometres from the TTC.

As they passed through immigration and customs, they were met by Dr Fernando Moraes. He held a single A4 piece of paper with 'TTC' typed in thick black lettering on it. Penny, who had made the contact arrangements, had been in touch with Fernando by email, and, as such, recognised him immediately. She had to admit he looked even better in real life than he did in his profile picture on the CTC server. He was of average height with well-coiffured black hair and a neatly trimmed beard. He had large round eyes and a dusky hue to his skin. Fernando was immaculately dressed in a Salvatore Ferragamo suit, white shirt and matching Salvatore Ferragamo tie. A broad smile appeared on his face as he shook hands with Penny.

"Fernando?"

"Yes, you must be Penny?" he said, without releasing his grip on her hand.

Beginning to blush slightly she replied, "That's me," then hurriedly went on to introduce the rest of the team.

With the introductions over, Fernando led them to the subterranean parking lot beneath the airport. He had arranged a minivan and driver for the trip to the TTC. The TTC site was located on the campus of the largest and one of the most prestigious universities in Latin America, between the Institute for Physics and the Department of Computational Science.

They pulled out into the traffic and bright sunshine and were immediately assaulted by the maelstrom of movement and noise that is so typical on the streets of Sao Paulo. Fernando was sitting up in the front seat, next to the driver. He turned to face the team and welcomed them once more. *"Bem-vindo ao Brasil. Tudo bem?"*

"*Tudo bom*," replied Maria. Surprised, he looked at Maria. "You speak Portuguese well! It's a pity about your Carioca accent."

They both laughed, and Fernando explained the rivalry between Brazil's two principal cities, Rio de Janeiro and Sao Paulo. He said it was easy to spot someone from Rio de Janeiro, a Carioca, by the way they spoke. He went on to tell the team a little about Sao Paulo and warned them not to be too alarmed by the drivers. "You know, here in Brazil we drive more by instinct and intuition than by blindly following the rules of the road."

The team members chuckled, and Charu added, "Yes, it's the same in Mumbai. I had real problems when I first started driving in the US. I must admit, I picked up more than one ticket for running red lights."

"You little devil!" said Philippe mockingly. "So, you do have a mischievous side to you?" Charu blushed slightly, as she smiled back at Philippe.

Suddenly, Maria touched Fernando on the shoulder and said "Can you get the driver to turn right up ahead?"

"But we need to go straight on," replied Fernando.

"Please, just do it," she urged, in a more serious voice. Fernando told the driver, and he turned right into a side street.

"OK, slow down slightly," said Maria. Checking behind her, she then said. "Now turn right again and make your way back to the main road."

Fernando complied but looked confused and a little annoyed.

"What was all that about?" he said.

"We are being followed," Maria said.

"From the airport: a silver Volkswagen, two men both in dark suits wearing sunglasses," Andrei cut in.

The other team members hadn't noticed a thing and were all a little confused and worried. Fernando breathed a sigh of relief and smiled. "Sorry, guys, I forgot to tell you. The two guys in the silver Volkswagen are with us." He looked a little embarrassed as he continued to speak. "You see, we have some extra security issues to deal with here in Brazil. Only last month one of the team from the TTC was carjacked at gunpoint. He was driven around the city from ATM to ATM, until the carjackers had emptied his bank account. It is not uncommon, I am afraid. They target wealthier students, especially on the campuses."

They arrived at the TTC without incident, and, as they entered the building, they saw the silver VW pulling up in the car park behind them. Despite being only thirteen kilometres from the airport, the drive had taken nearly an hour in the dense and chaotic traffic of Sao Paulo.

"Guys, please sit down," Fernando said, gesturing to the seats around a conference table. "I will call the other members of the Mini-Drone Project team and we will get started with a quick overview of where we are with the project." A few moments later, Fernando returned with his two colleagues, Dr Joe Delany from MIT and Ernst Baumgartner from Hannover University. Joe's Ph.D. was in electronic systems, and Ernst had specialised in computational avionics.

It had long been recognised in the military world, as well as the corporate world, that the use of pilots to direct aircraft was becoming rather outdated and redundant, and, particularly in smaller aircraft they were seen as a burden by the design engineers, as much of the aircraft's power and space had to be given over to housing and supporting the humans. This affected space, weight, aerodynamics and a whole host of other variables.

"Joe!" exclaimed Charu, jumping up and hugging the bigger American. "What, how, er, I mean, why are you here?"

"Surprise!" Joe replied. I am only on loan from MIT. When I heard you were on the team, Charu, I jumped at the chance to spend six months in Brazil helping the CTC get this project started."

"Really good to see you, Joe," said Charu, squeezing his hand, and wiping away a tear.

Joe had been Charu's rock at MIT after the attempted rape. In fact, it was he who had caught the guy trying to attack Charu, and had beaten him almost to a pulp. "Now, er, the reunion is over with shall we continue?" said Ernst. Ernst was the epitome of Teutonic efficiency. Passing time with small talk and introductions appeared inefficient to Ernst, as he immediately launched into his prepared brief. He spoke in a clipped and precise manner, which, on the one hand, was very easy to understand, despite coming across as soulless. Drifting off slightly, Charu wondered to herself how easy it would be to write an algorithm that would make a robot speak like Ernst.

"So, the project status is as follows: We currently have a swarm of seven hundred and forty-two mini-drones, covering the entirety of the Brazil-Bolivia border up to a depth of ten kilometres into the rainforest on the Brazilian side. At nearly three thousand five hundred kilometres in length, this border was by far the longest individual border that Brazil had." Charu did some quick calculations, to estimate the size of the area and the granularity of the coverage.

"Firstly, I will describe the drones; then Joe will describe the sensor arrays and communication systems. The drone looks like this." He handed a mini-drone to each of the team members.

"Careful, they may still be hot!"

"Hot?" retorted Matthias. "Why, hot?"

"Simple! We finished printing them on our 3D printer about half an hour ago."

"Really, you produced these intricate machines in a printer?"

"Sure, it is quite common now. It is a much more effective means of production, but it is also integral to the project, because it means that the drones can be printed or produced, if you prefer, locally, whenever they are needed."

"Incredible," murmured Matthias, playing with the drone between his fingers. The drone was cuboid in shape, about the size and shape of a Rubik's cube. It had four arms which extended from its body. Each arm had a propeller fixed to it. Unusually, the propellers were side mounted, and pointed outwards instead of upwards.

"It's quite heavy, isn't it?" declared Maria, weighing it in her hand.

"Yes; actually we have added weight to the device to keep it more stable in flight, and prevent it from being too susceptible to high winds." replied Ernst.

"But I guess it must need a lot of power to keep it airborne?"

"Not at all," replied the serious German in a triumphal tone. "You see, we attach the drones to this." Like a conjurer, from behind a black screen he produced a large shiny balloon. The balloon was almost as large as a small car. It was spherical in shape, not dissimilar to a flying saucer.

"You see, we use the propellers on the drone only for repositioning purposes, rather like a satellite uses its jet thrusters. The balloon is helium filled and can maintain a neutral altitude simply by altering the amount of helium in the main chamber."

"How do you do that?" said Philippe. As an avid engineer and lifelong tinkerer, Philippe knew, as did nearly everyone, that a balloon relied on losing ballast to go up, and, to come down again, you had to release the precious gas from the balloon. Surely this would limit their maneuverability?

"Actually," replied Ernst. "Building on work from the mainstream airship industry, we have miniaturised a process of compressing the helium gas, so that we can modulate the amount of lift it gives without losing any gas. Oh, and the cherry on the cake, as I think you English speakers say, is that the balloon's surface is covered in photovoltaic cells. This is partly the reason for its size. You see, under normal conditions these drones can remain in the sky as long as we need them to."

"Thank you, Ernst," began Joe. His style was far more relaxed than Ernst: more California cool than Prussian precision.

"OK, now to the sensors. I guess we could mount whatever you wanted on the drones; however, in our example we have gone for heat sensors and infra-red/normal light cameras. They could be equipped with chemical detecting equipment or vibration sensors. Whatever you like, really."

"What's the resolution on the cameras, Joe?" said Charu, from her seat by the table. She needed this information to complete her mental calculation of the coverage and altitude that the drones would fly at.

"Just about as good as it gets. Day and night, we can distinguish men from women, and, up to a certain altitude, we can recognise facial features.

"When I say 'recognise facial features', I mean the computer can. You or I would only see a blur, but the computer uses an algorithm to translate the information from the camera and build a composite of the face. It can also compare this image to older images, stored on police databases." Joe summarised the rest. "These seven hundred and forty-two drones are covering an area of thirty-five thousand square kilometres, flying at an altitude of fifteen hundred metres. If we wanted to, we could increase the coverage by one half again, simply by increasing the altitude of the drones. Sure, we would lose some granularity, but you would be able to generate a general picture of what is going on."

Joe handed back over to Fernando to complete the presentation. Still immaculately dressed in his Salvatore Ferragamo suit, he rose from the table and addressed the group. "Are you still with us? Great! I will briefly explain how these things work as a swarm. Charu, I know you are already up to speed on this. Indeed, we actually borrowed heavily from some of your post-doctoral work in our initial design work." Charu smiled and inclined her head graciously.

"Basically, for the non-scientists amongst you, the principle is really simple. We programme each drone only to consider the environment immediately around it. So, for example, we might tell the drone, 'You must always remain within five kilometres of the nearest four neighbouring drones.' The drone is then simply commanded to maintain a specific altitude and given tasks such as monitor a specific geographical area with a certain degree of granularity, as described using its on-board GPS."

"Actually, the whole is far greater than its parts," interjected Charu. "You see, this system then displays Swarm characteristics. For example, if one or several of the drones falls from the sky, then the remaining drones will automatically readjust their position relative to each other. You see, it is the commands which are the secret. You give the drones the end state you want them to achieve, and they always try to achieve that end state. If it is stated that they must maintain a certain level of granularity, and you lose several drones, then, as a swarm, they may lose altitude in order to maintain the level of granularity you have prescribed."

"Yeah, that just about sums up what I was going to say," said Fernando. "If I could just add one more point, it is that we use a composite picture made up from all the drones to compile our reconnaissance photos. Where their images overlap by nearly a kilometre in these areas, we get a much more detailed image. It is rather like being able to look at something from different sides or aspects at the same time." Fernando spent a further five minutes outlining the drones' data-collecting capabilities, describing the satellite uplink which they used to control the drones and to collect the data.

Chapter Twenty-Two

Eyes in the Sky

"Right, that's the boring stuff over with," said Joe. "Let's get some lunch." They followed Joe through the TTC to the canteen, which was shared with the physics lab. Andrei found it particularly interesting. It wasn't anything like he had expected. He thought he would see white-coat-clad middle-aged men, bent over their plates of food, deep in hushed conversation with each other. Nothing could be further from this vision. The cafeteria was a riot of noise and colour. More than half the people inside were female, and Andrei could only count about six whom he considered to be over forty. People were chatting loudly to each other across the tables and gesticulating wildly whilst doing so.

For the most part, the uniform seemed to be casual trousers, a smart casual shirt with the sleeves partially rolled up, and a pair of brown brogues or slip on shoes. The women were even more stylish. Elegant jewelry hung from their necks and ears, and they sported the very latest Versace and Karen Millen dresses.

"Not what you were expecting?" Matthias said to Andrei.

Maria heard the comment, and, before Andrei could reply, said. "Yeah, not at all. No wonder they are targeted by the kidnappers. Imagine how wealthy they must be to afford to come to work wearing those clothes?" The two men nodded in agreement, as they sat down on either side of Maria at the dinner table.

Fernando addressed the group. "To try to keep the timings for today, I ordered a set menu for us all: some meat and some fish. Two very typical Brazilian dishes. Over here." Fernando pointed to a large clay pot of steaming red sauce with chunks of delicious white cod floating in it. "We have *bacalhao*. This is a simple fish dish of cod in a tomato-based sauce. And over here, we have my favourite, *feijoada*. It is basically a thick black bean stew with chunks of pork and spicy sausage in the sauce, and of course we have plenty of rice to go with both dishes."

The team helped themselves to the two dishes, and, whilst they ate, Fernando described the plan for the rest of their visit. "When we get back, we will look at the drones working in real time. Now that you know the theory, it will be much easier to understand what we are doing. After that, we are pretty much free for the night. Tomorrow, we will look a little more closely at the drone construction and talk some more about how they can be deployed. You can even have a go at printing your own drones!

"Apart from that, the time is your own. If you wish, I could take you all out and show you some of our Paulista nightlife?" Maria and Penny nodded immediately. Andrei also nodded eagerly, and even Philippe said he was up for it. Only Matthias said that he was too old for that sort of thing and made his excuses.

Back in the TTC, the team were sitting once more in the briefing room. A live feed from the drones was being projected on to a huge series of plasma screens in front of them. Ernst began speaking, "OK, so here we are looking at the entire border area between Brazil, on the North-East of the picture, and Bolivia, on the South-West. This is real time information, not a Google maps snapshot," he said, with a derisory snort.

The image appeared to have thick gridlines dissecting the screen into hundreds of tiny squares. "What's that?" asked Maria. "Remember that we said that in some places we got a multidimensional view of the ground? Well, those darker green areas that look like grid lines are where this is occurring. Here, let me show you."

He typed a command into the computer and in less than four seconds, the image started to zoom into a specific area, just over a small Brazilian border settlement called Costa Marquez, which lay on the river Guaporé.

"OK, now we are just seeing the feed from two drones. By zooming in and out, and by switching between the drones, we can create images similar to those you would see on Google street view."

Awesome, said Penny to herself. Imagine what the team back at MI6 could do with this tech!

Both Andrei and Maria were both having similar thoughts about how their respective agencies would deploy this type of drone technology. Ernst retyped a couple of lines of code, and said, "Now compare these six images." The large plasma screens displayed what, at first glance, appeared to be the same image six times over. "Look carefully," said Ernst.

"Got it!" shouted Philippe triumphantly. "There, in the bottom left hand corner of the picture: do you see that brown dirt strip? See how it grows in size over the sequence of pictures."

"Exactly," said Ernst. He was impressed by Philippe's powers of observation. It took a trained eye to be able to scan so much detail quickly and thoroughly enough to pick up such small changes.

"You are looking at a piece of the border area roughly seventy kilometres by twenty kilometres in area. That patch that Philippe noticed" – Ernst circled the area with his mouse – "is an illegal runway, used by a drugs cartel to bring drugs illegally into Brazil from Bolivia. This type of activity can take months, if not years, to detect using foot patrols or aircraft overpasses. Our images are recorded twenty-four hours a day, and we keep the archived images. What we are currently working on is an algorithm to flag up any changes in the appearance of the ground surface, without us having to look at the images week by week."

Charu said that she had given the idea some thought when she had read the pre-briefing pack before they had started the trip and would like to discuss them tomorrow.

The team spent more time examining the images and having a go at controlling the drones and giving them specific commands. Matthias, who wasn't a big technology fan, had been silent for most of the afternoon's session. He turned to Philippe, and said, "You know, it would be a great way to protect indigenous peoples. I mean, you could see in real time any ecological or man-made events that were going to impact on them, and have enough time to try and stop it, instead of waking up one morning and reading in the Sunday newspaper that yet another lost tribe had been 'found', as their habitat had been cut down in order to create yet another super-farm or mineral quarry."

Philippe nodded gravely. It was one of the reasons he had left the oil industry. One day at work in his company's headquarters in Quebec he had overheard some senior board members discussing the fine details of their impending oil exploration in the Arctic. He just couldn't bear thinking about the pollution and harm this exploration could do to this pristine environment. Realising that he personally was impotent to act and change the company's decision, he had handed in his resignation, and had then, with his friend, Matthias, started work on the Inuit Power project.

"That concludes today's presentation," Ernst said, in his clipped Prussian voice. "I think Fernando has some plans for you tonight. I will not be joining you; my wife and I have tickets for the Opera."

As they were leaving, Joe said, "See you tonight. Shall we meet up at the hotel for a drink first?" Fernando agreed, and bundled them all back into the minivan. Accompanied by the silver VW, they left the university car park and headed to the hotel. The hotel, Faria Lima, lay just across the river Tiete from the university. The river bordered the south-west part of Sao Paolo and separated the university from the inner parts of the city. After about twenty minutes of 'edge of the seat' driving through the intense Sao Paulo traffic, the team arrived at their hotel. Fernando bade them farewell, and said that they should get some sleep, and that he would return with Joe at around ten p.m. to start the evening with a quick drink at the hotel, before heading into the milieu of downtown Sao Paulo.

Chapter Twenty-Three

A Good Time Had by All

Thump, thump, thump! There it was again. The room was dark, and Penny lay fully clothed on the bed. Thump, thump, thump! Again.

My God, why can't these people be quiet? All I want is a peaceful night's sleep, thought Penny to herself.

"Penny, are you awake? *Penny?*"

The voice was familiar, Penny thought, and they were shouting her name, weren't they? Shit, damn, bugger! Penny sat bolt upright in the bed. She immediately regretted moving so quickly and lay back down again. Grabbing her mobile phone, she checked the time. Three p.m. in the afternoon. That couldn't be right, could it?

"Penny, we're leaving in thirty minutes; just thought you might need a wake-up call." It was Philippe. She knew she had recognised the voice.

"Philippe, what time is it?" she called feebly from her bed, unable to lift her head from the pillow.

It's eight in the morning. I'm just rounding everyone up we are leaving at eight thirty."

"Thanks," she whispered back, as she once more tried to lift her head from the bed.

It was coming back to her now: her phone wasn't working, as it had stopped updating the time zones as they travelled around the world. It was probably still on Oman time or something like that. She couldn't think well enough to do the maths; her head hurt like hell. And why was she fully clothed? She had no recollection at all of last night. All she knew was that she had less than thirty minutes to be outside in a minibus travelling to the TTC. OK, priorities, she thought to herself. Shower, clean your teeth and change your clothes.

It was a Herculean effort to lift herself from the bed; she stripped her clothes off, discarding them on the hotel floor as she made her way to the shower. She tried to take her socks off, but the effort of bending over made her feel sick. Sitting on the toilet, she lifted her leg gingerly and used the other foot to scrape off her sock. Standing slowly, she squirted toothpaste directly into her mouth, grabbed her toothbrush, and entered the shower. Initially, she felt nothing under the shower, she couldn't even tell if the water was hot or cold, she just stood with her back leaning against the tiled wall hypnotically brushing her teeth. Soon the hot water began to sting her body; at first, it was like tiny pin pricks, but it soon became unbearable. She quickly turned the shower to cold, lifted her face up towards the shower head and shivered violently for thirty seconds as the freezing cold water began to clear her head.

"Time check," she said to herself. "8.20 a.m. Hmm, ten minutes." Leaving the shower, she stood freezing in front of the mirror and examined herself. My God, she thought, Penny, my girl, you look rough! She towelled herself dry, and, ignoring her clothes, which now lay strewn around the bedroom, she slipped on a pair of grey slacks and a cream-coloured silk top. Giving her hair one final rub with the towel, she applied a thin layer of lipstick, slid into her shoes and shuffled out of the hotel room. I hope we have time this afternoon to pack our bags before we leave for the plane, she thought, as she pressed the elevator button.

She met the rest of the group downstairs. Matthias was just entering the hotel. He had been outside for a walk. Charu looked like Penny felt, she thought. But the rest of them seemed wide awake. There was something odd, though, something incongruous that she couldn't put her finger on. Wait a minute; she refocused her bleary eyes. Weren't they still wearing the same clothes as they were wearing last night? She pinched herself. Was she still dreaming? Looking again, she noticed that Andrei and Philippe were grinning and giggling away to each other, and Maria was having an animated conversation with the hotel receptionist. My God, she thought. They haven't been to bed yet!

Moving closer to Maria, she could hear Maria telling the male clerk all about her great city of New York, and how good the Yankees were that season. The clerk seemed mildly amused and seemed to be happy to have the attention of this attractive American woman, even though she was clearly drunk beyond belief.

Fernando came bowling into the hotel reception, immaculately dressed as usual, this time in a different designer suit, but no less elegant. Surely he hadn't stayed out all night as well, had he, thought Penny. Her mind was still foggy. She needed a strong black coffee to clear it. *"Bom dia todo mundo,"* said Fernando.

"Good morning," they chorused back.

"Vamos?"

"Maria," Andrei shouted. "Put him down. The poor boy looks petrified. He's too young for you, anyway." Maria turned to the group and pulled a sarcastic face. Reluctantly, she left the hotel receptionist, promising him that he could come and visit her in New York.

They bundled into the taxi and headed to the TTC. Unable to stand the stench of alcohol any longer, after less than five minutes in the minivan, Fernando opened the window, to let some fresh air into the vehicle. He turned to the driver and murmured something unintelligible in Portuguese and the driver pulled over at the side of the road outside a bakery. "Uggh, what's happening, why have we stopped?" moaned Charu from behind a set of dark sunglasses.

"I think we are stopping for breakfast," whispered Philippe in reply.

They all piled out, shielding their eyes from the already bright sunshine, and entered the bakery. Fernando ushered them to two stand-up tables in the corner and went to order. The team all stood around the tables in the cool, air-conditioned bakery. "Now, that is what I call a good night out," said Andrei, looking across at the others. Andrei, Philippe and Maria had managed to last the whole night in the ultra-chic Sao Paolo club. Sure, it had been expensive, but the club, which was inside a converted luxury mansion, seemed to Philippe to have attracted all of the beautiful, rich and famous people in Sao Paolo. The atmosphere had been electric; all three had danced and drunk through the entire night. Penny and Charu hadn't been so lucky. After their third drink, Penny and Charu had decided to challenge Andrei at drinking vodka shots. It hadn't taken long for Charu to start feeling dizzy and sick, and, escorted by Fernando she excused herself and was taken up to the rooftop chill-out area and left in a chair to sleep off some of the alcohol. No sooner had Fernando returned to the group than he had found himself repeating this action and half carrying, half supporting Penny as she went upstairs to sit on the sofa in the rooftop bar area.

Eventually, after what seemed like an eternity to the hungover team members, Fernando came over to their tables, carrying a large tray. "*Sete cafés com leite forte, pão na chapa com manteiga e pão de queijo.*" He quickly translated into English. "Seven strong milky coffees, freshly toasted thick bread rolls dripping in butter, and small cheesy flavoured doughy balls. The perfect hangover cure," Fernando said, as he handed out the thick warm bread rolls and the coffee.

The team ate and drank in silence; after they had finished the food, Penny said, "My God, that coffee tasted so good! I don't know about you guys, but I need another one of those. Do we have time before we go?"

"Sure," replied Fernando.

The team sipped their coffee and ate their bread in silence. They were beginning to come down from their drunken state now, and it wouldn't be long before the hangovers began. Penny, who was sitting next to Maria, whispered to her, "What the hell happened last night? I woke up this morning fully clothed in my bed."

Maria, who was clutching her coffee, and beginning to regret drinking so much, whispered back, "You really don't remember?"

"Nothing, I mean, I remember that we were drinking shots."

"Yeah," said Maria. "You and Charu were really going for it. It looked like you were both enjoying yourselves, anyway."

"What happened then?"

"Well, you and Charu said you were going up to the roof bar for some fresh air."

"Did we go?"

"You tried; it was Fernando who initially took you both upstairs, where you both passed out on one of those big sofas they have up there."

Shit, thought Penny. How embarrassing.

"It was Fernando who, later, took you both back to the hotel in a taxi, and got you back into your rooms. If it's any consolation, Charu looks even rougher than you do."

"Thanks; er, I guess I should thank Fernando for getting us back safely. What about you guys?"

"Ha, we just carried on partying and dancing. You know, once he gets some drink in him, that robot Andrei is not a bad dancer." Maria said this last part in a hushed and conspirational tone. "It was a great night out. Joe, Charu's friend, was good company but he left earlier. I guess he wanted to stay focused for today."

The team eventually arrived at the TTC; even big old Philippe looked fragile as he climbed out of the minivan. "I am definitely too old for this," he said to no one in particular, as he stumbled across the car park and into the TTC reception area.

They were met by Ernst, who made a point of checking his watch and audibly tutting to himself as they entered.

Keen to defuse Ernst's frustration, Penny asked, "How was the opera?"

"It was one of the worst performances of *Tristan and Isolde* I have ever had to endure. Simply ghastly."

Penny knew that Ernst had probably enjoyed the opera and was actually annoyed at the team for being late, and for the fact that they all still looked very drunk.

"And you, Penny. I trust you had an enjoyable evening?" he said, in a slightly acidic tone.

"Lovely, thank you!" She honestly couldn't say any more, because she still couldn't remember it.

Just then, Joe came around the corner. "Hi, gang! Some of you look a little fragile this morning. Sorry I bailed out early. I had the school run to do this morning with my little girl, Emma Jane. It's her first day at big school today."

Joe was the complete antithesis of Ernst; how they could work together, Penny would never know.

"OK, let's get started then, shall we?" Fernando explained the outline of the day, and said, "If we can split into two groups first of all; Charu, can you, Andrei and Maria join me? We are going to talk about the algorithm for detecting anomalies in the pictures that we discussed yesterday. I was thinking that although you and I might be able to write the algorithm, neither of us would know what to tell it to do. I know that Andrei and Maria both have counternarcotic and people-trafficking experience so I thought they could tell us what things we should be asking the computer to look out for, when we tell it to scan the images."

"Good thinking; do you think we could grab a jug of water and some painkillers before we start?" Charu said, with a pitiful look on her face.

"Sure!" Fernando said, giving her a knowing smile.

Joe addressed the others. "OK, you guys are with me and Ernst. We are going to let you have a go at using the 3D printer to make your own drones; then we will assemble the rest of the parts by hand, to show you how quick and easy it is." Matthias, Philippe and Penny followed the two scientists down a long corridor into a fairly large workshop area. Matthias was in his element. The walls were lined with plastic boxes containing circuit boards, batteries, capacitors, sections of solar panels: in fact, everything that was needed to assemble the mini drones.

Everything was meticulously laid out. Every box was labelled with the same font and colour of label. The items were categorised alphabetically and placed around the room in the precise order in which they would be needed as the drones were assembled. Near the door of the room, connected to an exhaust extractor unit, was the 3D printer.

Joe said, "This is Ernst's area; I just pop in now and then when he needs my help."

Once more, without preamble and with no humour in his voice, Ernst went on to explain the production process. "This is a Selective Layer Sinterin 3D printer." The printer sat on a bench and was roughly cube-shaped. It was larger than Matthias had imagined it would be, standing over a metre and a half tall. Ernst continued, "It is an industrial-standard printer, and has the capacity to print metal as well as plastic components." Ernst droned on about the printer's capabilities and specifications, then went into a lengthy speech about the importance of health and safety.

My God, is he even aware of how uninterested we are, thought Penny to herself. I would kill for another cup of coffee.

Meanwhile, on the other side of the building, the atmosphere was a little lighter. They had spent the first twenty minutes chatting about last night, whilst drinking more coffee and washing it down with large glasses of water. Fernando did a great impression of Philippe's rather old fashioned and unusual dancing style. They all laughed, as Fernando strutted around the computer lab, doing his dancing impression.

After the laughter had died down, Fernando said, "I guess we should get some work done. Maria, Andrei, can you tell us from the aerial photo images that you examine in your work, what are the telltale signs that you look for that tell you that there is illicit activity happening in that area?" They discussed different types of activities, and how images like the roughly-built airstrip seen in the image yesterday were seen a lot; and also that looking for straight-sided angular shapes in jungle photos was a clear indicator that maybe a jungle heroin or cocaine plant was being operated.

"OK, I think I understand now. Charu, how long do you think we would need to get an algorithm written that could get our computers searching our databases for these types of anomalies?"

"I figure we could get a basic working model written in about three days. But we would need to beta-test it extensively using known images, and it might take a week or two to fine-tune the algorithm."

"Thanks, Charu; don't worry, I am not going to ask you to start it now, knowing how delicate you are feeling. I will script out some basic code today, then let you look over it when you are feeling a bit better. It should be available for you to look at on the CTC servers by the time you land in Gander."

Charu smiled and sighed a sigh of relief that Fernando hadn't insisted they start right away. "So, Fernando, what's the aim again?" said Maria.

"Sorry, Maria; as you know, the CTC is a small organisation, and we don't have the skilled analysts or the time to pore over hundreds of hours of photos hoping to spot anomalies. That is a very specialised field, and only a handful of the major militaries in the world have that sort of capability. What we want to do is tell the computer to examine the new video data feeds coming in and compare them with past images to see if they notice any of the obvious anomalies that you and Andrei were talking about."

"I think I am with you; so, when the computer recognises this illegal activity, it can filter all of the relative images, and we will have a complete timeline of the events, dated accurately."

"Exactly," said Fernando.

Andrei interrupted. "But we are talking about crime here; I didn't think the CTC's job was to catch criminals?"

"Exactly right; it just so happens that, in this test phase, that is how we are using it. But it could just as easily be used by smaller communities to monitor crop yields, give advance warnings about droughts or floods, be used to aid rescue workers after natural disasters, or protect wildlife from poachers. Actually, the applications are limitless. What we are trying to do here is to develop a robust system that is cheap and easy to use."

"I see," said Andrei, stroking his chin thoughtfully. "And just how easy and cheap is it to make these drones?"

"Depending on scale, we figure a unit price of around eight dollars per drone."

"That is cheap," said Andrei. "But surely you need to be some type of engineer to build them and run them?"

"Not really," said Charu. "You see, that is the beauty of this swarm behaviour that we are using. We do all of the programming here; all the customers need to do is decide what they want their drones to do: you know, take video images, detect heat sources, etc."

Fernando looked at his watch. It was nearly two p.m. In a few minutes, we should be joined by Ernst, Joe and the rest of your team. You will see then how easy it is to make these machines. The whole team reassembled in the briefing room, and, despite their hangovers, it appeared that Matthias, Philippe and Penny had enjoyed themselves with Ernst and Joe. It turned out that despite his obvious distaste for their hung-over state, Ernst's passion for his work had rubbed off on the rest of the team, and they had enjoyed building their mini-drones. They had even programmed the 3D printer to print them in the colour and design of their respective national flags of Denmark, Canada and Great Britain. Philippe was like a little boy, excitedly showing off different aspects of the drone's design to Maria and Andrei.

"I am sorry to spoil the party," said Joe, "but the clock is ticking; I know you guys have to fly all the way up to Newfoundland today, and, after last night, I guess you are all looking forward to a good sleep on the plane?" As one, the team nodded their agreement.

"I will give you two options for lunch. We can play it safe and have a chicken salad in the cafeteria here?"

"Or," interrupted Fernando. "We could have a true Brazilian experience, and visit a good *churrascaria*?"

"What is a *churrascaria*?" asked Charu.

"It is a totally delicious BBQ. You just sit there, and the waiters just keep bringing around skewer after skewer, loaded with delicious cuts of different meats. I'm certainly in."

"Me too, said Philippe; I am looking forward to a good bit of red meat, after all the fish we have been eating."

"Let's go, then," said Fernando. "Unless any of you would prefer to go for a salad with Ernst?"

Ernst had already left the room, and Fernando thought it would be safe to poke gentle fun at 'Earnest Ernst', as Joe had nicknamed him.

Once more the team found themselves driving through the chaotic Sao Paulo traffic, accompanied by the ever-watchful silver VW. From the outside, the Churrascaria didn't look too special. Once inside, the entrance area opened up into a large hall; at the top end of the hall, behind huge windows, the chefs could be seen tending to rack after rack of meat that was slowly being barbequed. The centre of the room was dominated by a huge circular table that was groaning under the weight of the salad bar, and a fresh sea food selection. They entered en masse, and Fernando asked for a table for eight.

"OK, the rules are really simple. Eat as much good meat as you can. To start with, they will come around offering you anything and everything. Use this." Fernando held up a small red and green wooden block that sat in front of each place setting. "It's simple, keep this on red. When you see something you fancy coming your way, then simply turn the block over to green, and the waiters will come over with the skewer, and serve you as much meat as you want." They all nodded their understanding, and the feast began.

Chapter Twenty-Four

Latitude 48° 58' 4.8720'', Longitude 54° 35' 53.1708''.
Technology Translation Centre, Gander, Newfoundland,
Canada. – May 2017.
Nikola Tesla

The atmosphere on the plane was more than a little subdued as the pilot taxied off and headed due north towards the Newfoundland coast. Most of the team had got over their hangovers by now. Only Penny and Charu were still suffering. Without exception, each of them was full to bursting after the mountain of meat they had consumed at the Churrascaria. When Christi came around to give them their melatonin shots, most of them declined. The time difference between Sao Paulo and Gander was only one hour, and, after looking around the cabin at the faces of the team, Christi could see that most of the team would sleep through the entire ten-and-a-half-hour flight. It must have been one hell of a night out, she thought to herself.

The approach into Gander was a nerve-racking affair. The wind outside was gusting up to ninety miles per hour, and the thunderstorm, driven by the unusually cold north-easterly wind, buffeted the Gulfstream G550 mercilessly. Even the most hung-over team members were awake, and busy strapping themselves in tightly to their thick beige leather chairs. Christi too was strapped in, and in constant contact with the two pilots in the cockpit.

She had expected bad weather. Gander sits on the Newfoundland Island surrounded by water. Not only is it about the same size as Ireland; it also shares Ireland's exposure to the Northern Atlantic. Gander is the first spit of land that an Arctic storm like the one outside would hit before heading inland. It is the most easterly point of North America, and one of the most exposed places on the continent.

Both Guenther Kramer and Fabio Cancerelli had flown in worse conditions, during their time with their respective militaries. Fabio had nursed a damaged Italian Air Force Hercules C-130 in to land at a dirt airstrip just north of the border between Somalia and Kenya, after being shot at by Somalia militiamen. Guenther had never been shot at, but whilst on loan to the US Navy he had had many nerve racking experiences landing F 16 fighter planes on the deck of the aircraft carrier, USS Abraham Lincoln, in tropical typhoons off the coast of the Philippines. Both men would openly admit, to anyone who asked them, that they were adrenalin junkies.

The plane touched down on its second approach. On the first attempt, a strong side wind blew the light aircraft dangerously off course and almost into the control tower. Remaining calm, both pilot and co-pilot had carefully brought the plane back round for the second landing attempt.

It was still raining heavily when the team left the aircraft and entered the Royal Canadian Air Force Terminal building in Gander. "*Bonjour mes amis, bienvenue au Canada,*" said a large, rosy-cheeked middle-aged woman wearing a thick woollen jumper, green military-style fatigue trousers and brown quilted cold weather boots.

"*Bonjour, Charlie!*" said Philippe in reply. "Hey, everyone, this is Charlie Armand." Charlie hugged Matthias effusively. Matthias hugged her back with genuine warmth.

"Charlie is the driving force behind our little power project here and has done so much to help Philippe and I with our own Inuit Power Project." The hugs continued. Charlie was clearly an affectionate woman, thought Andrei. Maybe she just didn't see that many people out here in the middle of nowhere.

"*Vous préférez Français ou Anglais*? Sorry, do you prefer French or English?" Andrei and Maria had very little knowledge of French, so it was decided that they would continue in English.

"We shall go now to my office, OK?" Charlie said in her accented English.

"How far is it to your office?" asked Maria.

Laughing heartily, Charlie replied, "Not far, not far at all."

Gander is a small town in Newfoundland, bordered to the south by the large serpent-like Gander lake. To give an idea of scale, the airport complex, runways included, makes up nearly half the size of the entire town. Since 1960, the population has doubled in size, to eleven thousand people. It is the type of town where everyone knows everyone else's business.

The five-minute drive took them down James Boulevard, then right on to Cooper Boulevard; on the way they passed a large Wal-Mart store and a Pizza Hut. The sky above was leaden with clouds and seemed to hang ominously over them. Charu turned to Penny, and said, "And to think that just twelve hours ago, we were partying in Brazil!" As she finished speaking, the vehicle turned right onto Navy Road and pulled over into a car park, where a cluster of very new dome-shaped buildings was arranged in two neat rows.

The buildings were connected by a series of glass-covered walkways, with a large atrium in the middle at the front. Getting out of the vehicle first, Charlie began to talk about the site layout, and to describe the purpose of each building. Charu and Maria started to shiver. My God, thought Maria, this moisture-laden air, with no sight of the sun, just seemed to suck the life out of you. She looked across at Charlie, who was happily chatting away, completely oblivious of the cold.

"Maybe we should enter Charlie? It seems that some of our team may require more than a couple of days to acclimatise to our lovely Canadian Spring weather," said Philippe, with a chuckle. He had caught the look of suffering on Charu's face and was certain that Maria's lips had turned blue already.

They entered the building's atrium and went straight on through to the Tesla Suite. "Wait, don't I know that name?" said Penny, to the group as a whole.

"Yeah, isn't that the new electric car company?" replied Andrei.

"It is, but for us the room was named in honour of Mr Nikola Tesla, a Serbian, who was raised in Croatia, and later started working for Thomas Edison after emigrating to New York."

"Right, wasn't he the crazy guy?" mumbled Matthias.

"Some would say there is a thin line between being crazy and being a genius, Matthias," Charlie said, with a raised eyebrow. "Back at the end of the nineteenth century, Tesla revolutionized not just our concept of what electricity is, but also of how to harness it and apply it to work for us. He experimented with invisible energy, or what we today know as X-Rays; he designed the first electric motors, and developed electricity generating and transfer plants. He was fascinated with what he termed invisible forces, and even invented a mechanical oscillator, with which he managed to cause specific objects, such as buildings, to shake violently when he tuned it to their resonance.

"He was truly a fascinating man. Anyway, we are moving ahead of ourselves slightly, shall we go into the briefing room and a have a cup of coffee, and I will introduce you to the rest of the team?"

The room was a little stuffy and cramped; it had a capacity for no more than twenty people. Andrei guessed they didn't get as many visitors up here as they did at the sunnier, more exotic, TTC sites.

"Ladies and gentlemen, can I introduce you to Professor Hideki Kobayashi?" The diminutive, bald-headed man bowed slightly and moved forward to shake hands with each team member in turn. The other research Head is Dr Semyon Volkov. Semyon was a tall, reedy-looking man with a pallid complexion. It looked like he rarely saw daylight. He stepped forward rather awkwardly, and, maintaining only minimum eye-contact, he greeted the group.

"Professor Kobayashi is from the University of Kyoto, and specialises in electro-magnetic induction. He has worked extensively on the Japanese magnetic levitating bullet train system." Still smiling, the Professor bowed once more. Dr Volkov formerly worked at the University of St Petersburg as an atmospheric physicist. I, as some of you know, have a Ph.D. in electronic engineering. I am responsible for the design and operation of the equipment. The good doctor and the professor are the brains bringing the theory to bear, as it were."

Both Matthias and Philippe knew that she was being self-deprecating. Charlie was one of the smartest people they knew; she was a natural engineer and could pretty much build anything you asked her to, as long as it contained a circuit board of some kind.

Semyon Volkov began the talk. "If I am not mistaken, I heard you discussing Nikola Tesla as you entered the room? It was this visionary man who first discovered and tried to harness atmospheric energy. Later in his life, he claimed to have developed a form of directed energy weapon, which, in his words would 'produce manifestations of free energy in the air'. Today, we now know that he was talking about the positively charged particles that we call ions."

At this point, Hideki Kobayashi took over. The presentation appeared smooth and seamless, but Matthias could not help wondering whether he didn't sense some friction between the diminutive Japanese man and the tall, pallid Russian. "Hello again." His English was flawless. You had to listen very hard indeed to hear the tell-tale signs, such as the slight humming R sound when the letter L was spoken. "Our research here at the TTC has been focused on three areas. Firstly, how the ions become charged in the first place, and what we can do to localise or increase the amount of charged ion particles in the air.

"Secondly – and this is probably the most difficult phase – how to capture these charged ion particles and remove the positive electrical charge. Finally – and this is by no means easy in itself – comes transporting and storing the energy in a usable form." He clicked the mouse button, and a slide showing what looked like hundreds of tiny atomic ball-like structures. "This is an image of an ion. Positive ions attract other particles in the air, such as dust. This was our first clue as to where to find them. In very dusty or cloudy areas," he said, looking skywards. "We can find an abundance of positively charged ions. In actual fact, some households have small air-ionizing machines that artificially charge the air with negatively-charged ions, so that dust particles clump more readily together, and then can be filtered out of the house air. They help many people with allergies, I am told. I shall defer to my esteemed colleague, Semyon, to tell you more about where the ions come from."

There it was again, Matthias thought; surely a professor doesn't 'defer' to a doctor, does he? No, these two men barely get along with each other. I bet they hardly speak to each other unless it's absolutely necessary.

Semyon began to explain how powerful cosmic rays from the deepest reaches of outer-space were constantly bombarding the earth's atmosphere; the rays collided with oxygen and nitrogen air molecules. These violent collisions were capable of knocking electrons off the air molecules, and thus creating billions of electrically charged airborne ions all over the world.

Matthias was only half listening to the Russian; instead, he was observing the Japanese man. He was sure he had caught the little man stifle a yawn as Semyon waxed lyrical about the cosmos. After about thirty minutes of the Russian doctor's diatribe about cosmic rays, Charlie looked around the room and could see the sleep-inducing effect it was having on the team. She stood, and, addressing the Russian scientist, politely said, "Semyon, I believe our friends may be a little tired from their long flight; maybe you could discuss the rest on a one-to-one basis tomorrow?"

It was phrased as a question, Matthias noted, but it was quite clearly meant as a command. It was obvious who was in charge here. "So, I hope you are still with us?" she said, with a conspiratorial smile. I will briefly summarise my part; then, after lunch, we will go and look at the system in action.

"Very briefly, then," she said, clicking on a new slide. The slide looked like a close-up of a particularly fine-branched sea coral. It had hundreds of tiny almost wispy tendrils that themselves branched off into smaller but exact copies of the larger tendrils.

"What you are looking at is our Ion Removing Integrated System, or IRIS, as we call it here. We actually don't do anything other than provide the right conditions for the positive ions to transfer to our IRIS. The IRIS collection sites are constructed from negatively charged carbon nanotubes, which have been suffused with alkali metals. The positive ions willingly transfer or dock with the negatively charge surface. In effect, the positive ions are then bundled and transferred to ever-increasing surfaces, until they are transferred down our cables like a regular AC current and stored."

"It's fractal, isn't it?" asked Charu. She had been sitting at the back, simply staring at the coral-like image on the monitor in front of them.

"Yes, exactly," Charlie replied.

Charu went on, "Each section of the IRIS is a scaled version of its closest neighbours. The charged particles are bundled together naturally by simply occupying carbon nano-tube structures of an ever-increasing size until they 'flow'" – Charu used her fingers to indicate inverted commas at the use of this non-scientific term – "yes, they then flow like a regular current down the cable to the capacitor bank." Both the Russian and Japanese scientists looked at Charu in disbelief.

"You should see what she is like when she is not hung over," said Philippe, this elicited a loud peel of laughter throughout the room.

Noticing Charu's obvious embarrassment, Charlie stood and said, "OK, I think that is about enough for this morning's session. Maybe we could go and get lunch, and meet back here in an hour?"

"What's for lunch, Charlie?" asked Penny.

"I'm afraid we are a slightly smaller set-up here than the other places, and we don't have our own canteen. Do you mind if we go to Pizza Hut?"

"Perfect," Penny replied. "Most of us got quite drunk last night, and I think we could all do with something delicious and stodgy to fill our stomachs with."

"Great, that's settled then. I'll grab my bag, and we'll leave in five minutes." Semyon had cornered Charu and was busy explaining his personal theory of cosmic dust accumulation in the outer atmosphere when Philippe walked over to rescue her.

Chapter Twenty-Five

Ions Ripe for Harvesting

They all sat at a large table in Pizza Hut. Philippe and Charlie pulled up extra chairs so that everyone could be seated. Everyone was there except for Semyon. Matthias asked Charlie, quite innocently, "Is the good doctor not going to join us?"

Looking a little sheepish, Charlie replied, "Dr Volkov is a good man really, but whereas Hideki…" Matthias caught the deliberate use of Semyon's title, and the less formal use of the Japanese Professor's first name. It was clear whose side Charlie was on. "Hideki and I have a, how shall I say, a stronger focus on translating technology into real world solutions. Dr Volkov is, er, shall we say, more attracted to the theoretical side of our work. As such, he prefers to remain in his lab."

A young girl, with a name badge declaring her to be called Yvonne, brought the pizzas to the table. She smiled at Charlie and asked how she was, as she placed four super-sized pizzas on the table. Hideki, Charu and Maria were sitting at the bottom of the table. The small-statured scientist seemed to be enjoying himself immensely, sitting between the two attractive girls. He was very animated and laughed regularly at the girls' stories. Matthias would find out later that, quite by chance, Hideki was a huge Bollywood fan, and he had been excitedly discussing the latest Bollywood releases with the two girls. Maria professed to having been hooked on Bollywood from an early age. She loved the huge dance scenes, and the perpetual, if slightly superficial, love stories that they often portrayed. It turned out that the Professor was particularly enamoured with one Bollywood star, Amrita Kapoor. When Charu admitted to having met her personally at a charity fund-raising event, the professor could not contain his excitement. "It looks like Charu just made an old man very happy," said Philippe, with a smirk.

Matthias and Andrei, who was sitting next to him, laughed out loud. "Hey, what's the joke?" said Penny.

"Oh, nothing," said Philippe, still with a broad grin on his face.

Back at the TTC, Charlie issued them all with a thick parka jacket and some stout wellington boots. I am afraid it is a little cold and wet out there today. These should keep you warm and dry, though. They set off once more in the TTC vehicles heading west out of Gander on the Route One. Once they reached the settlement of Appleton, Charlie turned the vehicle off the road, and headed over up over a heavily-rutted dirt track, gradually climbing until they reached what passed for a hill in Newfoundland.

The wind was picking up again outside, and it was beginning to hail again. "Now, before we get out, I thought I should explain. We do not need to locate the site on a hill, we just chose to, as sometimes we have a little electrical discharge that results in a highly statically-charged environment." Charlie went on to explain that the local community felt more comfortable if the 'scientists' did their experiments high up on a hill, well out of the way of the ordinary folk. "Of course, from a safety point of view we also didn't want the site too close to an airfield, which stores thousands of gallons of highly combustible aviation fuel."

In front of them was an array of what looked like giant wind turbine towers without the blades on top. Instead, the tall towers had what looked like a giant sleeve wrapped around the upper third of the tower. From each of the towers, a single cable trailed towards the earth, and disappeared into a manhole-sized opening in the centre of the array.

Now outside the vehicles, Charlie had to shout to be heard above the wind. "You see the thick sections at the top of the towers. They are filled with the carbon nanotube material; you know, the stuff that looked like coral. They are quite literally filtering out the positively-charged ions as we speak." The atmosphere was filled with a constant humming noise, and the very air itself seemed palpable. Penny could feel the fine hairs on her arms and back of her neck tingling with the static-laden air. Charlie led the group to a small concrete blockhouse. Inside, they descended a tight rubber-coated spiral staircase, and entered a large bunker. The room was easily fifty metres in length and probably well over thirty metres wide, Andrei thought. Along one wall sat a long row of what looked like large grey lockers. The row stretched the entire length of the room. At regular intervals sat a tiny platform with a touch-screen display mounted on each one. The displays were showing the actual charge state and flow rate of electricity in and out of each of the giant sections of the battery bank.

"Very impressive indeed!" said Charu. Both Matthias and Philippe had visited the site many times before, but never failed to be impressed. "How much energy can you generate?"

"That's what we are having some issues with at the moment. You see, the plant, at full capacity, can generate quite a lot of power. Enough to provide electricity to about forty homes around the clock. Our problem is in storing that much power.

"Remember, the idea is for small communities to set up 'puddles' of power generation, and not necessarily be part of a national grid system," said Charlie.

"Yes, but if you were close to the grid, you could feed the excess directly into the grid, couldn't you?"

"That's possible. We are also looking at ways of direct supply from the generating site to the local community. In fact, we're trialling one of the ideas whilst we speak," Charlie said, with a sly grin on her face. "If it is not successful, then we will be burning off all that pizza on the long walk home."

"The vehicles, they're electric?" Maria asked. Over the noise of the wind and hail, the team hadn't noticed that the vehicles actually made no noise at all. "Yes, all of our vehicles run off this power system; in fact we use the system to power the entire TTC," Charlie said, with no small amount of pride in her voice. The team spent a further thirty minutes looking around the site, then jumped back into the electric vehicle and drove back to the TTC in the silent vehicle.

"That's about it for today," Charlie said with a smile, as they arrived back at the TTC site. "Matthias and Philippe both know where the hotel is, and you can use this vehicle to get around town." It was only a short drive to the aptly named Hotel Gander. All of the hotels were located in the same area of town, down towards Lake Gander. The Hotel wasn't quite the same standard as the previous one in Sao Paulo; however, it was comfortable, and, as with everyone they had met in the small town, the manageress made them all feel very welcome.

Chapter Twenty-Six

Running for Respect

If you took a room on the fourth of its four floors you could see Lake Gander, just over four hundred metres away over the fir trees. The hotel building itself was a bright white building, which, unusually for a hotel, was wider than it was tall. "I guess that comes with having so much space and so few people," Penny said to Matthias.

"Yes, they certainly like their space up here. I noticed the same phenomenon in Northern Australia as well. Did you notice that, despite being pleasant, the manageress kept her distance from us?" Penny hadn't noticed. "Tonight, if we go out for a meal, try standing closer to one of the people in the restaurant. By close, I mean as close as you would normally stand next to someone in London without feeling weird. You see, people who live in large open spaces adapt to that environment, and actually require more personal space."

"OK, I'll try; let's see who can get someone to move away from them first."

Andrei was gazing out of the window, eyeing the paths that wove between the fir trees. He turned to the hotel receptionist. "Do you have a small-scale map of the area?" he asked.

"Yes, sir," she said, handing him a local map.

"What time's dinner? I'm going for a run," he declared.

Matthias had noticed how on edge Andrei became if he didn't get his regular bouts of strenuous exercise. "I suggest we meet down here at eight p.m. and take a drive over to a great Bistro that Philippe and I know."

"OK, I'm off then," said Andrei. He was straining at the leash to run. As an afterthought, he said, "Does anyone want to come with me?"

Most team members flatly refused, all except one. "I'd love to," said Maria. Maria had been getting on better with Andrei on this trip, but, with their imminent return to Singapore pending, she feared Andrei would go back to arguing about every decision she made if she didn't try to do something about it. Maybe I could show him that not all women are weak, she thought.

They met in the hotel lobby twenty minutes later. Andrei was wearing a lightweight pair of running shorts and a T-shirt, which was stretched taut over his muscular frame. Maria wore long black leggings, a long sleeved thermal top with a T-shirt over the top, gloves, and a head-warming band that covered her ears.

"Don't worry," he said to her. "I'll be gentle with you. We will just do a steady two hours around the woods down by the lake. OK?"

Maria couldn't remember the last time she had run for two hours. She was a good sprinter, and also practiced parkour, the newly emerging sport of urban free running, where you negotiated your way through an urban landscape using a series of flowing gymnastic moves to jump over, climb up or descend a whole assortment of man-made objects. It was very elegant to watch, and the trick was to keep the flow of movement going.

Mustering as much enthusiasm as she could get into her voice, she said, "Let's do this," as they left the warmth of the hotel and began to run towards the woods.

Maria noticed two things immediately. Firstly, unlike most people, apparently Andrei did not require a period of warming up before he ran at full pace. He was like the electric car they had spent the day driving around in. He silently and effortlessly accelerated from a standing start to the pace he would maintain for the entire run. The second thing she noticed was that he seemed impervious to the weather. It must have been close to three degrees Celsius outside; when you added the wind chill and the effect of the light drizzle, it would feel well below zero. When she had observed him running in Namibia from the helicopter, she had thought of him as robotic. Watching him now, though close up, she recognised a fluidity of movement and harmony with the ground that he ran across that she had never encountered before.

The paths through the woods were perfect; they were wide and sheltered from the worst of the wind and rain, and had a soft matting of moss and pine needles that cushioned every step she took. They had been running for about thirty minutes now, and, checking her pulse monitor, Maria was alarmed to see that she was running at one hundred and seventy beats per minute. This was over seventy-five per cent of her maximum effort. She still felt fine, but knew that if she were to maintain this tempo it would soon start to become very uncomfortable. She looked once more across to Andrei. He looked comfortable yet alert. How was it she had heard him describe his Special Forces Group? Yes, that was it, the Wolf Pack. The name could not have been more apt.

Andrei ran smoothly through the forest, taking in his surroundings, reacting to different smells and sounds by darting left and right through the trees to investigate the source of these stimuli.

An hour had passed before he even seemed to notice Maria. He began to study her out of the corner of his eye. She was too powerfully built to be a good endurance runner, he thought. But as he watched her skip over the tree roots and power herself up the hills, he slowly started to develop a little respect for the American agent. He descended a steep bank down towards the river and decided that he would open up the pace a little, as they ran along the lake shore back to the hotel, then ease off as they turned back up through the woods to the front of the building.

Picking up the pace slightly, he noticed Maria's gait start to become unnatural. She slid a couple of times on the loose gravel, and he could hear her breathing increase in both volume and intensity. For her part, Maria had stopped enjoying the run about ten minutes previously. By now, she was well into her red zone. Her lungs were burning, as her body concentrated on its sole important task of trying to remove as much of the lactic acid from her legs as she could. It seemed an impossible task: the longer they ran the greater the burning sensation became. She knew one thing for certain. She wasn't going to give up.

Andrei had moved ahead slightly, or had she dropped back? She didn't have the capacity to work it out any more. There! He seemed to be slowing now; a glimmer of hope appeared in the back of her pain-racked brain. Maybe this torture was coming to an end. Andrei slowed his pace slightly and allowed Maria to catch up with him. He was genuinely impressed by her. She had run almost as well as some of the men he used to train with. But more than that, she had shown a determination that he hadn't thought she possessed. He knew the run had been hurting her for the past hour, but she hadn't relented. It would come at a cost, Andrei thought. Tomorrow she would have very sore legs indeed.

As they trotted back up the path that led to the hotel, Maria watched Andrei. He seemed to skip almost gazelle-like up the few steps that led to the hotel entrance. He certainly was a wolf, she thought: a dangerous animal, only truly at home in the wild. The question on her mind was whether it was possible to tame this animal.

Dinner at the Bistro was exactly what the team needed after the night of drinking and the massive meat feast in Sao Paulo at the *churrascaria*, and the giant pizza portion at lunch time. The team were ready for something a little lighter. They weren't disappointed. Charu chose mushroom and lentil fritters, followed by pan-roasted salmon. Matthias and Philippe had their favourite dish of Blueberry and Newman's port scallops, preceded by a mushroom tart. Penny was feeling adventurous and tried the seafood chowder as a starter, followed by duck breast in maple sauce and dried cherries.

Maria and Andrei sat down together at the end of the table. Maria's hair was still wet from the shower, as she perused the menu. "What's the soup of the day?" she asked the waiter.

"Broccoli and blue cheese."

"Perfect, I'll take that, followed by your black Angus filet mignon, rare please."

"Make that two," said Andrei. "Although I prefer mine medium."

The food arrived, and Matthias watched as Maria tore off a huge chunk of crispy bread to mop up the remains of her soup.

That must have been a hard run; she looks hungry, he mused to himself. What he wasn't sure of was whether the food would satisfy her hunger or whether, out on the run, she had developed a different type of hunger. He had noticed how she and Andrei had started to get along a lot better together recently. He had also seen, first, her stolen glances at Andrei's legs when he went running against the buggy in Namibia, and, more recently, he had noticed Andrei checking out her body when she had appeared at the beach with Penny in her bikini. He put the thought to the back of his mind. "What will be, will be," he thought to himself.

"Penny!" he shouted across the table. "Remember our plan tonight?" She was sitting waiting for her duck breast to arrive. Nodding to Matthias, she stood up from the table, and walked towards the waiter, who stood by the entrance to the restaurant. She deliberately positioned herself in front of the waiter, standing about one metre away from him.

"Excuse me," she said. "Could you tell me where the bathroom is, please?"

She noticed the almost immediate sub-conscious reaction by the waiter. She had barely finished the words 'excuse me' when she noticed him flinch involuntarily and shrink back half a pace. It was as if he were sub-consciously trying to remove himself from a threat. The movement was subtle, and Penny wondered if the waiter was even aware of making the movement. "Right that way, madam," the waiter said, pointing with an outstretched arm towards the obvious bathroom sign. As she turned to head towards the bathroom, she glanced once more at the waiter. Did he look relieved that she was leaving his personal space?

When she returned to the table, her duck was waiting for her. As she began to eat she glanced over at Matthias who was sat with a wry smile on his face. Over coffee back in the hotel lobby, Matthias explained the little experiment to the rest of the group. "You know, some very interesting experiments similar to this one have been conducted in the past. In one, the participants were wired up with devices to measure their heart rate and body temperature, and, also, their exact location relative to the other people was tracked throughout the experiment. The experiment was to see how differently the people behaved when being forced to meet and greet people of different genders and races in a confined area.

"Obviously, in the pre-screening questionnaires everyone reported that they had no 'issues' with people of different genders, sexual persuasion or races. The data from the body temperature and heart rate devices told a different story though."

"Surely everyone is going to get warm in a small room where they are circulating and meeting each other?" asked Penny.

"Yes, but these people demonstrated what amounted to physical distress when they were kept in close proximity, or had to make contact with certain other ethnic groups."

"I wonder what would happen if we were wired up like that?" Charu mused aloud.

A slightly longer than natural silence passed over the group, then Matthias continued. "More interesting yet was the data on their location. You see, when these clusters were viewed over time, it became apparent that the people spent more time clustered closer together in groups of similar ethnic persuasion or gender. Indeed, the further they were from each other ethnically or physically, the further they stood from each other."

"That's fascinating, but doesn't it make our job at the CTC almost impossible?" piped up Maria.

"Not really; you see, if this group," – he gestured to the team sitting around the table – "If this group had been measured on the first day in the briefing room in Singapore, and then measured again today, the result would be different. We are able to adapt our behaviour and modulate our prejudices. Put simply, the more we know about other people, the more familiar we become with them, the more we relax around them, and, as a result, less hostility is generated between the groups."

"Fascinating as ever," said Philippe to Matthias. "But if I don't get to bed and get my eight hours' sleep, I will be very hostile indeed tomorrow!" The group laughed and slowly dispersed to their rooms.

The final morning at the TTC in Gander was spent digging deeper into the technology. Charu had drawn the short straw and sat with Dr Volkov discussing the opportunities that clouds presented to be harnessed and used as massive natural energy storage sites, instead of relying on the limited capacity of the lithium ion batteries. To be fair, she was probably the only one in the group who could keep up with the doctor's rapid stream of consciousness.

Matthias and Philippe were busy chatting to Charlie about the application of the ion power generation to the Inuit Project; and Maria, Andrei and Penny sat with Hideki in his lab, discussing the materials used. It had struck both Penny and Maria that creating a carbon nanotube material infused with alkaline metals would not be a simple process.

Hideki explained how the sheets were created and layered upon each other, admitting that this was one of the parts of the project that was causing them some headaches at the moment. He was busy working on ways to simplify this process, or even to automate it, so that regional hubs could have their own lab to make the material, as and when it was required.

The morning passed swiftly, and soon it was time to say goodbye to rainy Gander. Despite the gloomy weather, they had all been impressed with the technology, and had found the visit to be one of the most interesting on the trip. As they were saying goodbye, Charu promised to send Hideki a copy of the latest Bollywood blockbuster that her relatives had sent her. Charlie once more gave each team member a tight hug and wished them '*Bon voyage*'. Even the reserved Dr Volkov had seemed to enjoy his chat with Charu and made the effort to come and shake hands with everyone before they left.

Climbing aboard the Gulf Stream for the final journey, they had mixed feelings. They were all looking forward to getting back to Singapore, having a few days leave, then getting straight back into work, preparing for the Human Terrain Exercise in Iraq. But they had also had a fantastic trip, meeting many great people, and being privileged to see first-hand some of the most bizarre and cutting-edge science projects currently being conducted around the world.

The flight plan was long, yet simple. The first leg would see them flying just under four thousand kilometres across the Atlantic, and touching down at RAF Northolt, just west of

London. This RAF base was home to the VIP, or Queen's, Flight, and was where the British Royal Family and senior politicians flew from, when on official business. It was also a busy commercial airport for small, privately-owned jets belonging to some of Britain's wealthiest inhabitants.

They would leave London and fly direct to Singapore. This would be a long leg indeed; at nearly eleven thousand kilometres, they would be right at the limit of the plane's twelve-thousand-five-hundred-kilometre flying endurance. Around three hours before the plane touched down in Singapore, at eleven a.m. local time, the team found themselves sitting around the touch screen table, engaged in a conference video call with Li. He had wanted to welcome them all back home safely.

One by one, he questioned them about different aspects of the journey. Once satisfied, he restated the fact that he had given them all three days' holiday. He then spent the next forty minutes outlining the work the team had ahead of them. Primarily, he spoke about the preparations for the Iraq exercise. He told Penny of a group within the British Army who would be supporting them on their forthcoming exercise.

This group of cultural advisors, or CULADs as they were known within the British Ministry of Defence, were the perfect people to support the team in their Human Terrain Mapping exercise. "You are to get in touch with them as soon as you land, Penny, and arrange a meeting for three days hence. I have the contact details here of their Adjutant, a Captain Phillip Morrison." Penny took note of the details and promised to contact the Army Captain as soon as they touched down.

Shortly afterwards, the plane touched down in Singapore. Thanking the crew for their Herculean efforts in getting them half way around the world in so much style and comfort, not to forget safety, they left the plane. On stepping outside, they were immediately assaulted by the heat and humidity of the air. Less than twenty hours ago, they had been shivering in a rain-sodden island off the coast of the North Atlantic. It would take at least three days to acclimatize to the heat in Singapore, never mind adjusting to the time difference.

Chapter Twenty-Seven

Latitude 1° 17' 28.8348'', Longitude 103° 47' 13.3296''.
United Nations Centre for Technology and Culture
Headquarters,
Heng Mui Keng Terrace, Singapore – May 2017.
A Moral Dilemma

The older Chinese man stood looking at the CTC from inside the glass-walled smoking box. A lit cigarette burned lazily in his right hand as he gestured to some unknown point outside the box.

"So you see, Li, the committee are very pleased with your work so far."

The committee to which the older Chinese man referred was the Politburo Standing Committee of the Communist Party of China. This committee of seven people were responsible for making every single decision of significance in China. Their actions affected not only the 1.3 billion Chinese citizens, but also all of China's regional neighbours, as well as the global economy.

Li was also in the smoking box; he wasn't feeling as confident as the other man right now. He was sat slouched on the settee; his face was drawn and pale and his chest was tight, he was struggling to breathe. "Thanks to your use of Chinese Project managers, and their willingness to help Beijing, the People's

Republic of China now has access to all of the research and design that your organisation has conducted so far. Our state-run cyber penetration teams have managed to infiltrate the entire network. This information will give China an enormous economic competitive advantage. We will be able to reduce our reliance on foreign coal and oil, clear the smog from our cities, and increase our economic output."

"Father, I, I was unaware of this, this act of espionage! I am an honourable man, and…"

The older gentleman raised his hand to silence Li. Crouching down, he stared directly into Li's eyes. "Li, my boy. Have I not treated you well? Have I not educated you and guided you up through the ranks of power to get you to where you are today?"

"Yes, Father, but now I work for the UN. I gave my word to my friend, the Secretary-General, that I would be politically neutral in my running of the CTC."

"Ha!" snorted the older man derisively. "Who do you think secured this position for you? You would be wise not to forget who your real masters are."

"I'm not your puppet; I repeat, I am an honourable man…"

Li was abruptly cut off. The older man stood, and, as he did so, he struck Li across the side of his face with the back of his hand. "You always were weak. I knew you couldn't be trusted. Well, allow me to let you in to a little secret, my boy. When I met your mother, you were just a baby, a few days old. You see, your mother had been conducting an illicit affair with the Japanese Trade Minister for several years in the early 1950s. And you," he said, pointing an accusatory finger at Li. "You are the bastard child who resulted from this disgraceful affair."

Li was stunned. He could feel his cheek where he had been slapped reddening as it perfused with blood. He simply couldn't believe what he was hearing. "I am an illegitimate child born of a Japanese father and Chinese mother?" He repeated the older man's words. "No, this simply couldn't be. I am Chinese. I am Han."

"Your mother came from an important family. Her father was very influential in the politburo, and he asked me if I would marry your mother to save face. Of course, I knew that this act of face-saving would be very beneficial to my own political career."

Li was silent now. He had just been dealt not one but two shocking pieces of news. Firstly, the Chinese government had hacked the CTC servers and had stolen all of the Research and Development work; and, secondly, it had just been revealed to him that the man in front of him was not his real father, and that he was of mixed race. He was impure. Worse still, he was half Japanese: the race that had subjugated, raped, enslaved and exploited China in the 1930s and 1940s. He was one of the despised *rìběn gǒu*, or Japanese dogs.

"So you see, Li, if you do not do as I ask, and continue to allow us access to the data, then I will make public your racial impurity and that will mean the end of your career!" With that, the older man left the smoking room, and went to leave the building. As he was nearing the entrance, he noticed the tall, elegant young lady working quietly at a computer terminal in a corner of the building.

The melatonin therapy that had been devised to help the team travel more easily around the world had worked superbly. After only two days back in her apartment in Singapore, Penny felt refreshed, and was keen to get back into work and begin her preparation for the forthcoming exercise. She had to contact the Cultural Advisors from the British Army and try to set up a meeting with them. She paused, only briefly, and stole a sidelong glance at the older Chinese man as he left the building. Then she turned her gaze to the smoking cube, where Li was still sitting. He appeared catatonic. Still as a post and deathly pale, he sat alone in the room, ignoring the cigarette that was slowly burning itself to a stub in his hand.

Penny entered the room with two steaming hot cups of Jasmine tea. "Li, you look upset; who was that man?" she asked in Mandarin.

"Until today, I thought I knew who he was," he replied, again sticking to Mandarin. Penny sat a while longer, then, finishing her tea, she stood up and went to leave the room.

"Thank you for your concern, and the delicious tea," Li said, quietly, as she left the room.

The following day began with a planning meeting. The entire team sat around the round table and took it in turn to discuss different elements of the exercise preparation. Matthias described the purpose of the exercise, and the methodology behind Human Terrain Mapping. He explained that phase one of the exercise would involve gaining a clear picture of the societal hierarchies, ethnic groupings and other important anthropological data. Using this data, Charu would generate heat maps showing points of interconnectivity or potential points of conflict. Phase two would be to focus on a small regional group, and, by means of discussion and analysis, divine what type of technical intervention if any, would be culturally appropriate and would lead to independent economic development. Maria and

Andrei were to be the two lead agents on the ground. Charu and Philippe would provide technical support, which would include some of the mini-drones from the Sao Paulo TTC. Philippe and Charu would be working from a support base somewhere in northern Iraq, which, as yet, had not been identified.

Penny concluded the meeting with an overview of the logistics, and the partner agencies that would be supporting the team. She took the opportunity to introduce Captain Phillip Morrison. Philip was a twenty-eight-year-old captain in the British Army Reserve. Formerly of the Household Cavalry, he had served in Bosnia, Iraq and Afghanistan before leaving the army to work in the city as an investment analyst. He had soon tired of the mundane life and hankered after his old life.

After joining the Army Reserve, he had attended the Long Arabic Language and Culture Course at the Defence School of Languages, then was seconded on a two-year full-time commitment to the newly formed Cultural Specialist Regiment. "Hello, everybody." He smiled as he spoke and seemed completely relaxed. He spoke eloquently, with an accent that could only have been obtained by attending the very best public schools and universities that Britain had to offer.

"My unit has carried out similar operations to the one that you are proposing, and we also have a bundle of data specifically on the Iraqi Kurds that we are willing to share with you."

Li stiffened slightly when the captain suggested connecting remotely into the British Army databases. He made a mental note to speak to Penny about a secure way of getting access to the data. Philip spent thirty minutes highlighting the support they could offer, which included gaining access to the US Air Force bases in northern Iraq that could be used as logistics dumps, or a field HQ. He also promised that his unit could supply up to ten fully trained linguists and cultural specialists with direct experience of Iraq, to support the data collection.

The whole time he was speaking, Matthias was concentrating hard. He focused on every muscle twitch, on every overt gesture as well as the subliminal gestures that betray our intentions. He wasn't looking at the dashing army captain. Instead, he was looking at Penny. She had reacted to Philip's presence as soon as he began to speak. She kept casually brushing the hair away from her face. Her lips had suffused with blood, her pupils were dilated, and she barely blinked. Matthias could see that the pulse in her neck was beating more forcefully, and she had achieved an erect posture in her chair, almost pouting, Matthias thought. "I think our English Rose has caught the scent of a stag," Matthias mused.

The meeting broke up, and Penny escorted Captain Philip Morrison out of the building. Once she was sitting back at her desk, Matthias sidled over, with a boyish grin on his face. "What did you make of our British Army Liaison Captain?" Matthias asked Penny, grinning to himself. Penny didn't turn to face Matthias, knowing that she would only reveal the embarrassment on her face.

"Oh, you know, he seems capable enough," she replied, barely managing to contain the emotion in her voice. "Damn it, Matthias, how do you do that?" Penny asked, turning to face him. "How do you always know what people are thinking before they do?"

"I could teach you if you like. It takes some practice, but actually it is nothing more than knowing which micro-gestures to look for and being able to build up a picture of that person. You then simply combine it with some behavioral psych stuff, mainly based on the social lives of monkeys, I might add, and voila!"

"Well, it certainly is impressive, and I would love to learn."

"It would be my pleasure. Maybe we can start by my lending you a couple of research articles on the subject. Once you have read them, let me know, and we will start to improve your powers of observation."

"I would like that," said Penny. "And, as for Philip, he is rather dreamy, don't you think?"

Andrei and Maria had gone back to a large desk together and were deep in discussion about how they were going to deploy once they arrived in the country. "You know, there is a hell of a lot of material to go over here," said Maria.

Without looking up, Andrei replied in a hushed tone. "We could continue our discussion over dinner?" Maria stiffened slightly. Was Andrei asking her out on a date? What a difference ten days can make, thought Maria. Before we went on our whirlwind trip, I would have slapped his face and told him to take a hike. But now, hey, what could it hurt, just dinner, you know, discuss the planning needed for the exercise.

Maria's thoughts were interrupted.

"Maria, did you hear me? What do you say, shall we do dinner?"

"Yes," she replied, gazing into his deep blue eyes. "I believe I would like to have dinner with you. But I choose the restaurant, and we split the bill fifty-fifty. Deal?"

"It's a deal," Andrei said.

Before returning to his office, Li looked across the room at his team. Yes, he thought, they had become a team. It was actually quite impressive how these six people from such diverse backgrounds had managed to bond together so well.

Chapter Twenty-Eight

Latitude 33° 16' 6.7008'', Longitude 44° 23' 20.1408''.
The Al Abbasin Household, Baghdad, Iraq, former
Mesopotamia – December 2016.
A Strategy Revealed

"Mother, you're tired; you can't keep pushing yourself like this." Hamed was concerned about his mother; in the last month she had spent more and more time in her lab at the university. She would leave the house after dawn prayers, and not return home until late in the evening.

"I'm fine, my son," she whispered, gently stroking his face. "Not much longer now; everything has to be ready for the meeting in Mongolia. I need to take some materials with me, and I need a little more time to prepare them."

Ali entered the room. "Mother, do you have a confirmed date for this meeting yet? I need to go back up to Mosul to buy some more carpets from my contact there."

"I am afraid the meeting has been delayed," Fatima said, with a resigned look on her face. "Ganzorig sent a message this morning from Mongolia. The meeting will now take place at the end of March. He needs time for the dust to settle. It appears that the activities of Ganzorig's group of radical dissidents has attracted the attention of both the Russian and Chinese Security

Services. Nothing to do with our plan, of course. One of his men was caught moving drugs between China and Russia."

"Does that mean we have to change our plan?" said Hamed.

"No, just postpone it for a while." replied Fatima.

"But this man, surely, this idiot, could talk and leak information about the group, about our greater plan?" Ali said, with a look of anger in his eyes.

"That has been taken care of. This man was found dead in his cell this morning. One of Ganzorig's men, posing as his lawyer, slipped him a cyanide capsule. He will remain silent." If Fatima was upset at this waste of human life, it did not register on her face.

Hamed saw this lack of empathy on his mother's tired face, and wondered out loud. "Are we doing the right thing? Is it not futile, I mean, to try to re-order the world?"

"Ali, Hamed, we need to talk seriously now." Suddenly Fatima didn't seem tired any longer. "Let me explain the plan and its impact to you." The boys settled down into their chairs in the living room, and, as the ceiling fan lazily circled above them, Fatima began to explain the plan in detail.

"Please remember, boys, that what we are attempting is to enact a plan which has been germinating since the twelfth century."

The boys settled down to listen, both sensing that this was to be the second revelation that their mother had promised to tell them. "Ever since the last true Caliph, Al Mustansim of the Abbasid Caliphate, was brutally murdered by the Mongols, the birth line of the Caliph has been kept a closely guarded secret.

Your grandfather and I have devoted our entire lives to realising this plan."

"Hold on, Mum," Hamed interrupted. "So why are we trusting the Mongols now?"

"Good question; I am sure that, as I continue, things will become clearer. However, in brief, time changes some people. The Mongols who attacked Baghdad in the twelfth century were very different to those who later became Muslim. Ganzorig and his group are dissidents, disaffected by the way they have been treated by both the Russian and Chinese governments." Fatima didn't like the price that Ganzorig had extracted from her for his assistance. The loss of her only daughter had hit Fatima hard. She had consoled herself to the fact that the greater prize of achieving her family's reinstatement at the head of a new Caliphate was of prime importance.

"He will benefit, because our plan will help to strike a blow against these governments; I have also promised him a large payment when we are successful. For our part, we need people to act for us, people with experience; and, most importantly, we need a group that cannot be traced back to us." Hamed and Ali nodded in unison. "Let me continue," Fatima said. "The world has not always been divided into nation states. In fact, the idea is, from an historical perspective, very new indeed. Only after the old imperial system started to disintegrate, because of the two world wars and the Russian Revolution, was the world order that we know today established."

The boys sat in silence, listening to their mother as she slowly explained to them the complex web of systems of government that led to the world we live in today. "Over the centuries, many different forms of government have been devised. Interestingly most of these different forms have resurfaced on numerous occasions, and many still exist today, nestled beneath the nation-state system. In ancient Greece and mediaeval Europe, powerful city states were the way in which groups of people were ruled. Singapore, Monaco, Luxembourg and the Vatican are all states principally built around a city. In later years, these city states competed with the rising imperial systems, such as the Ottomans. But, of course, we know that the Romans had an Empire long before the Ottomans. Here in Iraq, we were once ruled by a Caliph, and this Caliphate held power over much of the current Arab world. We all know, too well, how those despicable terrorists called ISIS tried to recreate a Caliphate. Their biggest mistake was to try and create a regressive, isolated Caliphate, which excluded all other faiths. They just couldn't see that the world has moved on since Mohammed's time.

"Did you know that the Christians had a similar concept to a Caliphate?" Ali shook his head; Hamed said nothing but continued to stare at his mother, completely engrossed in the story. "Yes, they called it Christendom. In mediaeval times Christendom was the counterpoise to the rise of Islam. This is where we see the beginnings of western interference in Arabic life, as the Crusaders poured into the Levant, stealing our cities and enslaving our people in the name of Christ."

"Yeah, and the bloody Americans still think they are on a Crusade!" exclaimed Ali.

Fatima continued. "You see, every new organisation or religion is simply built upon a previous one. This is done to gain acceptance from the people. Consider Christianity. This has at its foundations the core of the Jewish beliefs. The Christians modified the Jewish faith to incorporate the teachings of their prophet Jesus. For political reasons, the Romans, when they adopted Christianity, superimposed some of their polytheistic beliefs and festivals on to Christianity, and selectively chose which books would be included in the Bible. After them came our religion, Islam, again built principally around the other two main religions; but, at its core, we concentrate on the teachings of our Prophet Mohammed, Peace be Upon Him."

Fatima paused and drank some water. "Sorry, boys; I didn't intend to give you a history lesson. In short, even today, when the inviolable rights of the nation state are the cornerstone of the world order, many different types of governance still exist. We still have tribes, kingdoms, principalities, autonomous regions, theocracies, dictatorships, and, more recently, historically at least, we have seen the rise of supra-state organisations, such as the European Union, which can, and do represent whole groups of countries."

Hamed had grasped the point first. His lightning-quick brain had seen where his mum was leading them a long time before she got to summarising her point. "What you are saying, Mother, is that different forms of government are tolerated and can coexist within the nation state system."

"Exactly, Hamed." Ali interrupted. "This is all well and fine, but most of these systems of governance were already in existence when the UN was established. What you are proposing is crazy, Mum. You expect to create a super-state by uniting all of the Arabic countries into a new Caliphate, right under the nose of the UN? It's impossible; the superpowers would never allow it. American tanks, Chinese aircraft and Russian ships would bomb Baghdad back to the Stone Age!"

"That is one scenario," said Fatima, with a glint in her eye. "Consider this scenario. What if Europe, China, Russia and the USA were all too preoccupied with another global financial meltdown? What if they suddenly lost all of their strategic oil supplies, and were incapable of waging war, because their war machines require oil?"

"And afterwards, after we have united the Caliphate?" Hamed asked. "What happens when they recover?

"That is the true genius behind this plan. We will have created a peaceful Middle East. This is something that has been one of the biggest problems facing the world for over a hundred years. Imagine a benign Caliphate which allows Muslims to live in peace: one that is tolerant of other faiths, big enough to allow different interpretations of Islam, to live peacefully together as neighbours; one that shares its wealth amongst these autonomous regions and allow local rule; a Caliphate that is willing to trade with the other countries as an equal partner. Imagine how this oil wealth could benefit all of the Arab peoples once we remove the dictators and despots who are currently draining our brothers and sisters of their wealth?"

Hamed began to summarise what Fatima had spent over an hour explaining. "So we will create a twenty-first-century Islamic Caliphate, a House of Peace (*Dar al Salaam*). Ali, as the Caliph, will have central control and co-ordination over these autonomous regions, with a development bank for the whole Caliphate, which distributes the oil revenues equally amongst the regions. As a consolidated group of ex-states in this new Caliphate, we have far greater power to control our own affairs, and will not be subject to the foreign ambitions of the big states such as Russia, China and America?"

"Exactly, my son," said Fatima with a warm smile. "OK. What is our next step, Mother?" said Ali.

"In order for this to work we need complete surprise. I have adopted a set of ancient Chinese strategies to help guide us through the plan. I have chosen these strategies so that any evidence of our acts will lead back to Asia and not here to Iraq. Some of the strategies are only for us to know. Others I will share with the Mongols at the meeting in Öndörkhaan.

"These strategies are ancient and come from both the book of Qi and the biography of a famous Chinese General called Wáng Jìngzé. There are said to be thirty-six stratagems. Through the passage of merchants along the ancient Silk Route, the original Abbasid Caliphate became aware of the Book of Qi, and, like many of the great texts of the time, they had it translated into Arabic. Your great-grandfather selected the first strategy, your father chose the second, and now that we are ready to implement our plan, I have chosen the final strategy. I have a copy of the book in English for you both. We chose English because it is the easiest language for us to be able to communicate with the Mongols in. I have highlighted the relevant chapters, so that you can read along with me."

Ali thumbed through the book that Fatima gave him. Ali wasn't as academically gifted as Hamed or his mother, but he possessed a sense of cunning. He could sense when an opportunity presented itself, and he knew damn well that the contents of this book, these Chinese stratagems, written hundreds of years ago were the key not just to creating the rebirth of the Caliphate, but the key to making him the most powerful man in the Arabic world. He was energized, and wanted to understand more about these strategies.

Reading aloud from a highlighted piece of text, he said, "This piece from Chapter Four: 'Slough off the Cicada's Golden Shell'. Is this the first strategy?"

"Yes, my son." Fatima was glad and a little relieved that Ali was showing a real interest in the strategy. If he was to become the next Caliph, he would have to be convincing not only to the Mongols, but also to the three principal Arab families which would help him rule over the vast Caliphate. "The meaning is simple enough. Your great-grandfather used it to describe what your forbears have been doing ever since the last Caliph was murdered by the Mongols.

"In simple terms, it means we should hide our true identities, to protect ourselves until we are ready to be revealed."

Hamed went next. "What on earth does this one mean, Mother? 'Borrow a Corpse to resurrect the soul'?"

"This is pivotal to our plan. It was your grandfather who had the foresight to think of this strategy. The strategy is about using a long-forgotten technology or idea and giving it a new purpose. It was your grandfather who saw the potential of his oil-destroying bacteria that he developed with the Nazis, to be used as a weapon. This, my sons, is why I have been working so hard recently. I have been improving the bacteria, genetically modifying them to replicate far faster and become far more virulent than they were when your father discovered them. Most importantly, I have developed a way of controlling them, so that when their immediate food source is exhausted, the bacteria will die off very quickly. This was necessary to prevent our own oil supplies from becoming infected."

Ali interrupted. "OK, I understand who we are, and the potential we have; but how do we attack the West with these bacteria?"

"Now we come to my part in the plan. I have chosen a strategy from the very first chapter to help us deploy our weapon and achieve victory. Look at the passage."

"To kill with a borrowed sword," read Ali aloud.

"This strategy refers to using a third party to do your work for you. My plan entails a dual approach to this strategy. Firstly, we will use the Mongols. If the plan fails, then we cannot be implicated. Secondly, and most importantly, it is what the Mongols are going to attack that is important. First they will deliver the bacteria to the Chinese Strategic Oil Supply sites. The destruction of their oil reserves will temporarily cripple their economy and make their government very angry. Of course they will suspect their arch-nemesis, Japan, and we shall leave several clues to help them reach this conclusion. This will lead to a counter-strike against the Japanese and Korean oil reserves, thus crippling the Japanese economy, and consequently sending the price of oil sky-high."

"I see," said Hamed, quickly grasping the strategy. "So the borrowed sword, as it relates to us, is that we will be using China, to attack Japan's oil supply?"

"Exactly, my son. Next, the Mongols will turn north, and attack the Russian strategic oil supply."

Ali cut in. "And the Russians will blame the Americans, and destroy the US oil reserves?"

Fatima smiled. "Exactly, my son.

"You do realise that, if Russia's oil supplies are threatened, then they will reduce or cut off supply to Europe?" Hamed said.

"I do, and it is part of my plan. This action by us should temporarily paralyse the United Nations, generate further distrust, and create potential conflict between the great powers; and, of course, to our benefit, we will see an unprecedented surge in the price of oil, which we will be more than happy to continue to sell to them. Only then will we strike, and in one swift blow remove the corrupt governments; and, using the three families from the secret society, we will create a power structure fit to rule our new Caliphate."

Both boys nodded in wonderment at their mother's plan. Ali, ever the calculating one, spoke first. "Mother, in chapter two I see that there is a strategy entitled 'Watch the fires burning across the river.' I think we should delay forming the caliphate until the major powers are completely exhausted, and tensions are so high that they are more interested in fighting each other. Then when their armies, or what is left of their military machine that can be deployed without using oil are ready to strike at each other, we should seize the moment and claim the Caliphate."

Fatima's face grew into a wide grin, and she began to weep. Seizing the two boys, she clutched them to her breast, and whispered, "We are the chosen family, and this is our time."

Chapter Twenty-Nine

Latitude 47° 19' 4.1160'', Longitude 110° 39' 12.7620''.
Secret Society Meeting Place, Öndörkhaan, Mongolia, –
March 2017.
The Meeting

The delay in the meeting had given Fatima the chance to complete her work on the bacteria in plenty of time. In the past few weeks, she had begun to work less and had managed to recover some strength, strength she knew she would certainly need. She had spent increasingly more time with her daughter, Zainab. At night, Fatima would hear her daughter crying herself to sleep. Initially, when the Mongol had named his price for their assistance, Fatima had been outraged. She knew, though, deep in her heart, that giving her daughter in marriage to the Mongol was a small price to pay for the services they were going to receive.

Zainab, for her part, had received the news initially with incredible composure. It was only natural that as the day grew closer she would become more emotional. Fatima thought, "Indeed, the women in this family are truly strong. It is a shame that we can only wield our power behind the scenes, that the Muslim world would not accept me as the next Caliph. Still, my son will be Caliph, and I will continue my influence through him."

It was late March, and Fatima and her three children Ali, Hamed and Zainab, arrived in Öndörkhaan at midday under heavy leaden skies. The town of Öndörkhaan lay in the East of Mongolia, half way between the capital, Ulaan Baatar and the Chinese border. The view from the tiny airport was of lush rolling pasture land that stretched out nearly to the horizon. The view was framed by steep-sided cliffs on either horizon, and the whole image was dissected by a slow, meandering river that wound its way through the centre.

Like the airport, most of the small town was located on the north side of the river, close to the lush grasslands that accompanied the river as it meandered through the town. The family had taken a circuitous route to get to the town, and had flown with Astana airlines from Baghdad, first to Astana, then from Astana onto Ulaan Baatu, and, finally, by light plane they had been brought to the small airfield that served the town of Öndörkhaan itself. They had flown for over twenty-six hours to get there, needing to take this particular route to avoid arousing suspicions by travelling through Russia or China. Despite only crossing five time zones, the journey had been tough for everyone, especially for Fatima, the septuagenarian mother of Ali and Hamed.

The meeting was planned for the following afternoon, where members from all twelve families representing the Arab nations that would unite to form the Caliphate would be present, along with Ganzorig and some of his key people, who would undertake the attacks on the Chinese and Russian strategic oil sites.

"Fatima! How good to see you again." Ganzorig was dressed in a traditional *deel*; it was an ornate, long jacket made of wool, which looked similar to a caftan. It was folded tightly around him and secured using a thick silk band. On his feet, he wore calf-length soft leather boots, and atop his head, he wore a thick fur hat that extended outwards above the ears.

"It is good to be here at last, Ganzorig. Is everyone else here?"

"Yes, as you requested, they will all come together tomorrow at midday for the meeting."

"Thank you, Ganzorig. Now, may I introduce my family? Zainab you know; Hamed is my youngest son; and this," she said, gently taking Ali's hand. "This is Ali, the next Caliph!"

Ganzorig bowed slightly as he met Ali; then, turning towards Zainab, he said, "Zainab, I would like you to meet my sisters. They can't wait to show you around your new home."

The other members of the meeting were representatives of the ancient families which would serve the Caliph and become regional governors of the new Caliphate. The Hashemite family, whose lineage can be traced back to the great-grandfather of the Prophet Mohammed (Peace be Upon Him) were represented by Faisal ibn Abdullah. Their family would govern over Syria, Jordan, and Lebanon. From Saudi Arabia, an older Prince and brother to the current King, very religious, would govern Saudi Arabia, Yemen, Bahrain, Qatar Kuwait and the UAE. His adherence to the strict form of Islam known as Wahhabism would guarantee him much popular support, as the Sharif of the two holy cities, Mecca and Medina. Tariq Al Khazari came from a very old family indeed; during the second Abbasid Caliphate Tariq's family had governed Egypt. Now, as head of their armed forces, he was perfectly positioned to become the next governor of not only Egypt, but of Sudan, to the South, and the now-fractured area known as Libya as well.

The men around the table had two things in common. They each had a genuine desire to reinstate a Caliphate and see a united and prosperous Arabic people. Secondly, they were all Sunni muslims. The schism between Sunni and Shia muslims was almost as old as Islam itself. It was one of those intractable problems that had led to numerous terrorist attacks in various countries across the Arabic world and had been the root cause of many of the religious conflicts. A resurgent and newly confident Iran stood ready to support Shias across the world.

A unified Caliphate would offer the Shia living within it the opportunity to live peacefully alongside their Sunni brothers, whilst, at the same time, offering a united front against an increasingly hostile Iran, which had taken advantage of the Arab Spring and recent overthrows of Arabic leaders by the West, and had gained a lot of political and military influence in Iraq, Syria, Bahrain, Eastern Saudi Arabia and the Lebanon.

The current ruling families of the Arabic world would face a simple choice; to accept the new Caliph and the redistribution of wealth, or to be forced to abdicate. Without the military support of the USA, they would stand little chance of stopping a concerted move against them. One thing all of those seated around the table possessed, was strategic control of their armed forces. If the current ruling families refused to abdicate or concede to the new Caliph's demands, and they were not persuaded to do so by mass popular uprisings, then they would be removed from power by force.

Fatima was still weary from her journey; however, she showed no sign of her tiredness, as she stood to address the meeting. This moment was the culmination of a lifetime's work, not only for her, but for many generations of her family before her.

"Brothers, welcome to Mongolia. May I start by thanking Ganzorig and his men for their hospitality and their support for our cause." A ripple of murmured thanks and head-nodding passed around the table. "Now, before we start, I would also like to introduce you to Ali Al Abbasin, my son, and our new Caliph, In Shah Allah."

The table erupted into cheers, as fists were banged on the table. All of the families represented stood and blessed Allah for the returning Caliph. "Now, on to business, gentlemen. In front of each of you, I have placed a copy of the book of Qi. It is from this book that I draw my strategies." Ganzorig had been especially pleased, when Fatima had explained her plan to him earlier, that the elements of the plan came from an Asian masterpiece of political and military strategy. Likewise, Ali had been both inspired and fascinated by the book, and along with the Koran, which he carried with him everywhere he went, he had taken to carrying the book of Qi with him and reading sections of it after his daily prayer sessions.

"Brothers, we have much work to do, and very little time left. I will briefly outline the first part of our plan; then we will meet once more after the successful completion of this phase, to coordinate the final part of our domination over the Caliphate. Part One, taken from the book of Qi, is to 'borrow a corpse to resurrect the soul'. In front of me are sixteen canisters of the most virulent form of bacteria that has ever lived." On hearing these words, there were murmurs of fear and discontent around the room.

"Do not worry. These sixteen canisters represent the lifetime's work of me and my father. The bacteria are virulent, but they do not seek out humans or other living animals as hosts. They seek out hydrocarbons: specifically, unrefined oil. Once they make contact with oil, they quickly multiply, as they feed on the oil, destroying the chemical bonds within the oil. The result is two-fold. Firstly, the bacteria population grows exponentially, requiring ever more oil to continue to survive, and secondly, and most importantly to our plan, they completely destroy the oil that they have used as a host. The oil becomes an inert, non-flammable viscous black sludge, which has no commercial value and no industrial properties at all."

Fatima read the reaction on the faces of her audience. "Don't worry; once the bacteria run out of immediate food they will die within hours." She could see admiration and respect on their faces, but also a hint of confusion and suspicion.

"Step two," Fatima continued quickly, trying to maintain their attention. "Step two of our strategy taken from the book of Qi is 'to Kill with a borrowed sword'. This is where Ganzorig and his men come in. Ganzorig, would you like to explain this part of the plan?"

Ganzorig rose to address the room. "My brothers, like you Arabs, we Mongols have been persecuted by the Russians and Chinese, and me and my group have made it our lifelong commitment to inflict as much damage on the Russian and Chinese governments as possible.

"Our plan is simple. My men will infiltrate first the Chinese strategic oil supply depots; then, some weeks later, the Russian strategic oil depots and we will deliver the bacteria into the oil. We will leave evidence of Japanese sabotage in the attack on the Chinese site. This is the true cunning behind the plan. This is where we begin to kill with a borrowed sword. The Chinese will be outraged by the attack and will naturally blame the Japanese. In order to save face, they will be forced to undertake a retaliatory strike against the Japanese oil reserves. This will destroy not only the Japanese but also the South Korean oil reserves. The effect of these attacks will be a massive destabilization of the Asian Stock markets, a huge reduction in world industrial output, and the threat of war between China and Japan. Of course, because of the several defence treaties that exist between Japan and the USA, this action would force the Americans into a confrontation with China which they would dearly like to avoid.

"Next we will travel north, and attack the Russian strategic reserves. Because of the enmity that exists between Russia and the USA over Syria, and an ever-expanding NATO, and the economic sanctions that the USA have already placed on Russia, the Russians will immediately suspect US interference. We will of course ensure that evidence is left at the site to encourage these thoughts. Angered and humiliated, Russia will strike back with their own conventional arsenal, and try to destroy the US strategic oil supply.

"The effect of these strikes will be a huge devaluation on the Russian, American and European stock markets, a reduction or complete stoppage of Russian oil exports to Europe over winter, and a ramping-up of military tensions between America and

Russia, with Europe caught in the middle." Ganzorig looked around to see if he still had their attention. "All of this, of course, is just a byproduct of the real effect. You see, without strategic oil supplies, these governments dare not mobilise their militaries. The UN Security Council will be unworkable, as Russia, China and the US refuse to cooperate. The price of oil will quadruple in a matter of days. It is amongst this panic and disorder that you will create your Caliphate."

When Ganzorig had stopped speaking, one by one the members of the group around the table began to rise and applaud loudly; they turned and hugged each other.

Chapter Thirty

Latitude 36° 18' 20.5956'', Longitude 43° 8' 49.1028''
Temporary US Air Force Base, Mosul, Autonomous
Kurdish Province, Northern Iraq – May 2017.
An Eye for an Eye

Fatima and her family arrived back from Mongolia exhausted and with mixed emotions. They were elated at the way the meeting had gone, and excited that the preparation for the first strike was underway, but all of them, especially Fatima, were deeply saddened at losing Zainab to the Mongolian. Fatima was in her room unpacking her bags when Ali knocked and entered.

"Mother, I am going back to Mosul to choose and order some more carpets from my Kurdish contact. I shall be gone a couple of days."

"But, my son, you don't need to concern yourself with your business any more; you are to become the most powerful man in all of Arabia."

"I know, Mother; I know," Ali said, slightly impatiently. "But I need to keep the business going, so that nobody suspects anything, and so that I can provide for my family until I become Caliph."

"I wish you wouldn't go, but I understand," Fatima said wearily.

Arriving in Mosul early in the afternoon, Ali went directly to his Kurdish contact's house. He had known the man for a little over two years, and, in that time, he had helped Ali do more than just buy carpets. Ayoub had helped Ali to track down the air force pilot who had blown up his father. The pilot worked at the US Air Force secure compound which had been established at the end of the runway at Mosul airport. There were only eight pilots who flew the drones from there, and it had only taken a few bribes to the locally employed catering staff who served the pilots in their canteen to learn who had been flying the drones on the day that Ali's father had been killed in Pakistan. It was even easier to identify the exact pilot, as it was US Air Force policy to give their pilots a period of two days' decompression after a kill operation.

During this decompression period, the pilots were not allowed to come to work, and had to undergo psychological evaluations. The cleaning staff employed to clean the small medical centre on base had identified the pilot concerned. Junior Lieutenant Paul Delaney, twenty-six years old, from Delaware, had been the pilot who had killed Ali's father. Ayoub, the contact from Mosul, had managed to get a copy of his shift rota, and knew that the Lieutenant from Delaware would be working day shifts for the next ten days.

Ali was sitting opposite the middle-aged Kurdish man at a café, which lay four hundred metres from the airport entrance.

"Ayoub, my friend, good to see you again. Do you have what I asked for?"

"Yes, my friend, I have everything you asked for. We will strike tomorrow night at dusk when the infidel leaves the camp and drives back to his apartment."

"No, Ayoub," Ali interrupted. "I will do this alone. I must avenge my father. An eye for an eye, isn't that what these American Kufar say?"

"Indeed it is, my friend. But tonight, you must stay with me and my family. We will eat, talk and pray together." The two men sat quietly in peace and drank their coffee whilst gazing at the perimeter fence of the air base.

"Shall we go, my friend? My wife is cooking a wonderful lamb stew for us, and I have a couple of bottles of Shiraz wine for us to sample." The smell from the lamb was mouth-watering. Ali had unpacked his bag and was sitting reading the book of Qi, which he had taken to reading ever since Fatima had first given it to him.

Ayoub entered the room, and said, "Shall we pray together, my brother, before we eat?"

"Certainly," said Ali.

"Tell me, what are you reading, my friend."

"It is an ancient Chinese book on strategy."

"You don't need a book on strategy to fire an RPG at this infidel's car!" Ayoub said, with a derisive snort.

"I have bigger plans, my brother, plans to rid us of all of these infidels." If Ayoub was shocked, he didn't show it. Smiling, he patted Ali on the back and led him downstairs to where they would pray.

"The food was even better than it smelled," said Ali to Ameera, Ayoub's wife. "I couldn't possibly eat another mouthful." She smiled demurely at Ali, and left the two men alone.

Ayoub was uncorking the second bottle of Shiraz wine, when he casually asked Ali, "You said you had bigger plans, my friend; would you like to tell me more?" Ali, who was starting to feel the effects of the alcohol, began to talk quite animatedly about all the injustices served upon the Arabic people by the West. "The time has come to take back what is ours, Ayoub," he said. He was starting to slur his words, and the last thing he remembered before passing out was his friend Ayoub smiling at him from across the table.

Ayoub carried Ali to his bedroom, then, taking the handheld satellite phone, he went outside into the building's outer compound to make a call. Using the pre-arranged codes he had been given, he punched a series of numbers into the encrypted phone.

"Homayoon, is that you?" Ayoub whispered into the phone.

"It is me, but I told you never to use my name on this line."

"Forgive me, but I have news of great importance." Homayoon was a colonel in the intelligence section of the Iranian Revolutionary Guard; he was sitting in his large, air-conditioned office in Tehran.

"Tell me what you know."

"The man, Ali; he revealed to me that he has great plans. Plans that will change the order of power forever in the Middle East."

There was a pause on the line. "Are you there? Did you hear what I said?"

"Yes, yes Ayoub. You have done good work. Now you must do the following. Allow this Ali to kill the American pilot; but as he attacks, I want you to have contacted our man in the police and have him ready to kill Ali at the crime scene, then hand over the body to the Americans."

Ayoub listened carefully, and replied simply, "It will be done."

Putting the phone down, the colonel left the room quickly, and went down the long corridor which led to the general's office. General Qusay Mohammed Hijazi was the general in overall charge of the Iranian Revolutionary Guard Corps. The Guards had been established in 1979, after the Iranian revolution, with the sole purpose of protecting the country's Shia Islamic system.

The colonel knocked and waited to be let into the general's office. "General. I have just received news from Mosul. The Abbasin boy will be killed tomorrow."

"Did he confirm his intended plan to our man there?" the general asked, in a quiet voice.

"He did, sir. It appears that the Abbasin family finally intend to try to claim their place as the Sunni Caliphs of all Arabia."

"He must be stopped. Do you understand?"

"Yes, sir," the colonel replied.

"He must be stopped at all costs. Today Iran possesses an unprecedented amount of influence across the Middle East. We are increasing our support to our Shia brothers from Iraq, Saudi Arabia, and Bahrain, all the way to Syria, Palestine and Lebanon. With the nuclear arms deal signed with the Americans, we no longer need to fear their military and economic interference.

Russia is a strong ally to us in Syria, and our forces in Palestine are finally bringing the Israelis to the negotiating table. Very soon, Colonel, maybe in our lifetime, we will witness the revival of the great Shia Crescent rising up out of Iran and arcing all the way to the Mediterranean, encircling these Sunni scum who have sought to enslave us for so long through their Caliphates."

Soon after being established by the then Ayatollah Khomeini, the Iranian Revolutionary Guard had been tasked with monitoring every possible opponent to the fledgling Shia theocracy. This, of course, meant rounding up many intellectuals or supporters of the old Shah within Iran, and summarily executing them. It also meant searching for and monitoring more esoteric threats. Historically, the Shia heartland of Persia had long been an enemy of the Sunni-dominated Caliphates to their West. They had rejoiced in Tehran when they had heard that the last Caliph, Mustansim, had been trampled to death under the hooves of the Mongolian horses in 1242. Since that day, news had travelled through Persia, which was also occupied by the Mongols, that the heir to the Caliphate had been sent to Mongolia. Persian spies, under many Shahs and Kings, had maintained a silent watch on the family of the last Caliph over many generations. They had nearly succeeded in capturing and killing the scientist who carried the formula to a weapon so powerful that the Nazis themselves had tried to eliminate him. Since then, they had been monitoring the Al Abbasin household closely. They had agents planted in the university to monitor Fatima's work, and they had even arranged a fortunate business contact for Ali, who would be more than happy to help him to import carpets from Iran and sell them on at a good price.

Ali awoke. Initially, he was disoriented and didn't know where he was. Then, as his foggy mind began to clear, he remembered back to the previous night and the wine. He must have drunk too much and passed out. How embarrassing! Just as he began to slide on his sandals, Ayoub entered the room. "How are you this morning, my friend?" He smiled as he said this and looked concerned. "Don't worry about last night. The shiraz wine is very strong indeed, especially for someone unused to drinking alcohol like you, Ali."

"Yes, sorry about my behaviour. It is true, normally I do not drink alcohol; but last night was a celebration of things to come."

"Are you ready for today, my friend?"

"I am, brother."

"Good, then I suggest we eat breakfast, pray at noon, then, after the mosque, I will teach you how to use the rocket-propelled grenade and we will get into position. I must ask one small favour my friend. Could I ask you to remove your clothes and books from my house before the attack? Maybe you can put them in the car. That way, if the police come around to search the house, they will have nothing suspicious to find."

"Certainly," replied Ali. "Ayoub, my brother, you have done so much for me already. How can I ever thank you?"

"No thanks are necessary, my brother. I only wish to help a fellow Muslim in his Jihad against the Kufar."

Dressed in a clean white Thawb, Ali sat behind the wheel of the car Ayoub had given him. The warm May air was becoming stifling. A thin trickle of sweat dripped down Ali's back, but he dared not turn on the air conditioning, in case he attracted attention to himself. Ali had placed the RPG on the back seat of the rented car, and covered it with a blanket. On the dashboard in front of him, he had stuck a picture, provided to him by Ayoub, of Lieutenant Paul Delaney from Delaware, USA. His target was due to leave the Air Base in twelve minutes. Ayoub had chosen the point for the attack for Ali, telling him that the quiet road just before the compound that housed the US Servicemen would be ideal. It was far enough away from the base so that the heavily armed guards could not interfere in the attack, and close enough to a major road junction to give him an easy getaway.

"Ali, is that you?"

"Yes, brother."

"Are you ready?"

"Yes, brother."

"The infidel has left the base and will be with you in five minutes."

After Ayoub put the phone down with Ali, he made one more quick call to the police officer. "The American must die before you kill Ali. Is that understood?"

"Yes," replied the policeman, putting down his phone and peering around the corner at Ali's parked car.

Just then, a set of headlights appeared around the corner. The lights belonged to the large Ford pickup truck belonging to the Lieutenant. The car slowed as it neared the junction, just in front of Ali's parked car. Ali climbed out, and, as he leaned into the back, to withdraw the RPG missile, he could hear the country music blaring from the American's car stereo. After clearing the junction, the Ford began slowly to accelerate over the rough potholed road.

Only a hundred metres away, thought Ali. He armed the RPG, hoisted it to his shoulder and pulled the trigger. For a moment, Ali was disoriented; a deafening roar exploded in his ear, and he was pushed back by the force of the missile leaving the launcher. Grabbing the side of his car for support, he looked up and saw the American's huge jeep erupt into a blinding yellow and white ball of flame. Smoke began to billow out of the ruined Ford, as it lay motionless on its side in the middle of the road. Ali could not know that this sight would be the last thing he ever saw. Without warning, the loud sound of subsonic ammunition being ejected from an AK 74 pierced Ali's left ear. He felt a wave of repeated pressure pulses as the 7.62 mm copper-headed bullets slammed into his torso. The force of the impact lifted him off his feet, and sent him sprawling over the blood-smeared car bonnet. As he slid to the floor, Ali neither saw or heard anything. All he felt was the intense heat on his face from the burning American vehicle.

After wiping down the weapon for prints, the Kurdish Shia policeman placed it in Ali's bloody lifeless hand. He withdrew his mobile phone. He tapped the screen once, to redial the last number he had dialled, and simply said, "It is done." Before driving off, he took out the phone, deleted his call list, withdrew the Sim card, and threw both the prepaid Sim card and phone into the burning wreck of the American's vehicle. When he was safely two or three blocks away, he picked up his police radio and called his station. "Abdul, this is Mohammed. I think I heard shooting and an explosion about five minutes from my location. I am going to investigate. Send back up as soon as you can."

Several hours later, after the American military police had finished processing the crime scene, they collated all of the evidence and returned to the US Air Force base with the charred remains of the lieutenant from Delaware. After some high level phone calls had been exchanged between the Governor of Mosul and the Chief of Police, the US military policemen, CIA and military intelligence were given primacy over the crime scene and investigation.

Latitude 33° 16' 6.7008'', Longitude 44° 23' 20.1408''. The Al Abbasin Household, Baghdad, Iraq, former Mesopotamia – May 2017.

A New Caliph

Hamed's phone began to vibrate in his jeans pocket. The Kurdish carpet seller had cloned all of Ali's phone contacts after he had passed out from the drugs that he had administered whilst they were drinking wine.

"Hello, who's there?" Hamed asked into the mobile.

The Kurd uttered five words only. "The Sunni prophet is dead." In shock, Hamed could hardly believe what he had just heard. The colour drained from his face, and, still clutching the phone, he slumped in his chair, opposite his mother. "We know who you are, and you are next," came the words from the Kurd. Then, suddenly, the phone was dead. Hamed dropped the phone on to the table and began to sob loudly.

"What is it, my son?" Fatima said, coming around the table to hug him. "What on earth happened?"

"Ali is dead, Mother, Ali is dead!" He was sobbing more loudly now and screamed the words into his mother's breast as she held him. Fatima stiffened, as her mind began to piece together what Ali's younger brother was saying.

"No, this can't be!" Her voice quivered slightly and rose in pitch as she repeated the words. "It can't be." Hamed thought first, and, jumping to his feet, he rushed to his computer, and googled Al Jazeera News Live. Flashing across the bottom of the screen was a banner saying 'News Flash: Middle-Aged Arab found shot dead at the scene of the murder of an American Serviceman in Mosul.'

"Didn't Ali go to Mosul to buy carpets, Mum?" Hamed already knew the answer but wished for it to be wrong.

"No, my son, he went to Mosul to avenge your father's death," Fatima said, flatly. "I tried to tell him not to go, but you know how he was." Hamed nodded sullenly and began to weep again.

Fatima had long ago reconciled herself to the cost of her lifelong ambition to reform the Caliphate. It had already cost her the life of her husband, and she had been forced to marry off her only daughter to the Mongol. Now they had taken her eldest son and the heir to the Caliphate. Stoically, she rose to her feet and strode over to the slumped, weeping body of her one remaining son. "Hamed, look at me." Hamed looked up; her piercing eyes seemed to penetrate through him and fix him motionless in their gaze. "Hamed, it is Allah's will indeed that you become the true Caliph. Your brother was impetuous and irrational. He always thought he knew better. You, my son, are clear-headed and good-hearted. You will make a good Caliph."

Hamed looked up into the strong eyes of his mother, and, seeing all the years of effort and sadness in her eyes, he began slowly to nod his head; rising from his chair, he stood to his full height and declared to his mother that her life's work, the death of his brother and the loss of his sister, would not be in vain.

"Good, my only son," said Fatima, her voice filled once more with a hint of sadness in her tremulous voice.

Chapter Thirty-One

Latitude 36° 18' 20.5956'', Longitude 43° 8' 49.1028''.
Mosul, Autonomous Kurdish Province, Northern Iraq –
June 2017.
Human Terrain Mapping

The CTC team had been given their own separate compound, which consisted of three linked portakabins, one hardened inflatable accommodation shelter, and a large storage shipping container. The facilities were rudimentary, but they were secure, and allowed the team to remain independent from the rest of the US Air Force personnel who worked on the base. The base commander, Colonel Larry Wozlawski, had also allowed the team access to the Mess Halls and sports facilities.

The team, led by Matthias, had flown directly from Singapore in their Gulfstream. At just over seven thousand kilometres, the flight had taken a little over eight and a half hours in the sleek private jet. The small detachment from the British Army Cultural Advisor Regiment, known colloquially as CULADS, was due to land the following day by Royal Air Force Hercules transport plane. On landing, the CTC team had been warmly received by Colonel Wozlawski, who had shown them their compound, and afterwards insisted that they ate lunch with him. "Colonel," asked Maria, after swallowing another mouthful of the delicious meatball and pasta bake. "You said in your brief that there had been an attack near the base. Is the area secure?"

"Well, Maria, isn't it?"

"Yes, sir."

"Well, Maria, some god-damned Jihadi decided to kill one of my pilots, then kill himself. If I ever catch up to the people behind this attack, God help me, I'll..." The colonel's face began to redden, and he spluttered, then began to cough up the food that he had been trying to swallow.

"I can see that the killing is still very fresh in your mind, Colonel," said Maria. "Sorry to have brought it up."

"It is just that, well, you know, I look upon all of the boys and girls here as part of one big family. We were all shocked after the attack. Our Police unit have taken all of the evidence, but, quite frankly, we can't make head nor tail of it. In fact, I would be mighty pleased if you could all take a look at the evidence. We were puzzled as to how a lone jihadi like this one would end up carrying around such a strange combination of books with him. What with your all being anthropologists and cultural experts, I thought you might be able to give us your thoughts?"

The team looked from one to another, then Matthias broke the silence. "We would certainly look over what you have, Colonel, but murder investigations aren't really our area of expertise."

"I understand, and just so you all feel a little more secure, I have assigned an armed plain-clothes security detail to accompany you at all times."

After lunch, the team returned to their own compound, and began to unpack their equipment. Charu and Philippe set to work testing the mini-drones, whilst Maria went over the day-to-day list of activities with Matthias, Penny and Andrei. They decided to have a final briefing session the following morning, after the British Army CULADS had arrived.

The next morning, at nine a.m., the whole team plus four CULADS were assembled in the larger of the three portakabins, which served as both a briefing and operations room. Maria was controlling the operation, and, as such, she led the brief describing how the Human Terrain Mapping teams would be configured, and what the daily goals and tasks were. After forty minutes of briefing, where she outlined tasks such as aerial reconnaissance, using the Minidrone swarms that would map the waterways, electricity and road networks, as well as foot patrols, which involved interviewing the local leaders of the different ethnic groupings, she handed the briefing over to Matthias, who, as the head of the operation from an anthropological perspective, was keen to set the scene.

"This is a fascinating first case for us. To demonstrate how ethnically diverse the area is, I will quickly review the local groupings. The dominant ethnic group by far are the Kurds. They can be further subdivided into four main groups. Sunni Kummanj Kurds, a few Shia Alevi Shabak Kurds, and Sunni Shabak Kurds. Then we have the Yazidi Kurds, who consider themselves Yazidis first and foremost. They are not trusted by their neighbours, because in their religion they have a peacock angel whom they worship, who is often misinterpreted by others as a representation of the devil. Finally, there are the Bajalan Kurds, who are Yarsan gnostics, and practice yet again a completely different religion. Thrown into this melting pot, we have Sunni

Jaziran Arabs, Sunni Turkomen, and Chaldean Assyrians who are essentially Catholics; Jacobite Assyrians, who are essentially Eastern or Orthodox Roman church, and as such are related to the Coptics. Finally, we have some small communities of the Shia Turkomen. These disparate diasporas are the result of hundreds of years of conquest and reconquest by the Arabs, Mongols, Persians and Ottomans. Then of course, you have to add into this the influence of the greater Kurdish people, the state of Iran, which supports Shia the world over, and the central government in Baghdad, which also has a Shia bias."

"Hey, listen, I'm from New York. I'm used to all these different groups: we got Korea Town, little Italy, the Irish side. You name it, we got it," Maria said, confidently.

"Yes, Maria; but, to be blunt, your history only goes back a couple of hundred years. These people were once part of different great competing empires, some of which still have ambitions today. Their history spans a thousand years, and they still have strong ties to their ethnic forbears."

"Er, OK; when you put it like that, it kinda does make sense." Maria blushed slightly, and a few grins appeared around the table.

Matthias continued with his part of the briefing. "Firstly, the objective is to see if it is possible to provide technical assistance, and, indeed, if that assistance is wanted. To do this, we need to achieve three things. Firstly, compare the current ethno-religious composition of the area to the one prior to the time when ISIS took control over the city, before the Peshmerga had eventually pushed them back out. Luckily, we have the mapping and data from the CULAD team to use as a reference. Philip, thank you very much for letting us have access to this data."

As he said this, he saw Captain Philip Morrison turn to Penny, who was sitting directly to his left, and give her a knowing smile. This caused Matthias to reflect briefly on whether the co-operation between the two organisations had been strictly professional, or, if he wasn't deceived by Penny's deflective body language, and her slightly reddened face, it seemed that Penny and Philip had become a little more than simple liaison officers for their respective units.

Matthias continued speaking. "Secondly, we need to establish what a state of ethno-equilibrium would look like. What I mean by this is that we should not impose our own biased view on how Mosul should be populated; rather we should speak to and observe the locals, and try to understand how they relate to each other, and note how much tolerance they have towards each other. Finally, using the data mapping taken from a mini-drone, we need to establish who has access to power, roads, water etc. You see, during Saddam Hussein's days, he favored the few Sunni Arabs in the area, and, as such they got most of the access to water and electricity. After the war, and with a Shia government in power, the benefits started flowing towards the few Shia Arabs in the area. Since defeating ISIS, the Kurds have stolen the initiative, and, to all intents and purposes, declared an autonomous area, and started ploughing resources into the mainly Kurdish areas."

Mathias finished his brief, and the meeting was about to be adjourned, with everyone keen to start their tasks, when Philippe stood up and asked for quiet.

"Before we start, I have an urgent message from Li, back in Singapore. It is unusual because it was delivered by fax straight to the US Air Base, and hand delivered to me. It reads 'CTC databases and communications compromised. All research data and communications have been hacked across all sites. DO NOT USE normal communication channels until the IT infrastructure is secure.'" Shocked looks were exchanged around the room.

Penny spoke first. "Listen, I hope I am not speaking out of turn, but I was in the CTC HQ just before we left and I saw a very old and angry looking Chinese man speaking with Li. It looked like a one-way conversation and it wasn't going Li's way. I can lip-read a little but I only caught a few bits of what the older man said. He was telling Li to accept his responsibilities as a Chinese diplomat and do what was best for the country. After this, Li told me to use an alternative channel when accessing the data from the British Army instead of using our own IT infrastructure. I think he knew then that the Chinese government had been playing him all along."

Philippe interrupted. "Well I guess from this fax, we now know which side Li is on."

The team left the briefing tent and prepared to start their specific tasks. Philippe and Charu were driven out to the airfield to launch their drone swarm, to begin mapping the local waterways, railroads, road networks and electricity grid. The task was relatively simple for the drones, but it was time-consuming, and would take them the best part of four days to complete. Matthias, Andrei, Penny and Maria each paired up with one of the British Army CULADS, and started a series of patrols and interviews, which, much to the annoyance of the US Close protection teams, took them through the toughest and most deprived parts of the town, and saw them speaking with religious elders, heads of tribes, local government committees and several women's groups.

On day three, Matthias was called to the Base Commander's office. Colonel Larry Wozlawski appeared to have recovered some of his composure from their lunch a few days earlier and had a determined look on his face.

"How's it going over there for you?"

"Fine," Matthias replied. "I mean actually, it is an amazing opportunity, and the team are learning a lot. Thanks once again for your support."

"It's nothing; glad to help."

"Is there anything we can do for you in return?" asked Matthias.

"Actually, I was wondering if you wouldn't mind taking a look at the stuff that we recovered from the man that attacked our pilot?"

"Sure, but how do you think I may help? I am an anthropologist, not a crime scene investigator."

"I know; I know," the colonel said, with a grim look on his face. "It's just that we are getting nowhere with this dammed investigation. We still have absolutely no idea who he was, where he came from, or which of these jihadi groups he was working for."

"OK, I see, but how can I help, exactly?"

"Your boss back in Singapore said you had a talent for reading people. Take a look at what we recovered from the trunk of his car, and let me know what you make of our perpetrator."

Matthias walked over to a desk at the back of the colonel's office, and saw several items laid out on it. "That is what I call an eclectic reading list," muttered Matthias to himself. On the table, next to a set of prayer beads, sat a copy of the Koran, an old and very well-thumbed book on Arabic Caliphic history, and a compilation of Chinese strategies called the book of Qi.

"Well, the prayer beads might or might not belong to a religious devotee; you see, for some people they are more of an affectation; you know, it is sort of a habit to keep them in your hand and play with them when you are thinking. As for the books, I notice that both the Koran and the book on Arabic history were printed in Baghdad. You wouldn't normally find them in the same collection, unless, of course, if the person was interested in Arab nationalism. You see, Arab nationalism has used Islam over the years to coalesce its followers and lend it some justification."

"That's interesting, our boys didn't pick up on where the books were published."

"However, this final book, the book of Qi, is most fascinating."

"Why?" asked the colonel.

"Well, you see, it is a book on grand strategy. When I say 'grand strategy', I mean the types of strategies required to conquer an Empire. It is not what we would expect to find amongst the possessions of a hit man out to kill an American Serviceman. Is it?"

"I guess not," said the colonel.

"Can I suggest, Colonel, that you get your forensic guys to track down the source of this book? It is written in English, and not in the original Chinese. Also, the colours on the cover look too bright. My guess is that it was printed somewhere in Central

Asia. Test the paper and leather on the cover; you may be able to trace it that way."

"Well, you have certainly given us something to think about, Matthias. But what are your initial overall thoughts?"

"Ahh, the million-dollar question! Well the guy was probably religious, but definitely driven by a sense of Arab nationalism. It looks as though he had a far grander strategy in mind, when you consider the book of Qi."

"Thanks, Matthias; the only good thing to come from this is that he was killed before he could do anything else."

"Yes, that's true, but something doesn't sit quite right, Colonel. I don't like unanswered questions. What was he doing with this copy of a Chinese book on strategy? And you said he was killed?"

"Yeah, that's right," replied the colonel.

"Well," said Matthias, a little impatiently. "Who killed him?"

"I'm afraid we have drawn a blank there. The local police unit that found him said they saw no one else at the scene."

"Ahh, the plot thickens," murmured Matthias to himself. "Colonel, I don't think I can help any more. Would you mind getting back in touch with me in Singapore, once you have found out where the book was printed. In the mean time, I will do a little research of my own." With that, Matthias stood and bade farewell to the colonel, then left the room.

Chapter Thirty-Two

Latitude 1° 17' 28.8348'', Longitude 103° 47' 13.3296''.
United Nations Centre for Technology and Culture
Headquarters, Heng Mui Keng Terrace, Singapore – June
2017.
A Spy in the Camp

The team, helped by the CULADs, had spent nine days in total conducting their Human Terrain Mapping exercise. They had collected masses of data, both electronically, using the mini-drone swarms, and by using face-to-face interview techniques. The team gathered once more with the CULADs for one final debrief, before they separately left Mosul for the UK and Singapore respectively.

After a day's decompression leave, the team were once more sitting around the round table in the CTC briefing room. The whole HQ building looked quite different than when they had left. Large chunks of wall had disappeared, and all of the ducting that carried the fibre optic pipes was laid bare. Also, the large server room was now just a shell of its former self with row after row of bare shelving visible, after having had their high-capacity state of the art servers removed and destroyed.

Li was the first to address the group. "Ladies and gentlemen: it appears that all of our data and communications have been monitored since the very start. I have been played for a fool. My own government demanded that I be complicit in this duplicity, and I, of course, refused. I have spoken with the Secretary-General of the UN, and, of course, I have offered my resignation."

Matthias observed Li closely. He wore the demeanour of a proud, yet defeated, man.

Philippe was the first to speak. "What did the Secretary-General say?"

"Oh, he said that he wanted me to stay, and was glad of my decision to inform him of the Chinese state cyber-attack. However, he did stipulate that I could only stay on if I had the complete confidence of each member of my team. That is why I have called this meeting."

There was a moment's silence around the table. Penny was the first to stand. "Li, you have my confidence and trust," she said in a clear voice.

Andrei and Maria rose simultaneously and began to speak the same words; after a slight, embarrassing pause, Andrei allowed Maria to speak first. "I believe I speak for Andrei and myself when I say, we want you to stay."

Each person stood in turn and confirmed their confidence in Li. Finally Philippe stood and said, "You have the support of your team, Li. Now tell us how we recover and move forward."

Li remained seated; he was humbled by the loyalty that his team had shown him. The personal cost of refusing to allow the Chinese cyber-security units to listen in to what the CTC was doing had been great indeed. He knew that his political career in China was now over. His name would be slandered, and his family disgraced. Was it worth it, he thought, looking around the table. He guessed that only time would tell.

"Well, firstly, thank you for your support, it means a lot to me, and also demonstrates exactly our purpose here, which is to act above the interests of individual countries.

"Now to business. I called in a team of private contractors to investigate the cyber-attack. They said that our servers had been infected with worms. So, as you can see, we will have to replace all of them, along with all of the terminals. Most worrying is the fibre-optic cable we use for communication and data transfer. When we uncovered the cables, we found that they had been spiked. Tiny sleeves had been placed over them. These sleeves were rerouting the traffic via wi-fi to an off-site server for storage. Therefore, as you can see, all of the cabling must be replaced as well."

Charu interrupted at this point. "Li, how can you be certain that the cables aren't spiked outside the building?"

"Very perceptive, as ever, Charu. The answer is that we cannot. That is why, from now on, we will transfer all data and communications using the UN's own encrypted satellites."

"Sounds feasible," said Charu. "Which satellites are we using?"

"The ones that have just been sent up to monitor global agricultural output."

"They're encrypted?" exclaimed Charu.

"Yes, you wouldn't believe how sensitive that information is. Many of the world's stock markets see investments of huge sums of money on a daily basis, where commodity traders invest in the future prices of grain and rice yields. This information could make you a fortune."

Andrei spoke next. "Well, now all of the geek chat is out of the way, what are we doing next?"

"Simple," replied Li. "First, we rebuild the infrastructure; then we repopulate the servers with stored data, and only then will you be able to analyse the data that you collected on your trip."

The meeting adjourned, and the team filed out, already discussing animatedly amongst themselves how they were going to go about reconfiguring the servers and IT system. As Li rose to leave, Matthias stopped him and said, "Would you care for a cigarette? You look as though you could use one."

Li glanced back, and, smiling, said, "I could always use a cigarette." In the smoking cube, Li drew long deep breaths, as Matthias sat and observed him.

"Something happened in Mosul that I want to talk to you about. But I see, looking at your reaction, that you know what this is about."

Li simply nodded, and continued drawing on his cigarette.

"I looked through the assassin's possessions, and found the most curious collection of books."

"I know," Li cut in. "A book on Arabic history, chronicling the different Caliphates, a copy of the Koran, and, most intriguingly, a copy of the book of Qi."

"You know the book?" asked Matthias.

"Very well, actually. I studied Chinese philosophy, and my passion for the subject has stayed with me. I can recite whole passages of that book verbatim. People refer to the book as the thirty-eight stratagems; actually, the number thirty-eight is just a notional number. The book has many more strategies than thirty-eight."

"Did the colonel get back to you with the results of the book analysis?"

"Yes, he did. The paper source comes from either eastern Kazakhstan or western Mongolia. But the leather used for the cover and the pigment in the colours can be traced far more precisely. The compounds used to create the colours differ from country to country, as do the exact colours used. The CIA analysis is that the books were printed in Mongolia; however, the paper may have come from Kazakhstan."

"Bloody hell," declared Matthias. "How was it Winston Churchill put it? 'This is becoming a riddle wrapped in a mystery inside an enigma'."

"Nicely, put, Matthias," Li said, withdrawing another cigarette from his pack.

"What do you think it means?" Matthias asked.

"I honestly don't know; and we are a little busy here at the moment to be concerned about it. However, I suggest we both do a little background reading on the books that were found. Don't bother with the Koran; read up on the Caliphate, and I will reinvestigate the book of Qi. The CIA forensic people also discovered which pages had been leafed through the most often by checking for DNA and fingerprint residue. That will help to narrow things down a bit."

"Isn't all this a bit irrelevant?" asked Matthias. "I mean, the guy is dead."

"He is, but, firstly, we can't presume he was acting alone, and any help we give the CIA will only stand us in good stead the next time Penny needs to ask them for assistance. Secondly, and probably most importantly, I hate being presented with a puzzle I can't solve. And looking at you, it appears you feel likewise."

"That's true," said Matthias. "If you turn anything up, let me know." With that, Matthias stood, and left the smoking cube.

Chapter Thirty-Three

Chinese Strategic Oil Storage Sites.
– Ten p.m., 15 August 2017.
Borrow a Corpse to Resurrect a Soul

The Mongol attack had taken almost four months to plan and prepare for. It was known from on-site observation and close target reconnaissance that the Chinese were employing monitor drones to act as an aerial observation over their strategic oil storage sites, or their SOSS, as they were called in government circles. The drones weren't merely being used as a silent security over-watch, they were also equipped with a sensor array that consistently monitored the temperature and chemical composition of the oil vapour. It was these drones that were to be the key to the attack.

Ganzorig had thought long and hard about how to infiltrate the heavily guarded oil silos. He knew he would never be able to get enough men in place to storm the three different SOSS without being detected. Even if he did, he knew it would be a grossly unfair battle against the regiment of Chinese special security police tasked with defending each of the sites. If they could get into the sites, and that was a big if, then they would certainly be killed to a man. This wasn't the Mongol way to fight. They were no team of suicide bombers. He would leave that type of lunacy to the Arabs. They were brave and cunning warriors who would use the enemy's technology against him.

Two weeks earlier, Hamed, the boy who would be Caliph, had sent Ganzorig an encrypted file. The programme that Ganzorig had received was the key to the whole attack. If the programme could be secretly placed on one of the servers that controlled the drones that were monitoring the sites, then Ganzorig and his men could infiltrate his own mule drones, which carried the canisters of bacteria designed to destroy the oil, in amongst the monitor drones, and deliver the bacteria directly into the oil silos. The programme that Hamed had written would simply command the Chinese monitor drones to continue to send the same data and images to the Chinese monitoring sites on a six-hour loop.

The part that Ganzorig liked best about the plan was that the server farm from where the controls were controlled lay some fifty kilometres from the principal SOSS at Tianjin, which lay south of Beijing in the Bohai Gulf and was only relatively lightly guarded. Over the last two months, a female in Ganzorig's team had managed to become 'romantically' attached to one of the software engineers, and often spent the evenings at his apartment. The plan was for her to place the malware programme onto the memory stick, used by the software engineer, and get him to upload the data when he went in to work. She had incentivised the software tech by hiding the virus within some self-taken explicit photos.

The exact date for the attack would be dependent on the Mongol girl's informing Ganzorig that the technician had put the files on his work computer. As soon as the technician clicked to open one of the files, a worm would penetrate deep into the servers' command files, searching out the files associated with the drones. The phone call came at ten p.m. on Thursday 10th August. All the female voice said was, "Hello, uncle, I am still in China. I miss you all so much." The word 'miss' was the activation word. Once spoken, it initiated a chain of events which would bring the current world order to the verge of disintegration.

Posing as tourists, Ganzorig's two-man teams approached the three SOSS's. The sites were located far from each other, and Ganzorig knew that, if his plan were to succeed, the attack would need to be coordinated with the utmost precision. The westernmost site in Karamay City was located in north-west China, and, despite the whole country's only having one official time zone, known as Beijing time, Karamay City was actually two hours behind Beijing and the other sites at Zhejiang, which lay just south of Shanghai and Tianjin, which sits south of Beijing. Together these sites represented a total oil storage capacity of one hundred and seventy million barrels of oil. Nearly the entire total of China's strategic oil supply. New sites in underground caverns were being constructed, but the recent contraction in the Chinese economy had slowed these projects considerably.

The implementation phase of the strategy was about to begin, as it was stated in the book of Qi. A Corpse had been borrowed to resurrect a Soul. The particular corpse in question was the secret Nazi bacterial formula, which had been developed by Fatima's father and passed on to her. Fatima had spent her whole life trying to improve the potency of the bacterial spores and enabling them to be stored in an aerosol form. She was happy with the result; her modified bacteria had a potency a thousand times that of her father's, and, when stored at low temperatures, they could survive in aerosol form for several months.

Ganzorig checked his watch once more, and then hit 'send' on his mobile phone. The pre-typed message was sent simultaneously to all three strike teams. Under the cover of darkness, in a well-coordinated and practiced action in Karamay City, Zhejiang and Tianjin, three pairs of men quietly removed small boxes containing the miniature mule drones from their car boots. They confirmed that the battery was charged on each drone, and that the bacteria canisters were securely attached. They then inflated the helium balloons, and, on receipt of the second text from Ganzorig, they all released the mule drones into the sky.

The drones had been released some five kilometres from the SOSS's, which gave the men ample time to get away from the scene. As the drones began to gain height, and reach a thousand metres, the onboard altimeters triggered the preset computer guidance protocol. From now on the attack would be completely autonomous. The attack was not only being monitored by Ganzorig and his team in Mongolia; it was also being monitored by Hamed and Fatima in Baghdad.

Hamed's computer monitor displayed three separate fields, with an image from each of the mule drones, as well as a status report, which would indicate when the drones arrived at the specific GPS coordinates; it would also confirm that the drones were communicating successfully with the Chinese Guard Drones; and, finally and most importantly, it would inform whoever was watching the monitor as soon as the bacterial spores had been released.

Ganzorig checked his watch once more. He was getting nervous that he hadn't heard from his men in China. They were supposed to report to him as soon as they were clear of the immediate area. Then, abruptly, in three successive beeps, he received three separate text messages, confirming the safe exfiltration of his two-man teams. Ganzorig had been told by Fatima that the modified bacteria spores would begin to decompose the oil within forty-five minutes of contact. After eight hours, the strategic oil reserves of the People's Republic of China would be little more than one hundred and seventy million barrels of closely guarded, and, more to the point, worthless black gum.

The Chinese would have no time to react, as their own over-watch drones would continue to report the same chemical signature from the oil for the next six hours; and by the time the monitoring teams of the Chinese special security regiment were alerted to the bacterial spores that were destroying the chemical structure of the oil, it would be too late to prevent any more damage.

There was only one small part of the plan left to complete. Fatima sat behind Hamed in Baghdad, and watched with fascination, and with a growing smile on her face, as the drones reported one by one that the Bacterial spores had been delivered. "Hamed, why do they not all report release of the bacteria at the same time?"

"Oh, that's out of our control, I am afraid. You see, the local wind and atmospheric conditions will cause each of the drones to fly at slightly different speeds. But, there, you see," Hamed prodded the screen with his index finger. "All of the canisters have been released."

Fatima then spoke in a quiet and commanding voice into Hamed's ear. "I think it is time to begin our next strategy. Let us watch 'the fires burning across the river'. Let us see how the People's Republic of China react, once they have evidence that Japan was behind this crippling attack." At a keystroke, Hamed commanded the mule drone, with its spent bacteria cartridge, to drop out of the sky, and silently land at the SOSS in Tianjin.

It was dark in Tianjin, and the drone had fallen to earth in a dark corner of the site which would not be discovered until later on that day. This particular drone differed from the others in one particular way. On the canister's base, barely legible, were three Japanese characters, describing with pride that the drone had been manufactured by Mitkasishu Industries. Mitkasishu Industries was a well-known Japanese electronics company that had many contracts with the Japanese Defence Forces.

Chapter Thirty-Four

Latitude 1° 17' 28.8348'', Longitude 103° 47' 13.3296''.
United Nations Centre for Technology and Culture
Headquarters, Heng Mui Keng Terrace, Singapore
– Two p.m. 17 August 2017.
Unbelievable News

"Li, are you alone in your office?" Guilherme Oliveira, the Secretary-General of the United Nations, had an unfamiliar edge to his voice.

"Hello, Mr Secretary-General, good to hear from you. But I detect from your voice that this is no social call."

"You are right, my friend; I am calling you in an unofficial capacity, partly because, if you still have any ties to the inner sanctum of the Chinese Politburo, we would greatly appreciate your help."

"Well, you certainly have my attention, although I am not sure how trustworthy any of my connections might be."

"I know, Li; but at this stage, I am only interested in what the feeling is inside the Politburo Standing Committee of the Communist Party of China!"

Li felt himself stiffen. My God, what had those power crazy old fools in Beijing done now?

"It's not what you think, Li. They haven't started World War Three or anything. Not yet, at any rate."

"I don't understand; what has happened? Have they started populating the Senkaku Islands?"

"Not yet, but I wouldn't rule it out. I have been receiving unconfirmed reports all day from several very respectable sources that last night three of China's largest strategic oil sites were attacked, and the entirety of China's strategic oil reserve have been rendered useless."

The other end of the phone went silent. "Li, are you still there?"

Li sat motionless in his chair, unable to comprehend the news he had just received. "Sorry, er, yes, I am still here. You say attacked? How, by whom?"

"We have no independent confirmation, and we also don't know how they are going to react over this. That is why we need your insight. All I know is that the Chinese Ambassador to the UN stormed into my office this morning, demanding that the UN Security Council be convened tomorrow afternoon. He said he had incontrovertible evidence that Japan had just launched a successful attack against its oil storage sites. He called it an act of war against the People's Republic, and told me in no uncertain terms that his government would react with extreme measures."

My God, thought Li, had the years of tension between China and Japan finally reached boiling point? Had the new right-wing Japanese Prime Minister actually decided to use the recent change in Japanese law that permitted its "Defence Force" to exact a pre-emptive strike against a foreign aggressor if it felt it was in immediate danger of attack? It was well known that, with the Japanese economy still stagnating after twenty years, and with the growing military, economic and political might of China, Japan was rapidly becoming an irrelevant inconvenience to China and its expansionist ideas in the East China Sea.

"What do we know exactly?" After recovering his composure, Li asked the question.

"Not too much. The Chinese Ambassador says that Chinese Security Forces recovered some equipment from the site of one of the attacks, that proved beyond doubt that the Japanese orchestrated the attack. He will not, however, release any more information about the equipment. As we speak, the US Seventh Fleet is sailing up from Australia to stand ready to honour their defence treaty agreement with Japan, should the Chinese feel obliged to act aggressively. However, the fleet was docked in Australia for a period of overhaul, and they won't be up to strength for a couple of weeks yet."

My God, thought Li, this really could get out of hand.

"Li, I am asking you and your team to unofficially investigate the attacks; I would like you to send me some policy recommendations from a cultural perspective as to how you think this is likely to play out."

"I understand. When do you need the paper?"

"Yesterday!" replied Guilherme.

Li replaced the phone in its cradle, and sat for a moment, still trying to digest the news he had just heard. He left his office, and went into the main open office, where most of the team were sitting at their new computer terminals. Charu and Philippe were concentrating on trying to restore their lost data after the cyber-attack; and the rest of the team were busy inputting and analysing the data from their first exercise in Northern Iraq.

"I need everybody's attention. I am calling a crisis meeting. Everybody is to be seated in the briefing room in five minutes. Where's Penny?"

"Oh, she is just downstairs, getting us some fresh coffee," replied Charu."

"Go and fetch her! This is a matter of the utmost urgency."

In a little under three minutes, the whole team were assembled around the circular briefing table. On the LCD display behind Li, a simple statement had been typed. 'If the entire stock of Chinese strategic oil reserves were to be wiped out in one go, what would be the consequences?'

Li began the meeting. "I want to conduct a little exercise with you. Imagine the scenario typed on the screen behind me and consider the consequences."

Andrei spoke first. "Isn't this a little far-fetched?" he said. "My colleagues at the FSB have spent many hours analysing the Chinese security at the sites, and it would be impossible to destroy all of the oil in one attack. For a start, the sites are located hundreds of kilometres from each other, and any fire at the sites would be noticed by satellite, or by the hyper-alert Security Regiments that guard the sites."

"I know, I know," said Li. "Let us forget the 'How' question for a minute and focus our thoughts on the 'Why', and then on the consequences of such an attack."

Penny spoke next, "If we look at it from the perspective of who could gain from such an attack, then the finger would naturally point to Japan. There is a lot of enmity between the two countries, dating back to the colonisation of eastern China and Korea in the 1930s. Today, the arguments are over possession of the Senkaku Islands, or, if you are Chinese, you would call them the Diaoyu Islands. Japan is no match militarily or economically for China; but if it could destroy China's strategic oil supplies in one strike, it would all but cripple the People's Liberation Army and Navy."

Whilst Penny was speaking, Charu was flicking through a news site on her tablet computer. Quick as ever, Charu had been contemplating other ramifications of such an attack. "My God. Is this true? Did it really happen?" she asked, placing her tablet on the table. Li looked at her inquiringly. Charu picked up the tablet, and turned it to show a news article from the financial pages' section. 'Chinese Stock Market ceases all trading, citing software glitch.'

"If this attack took place, then the ramifications for the share prices of Chinese companies, their currency and for world oil prices would be immense." The assembled group turned back to look at Li.

"What do you know?" asked Matthias.

"I have just been informed that the Chinese Ambassador to the UN has called an emergency session of the UN Security Council to discuss an attack on their oil storage facilities. They say they have incontrovertible proof that the attack was conducted by Japan." There was stunned silence around the room.

"No more details have been released to the general public, and all members of the Security Council have decided unanimously to keep the news quiet until China decides how to act. As you quite rightly said, Charu, the economic consequences alone would be staggering."

"Hold on a minute, Li; you say they have proof, but won't release any evidence? I think we should look a little wider and decide who else could benefit from such an attack," Maria began. "Our State department has done a lot of analysis on oil security. There are over a dozen climate change activist groups against global warming that want to see an end to fossil fuels. With China being the largest greenhouse gas emitter, and with its smog problems, it could have been an environmental activist group."

Philippe spoke next. "Ever since the US and Canada started large-scale fracking, it has driven the price of oil down to the lowest prices recorded. Some countries' economies rely almost entirely on oil. The governments of Venezuela, Russia, Iran and Saudi Arabia are all currently running massive current account deficits, because of the low price of oil, and there are regular anti-government rallies and riots in these countries, as the economic reality begins to hit home."

"It could also be internal dissidents. Don't the Chinese have one of these sites in the autonomous Uighur region?"

"Yes," replied Li. "In the far North-West of the country; and it is true that the Uighur separatists have been fighting for a long time for an independent State."

Li now stood up and took control of the meeting. "So, in summary, we have a whole range of potential attackers: disenfranchised governments of oil-producing states who fear their regimes may crumble, environmental activist groups, the Uighurs of North-West China, or Japan!"

"That about sums it up, Li," said Penny, looking once more over her notepad. "What have we been asked to do?"

"The Secretary-General asked me to use back channels to Beijing to get a sense of the mood there. From us as a team, he would like some recommendations as to how we think the Chinese will react."

Li closed the meeting by asking each of the team members to reach back to their respective former organisations to try to establish as much information as possible. For his part, Li picked up his phone, and began to dial a number in Beijing. He called his father's brother, unsure as to the reception he would receive.

"Who is this?" came the older voice, in Mandarin.

"It is I, Li Qiang Wu."

"Li! Well, I certainly didn't expect to hear your voice again. Not after what your father told me. You know you are 'persona non grata' here in Beijing?"

"I know, I know, Uncle," Li said, in a resigned tone. "Can you tell me anything about what is going on?"

"You know full well I can't do that, Li. You are no longer in the privileged position that you once were. I can say that the Politburo Standing Committee of the Communist Party has been in session all day. At lunchtime today, one of the five members was removed from the Committee under Armed Guard and declared an enemy of the People's Republic of China. The remaining four members, including your father, are still in session."

"Thank you, Uncle. I apologise once more for bringing shame to you and our family, and I will not bother you any more."

Replacing the phone receiver, Li got up and strode to the smoking cube. Checking his watch, he thought, just enough time to do some thinking, before I send off my report to Guilherme. Lighting one of his favourite Marlborough cigarettes, Li slumped back in the chair, and began to think about the conversation he had just had with his uncle.

The conversation had been both useful and very alarming. With the only moderate member of the Standing Committee silenced and removed from the committee, and with people like his father, who bore massive anti-Japanese sentiment, running the country, Li was sure that a military reaction of some form would be the response from China. People like his father, who had witnessed the savage period of Japanese occupation and the shame it had brought upon China, would not lose face today by de-escalating the situation. His father was one of four men who now controlled the largest armed forces in the world.

At five p.m. that day, Li sent a simple encrypted message to the Secretary-General of the United Nations.

"To the Secretary-General of the United Nations.

Following your direct request, please find below the CTC's analysis of the Chinese reaction to the unconfirmed attack against its strategic oil reserves.

My team have analysed the problem, and the method of attack, which is as yet unknown, seems to be the key to this problem. Apart from Japan, several different actors could have cause to conduct such an attack, ranging from internal dissidents, through to environmental groups, to foreign oil-producing states who are currently suffering due to the low oil price. Japan itself, which is reliant on daily imports of crude oil, would not benefit from a sharp increase in oil prices in its current economic state. Of critical concern is that, as of this afternoon, the Standing Committee of the Communist Party now consists of four and not five members, and each of these members is known for his hardline anti-Japanese rhetoric.

Our concern here is that the attack may not have been initiated to simply destroy China's oil supply. It may have been deliberately perpetrated to bring the two regional powers into conflict. If this is true, then it's not inconceivable that a third party may have been involved in the attack. My final point is that I would caution that China has been looking for a legitimate reason to attack Japan since the end of the Second World War. I believe that, under international law, if they can prove that Japan was the aggressor, they would be quite within their rights to counterattack.

Yours, Li Qiang Wu."

Chapter Thirty-Five

Japanese Strategic Oil Storage Sites –18 August 2017.
Kill with a Borrowed Sword

Sixty hours had passed since the attack on the Chinese strategic oil storage sites. The Chinese Ambassador to the UN was in his office, preparing for the two p.m. extraordinary meeting he had called of the UN Security Council. At 1.55 p.m. exactly, his encrypted cell phone buzzed once. The one-line message read, 'Ten strategic oil storage sites targeted by ground-launched ICBMs. Damage report to follow.' He smiled, replaced the cell phone in his pocket, and left his office to attend the UN Security Council meeting.

The other members of the Permanent Five Security Council, representing America, Russia, Britain and France, were also joined by a Japanese delegation. They had been waiting in the meeting room for five minutes before the Chinese Ambassador arrived. As the older Chinese Ambassador strode into the room, a series of beeps began to emanate from the cell phones belonging to those assembled in the meeting. The Chinese Ambassador ignored the shocked look on the faces of the other ambassadors as he took his seat.

Guilherme, who had as yet not heard the news about the Chinese counter-attack, stood to open the meeting.

"Ambassadors, we are gathered here to discuss the report of an unprovoked attack by one member state upon another. The Chinese Ambassador…" Before he could finish his introduction, the US Ambassador held up his mobile phone for Guilherme to read. Guilherme read the simple message that read 'Japanese Oil Storage sites hit by explosions. Suspected missile strike.'

Guilherme froze; without removing his eyes from the screen of the phone he slowly began to speak. "Gentlemen, it appears that events have moved on considerably since this meeting was called. Indications now are that Japanese SOSS's have been destroyed as well. I will permit a brief comment by the representatives of both the Chinese and Japanese delegations, then I will close this meeting and reschedule another for ten p.m. tonight."

The Chinese Ambassador rose and quickly read out the pre-prepared Chinese position. "On the evening of 15 August 2017, at an undefined time, an attack was perpetrated against the sovereign territory of the People's Republic of China. We have evidence from an unmanned aerial vehicle captured at one of the attack sites that the Japanese government is behind this attack.

"Within existing international law, the People's Republic of China has exercised its right to defend itself by launching a counterstrike against the Republic of Japan's oil infrastructure. I believe that this committee will agree that this was a most measured approach by the People's Republic of China. My country will be demanding economic reparations from Japan for the one hundred and seventy million barrels of oil that were destroyed in this attack."

Sir Richard Belmarsh, the British Ambassador, nearly choked when the scale of the attack was revealed. Next, the irate and confused Japanese Ambassador stood up. "Gentlemen, my government completely deny any allegation of an attack against the sovereign territory of the People's Republic of China. My intelligence sources have reported no fire or explosions from the Chinese sites. We are grief-stricken to hear of the heinous and cowardly strike by the Chinese government against our state, and will take all measures to defend ourselves against further attacks. The government of Japan will be pressing for full compensation for the lives lost, as well as the economic value of the oil and infrastructure.

"Ten sites were struck, and, because of the massive heat of the explosion, and the danger of further explosions, the Japanese government can do nothing to prevent the oil from being burnt up. The government is co-ordinating an emergency response as we speak, to try to isolate the sites, and search for the dead or injured."

Before Guilherme could stand to draw the meeting to a close, Chuck Henderson, the US Ambassador, rose to address the assembled group. Staring directly at the Chinese Ambassador, he said, "Before you all leave, I would like to inform all present that the US 7th Fleet is sailing towards Japan as we speak, to stand ready to honour our defence treaty with the Japanese Government."

The effect of the strike against the Japanese oil storage sites was more critical than had at first been imagined. Since the Fukushima Nuclear power plant meltdown, the Japanese government had required a lot longer than was first estimated to get the country's nuclear power production back up to its full capacity. Nuclear energy used to be responsible for around twenty-six per cent of Japan's energy needs. Currently, it still only accounts for around fourteen per cent. This situation had become even more inflamed, because of the method of attack. Japanese civilians near the sites had filmed the incoming missiles on their mobile phones, and some of the more popular social media platforms had actually crashed that day with the uploading of images of Chinese intercontinental ballistic missiles striking Japanese soil.

The Japanese government was in emergency session; there were protests in the street by Japanese citizens demanding protection from further attack, and revenge for the strike against them. The Japanese Defence Force had been placed on full alert, and the Japanese Nikkei stock market had been closed for the next two days.

To further widen the spreading global alarm about an energy crisis, both New Zealand and South Korea shared Japan's strategic oil storage facilities which meant that economic and industrial output would be severely affected in these countries as well. China, Japan and South Korea combined, account for over thirty-five per cent of total global industrial output.

Russian Oil Pipeline Network – 01 September 2017.
Attacking a Network

Despite the three Chinese SOSS sites' being located a long way from each other, the attack using the mini-drones had been a relatively simple affair, and had not exposed the lives of the

291

Mongol separatists to an unacceptable level of risk. The attack on the Russian sites was an altogether different proposition. Russia's oil exploration, refining and export infrastructure was highly developed, and the new government had decided quite wisely to diffuse the risk to its strategic oil reserves, by storing the oil at a multitude of refining sites across the breadth of the entire country.

Ganzorig had initially refused to believe that his group would be capable of such an attack. Again it was Hamed, the future Caliph, who had designed the mode of attack. It was brilliant in its simplicity. Instead of exposing most of Ganzorig's men to capture or death, as they tried to infiltrate the tens of refining and storage sites, Hamed had realised that he could use the Russians' own highly extensive network of oil pipelines to transmit the bacteria around the country.

The additional bonus was that the bacteria would also flow through the Druzhba, or, to give it its English name, the Friendship Pipeline. This one single pipeline was responsible for the majority of the oil sold by Russia to Western and Central European countries. The self-replicating bacteria would lay waste to millions of barrels of oil throughout Russia and Europe. This one single attack epitomised to perfection the Chinese strategy from the book of Qi, of 'Killing with a Borrowed Sword'.

For his part, Ganzorig had managed to get hold of the digital schematics for the entire Russian oil pipeline network from a disgruntled Russian oil executive, who had been amenable to receiving an international bank transfer to an unlisted Cayman Islands bank account. Hamed had scrutinized the interactive pipeline schematic in detail. His sharp physicist's brain quickly identified flow rates, nodes of confluence and critical access points.

Ganzorig had been given four sites to attack. The plan was simple and low tech, and, most importantly, thought Ganzorig, it didn't place his men under undue threat of discovery. His four teams, each consisting of three men, would infiltrate the porous Russian-Mongol border by car. Once across the border, they would dress once more as nomadic horsemen, so typical of the Steppe region that covers the border area between Russia, Mongolia and Kazakhstan. Just like Mongolia's most famous son, Genghis Khan, Ganzorig and his men would sweep across the Russian steppe, causing havoc and destruction. This time, though, it would be a far subtler method of attack.

Even though the pipelines were regularly patrolled by armed government security forces, as well as Russian oil company personnel, the pure size of the network meant that, in many areas, the terrain was too difficult, or the pipeline simply too long, for it to be monitored accurately. In addition, the advantage of a horse-borne attack was that they could easily outrun the all-terrain vehicles used by the security forces.

The attack was simple. The horses in each of the four groups would carry the bacteria, and the device contained a tiny conical explosive charge, which was needed to couple with the pipeline, to inject the bacteria into the system. The only slight concern was whether the explosives would be picked up at the border crossing. Ganzorig was satisfied, though, that the crossing they had chosen was one that he and his men had used many times before on other operations, and that they would be able to get across safely.

Hamed put his mobile phone down, and turned to look at his mother. "Ganzorig and his teams have crossed into Russia and they are making their way to the attack sites."

"Perfect, my son. How long will they need to get into position?"

"Riding, as they are, over the steppe land, two of the teams will have over two days' riding before they are in position. Don't worry, Mother, Ganzorig's network extends far into Russia; he will have people and fresh horses available to him when he needs them."

Fatima seemed tense. "I am concerned that we need to co-ordinate this attack carefully. The Russians have already increased the security around their refineries and storage sites. If any hint of what we are trying to do gets out, the whole plan, my life's work, will be for nothing."

"I know, Mother, I know. That is the beauty of our plan. We are not directly attacking points of strength. We are deliberately attacking sections of the pipeline in remote areas, where our intrusion will not be noticed for many days probably. 'H' Hour is set for three a.m. on the 4th of this month."

Ganzorig never tired of the thrill of riding the short stocky pony over the rolling steppe land. He had been riding a horse before he could even walk. It was in his blood, and in the blood of his people, he thought. Glancing across at his two fellow saboteurs, he grinned wildly, spurring his horse on even faster, until he reached the brow of a hill.

He reined in the galloping horse just before reaching the brow of the hill, and dismounted. The horse was breathing heavily, venting thick clouds of moisture-laden air from its nostrils. The two men with Ganzorig arrived and slowed their horses to a walk, then dismounted. Leaving the horses out of sight below the brow of the hill, Ganzorig and his two comrades crept forward slowly to peer over the crest of the hill and down into the valley below.

It was nearly six p.m. and the sun was beginning to set. One of Ganzorig's men removed the US military issue GPS device from his jacket pocket and passed it to Ganzorig. Glancing briefly at the screen, Ganzorig confirmed that they were at the correct location and that the section of pipeline that stretched out into the distance, as far as the eye could see, just eight hundred metres in front of them, was indeed the same section identified by Hamed.

Hamed, for his part, had recorded the exact strike locations on the US military GPS devices, and had had them delivered to the Mongolian separatists, prior to the attack. Of course, hitting the exact section of the pipeline was important, but of far greater significance to the overall plan was to be able to leave behind some evidence at the scene of the crime that would deflect the attention of the Russian Security Forces away from the Mongolian separatists, and encourage them to believe that the USA was behind the attack.

Crawling back to the horses, Ganzorig once more checked his watch, and signaled to his men to unpack the equipment and to prepare to wait until it was time to attack. It was seven p.m. when he sent a single message to the other three teams, indicating that he was in position and waiting for their status confirmation. Teams Two and Three replied immediately. They were waiting in the pre-attack positions, and the equipment was ready to go. No reply came from Team Four. This worried Ganzorig a little as Team Four had the shortest distance to travel to reach their target. Still, he mused to himself, it was early; the attack wasn't due until three a.m. He turned his attention to the equipment that the men had unpacked from the horses.

On the floor in front of him were two long lengths of rubber-coated, steel-reinforced chain, attached to ratchet straps. The chains would be used to clamp the device that would inject the bacteria into the pipeline, on to the outside of the pipe's casing. The device itself was made up of a large metallic heavy cylindrical container approximately ten inches in diameter and about twenty inches long. On one end it had a curved metal flange which had been carefully engineered to match the curve of the pipeline's exact diameter. Through this flange, the two rubberised metal chains would be threaded to secure the device to the pipe. Despite its being relatively small, the whole device weighed about ten kilograms. On the inside was a very small, yet extremely powerful, conical explosive charge, that, once detonated, would pierce a neat one-inch hole in the skin of the pipe.

On the exterior of the cylinder were two valve-like attachments. The lower attachment was where the handheld electrical detonator was inserted prior to firing. The upper attachment was a threaded valve, similar to those found on camping gas canisters. It would be on to this thread that the aerosol-can-shaped cartridges that were filled with the devastating bacteria would be screwed. Having checked the equipment once more, Ganzorig sat back on the damp grass with his two colleagues and began a simple meal of dried meat and fruit.

At eleven p.m. his phone vibrated in his pocket. Checking the illuminated display, he saw that it was Team Four reporting in. They were in position. It appeared that one of their horses had become lame on the final approach to their target, and they had been forced to transfer the rider and equipment to the two remaining horses, which had caused them a considerable time delay. Sitting back once more, and visibly more relaxed, Ganzorig continued to eat and talk quietly with his friends.

By two a.m., it had been raining for over an hour. It was no discomfort for Ganzorig and his men, who were used to the outdoor life; however it would mean that the security patrols would be even less inclined to get out of their vehicles to inspect the pipeline properly. Alerting the other three teams once more by text, he nodded to his two colleagues, who were sitting ready, with the chains and canister of bacteria clutched in their hands.

"Today, my brothers, we strike a heavy blow against those interfering Russian dogs. Today they will feel the might of the Mongolian sword as it is plunged deep into their economic heart."

Two smiling and determined faces looked back at him, as they carefully began to make their way down the hillside, through the long grass, to the point of attack.

Once in position, the team moved quickly; they had practiced this exact manoeuvre a hundred times back in Mongolia. The chains wrapped around the pipe were quickly ratcheted tight and the cylinder containing the explosives was secure. Pulling a small battery pack with a cable attached from his pocket, Ganzorig carefully connected the detonator to the device. He screwed in the contact switch until he felt a pulse of electricity.

The explosive charge detonated, and a sound similar to a heavy stone landing from a height onto damp earth could be heard. A small pressure gauge on the side of the container confirmed that the pipeline had been punctured. One of Ganzorig's men carefully handed him the aerosol canister containing the bacteria. Ganzorig threaded the container into position until he could feel the thin metal seal on the bacteria's container puncture and hear the release of pressure as the bacteria were delivered under high pressure into the flowing oil mass that coursed through the Russian pipeline.

The three men grinned at each other through the dark rain filled night. Swiftly, they turned and began to quickly make their way back up the hill to the waiting horses. Ganzorig was last to leave, and, before he did so, he removed the US military-issue GPS device, complete with serial numbers, and dropped it on the floor, twenty metres from the site of the attack.

The simultaneous attacks occurred within two minutes of each other, and the release of the destructive bacteria into the Russian oil supply pipeline was complete by 3.05a.m. on the 4th September, 2017.

It would take nearly seven hours before the first reports of increased pressure in some of the major oil pipelines were being reported by the regional control centres to the head of the Russian state oil company. By eleven a.m. Moscow time on the same day, the chairman of this oil company was holding frantic talks with a committee comprising of several senior FSB officials, the Russian oil minister and senior technical heads of department. Filter and monitoring stations at key pumping sites along the entire extent of the pipeline were reporting blockages and a silting up of the filters.

By midday on the 4th of September 2017, the pumping of refined oil through Russia and onwards to its many customers in Europe and Central Asia had been stopped. Emergency strategy meetings were being held in the Kremlin and the FSB had deployed over twenty thousand Internal Security Force personnel to search the entire length of the pipelines, looking for any attempted sabotage.

A little earlier, at 11.30 a.m. Moscow time, just north of the great Uvs lake in the North West of Mongolia, at a border checkpoint near Khandagaty, a bus load of Mongolian visitors were returning to Mongolia on their way back from a regular shopping trip to the larger Russian town of Chadan that lay some seventy kilometres inside the Russian border. Amongst the happy shoppers were Ganzorig's twelve men who had taken part in the attack. They sat separate from each other, dressed as simple Mongolian visitors, each man carrying plastic bags filled with Russian vodka and cigarettes.

Chapter Thirty-Six

The flow of Russian oil into the states surrounding Russia is a never-ceasing operation. It would be impossible for the incident affecting the Russian pipeline to go unnoticed for very long. Penny, the former MI6 officer and head of liaison at the CTC, knocked on Li's door.

"Do you have a minute?" she said.

"But of course; please come in, sit down, won't you?"

"I'd rather not. I think we have a big problem."

"Oh," said Li, looking up once more, this time noticing Penny's agitated state.

"I have been receiving reports from several European Intelligence agencies since late last night. They are all reporting a similar pattern of events. The oil storage and onward pumping stations across Europe had been noticing increased pressure."

"Oh," said Li, raising an eyebrow, suddenly fully focused on Penny.

"The timing of the events shows a pattern. Charu and Philippe have confirmed my analysis. In the north, the incidents were reported first in Belarus, then Poland and finally in Germany. In the centre, Slovakia were the first to signal a problem, followed by Hungary and Austria, and, in the south, Ukraine reported problems at just after eleven thirty a.m., and the problems continued downline through Romania and Croatia."

"My God," spluttered Li, suddenly standing up from his desk. "If what you are telling me is correct, then the entire European oil supply network is affected. What else do we know?"

"Well, these effects were reported between eleven thirty a.m. and two thirty p.m., Central European Time. Then, well, I don't know how to put this. Well, then the oil just stopped flowing completely!"

"Come with me," said Li, with an urgency to his voice that Penny hadn't heard before. "Get everyone assembled in the briefing room. I am ringing the Secretary-General."

Twenty minutes later, the entire CTC team was assembled around the briefing table. "It seems that the recent madness in the world over oil is spreading like a virus," Li addressed the assembled group succinctly. "We have been formally asked to support the effort to establish just what is going on, and, more importantly, what events may occur as a result of this oil stoppage."

Philippe was the first to stand up and address the group. "I have friends in Germany at one of the receiving stations. They say that their pumps and valves are jammed solid. My friend says that the entire system seems to be clogged with what he describes as a tar-like substance. He is flying over a sample for us to analyse."

"Thank you, Philippe," said Li, turning to Maria. "What's the global outlook?"

"Well, the Russians have stopped pumping oil. If the entire network is offline, then, potentially, we will see another major world economy economically crippled. After the attacks on China and Japan, which have reduced world industrial output by over one third, now we see attacks on Russia, which is completely reliant on its oil and gas exports to be able to service its debt, and to be able to provide public services."

"Thanks, Maria, anyone anything else to add?"

"Well, said Andrei, I have had a phone call from an old FSB friend who wanted to warn me that his boss Dimitri Podoyenko…" Hearing that name struck Maria like a knife through her heart. Dimitri Podoyenko had been one of the two Russian agents on the drugs bust when her husband had been shot in a 'friendly fire' incident.

She sat motionless for a second, her face completely drained of colour, and sick to her stomach. "I, er, need to leave for a minute," she stammered, as she shakily got to her feet and went to leave the room. Five pairs of eyes watched her make her way out of the room.

"What happened?" asked Andrei. "Maria, are you OK?" he shouted after her.

"Please, Andrei, I am sure she will be OK; can you continue with your brief? This matter is of the highest importance and I fear we have no time to lose."

"Yes, sorry; as I was saying, an old FSB colleague of mine told me that they have been tracking a group of Mongolian separatists for some time now, and they have noticed a large spike in recent activity. Travelling under different passports, several members of the group have been identified crossing the border into both Russia and China over the past several months. They cannot establish a pattern, but feel sure that the attacks may be linked. He also told me confidentially that that the Kremlin is really in a panic over this at the moment, and the noises from the President are that when he discovers who undertook the attacks, retribution will be swift and merciless. Some of the more nationalist members of the government are already pointing the finger at the US."

"Thanks, Andrei;" Li said.

"Would you mind if I checked on Maria?"

"No, please do, but hurry back in, won't you?"

Andrei left the briefing room and began looking for Maria. She was nowhere to be seen; knocking briefly on the ladies' toilet door before entering, Andrei pushed open the door to see Maria by the wash basins rinsing her face with cold water. Her eyes were red and puffy; he could see she had been crying.

"What is wrong, Maria?"

She looked coldly into his eyes. "How well do you know this Podoyenko?" She almost spat the man's name out, her eyes never wavering as they stared into Andrei's deep blue eyes.

"He's the boss of a friend of mine. I have only seen him once, in the car park talking to my friend. He introduced himself, he seemed all right to me. Why do you ask? What is troubling you?" He reached forward to try and stroke the hair out of her eyes, but she pushed his hand away.

"I need some time, Andrei, that's all. I just need some time." With that, Maria threw the paper towel into the rubbish bin, and left the toilet. Andrei stared after her in bewilderment. Women, he thought. I'll never understand them!

Back in the briefing room, Matthias was giving a summary of the global picture, and, more specifically, commenting on how the CTC could assist the UN. "As it stands today, the majority of Russian, Chinese, Japanese and South Korean strategic oil stocks have been destroyed, or, should I say, made unusable. The downstream effects of today's strike are that, as of this afternoon, Europe has stopped receiving oil supplies, too."

"If I may?" cut in Philippe. "Europe is important because, unlike the other countries so far affected, most European countries rely on companies to hold their own strategic fuel reserves to cover ninety days of net imports; however, as with many agreements within the EU, most countries have been relaxed about this, and many are well below this level of contingency. I would estimate that, realistically, most European nations have between one and a half and two months' worth of fuel stocks. Government-enforced rationing and controlled power outages would begin within three weeks if alternative sources cannot be found."

"Thank you, Philippe," Matthias continued. "So, as you can see, apart from the US, most of the industrialised world is running dangerously low on oil. Trading has been suspended on the Chinese, Japanese, Korean, and now on the Russian stock exchanges. The price of a barrel of Brent crude is currently hovering at one hundred and twenty dollars per barrel, up from thirty-six dollars per barrel since the first strike on the Chinese sites. The UN Security Council was log-jammed before this attack. Now, with Russia affected, it will be damned near impossible to get any sort of agreement between the major powers.

"As I see it, we have three concerns. The immediate concern is whether Russia will lash out with a military response to the attack. Secondly, how are we going to deal with the global fuel shortage? Finally, who is behind this, and how do we stop them?"

Li stood and addressed the entire room. "Ladies and gentlemen, we are facing the gravest of times; the stability of the entire world order is being threatened. We have no time to lose. The time now is four p.m. here in Singapore; that makes it just gone midday in Moscow. We will reconvene at ten p.m. tonight. I want your ideas on how we are going to solve these three problems by then. It will be a long night, maybe even a long few days for all of us. You are dismissed." The team filtered out of the briefing and rushed to their terminals, to begin trying to work on the problems outlined by Mathias.

"Matthias!" Li looked at Matthias, then looked over to the smoking cube. "Would you join me for a few minutes, please?"

Once seated in the smoking cube, Li reached into his pocket and withdrew his customary packet of Marlborough cigarettes. "You know, Matthias, I have been thinking about these oil attacks, and who actually benefits from them."

Sitting opposite Li, and accepting one of his proffered cigarettes, Matthias nodded in agreement. "Me too. It just doesn't make sense that the Japanese would initiate such an attack against the Chinese in the first place. Japan suffered horrendous casualties during the Second World War from fire bombing, and, ultimately, with the two nuclear bombs dropped on Hiroshima and Nagasaki. I don't believe that after spending seventy years rebuilding their country, they would risk certain devastation again from Chinese nuclear missiles."

"I agree, and, for some reason, I can't stop thinking about what you found in Mosul amongst the belongings of the man that killed the US airman. Finding the book of Qi there was most incongruous indeed. I have been re-reading the book and its stratagems, and I am becoming increasingly convinced that a third party is behind these oil strikes – a third party with a lot at stake. There is one strategy in particular that I read in Chapter Two. The name of the strategy is 'Watch the fires burning across the river'. The concept has been used countless times to great success. In effect it means that once your enemies are fighting amongst themselves you wait until they become depleted and exhausted before you move in to seize what you want. The problem is, I can't identify who this third party might be, or what their aim is."

"Interesting," replied Matthias, drawing deeply once more on his cigarette. "I have been re-reading the history of the Arabs and their Caliphates. Two things struck me; firstly, the preferable natural state of order amongst the Arabic countries seems to be when they are loosely governed by a Caliph or sitting within an Empire. It is only relatively recently, with the artificial invention of many of the states such as Syria, Palestine, Libya, Iraq, etc. that the Western democracies have tried to push for these states to be completely autonomous.

The second revelation which I noticed when reading about the Caliphs was that the last truly great Caliph, who ruled from Baghdad in its heyday, was a guy called Al Mustansim Billah of the Abbasid Caliphate. He died in 1258. Do you know how he died?" Matthias looked quizzically at Li. "He was killed; to be specific, he was rolled in a carpet and trampled to death. The thing that struck me most about his death was that it was done by Mongol horsemen!"

"This is becoming more interesting by the minute," Li said, exhaling the strong tobacco smoke.

"I haven't finished," interrupted Matthias. "In the texts I read, there are some abstract references to the Mongols removing one of the Caliph's sons and his daughters and taking them back to Mongolia."

"So, if I understand correctly," started Li, suddenly becoming more animated. "In Northern Iraq, amongst the belongings from the attack, you were shown a book on Arabic history, the Koran and the book of Qi which we believe was printed in either Kazakhstan or Mongolia. Coupled with that, we hear today that there has been increased activity amongst Mongolian nationalists, who are upset at how much influence Russia and China still have over Mongolia."

"That about sums it up," said Matthias. "Do you think the Mongols are behind the attacks?"

Li looked unconvinced. "A lot of evidence points that way. But two things confound the situation. Firstly, what does Mongolia stand to gain by destroying the economies of China and Russia? It is almost completely reliant on Russia for energy and China for manufactured goods. Secondly, why were these books found amongst the possessions of an Arab, most likely an Iraqi, who died whilst trying to kill a US airman?"

"I honestly don't know," replied Matthias. "But I know where we can start looking. I suggest that we get some of our collective brain power working on this. With your permission, Li, I would like to request that targeting information from the US drone unit based in Mosul. I want to know how many Iraqis were targeted in the six months prior to the attack on their airman."

"They will never release that sort of information to us, Matthias; you know that."

"Maybe not; but they may allow Maria to look at the data. She is cleared for that sort of thing. Secondly, I think we should ask Andrei for a favour from his FSB colleagues. Would you mind asking to see whether they can pull in one of these Mongolians for questioning? We need to know how they are involved."

"OK, I'll get on to it right away. I am going to enlist the help of our resident puzzle solver Charu, to see if she can make any more sense of this than I can."

Chapter Thirty-Seven

Latitude 55° 45' 7.2828'', Longitude 37° 37' 2.9964''
The Kremlin, Moscow, Russia – 6 Sep 2017.
Watch the Fires Burning Across the River

The Russian President, Oleg Vasilienko, slammed his fist down hard on the table. Immediately, the council of collected ministers and security personnel ceased their squabbling, and looked up to the head of the table. Oleg was a short, muscular man with a slightly flattened face, and the pronounced cheekbones so typical of his Georgian ancestry. His hair was dark black, although only his closest aides knew that, out of vanity, and in an attempt to maintain his masculine image as a man of Russia, he regularly dyed it.

"Gentlemen, don't you see who was behind this cowardly attack on mother Russia?" Withdrawing a small hand-held device from his pocket, he threw it across the large wooden meeting table; it hit the table with a loud thump, spinning a couple of times before coming to rest by a large jug of water. "That," the red-faced leader of Russia said, barely able to contain his anger. "Is a mobile GPS device. Not our GLONASS system but American GPS. Yuri, pick it up and read the inscription on the side!" The head of the FSB picked up the small rubber-coated device, and, because of his deteriorating eyesight, and his vanity, which forbade him from wearing glasses in public, he passed the device to one of his aides to read the words that had been embossed by the manufacturer on to the side, next to a small moveable antenna.

"It says, 'US Department of Defense. NATO Serial number: 4536 2332 4878'."

Those assembled at the table turned once more to face the glowering President. "That little box is an American military GPS device; it contains pre-programmed coordinates of one of the attack sites, and it was found no more than thirty metres from one of the attack sites." The assembled men at the meeting broke out once more into shouts of indignation and rage. Holding up his hand to silence them, Oleg Vasilienko spoke once more.

"For years, the Americans have been afraid of a resurgent Russia. They have interfered in our attempts to support the Assad regime in Syria; they have placed economic sanctions on many of our leading citizens and they tried everything they could to stop the new Chinese-Russian oil supply deal. They are weak and we are strong. They are afraid of a united Russia and China being able reassert their rightful place in the world. I have ordered our military on to full alert, and the Russian Aerospace Defence Force will strike back at the American oil sites within forty-eight hours." The President then turned to face the head of Russia's Aerospace Defence Force.

"General Bukharev, please brief this committee on the attack." General Pyotr Bukharev, head of the Russian Aerospace Defence Force, rose to address the group. In a brusque and efficient style, he outlined the plan.

"Gentlemen, within thirty-six hours of this briefing, our air force will have released a total of twenty-four AS-15 Kent Cruise missiles against the four major underground strategic oil storage sites in the USA. The target sites are located at Bryan Mound, Big Hill, West Hackberry and Bayou Choctaw. These sites lie between Texas and Louisiana in the USA."

Pointing to a map on a projected screen, he launched into the details of the attack. "Five TU 160 stealth bombers will leave our joint Arctic command base at Tiksi in the East Siberian Sea, and fly over Russian Territory towards the Kamchatka Peninsula in the Bering Sea. From here, they will alter course, head out over the Aleutian Islands, and chart a course heading half-way between Hawaii and the western seaboard of the USA. Before getting within range of any early warning radar on Hawaii, the aircraft will turn towards the US / Mexico border. Flying along the Mexican side of the border, at a maximum cruising speed of two thousand two hundred kilometres per hour, the aircraft will be within launching range for the Cruise missiles within fifty minutes."

The general stared at the group for hints of comprehension of his plan. The FSB head was the first to raise his hand with a question. "You say they will be within launching distance using Cruise missiles; my sources tell me that the US oil is kept deep underground, in salt caverns. How will you be able to strike so deep underground?" With a wry smile, the general clicked the mouse, and showed another diagram on the projected screen.

"Quite simple really, Comrade. You are right; we could never penetrate deeply enough to ignite the oil. So each site will be hit by four missiles. The first two missiles are designed to bury into the rock formation and create a crater, using conventional explosives. The second two missiles contain a mixed payload consisting of high explosives and radioactive material. I believe the Americans call it a dirty bomb. These missiles will be guided into the craters formed by the first two missiles; when they detonate deep under the ground, they will cause fissures in the rock, some of which will lead to igniting the oil but most of which will simply allow the radiation in the dirty bomb to seep into the salt caverns. We cannot guarantee that we will destroy all of their oil; but we can guarantee that we will irradiate it, and make it useless for the next thousand years!"

There was a sigh of appreciation around the table, as the committee began to realise the enormity of the strike. "I have one more question, General," said the Head of the FSB. "How will our bombers fly back to Russia after the attack, with no fuel on board?"

"They won't. Instead they will fly over Cuba, and directly on to our air base near Caracas in Venezuela."

The older FSB man sat back in his chair, and began to grin. "General, my compliments to you and your staff. It is a brilliant plan."

The Russian President had been watching the reaction of his council as the plan had been unveiled to them. He couldn't sense any opposition to the plan. The men from the state oil company looked a little uncomfortable, but as long as they received their regular payments to their overseas accounts, they wouldn't cause any trouble.

"So, now you have heard our response to the cowardly attack on our nation. I am also proposing further sanctions. This attack is an opportunity for Russia also to punish the European Union. As of today, we will use the damage to our pipelines as the excuse we needed to stop pumping oil and gas to Europe.

"The EU is a fractious organisation and they only have, by our estimates, about forty-five days' worth of oil reserves." Turning to the head of Russian oil production for confirmation, the President continued. We will increase our production and export to China to offset the loss in income from the European markets. The Chinese are ready to buy as much oil and gas as we can sell them at the moment, and, because it is not due to go online for another month, the new China-Russia pipeline was not affected by this attack."

After agreeing to reconvene the committee some thirty hours later, so that each man assembled around the table would be seated together when the strike occurred, Oleg Vasilienko dismissed the committee and left the room. The men filed out one by one; some of the oil men headed down the corridor to the Trade Ministry. The air force general returned to the air force HQ to finalise his attack plans, and issue the clearances required to remove from storage the nuclear materials that were to form the core of the dirty bomb.

The FSB Chief left with his junior aide. Responding to a message on his encrypted phone, he made a swift call to his operations officer for Mongolia and ordered that two of Ganzorig's men be picked up for questioning. He made the call as he and the aide travelled back together the short drive to the FSB Headquarters at Lubyanka Square.

Once the vehicle had arrived at the square, the FSB Head turned to his younger aide, and said, "You should go home now to your wife. Eat, drink and sleep. Who knows, in just over twenty-four hours we may all be very busy people indeed." The younger aide nodded curtly to his Director, and began to walk away, his mind in turmoil, desperately trying to make sense of what he had just witnessed in the meeting. He needed to talk to someone about it. He couldn't speak to his wife. No, he needed to talk to someone he could trust, but someone outside of the FSB.

Chapter Thirty-Eight

Latitude 1° 17' 28.8348'', Longitude 103° 47' 13.3296''.
United Nations Centre for Technology and Culture
Headquarters, Heng Mui Keng Terrace, Singapore
Ten p.m. Singapore time – 6 Sep 2017.
Finding Solutions

Seated once more around the round conference table, Li opened the discussion by scribbling out the three questions on a white board. 1. How will Russia respond? 2. How can we respond to a global fuel shortage? Finally, 3. Who is behind this and how do we stop them?

"OK, who is going to start us off on the first question?" Li said, glancing around the room.

Matthias spoke first. "I find the silence from Moscow the most interesting and telling sign. I believe they are going to strike back."

"At whom?" asked Maria.

"Well, they haven't stated who they think is behind the attack, but with relations with China at an all-time high, and relations with the US at their lowest ebb since the end of the cold war, I would say that the US would be the obvious target."

"What?" exclaimed Maria. "We need to warn them!"

"We will," interrupted Li, trying to calm Maria down. After this meeting, I am writing up a report to go to the Secretary-General of the UN. He will ensure that the US get the information. Remember, all we have is speculation. How ready is America to defend itself?"

"Good question. I would say, not very ready at all. All the budgets for the military defence of the US continent were slashed in the early 1990s, at the end of the Cold War. With the new government's pivot towards Asia, most of our best equipment and resources are now in Japan or Australia. The high oil price has restricted many exercises and routine maritime and air patrols, and the bloated defence budget is under real strain because of many expensive equipment procurement overruns. I don't think we have ever been in a worse position to try to defend America from a direct attack. Besides, we don't even know how they would try to attack."

"Thank you for that very frank assessment, Maria. Next, how do we deal with a global fuel shortage?"

Philippe started to speak first. "Charu and I have been on the phone to our Technology Transfer Centres around the world. The good news is that, from a technological perspective, we can make up a lot of the shortfall in energy demand through other means. I'm not sure how it will go down politically…"

Philippe continued to outline how the technologies developed by the CTC could be used and deployed around the world. "The bottom line is that we already have proven technologies, and we are prepared to give away the patents through the United Nations, so that countries can rapidly develop their own carbon-free energy production. Most of the world's coastal cities could employ a scaled-up version of the wave technology that we have developed in Girona. Charu and I estimate that these hydropower generating farms could contribute nearly eighty per cent of the electricity requirements for the world's major coastal cities."

As Philippe spoke, Charu flashed up graphs and charts on the wall-mounted LCD display screen.

"The snake-like devices that we use to convert the wave energy into electrical current are easily manufactured, and would take skilled engineers no more than three weeks to manufacture, and another week to install, if the governments applied sufficient resources to the task. The Ion Removing Integrated System which we have developed in Gander collects ions from storms either from vapour or dust clouds. Well, because of global warming, the one thing that we seem to have much more of at the moment is storms. The plants are actually easy to set up, and would be ideal for power generation in the American Mid-West, Central Europe and China. They supply a local network with power day or night; the only restriction is that they need friction in the air. The current El Niño effect in the Atlantic should be strong enough for the next few months, and, further south, the Asian Monsoons will keep power generation going for at least two months."

Matthias interrupted, commenting, "It's a little ironic, isn't it, that climate change, caused through man-made global warming, will now actually work to our benefit?"

Philippe concluded his presentation. "Finally, if we can convince governments to install piezo-crystal pads into public infrastructure such as railway stations, major pedestrian walkways, even inner-city congested roads and electrified railway lines, we could see a dramatic increase in human-powered electricity generation within the major population centres."

"Thank you, Philippe. I will pass on your report, and the figures that you and Charu came up with the to the Secretary-General. I also think that our colleagues at the World Bank and IMF will need advance warning of this."

Li now stood to add substance to what he was about to say. "Finally, we must now look at the most vexing question of the three. Who is doing this? Why are they doing this, and how are they doing this?"

Philippe once more began to address the group. "I have been examining the oil sample sent to me by my German colleague, as well as discussing the events with my former professor in Canada. The curious thing about the attacks is that in the case of Russia and China, both governments reported that the oil had been destroyed, yet no oil fires had been witnessed. This got me to thinking about how oil could be destroyed without burning it up. The sample from Germany clearly shows that the chemical structure of the oil has been changed. It has undergone some form of biodegradation."

Philippe then went on to explain how the oil might have been affected. "You may know that the oil industry uses bacterial detergents at major oil spill sites to clean up the polluted water. In essence, the detergents degrade the oil until it can be absorbed by the sea. I asked my old professor whether there was anything commercially available that could have been used. He said quite adamantly that nothing on the market today could have such a great effect in such a small time. He did mention, though, that there was some talk that, years ago, during the Second World War, the Nazis had been working on a way to destroy large quantities of oil, to stop it falling into Allied hands. I have sent a priority research request to the German National Archives for any papers or information they may hold, related to this type of research."

Li interrupted. "OK, so we have the 'how', despite its being a far-fetched theory at the moment. What about the Who and Why?"

Matthias was the next to stand up. "Li and I are convinced that this is not the work of a specific country, but rather of a non-state actor with a lot to gain from seeing the economic paralysis of the major powers and the chaos that it brings with it. As Charu will explain further, we have linked it to some clues that were found during your exercise in Northern Iraq. Firstly, there is strong evidence of some sort of Mongolian involvement. Andrei's FSB colleagues are currently questioning several known Mongolian nationalists about their recent activities. We hope to find out more about their involvement soon. However, I don't think the Mongolians stand to gain a great deal from a destabilised world order.

"Today, thanks to Maria's contacts at the US Department of Defense, we received a list of names of Arabs targeted by drone strike within the last six months. We found no Iraqi nationals on the targeting list; however, when Charu went back through the data her algorithm managed to extract the name of an Arab who was killed as collateral damage in a strike against a Pakistani target. His name is Dr Faisal Al Abbasin, a Baghdad based physics professor. We have checked out his background, and neither he or his family have any history of political activity. So it seems that we are at another dead end."

"Charu," Li said. "What have you made of this puzzle so far?"

"Well, I confirmed that the book of Qi was indeed printed in Mongolia. We located the publisher. They couldn't give us any details about the purchaser, as the purchase was completed in cash. They can confirm that it was a small order. Only twenty copies were printed. Based on DNA evidence left in the book recovered from the attack in Mosul, I scanned the pages from the Book of Qi that were most thumbed through. I then wrote an algorithm with Li's help, searching for key words pertaining to the current situation that might appear in the strategies written in the book. My algorithm produced the following results."

Charu flashed up a list of five strategies most commonly read in the book of Qi belonging to Ali.

"One. Borrow a corpse to resurrect the soul: Chapter Three.

"Take an institution, a technology, a method, or even an ideology that has been forgotten or discarded, and appropriate it for your own purpose. Revive something from the past by giving it a new purpose or bring to life old ideas, customs, or traditions and reinterpret them to fit your purposes

"Two. Kill with a borrowed sword: Chapter One.

"Attack using the strength of another (in a situation where using one's own strength is not favourable). Trick an ally into attacking him, bribe an official to turn traitor, or use the enemy's own strength against him. The idea here is to cause damage to the enemy by getting a third party to do the deed.

"Three. Watch the fires burning across the river: Chapter Two.

"Delay entering the field of battle until all the other players have become exhausted fighting amongst themselves. Then go in at full strength, and pick up the pieces.

"Four. Slough off the Cicada's golden shell: Chapter Four.

"Mask yourself. Either leave your distinctive traits behind, thus becoming inconspicuous, or masquerade as something or someone else. This strategy is mainly used to escape from an enemy.

"Five. Make the Host and the Guest exchange roles: Chapter Five.

"Usurp leadership in a situation where you are normally subordinate. Infiltrate your target. Initially, pretend to be a guest to be accepted, but develop from inside, and become the owner later.

Li took over at this point. "I think you will agree: quite amazing work by Charu. When we examine these stratagems, it is possible to divide them into two groups, those that may already have been used, and those yet to be put into use. The first strategy may well apply to the technology, as yet currently unknown, that is being employed to destroy the global oil stockpiles. The second strategy, we believe, is pointing at how the original attackers of the Chinese site managed to get the Chinese to counter-attack the Japanese storage sites; and, unless I am mistaken, how it may cause the Russians to strike back at America. The third strategy is the final one in the group of strategies that have already been used. Matthias and I believe it is their most important strategy. The reason behind implementing strategies one and two was simply to sow the seeds of global chaos and economic fragility; a type of deception, if you like. We believe that the aim is to limit the ability of the major powers to interfere in whatever the ultimate goal of this group is.

"The last two strategies relate in some way to a rebirth, renaissance or re-genesis if you like. Again, at this point, we are uncertain whether we are talking about a new country being formed, or a new ideology becoming reborn." Li looked to Matthias for a summary.

"Well, it is certainly a mystery, but based on the evidence from the attacks and considering who would have the most to gain from the escalation in oil prices, we think the group is Middle Eastern, maybe Iranian, although there seem to be a lot of clues linking back to Iraq.

"Some sort of chemical or bacterial agent that is not commercially available is being used to destroy oil supplies, which points to a group with access to advanced scientific research. That is about all we can say at this moment."

"Thank you, Matthias," said Li. "Does anyone have anything to add at this stage?" There was silence around the room; it was midnight in Singapore, and Li could see how tired the team were. "In that case, thank you all for your input. I will send our findings to the UN Secretary - General in New York. Andrei and Maria, please let me know as soon as you hear anything further from your governments. I suggest you all get some well-deserved rest. We still have a lot of work ahead of us. I will expect to see you all in here at seven a.m. sharp."

Chapter Thirty-Nine

Birds in the Air

Li returned to his office and started to type up the report for his friend Guilherme, the Secretary-General of the UN. The rest of the team left the building one by one. Maria had told Andrei that she was tired and preferred to go back to her apartment to sleep.

"Is everything OK between us?" asked Andrei.

"Sure," replied Maria. "I just, you know, need some time to myself."

"OK, I'll see you in the morning. Do you want me to pick you up on the way into work?"

"Yes, that would be good. I'd like that."

Andrei drove back to his apartment on his own. He was worried about Maria; she had been odd ever since the meeting when he had been discussing the information sent from his FSB contact. He didn't feel tired, and, after being trapped inside the office all day, he decided to take himself out for a run. The temperature was perfect at midnight, the streets were quiet, and it would give him the opportunity to think. He quickly pulled on a pair of running shorts and a tight fitting vest top, and exited his apartment.

It felt good to run, to move unhindered, to be able to think. He never ran with music or headphones, and he had left his phone at home. Completely unencumbered, he began to pick up the pace and gradually felt his body relaxing into his comfortable loping stride. Gliding effortlessly forward, he steadied his breathing and entered his trance-like state that he so enjoyed when running. It had been a long time since he had enjoyed a run as much as this. Arriving back at his apartment, he checked the time on his mobile phone and saw that he had been gone for over two and a half hours.

Standing on his balcony, he began his regular post-workout stretching routine; as he was looking across the Singapore skyline, he noticed in the corner of his eye, a light blue light flashing on his mobile phone. Realising that he had a voice message, he pressed play. The voice belonged to Russian male. Andrei immediately recognised it as his old friend from FSB headquarters. His words were slurred and he sounded quite drunk and very upset. He didn't say what the problem was but kept pleading in the message for Andrei to call him back.

Snatching up the handset, Andrei quickly redialed the number. "Pyotr! Is that you?"

"*Da*, my old friend Andrei; thank God you called."

"Are you OK? You sound drunk."

"Ha, I am drunk, my old friend. I have not slept. I must speak to you. Is this line secure?"

"Certainly, what is it? What is so important?"

"Our fool of a President is launching missiles at the USA. Missiles with nuclear material inside, which will pollute most of the Gulf of Mexico for decades." Andrei could not believe his ears. Rushing inside, he grabbed a notebook and pen and sat down.

Returning to the phone, notepad in hand, Andrei tried to clear his head and understand what his old friend was saying. "Pyotr, what are you saying. Are you serious?"

"I was at the meeting myself. I saw the evidence with my own eyes. Our government has recovered a US military satnav from near the site of one of the oil pipeline attacks."

"But then surely they should take this evidence to the UNSC and discuss it?"

"That would be the action of a sane man. I fear our President is not a sane man. He has found his excuse to strike back at the USA and he has done so."

Barely able to comprehend the words his old friend had just spoken, Andrei interrupted. "Did you say he HAD launched an attack against the US?"

"Yes, my friend, that is why I was so desperate to contact you. We must stop this madness before he starts World War Three."

"Give me details," Andrei said. He was slowly regaining his composure, and his years of training as an FSB agent were beginning to kick into action.

"Pyotr, sit down, take a breath and calm yourself. I need you to tell me exactly what you know."

"*Da*, OK, I will tell you all I know. A strike will be launched by our long range stealth bombers. They will fly from Russia and target the US underground salt caverns containing the strategic oil reserves with Cruise missiles. Some of the missiles have nuclear material in them. The idea is to irradiate the oil and make it and the surrounding area unusable."

"That's good, Pyotr, keep talking. How many planes are they sending, and how will they fly to America?"

"Five bombers will fly low from our sub-arctic base on the East Siberian Sea. They will fly over Russian territory to remain undetected as far as the Bering Sea; only then will they cross the Aleutian Islands and head over the Pacific. The ocean is so vast that unless you knew the planes were there, or where to look, you would never find them. Then they will turn towards the US, but remain on the Mexican side of the border until they reach the Gulf of Mexico."

Scribbling down notes furiously in his pad, Andrei was already thinking of how he should act. "Pyotr, when is this going to happen?"

"It has already started."

"What?"

"It has already started; the planes are being fuelled and armed as we speak. They will leave the Arctic Command HQ in around two hours, to begin their long flight south. They will refuel over the Bering Sea, before they reach the Aleutian Islands; then they will lose altitude, and fly at nearly Mach Two all the way to the target.

"My God," thought Andrei. He had joined the FSB after the Cold War had ended, and thought that this kind of madness had finished for good. "Listen, Pyotr. You have done the right thing. Thank you, my friend. I will ensure that none of this is attributable to you."

Hanging up the call, his head buzzing, not wanting to comprehend what he had just been told, he forced himself to calm down and think logically. What should he do? He had to tell someone. Picking up his phone once more, he dialed Li's number. After recounting the story to Li, and promising to meet him at the CTC HQ, he called Maria and told her he was on his way over to pick her up. "What is going on, Andrei? I got a Maximum Priority Flash message from Li saying we had to be in work as soon as possible?"

"I'll tell you in the car. We have no time to lose."

A confused and tired group of people assembled in the briefing room, to hear Andrei recount his conversation with his FSB contact. "Whatever happens, those planes need to be stopped before they reach the US. Apart from the economic and environmental damage those bombs will cause, there is absolutely no way on this earth that the US government will allow an attack by Russia to go unpunished. This could escalate into a major confrontation between the two most heavily armed countries in the world."

Matthias didn't need to stress the point any further. He had made his point. The team were the only people in the world outside of the Kremlin that were aware of an impending nuclear attack by Russia on the USA.

"OK, let's focus," said Charu. "What do we know? And how can we use the information?" The team went back over the details of the attack that had been relayed to Andrei from the FSB contact. Dividing themselves into smaller groups of shared expertise, Maria and Andrei examined the details of the TU 160 Stealth Bombers and the AS 15 Kent Cruise missiles they were carrying, trying to uncover any weaknesses in these superfast stealth bombers and high tech guided missiles. Philippe and Penny spent their time examining the impact of any such strike and the effect of the nuclear fallout.

They were busy calculating the latest time at which they would have to tell the Americans about the attack, so that civilians could be evacuated from the area, when Charu interrupted the group. "Listen up, you guys. I may have something here." The team crowded around her multi-panel computer display screen and she began to talk excitedly. OK, I have inputted everything we know as fact about the attack: the type of plane, flight speeds, point of departure and attack site. Then I ran a simple programme to determine probable flight paths, considering their need for speed, fuel efficiency – it's a long way from the East Siberian Sea to the Gulf of Mexico – and then I had to factor in their desire to remain outside of radar detection."

Penny cut in. "That's this red line here, is it?" She stubbed her finger on the left-hand monitor, which displayed a map of the world with a red line of trajectory arcing down from northern Russia to the southern United States.

"Yeah, that's it," replied Charu.

"Do you notice anything unusual?" Li interrupted. "Charu, we haven't time to play games. This is…"

Li was interrupted as, in unison both Philippe and Matthias shouted out "UNALASKA!"

"What?" said Li, already annoyed at being cut off. Philippe spoke first. "The planes have to fly over the Aleutian Islands, where we have our Inuit power project."

"Exactly," replied Charu. "Do you remember when we visited Gander in Newfoundland, and that sweet old Japanese Professor Kobayashi, and the Director, the lovely Charlie Armand, never stopped talking about Nicola Tesla?

"Yeah," cut in Penny. "It was almost like they worshipped him."

"Not far off," said Philippe.

"Tesla was a genius who pioneered work on electricity, which has led today to such things as our use of wi-fi; I do remember reading that he worked in secret for the US Department of War and that he claimed to have developed a directed electrical energy weapon that could destroy whole buildings."

"It wasn't just a myth," Charu interjected, now speaking quickly and excitedly. "His idea paved the way for the invention of a weapon that, although it has never been used in anger, certainly exists in more than just theoretical terms."

"Will someone tell me what they are talking about?" moaned Matthias.

Philippe patted his old friend on the shoulder to calm him down and began to explain. "An Electro Magnetic Pulse weapon, or EMP. It is actually super-easy to build and operate, although directionality can be a little difficult."

"Can anyone explain to me in English just what he is talking about?" retorted a frustrated Matthias. Charu took over.

"Simple, you release a large amount of stored electricity into the environment in one burst. This has the effect of frying any electronic components or electrical circuits in the surrounding area."

"Would it work? I mean would it bring down those aircraft?" Maria asked.

Andrei was the first to answer. "It could; you see, although the cockpits of those TU 160's look outdated, with their analogue dials, the whole plane is actually flown by wire. You know, there are no hard linkages between the controls and the wing surfaces or engines; it is all electronic."

Catching up at last, Matthias summarised. "So what you are suggesting is that we send an electro-magnetic burst into the air above the Inuit settlements as these planes are flying over? And this burst of energy will be enough to knock them out of the sky?"

"Exactly," said Charu. "We have everything we need right there on Unalaska. The Inuit power project uses the Ion Removing Integrated System, which collects positively charged ion particles from the storm clouds and stores the energy in the large capacitor storage facility. All we need to do is reverse the process and release the stored energy in a concentrated burst, straight up into the atmosphere."

"I think you are forgetting something," cut in Andrei. "Those are stealth planes, which will be flying at approximately two thousand kilometres per hour. How the hell are you going to fire your homemade energy weapon at the right time?"

"He has a point," interjected Li.

"The fishing fleet," said Matthias.

"What?" exclaimed Li. "The fishing fleet. All the trawlers in Unalaska are fitted with radar and good communications gear, as well as GPS guidance systems. We send out the fleet to form a cordon at known intervals in waves above the Islands, say, ten kilometre distances. Then they report by sight or sound as the planes fly overhead. By triangulating the reports from the boats we will know the speed and direction of the planes."

"You know, it might just work," said Philippe. "But we are going to need some serious help."

In thirty minutes, a rough plan had been formed. It had been decided that if the plan failed, and they didn't knock the planes out of the sky over Unalaska then they would have to inform the US and UN of the impending Russian attack. Charu had worked out approximate timescales, and Philippe and Matthias were busy contacting everyone they knew in the Inuit community on Unalaska, to get the trawlermen briefed up and ready to put to sea. Luckily, it was ten a.m. in Unalaska, and most of the trawler men would already be in the harbour, working on their boats.

In Gander, it was nearly five p.m. when Charu contacted Charlie Armand and Professor Kobayashi to explain her idea and see if they agreed. Charlie, ever the pragmatist, and thrilled at the thought of attempting to recreate one of Tesla's inventions, said it could be done. The Professor was a little more reticent, and explained that the emission of so much energy through the delicate IRIS collector array would certainly destroy the equipment and would be hazardous for any humans standing nearby. With that said, they got straight on to the phone with their technicians who were working at Unalaska, monitoring the progress of the Inuit power programme, and began briefing them on what they had to do.

Chapter Forty

Three thousand kilometres to the North of Unalaska, the Commander of the five TU 160 long-range strategic bombers was queued up behind another of his aircraft as they circled high above the Bering Sea in a holding pattern, waiting for all five giant bombers to be refuelled. This was always a perilous and nerve-sapping task, trying to couple two jet aircraft with a hose supplying thousands of gallons of highly flammable fuel, whilst flying at over five hundred kilometres per hour. Today, the task was even more dangerous, thought the colonel in charge of the operation, considering the cargo of cruise missiles that each plane carried.

The colonel, a veteran flyer from the Soviet Afghanistan conflict, and from the more recent Chechen war, was a proud ex-Soviet officer who had believed that, when he had been posted to the command of a long-range strategic bomber squadron in 2015, it had meant the end of his career. I mean, everybody knew that these planes would never leave the ground again, except for the odd air display or training exercise. Now here he was, circling over the Bering Sea, with four other planes armed with a full complement of cruise missiles heading out over the Pacific, on a mission that would see him strike at the heart of his country's former enemy, the USA.

"Colonel," came the voice over the radio. It was the commander of the refuelling tanker. "Colonel, all aircraft are refuelled, we are turning back now. Good luck on your mission, sir." The colonel acknowledged the tanker pilot with a brief message, then addressed the other four bombers under his command.

"Eagles Two, Three, Four and Five. This is Eagle One. We are now about to leave Russian airspace. In approximately three hours, we will pass over the Aleutian Islands, then on over the Pacific. We will head due east, towards the US-Mexico border approximately six hours later, depending on the head-winds. Our estimated time for missile release will be eleven a.m. tomorrow, Moscow time. I wish you all good luck. We will be on radio silence from here on. Remain on the pre-programmed coordinates until or unless I tell you otherwise. Eagle Four, confirm Over." Eagle Four confirmed the Colonel's orders, and the radios went silent.

Charu figured that the EMP device would affect an area roughly twenty cubic kilometres in size and had calculated that the EMP device would have to be discharged or fired in a time window of just thirty-six seconds. The maths was relatively simple. Five objects, travelling at two thousand kilometres per hour, flying in close formation, displaced no more than one hundred metres apart from each other, would pass over the area of the electro-magnetic pulse from the IRIS site in under forty seconds. Of course, the reports from the triangulated signals from the trawlers would confirm the exact speed, and the technicians at the IRIS site in Unalaska would be able to fine-tune the energy release accordingly.

Tulugaq and Tikaani, the two Inuit brothers who had hunted walrus several months before with Matthias and Philippe, had been joined by Taliriktug, Uki and Tikaani's wife Tapeesa. It was eleven a.m. in the morning, and, having received the message from Matthias and Philippe, they had sprung immediately into action.

The Inuit people had no love for the Russians. It was the Russian fur traders who had brought disease and alcohol to the islands, and nearly wiped out the entire Inuit people. Uki, Taliriktug and Tapeesa had jumped into their vehicles, and driven around the small fishing community corralling the boat crews and setting up a temporary briefing room in the harbour-master's office. All of the boats were ready and fuelled. The fleet and its crews had been in harbour for a little over a week, because of the bad weather, and were itching to get back out to sea.

Tulugaq and Tikaani were with the two technicians from the TTC in Gander. They had brought a short wave radio with them and set about helping the technicians set up the IRIS equipment, so that, instead of charging the capacitors, it would discharge a huge electro-magnetic pulse in a little under a second. Tikaani now monitored the radio, and was carefully recording the messages from the trawlermen, who were sitting in their boats off the shore of Unalaska, in three rows set ten kilometres apart.

Effectively, they formed a huge, all-seeing radar and visual detection barrier. The trawlermen had no military training, but every single boat's captain knew how to report his course, using GPS co-ordinates and compass bearings. More importantly, they knew what to look for out in the rough seas and skies north of Unalaska. The only thing not in the Inuits' favour was the weather. For the past week, a huge block of low pressure had sat over their section of the Aleutian Islands and had stubbornly refused to move.

The seas were a roiling mass of churning water and the rain hadn't stopped for five consecutive days. The men were unhappy at the thought of leaving the safety of the harbour in the rough seas. However, these were brave, patriotic men, and, after they had listened to the impassioned pleas for help in the recorded message from Philippe at the CTC, that had been played to them during their hasty thirty-minute-long brief, they had unanimously agreed to help.

Tikaani was sitting at a table in the hut on the hill top where the large IRIS array had been set up. He was hunched over the sea charts, listening to the radio reports and carefully continuing to mark the positions of the boats on the map in front of him.

"Bob," he shouted to one of the technicians. "Say, Bob, just how many volts will this thing produce?"

"Good question, Tikaani. To be fair, we are not too sure. We calculate around five thousand volts per minute."

"Wow, that's some power, man."

"Yeah; actually it's only about half what a purpose built EMP weapon would produce. But the point is how quickly we can discharge the electricity. You see, what we are aiming for is to create a violent and intense magnetic field. It is this magnetic field that will fry the circuit boards on those planes."

Tikaani was just about to respond when his radio crackled into life. "Ground station, this is the Arctic Corsair; we spotted four to five planes heading one hundred and ninety-two degrees from our position."

"Arctic Corsair, this is Ground Station. Roger that, I confirm one hundred and ninety-two degrees."

"Roger." As he was speaking, Tulugaq had drawn a straight line from the boat's position towards the islands.

"OK," said the technician, "We know where they will appear, and it is in range of our little EMP machine; we just need to confirm when."

Tikaani checked his watch; it was just before one p.m. He made a note of the time in his radio log.

He had barely finished speaking when the radio sprang back into life. "Ground Station, Ground Station, this is the Northern Warrior. I see planes heading one hundred and ninety-four degrees."

"Northern Warrior, I confirm one hundred and ninety-four degrees. Thanks and Out." Before Tikaani had even put down the radio, Tulugaq had drawn the second line on the chart from the last reported sighting. This boat was twenty kilometres closer to the islands. The two technicians briefly conferred with each other, then ran to the main control box.

"Guys, you gotta get out of here. This is going to be real loud, and mighty dangerous," said one of the technicians. Tulugaq and Tikaani didn't need telling twice; they jumped up and sprinted for the door. "There! I've set the timer; we have twenty-six seconds before this thing blows." Running frantically, the two technicians left the hut out into the stormy night sky and stumbled down the rain sodden slopes of the hill.

Suddenly, as if they had been pushed in the back by the hand of a giant, all four men fell forward and began to tumble down the side of the hill. The air was rushing past them, and all they could feel was an intense pressure in their ears. Coming to rest at the foot of a muddy boulder field, the four men looked back up the hill towards the hut and the IRIS antenna array.

The hut was on fire, and what remained of the intricate fractal like antenna array was a mangled mess of charred and molten materials. Looking skyward, hoping to see the bombers fall from the sky, all they saw was a dark swirling maelstrom of cloud and rain. Had it worked? Tikaani was the first to catch his breath and speak.

"Did we do it?" he shouted, to be understood over the noise of the howling wind.

The technician replied, "We certainly caused the EMP. I just don't know if we hit the planes."

Flying at an altitude of only three thousand metres, the crew of the lead bomber were being buffeted about by the violent storm raging around them. Since leaving their arctic base, and with the inevitable delays that air to air refueling causes, the aircraft had been in the sky for well over nine hours by now. As the lead stealth bomber drew within a hundred kilometres of the Aleutian Islands, the navigator confirmed course and the radar operator pointed out the fishing boats near the sea.

The aircraft's crew thought it strange that the trawlers would be out in such bad weather, and, even stranger still, they couldn't understand why the fishing boats seemed to be clustered together so tightly. Surely fishermen needed space to tow their huge trawler nets? What do I know, thought the Air Force Colonel. He turned to his navigator, and said, "This weather is getting worse. I want to lose some more height to try and get beneath this low pressure front."

"*Da*," said the navigator.

Tilting the wireless joystick forward slightly, the colonel caused the huge, heavily-laden bomber to begin a gradual descent. Just as the aircraft's sleek pointed nose began to pierce the cloud cover, 'BANG!'

"What the hell was that?" screamed the colonel. No reply came from his crew. His voice had not been transmitted through the intercom. He tried again, looking at his radar operator, who was staring uncomprehendingly at a blank screen.

The entire cockpit had gone dark, and the colonel struggled to see his radar man and navigator. Pulling back on the tiny joy stick, to try to come out of the shallow dive and level the plane out, the colonel felt no reaction. He knew he wouldn't feel anything through his fingers: no strain, no pressure. But he expected to feel it in his body, to feel the sensation as the plane levelled itself out. Nothing.

"Yuri!" the colonel cried, removing his radio mask. "Yuri, status report!"

"We have lost all power. Have we been hit?"

"The radar reported no missile lock before it went dead."

"Systems check!" screamed the colonel, desperately trying to stop the plane from diving into the cold Northern Pacific. "We have no power to the engines. Weapons systems are offline, and we have no navigational support."

"My God!" said the colonel, as the sleek nose-cone of the bomber once more burst through a patch of cloud to confront him with the horrifying site of the cold Pacific Ocean seemingly bearing up towards them at great speed.

At a little past one p.m., on the 7th of September, 2017, during a violent storm, just south of Unalaska, the Russian TU 160 stealth bomber, with its full complement of four Cruise missiles, struck the surface of the Pacific Ocean at over nine hundred kilometres per hour. It disintegrated on contact with the roiling ocean surface, and many of the heavier sections, including the missiles, plunged downwards to the ocean floor below. The other four planes followed their lead plane on its spiraling journey to their graves at the bottom of the freezing ocean. No signal was sent by the brave crew reporting their position.

Tulugaq, Tikaani and the two technicians had recovered their senses, and had begun to descend the mountain to their SUV. Tikaani tried the ignition but nothing happened. Just as he was about to try again, the technician stopped him. "Don't bother," he said, with a smile on his face. "The electrics are fried. I guess if we needed confirmation that the EMP was actually produced, then here it is."

The other technician interrupted. "I guess we aren't that clever after all."

"What do you mean?" replied the first technician.

"We just blew five nuclear stealth bombers out of the sky!"

"Well, firstly, all we know at this stage is that we recreated Nicola Tesla's famous electro-magnetic pulse. We need to see if the trawlers find any evidence of wreckage in the ocean. Secondly, and at the moment more importantly, we are five kilometres away from the harbour, in the middle of an arctic storm and we have no car!"

"Oh," said the other technician, a little sheepishly, turning to look at Tulugaq and Tikaani.

"Don't worry," said Tikaani. "We know this land like the back of our hand. If we move quickly we will be back in the harbour master's office, drinking hot coffee, in a little under two hours."

Two hours later, Tulugaq and Tikaani arrived at the harbour-master's office, where, only a few hours before, the trawlermen had gathered to be briefed about the situation. Two Inuit, and two very tired and wet technicians, entered the office. Once inside, they removed their mud-stained and rain-soaked parkas, grabbed a hot cup of coffee, and began to explain what had happened to Tapeesa, who had been monitoring the radio sets from the harbour master's office.

After embracing his wife for a long time, Tikaani began to speak. "Tapeesa, call the fishermen back in. We did it!"

"It worked!" she replied in surprise.

"Well, we certainly sent five thousand volts into the sky above the mountain, and nearly blew ourselves up trying to do it."

"Did you see the planes fall out of the sky?"

"Er, no. When the explosion happened, we were outside in the storm, and the EMP blast knocked us over and threw us down the hill."

"Oh my!" declared Tapeesa, tears of relief in her eyes.

"You need to send two teams of trawlers around the south and north of the Island to begin a search for the wreckage," one of the technicians broke in.

"I have a rough set of co-ordinates, based on their bearing, altitude and speed, that should help the trawlers start their search. Philippe and the CTC said that it is vital that we find some wreckage, otherwise the Russians will deny that the event ever happened."

Latitude 55° 45' 7.2828'', Longitude 37° 37' 2.9964'' Kremlin / US Strategic Oil Storage Sites – 8 September 2017.
Countdown

Bob Johnson had been working at the Bryan Mound Salt Caverns in Freeport, Texas for over five years. He knew his government job was important. Bryan Mound was one of only four major strategic oil storage sites belonging to the US Government. Beneath his feet sat millions of barrels of crude oil, millions of barrels of oil that would protect his country if those dammed Arabs decided they wanted to go to war again in the Middle East, he thought to himself, spitting out his chewing tobacco on to the dusty floor as he walked to his four-wheel drive truck.

Bob's job was a simple one. He was responsible for the surface site. This meant that he and his men did a couple of patrols around the perimeter twice a day; they conducted guided tours for new congressmen who bothered to travel all the way down from Washington to see the sites, and, once every twelve hours, he checked the five monitoring sites that gave him real-time readings about the atmosphere in the salt chambers where the oil was stored. Recently, Bob had noticed a sharp increase in the number of visitors to the site. In the last couple of weeks, all manner of agencies had descended on the site: NSA, CIA, FBI, along with a whole host of Senators from Capitol Hill. Bob wasn't a technical man; he'd barely scraped through high school, but he was a patriot and he was glad of his government-paid job. Today, on this bright sunny August day, he set about doing his work at the site, much the same as he had every day and much the same, he mused to himself, as he hoped to do until he retired in ten years' time.

Over nine thousand five hundred kilometres away, in Moscow, it was ten thirty in the morning; a very select committee of some of the most influential people in Russia was sitting in the President's private briefing room, awaiting news of the missile strike. The heads of Russia's oil industry, intelligence services and armed forces sat around the large boardroom table. President Oleg Vasilienko sat at its head. He was in an unusually ebullient mood. He knew himself that this moment would be the defining moment in his political career, and he wanted all of these men of power to be here to witness it.

The large projector screen showed images from one of Russia's weather satellites that had moved position, and now showed real-time pictures of the Gulf of Mexico. General Pyotr Bukharev, the chief of the aerospace command, was sitting next to the President, anxiously looking at his watch.

"Relax, Pyotr," purred the President. "In a little under thirty minutes, the whole world will once again witness the awesome power of Russia, and you, General, will be remembered as one of Russia's great patriots."

The talk in the room gradually petered out, as the countdown clock ticked down towards zero hour. Every man in the room was transfixed on the live satellite images being beamed halfway around the world into the President's office. One minute remaining: Pyotr Bukharev was beginning to sweat inside his dress uniform. Surely they would have seen the five bombers by now on their screen. I mean, the satellite image covered an area of over one hundred kilometres. 5.4.3.2.1. The countdown clock stopped.

The atmosphere in the room was palpable. A flushed-faced Oleg Vasilienko, the Russian President turned to his head of aerospace, and, in a quietly menacing voice, said, "Where are the explosions, General? Where are the bombers? Did they just vanish?"

Flustered, and, by now, sweating profusely, the general stammered a reply. "Because of the radio silence, we do not know whether they had problems on the way. Maybe they had strong head-winds, or ran into a storm?"

"Supposition! Speculation! Bluster! General, you told me that today I would witness the destruction of the American oil reserves. Well, when is it going to happen?"

The other men sitting around the table were silent, despite more than one of them having spent the previous evening drinking vodka with the air force general, every one of them knew it would be career suicide if they tried to side with the general now.

Briefly recovering his composure, the general spoke once more. "Mr President, gentlemen, I cannot explain what has happened. Maybe there is a problem with the satellite feed, or maybe the planes were delayed for some reason. We have been monitoring the US radar sites, and we can confirm that no aircraft or ships were scrambled to intercept our bombers. They simply appear to have vanished."

"Vanished!" spluttered the apoplectic President, his face now a bright crimson red. Turning to the FSB head, he raged, "Dimitri, take the general to the Lubyanka, learn all you can from him about this mission, and personally investigate what happened. I shall expect a full report in eight hours. Gentlemen, you are dismissed."

The group of Russia's most powerful business and military leaders could not wait to escape the President's office, nearly tripping over each other in their haste to leave. Only General Pyotr Bukharev remained. Standing up from his seat, and looking over at the waiting FSB man, he turned to the President; his body rigid to attention, he saluted, then, removing his hat, he walked out of the office and into the custody of the FSB.

The President remained at the table after the others had left. He was trying to figure out what his next move should be. The first task had to be to try to cover up any trace of the attempted retaliatory missile attack. Then he would take up the matter at the UN Security Council, and deliver an ultimatum to the US Ambassador, stating that the US government should either publicly admit that it had attacked the Russian oil pipeline infrastructure, or it would face Russian military retaliation.

Chapter Forty-One

Latitude 1° 17' 28.8348'', Longitude 103° 47' 13.3296''.
United Nations Centre for Technology and Culture
Headquarters, Heng Mui Keng Terrace, Singapore – Nine
a.m.
8 September 2017.
Mission Accomplished

A loud cheer went up from the exhausted CTC staff, as the phone conversation was broadcast on loudspeaker throughout the building. "We did it!" Tapeesa's voice sounded crystal-clear on the encrypted Satellite phone. Matthias and Philippe could tell she was emotional and probably very tired.

"Tapeesa, tell us what happened?"

"Everything went exactly to plan; the ships managed to send the co-ordinates to the guys on the hill at the IRIS power generating site. We didn't have much time to act. The planes were travelling really fast."

"Hi, Tapeesa, it's Charu. Did they manage to release an EMP?"

Tapeesa looked across the harbour master's office to the two technicians, who, by now, had just about recovered from their ordeal and were sitting drinking hot coffee and listening to the call. "Guys, the team in Singapore want to know if we really did release an electro-magnetic pulse." With sheepish grins at the thought of the long walk back from the site, they both nodded and gave a thumbs up sign. "The tech guys reckon it worked."

"OK, Tapeesa," cut in Li. "We need confirmation as to whether we managed to destroy those bombers, and we need to know we got all of them."

"I understand. We have the trawlers out looking for the wreckage now. We are trying a two-pronged approach. Half of the ships are searching with their high powered sonar – you know, the ones they use to hunt for shoals of fish – and the other half are trawling with their nets to try to catch any debris."

"Thank you, Tapeesa," Li said. "Thank you very much; I cannot express how grateful we are for all that you and your people have done for us today. Please keep in touch and let us know as soon as you have an answer."

Li left the rest of the team celebrating in the main office area.

"I have to go now and report to the Secretary-General. God only knows how he will react?"

Returning to his office, Li picked up his desk phone, and dialled the personal number of the Secretary-General of the United Nations.

"Li, is that you? It's a little late for a call, isn't it?" Guilherme had been sitting with his wife in their apartment, enjoying one of their very rare moments of relaxation together. They had spent the evening enjoying a fine bottle of Californian Shiraz, and, by now, at nearly eleven p.m., both Guilherme and his wife were preparing to go to bed.

"Sorry to disturb you, Guilherme, but I have something of the utmost importance that I need to tell you, and it simply can't wait."

Guilherme knew that the usually calm Chinese man was not prone to exaggeration. "OK, hit me with it. Tell me what is so important," Guilherme said, as he climbed out of the bed, and headed down the hall to his study.

Li began to recount the whole story, from the phone call that Andrei had received, to their detonation of the EMP. Unsure as to how Guilherme would react, Li finished speaking and waited patiently. It was several seconds before Guilherme began to talk.

"Do you mean to tell me that you have singlehandedly stopped a nuclear-armed cruise missile attack against the USA by Russia?"

"Yes, sir; well, at least, I think we did." Guilherme continued to interrogate Li. The questions held no menace. It was simply Guilherme's logical brain trying to make sense of the situation.

"Why didn't you call me the moment you heard about the attack?"

"I own up. That was my decision alone, sir. We discussed the problem amongst the team members, and, collectively, we believed that alerting the US government would have escalated the situation, and maybe led to counter-strikes. Also we believed that stopping those aircraft with their nuclear material and cruise missiles, over the open ocean, and not over heavily populated parts of Texas or the Gulf of Mexico, was important as well."

"I see," said Guilherme. Li was anxious; he couldn't tell if his gamble had paid off. "Li, how long have we known each other? Ten years, fifteen years? In all that time, have I ever questioned your actions?"

Li knew the questions were rhetorical, and just kept quiet at the end of the line. "I need to wake the US Ambassador and speak to him urgently. But if what you say is true, you and your team over there in Singapore may have prevented a global meltdown of unprecedented proportion.

"That international multi-disciplinary team of yours has managed to achieve incredible deeds against nearly impossible odds, whilst the rest of the international community could only sit bickering, finger-pointing and levelling accusations at each other. Thank you, Li, and please pass on my personal thanks to your team. We still have a long way to go on this one, but your actions so far have certainly vindicated my decision to establish the CTC in the first place. Let me know when you find the wreckage of those planes. We need to find the evidence."

Palpably relieved, Li replaced the receiver with the UN head in New York and returned to the main CTC open plan office.

The team turned to look at him, and, with a broad smile, he said, "We're in the clear. The Secretary-General wants me to pass on his personal thanks to you all. It has been a long couple of days, and you all look as though you could do with some sleep."

"There's an understatement if ever I heard one," said Maria, through her teeth.

"Yeah, I know I have been pushing you all pretty hard recently. I promise you can all go home and rest soon. But first, we still need to spend a couple of hours working on the rest of this puzzle."

As the team were exchanging smiles and hugs with each other, Matthias began to speak. "OK, well done for now; but all we have done is to stop the most recent attack. But we are still no closer to establishing who is behind this."

Charu spoke first. "We do have a few more pieces of the puzzle, though. Thanks to Andrei's and Li's contacts we have photographs of the devices used in the attacks."

"Only photos!" declared Penny.

With a resigned shrug of her shoulders, Maria said, "Yeah, the Chinese and Russian governments are still embarrassed over these attacks and won't release any hard evidence until they have completed their investigations. We have tried every channel possible. I guess I can understand their reluctance to share the information."

"OK," Charu continued. "Matthias and I have analysed the photos, and, although the delivery mechanisms were different, there does appear to be at least one thread of commonality. Both attacks were designed to deliver an agent of some kind into the oil supply."

Charu finished speaking and looked around the room for a response. In the corner of the room, Matthias was hunched over a whiteboard, busily sticking bright pink Post-It notes onto the board. "Come over here, quickly! I think I might have something."

"The team moved over to the corner of the office, where Matthias stood in front of the whiteboard, clutching a large hardback book."

"I think I know who is behind the attacks," he declared, barely able to contain his excitement. He began rapidly drawing interconnected lines in coloured marker pens between the Post-Its stuck to the whiteboard.

"To recap quickly, I have scribbled down on these Post-It notes all of the verifiable facts that we are certain about." One by one, Matthias went through everything the team had learned so far. "We have a link to Mongolia in the printed book of Qi that was found on the unknown dead Iraqi boy. Faisal Al Abbasin was the Iraqi physicist from Baghdad killed in the drone strike. We believe it was his son who died whilst killing the US Air Force pilot in Mosul. We found the book of Qi, Koran and a book of Arabic history at the site of the attack.

Philippe gave me the last piece I needed in the puzzle, the name I was looking for. German Second World War archives revealed the name of a young Iraqi physicist from Baghdad who had been working with Professor George Wittig on his bacteria experiments, designed to degrade the structure of oil molecules. The young scientist's name was Mohammed Al Abbasin." Matthias looked up at the group, smiling, and said, "So what do you think?"

"I'm lost," said Penny.

"Me too," said Andrei. Matthias looked from face to face. They all held the same blank expressions.

"OK," he said. "It really started to come together when I thought about Li's words. He spoke about a renaissance or re-genesis. And then, bingo! The pieces of the puzzle started to slot together." He looked up once more and was still met by perplexed stares. "Oh, come on. Think!"

No one spoke; they simply looked from one to another, with bemused expressions on their faces. "Well, to tell the truth, the real breakthrough came when I re-read a chapter from this book." He held aloft the thick hardback book on Arabic history and culture. "It was the chapter on the Abbasid Caliphate that caught my attention. You see, the Caliphate came to a sudden end when the Mongol hordes captured Baghdad, and ended the Arabic age of enlightenment. It is also hinted that a surviving member of the Abbasid Family was taken back with the Mongols, who were, by now, new converts to Islam, to Mongolia. You see, the answer has been staring me in the face. If you replace the Al Abbasin name for Al Abbasid, then it all makes sense."

"Are you saying what I think you are saying, Matthias?" said Li. "Do you think that the Al Abbasin family are really the rightful heirs to the Abbasid Caliphate, and that everything that has happened is part of some enormously protracted eight-hundred-year-old revenge plot to restore the Caliphate?"

There was silence for a while, then Charu spoke. "It could add up," she said, peering closer at the whiteboard and its scribbled lines. "That most famous of English authors, Sir Arthur Conan Doyle, once wrote in one of his Sherlock Holmes novels that 'Once you eliminate the impossible, whatever remains, no matter how improbable, must be the truth'. I believe, as fantastic as this may sound, Matthias could very well be right.

"The Al Abbasin or should I say, Al Abbasid family are the key. Penny has checked up on the family for me through her Interpol contacts. The only surviving members of Mohammed al Abbasin, the guy who worked with the Nazis on their bacteriological experiments, is Fatima, his daughter. Fatima's husband, the physicist, was killed by a US drone in Pakistan six months ago. We also know from Iraqi police sources that her eldest son, Ali, is recently deceased. No explanation for his death exists. She has another son called Hamed, who still lives at home with her.

"Fatima is a tenured professor at the University of Baghdad, and she is a petro-chemical engineer."

"It makes sense," said Philippe. "Fatima had the motive and knowledge to carry out the attack. But she needed someone to do the dirty work for her. *Et voilà*, enter the Mongols. I was re-examining the oil supply strikes, and realised that only two of the strikes could have been committed by this group. The other strike, by China on Japan, and the attempted Russian strike against the US, were simply retaliation.

"Look at the geography. Mongolia sits between Russia and China. Both countries have a history of conquering and suppressing the Mongols. It wouldn't take much for Fatima to convince the Mongol nationalists to help orchestrate the attacks."

Li cut in, "Exactly as Fatima had planned all along. Her strategies really start to make sense. 'Borrow a corpse to resurrect the soul', 'Kill with a Borrowed Sword', and 'Watch the fires burning across the river'. The borrowed corpse could relate to the bacteria formula that Fatima's father developed with the Nazis.

"Killing with a Borrowed Sword is twofold. Firstly, I believe we will discover that Mongol separatists were behind the attack on China and Russia; and, secondly, these attacks encouraged both Russia and China to attack Japan and the US. Finally, Watching the Fires burn across the river is what her group are doing as we speak. They are watching the great powers attack each other, and the UN become weaker every day, as the oil shock cripples industrial output and distorts the global financial markets. All of this, everything that has happened, has been planned by Fatima Al Abbasin, with one goal in mind. She is an engineer, and she has been cleverly engineering the conditions needed for the new Abbasid Caliphate."

Chapter Forty-Two

Time to Strike Back

Just then, Li's phone rang. "Li, is that you?"

"Yes, it's Tapeesa, isn't it?"

"Yes, sir. You told me to call you as soon as we found anything. The trawlers have been picking up pieces of fuselage and wing for the last hour. We cannot confirm at this stage how many planes the debris belongs to, but judging by the position of the wreckage, we think it is certainly more than three planes."

"That's good news indeed. Keep up the good work, and keep us informed. Oh, and tell those fishermen that they will all be receiving compensation for their time, and for any damage suffered to their equipment."

Li immediately called Guilherme in New York. "Thanks, Li. I can't tell you how relieved I am to hear the news. I won't repeat what Chuck Henderson, the US Ambassador, said to me when I woke him after your call to inform him of the foiled attack on his country. I will call him back right now. Hopefully, this news will placate him somewhat."

"Good luck with the US Ambassador. I don't know if it will help at all, but you could mention that it was your Chinese-led CTC team, and a tip-off from the Russian FSB, that were the only things that stopped the attacks."

"Yeah, I'm not sure how he will take that one. But I might throw it in anyway. It is about time Chuck realised that the UN isn't a US think-tank." Li chuckled to himself.

"Before you go, Guilherme, we are moving forward quite rapidly with our investigation. We think we know who is behind the attack, and I think I know what their endgame is. I will let you know when we are sure. But if we are correct, this group needs stopping, and fast."

"That's great news," agreed Guilherme. "I agree, they will need to be stopped, but it can't be done by the US, Chinese or Russians. I will speak with Sir Richard Belmarsh, the British Ambassador, and see whether the British Special Air Service might be persuaded to help out."

"Thanks, Mr Secretary-General. I will get our British liaison officer, Penny, on to it from our end to sort out the details, once you give me the green light."

Li finished speaking with Guilherme and turned his attention back to the group. "That was the Secretary-General. He is over the moon with our work, and I said we would get in touch with him once we have figured out the rest of the puzzle. Potentially, we might be looking at an SAS strike on the Al Abbasid household. Penny, Maria and Andrei, I want you to start working up some contingencies."

Penny, Maria and Andrei left the group assembled around the whiteboard, and moved over to a corner of the office, to begin planning the strike against the Al Abbasid house in Baghdad.

Li, Matthias, Philippe and Charu remained grouped around the whiteboard. "Do you think we are correct in our assumptions?" Matthias asked his two colleagues.

"What I do know," said Li, "is that this is one very determined lady, who has spent her entire life building up to this point. Indeed, you could say that her family have spent generations trying to recreate this Caliphate."

"That's true," added Philippe. "I would say that there has never been a better time for her group to make their push."

"What do you mean?" asked Li.

"Well, through the oil strikes, she has generated a massive income boost from oil sales for many Arabic countries. She only has to reveal that she was behind the attacks, and she will win massive popular public support. Also, remember that, a few years back, we had the Arab Spring. Well, there are still millions of Arabs, from Yemen to North Africa, who are unhappy with their current governments."

"That's right," cut in Matthias. "Then, when you factor in the dire global economic position, and the lack of strategic oil supplies, she has effectively ruled out any interference by the major powers."

Both Russia and the US have painful memories of the cost in terms of lives, money and *matériel* that engaging in Middle Eastern wars carries with it."

"So what's her next move?" Philippe said, as he hastily removed the Post-It notes from the whiteboards, and wrote the words 'How to create a Caliphate'. The question was partly rhetorical; he had asked it of himself, and the other two men stood by as he began scribbling quickly on the whiteboard, speaking out loud as he did so.

"You know, this Fatima is a scientist, and, from what I read about the Abbasid Caliphate in Baghdad, the city was considered the centre of knowledge and culture centuries before the enlightenment in Europe. I think she is trying to recover some of that prestige for the Arabs."

"In that case, it is simple," said Philippe. "At this point, I am assuming that her son Hamed will be the new Caliph? She simply has to let the Arabic world know that the new Caliph single-handedly crippled the major powers and brought untold wealth to his people. If she is clever, and promises to distribute some of this wealth more evenly than the current governments, and generate industry and build schools and universities, I think she will gain a lot of popular support."

"I agree with you, Philippe," Li said, scratching his chin and secretly yearning for another cigarette. "But even then, we have seen popular democratic uprisings brutally repressed in the past. If she wants to achieve regime change, then, as well as having the people on her side, she will need key people, high up in the societies or regimes of these countries, on whom she can rely to neutralise the existing governments, people with real political clout."

Catching on quickly, Matthias scribbled some more on the whiteboard. "She needs to hold another meeting. She needs to co-ordinate the next phase of her attack."

"Exactly," said Li, grinning from ear to ear. "And that is how we will catch her. She has no more use for the Mongols. So, any meeting she holds will be held on Arabic soil. My bet is that the meeting will be held in the capital of the new Caliphate, in Baghdad itself. We need her watched night and day."

Li ran quickly, across the office to where Penny, Maria and Andrei were busy planning how to take out Fatima and her followers. "Penny, we need Fatima watching. We need surveillance."

"Don't worry, Li, we are ahead of you on that one. When I left MI6, I didn't leave without keeping some contact with some of my colleagues. A chap named Donovan Utteridge is Head of Station in Baghdad. I called him twenty minutes ago, asking if he could prioritise surveillance of our suspects. I am afraid I did rather take your name in vain, and suggest that higher-level authority would be sent to him in short order."

Penny looked nervously across at Li as she said the last few words. "Don't worry; you did the right thing. I will ask the Secretary-General if he will speak to the British Ambassador, Sir Richard Belmarsh." Walking, now a little more calmly, back to Philippe, Charu and Mathias, Li looked once more at the mass of scribbled writing on the whiteboard.

"What are you thinking?" asked Philippe.

"I am just considering how the final two strategies fit in with our guess of what is going on.

"The final two strategies are, 'Slough off the Cicada's golden shell' and 'Make the Host and the Guest exchange roles.' If my thinking is correct, the first strategy relates to the Caliph's being revealed to the world. The second strategy could be two-fold; firstly, in a more limited geo-political area, it may relate to the change in governments that will have to happen for the Caliph to take power. In a far wider geopolitical sense, it may imply a resetting of balance between the West, or the larger developed countries, and the Arabic world in general, harking back to the glorious days of the last Abbasid Caliphate."

Philippe and Mathias were nodding their agreement

enthusiastically. "You know," began Mathias. "I don't see too many down sides to this new arrangement. I mean, if the new Caliph could pacify the Middle East, and bring prosperity and development, what's not to like?"

"You make a good point, Mathias," Li said, sagely. "However, unfortunately, I believe there are too many powerful people high up in many governments that have too much invested in the current world order. Not forgetting, of course, that the new Caliphate, like the one it is trying to emulate, would be a purely Sunni Caliphate. Benign or not, I really can't see Iran settling for so much Sunni dominance across the Arabic world.

Latitude 35° 38' 23.8524'', Longitude 51° 26' 45.0528''. Residence of the Supreme Leader (Ayatollah), Tehran, Iran. – 17 September 2017.

The Enemy of my Enemy is my Friend

The attempt to re-establish the Abbasid Sunni Caliphate had been one of the greatest existential threats to the state of Iran since the creation of the state of Israel, thought General Qusay Mohammed Hijazi, the Commander in Chief of the Iranian Revolutionary Guard Corps. His country owed a debt of gratitude beyond words to the young Colonel Homayoon in counter-intelligence. It was he who had first identified the threat, through his network of spies in Iraq. It was also he who had first suggested that they use the Al Abbasin family and their plan to destabilise the United Nations for the benefit of Iran.

Yes, thought the general, as he sat waiting to speak to the Ayatollah, the supreme leader of Iran. Yes, indeed; this colonel deserves the highest recognition his country could bestow upon him. "General, the Ayatollah will see you now." A tall guard escorted the general into the Ayatollah's private quarters. The general stood to attention, and saluted when he saw the old, white-bearded cleric.

In response, the cleric placed an old wizened hand on his shoulder, and beckoned him to sit and take tea with him. "General," began the Ayatollah, in his usual calm voice. "I believe you have something to report to me?"

"Yes, sir," began the general, unable to remove his gaze from the older man's steely grey eyes. "Sir, we are about to terminate the Al Abbasin operation. That is, we are about to terminate the Al Abbasin woman and her son. This will bring to an end the line of succession of the Al Abbasid Caliphate."

The older man nodded sagely. "You know, General, this affair has been most beneficial to Iran. Through the actions of the Abbasin family, the great powers that seek to repress and threaten Iran have been dealt a severe economic blow that will limit their ability to meddle in our affairs for a very long time indeed. As a by-product of the oil crisis, our economic output has never been greater. We cannot pump the oil fast enough. Those fools will buy this black gold at any price. They are so scared of being without their reserves. But do you know what will be the most important outcome from this affair?"

"No, your grace," replied the general.

"It will be the debt of gratitude that the world will owe Iran when they discover that Iranian agents uncovered the Sunni plot to create a Caliphate in the Middle East. We will no longer be pariahs in the international community. We will be seen as serious power-brokers in the Middle East, as a country that is supportive of the international community."

Chapter Forty-Three

Latitude 33° 16' 6.7008'', Longitude 44° 23' 20.1408''.
The Al Abbasin Household, Baghdad, Iraq, former
Mesopotamia
— 20 September 2017.
Maintaining Momentum

Nearly two weeks had passed since Ganzorig's men had successfully crippled the Russian oil pipelines. Fatima had expected the Russians to enact swift retribution for the attack on their country, as had been the case with the Chinese. She and Hamed had been monitoring every media outlet they could think of, and had heard nothing about any Russian reprisals.

She had heard about the bickering and protestations at the UN Security Council. China was still blaming Japan for the attack on its oil sites; and Japan was still vehemently denying any involvement and requesting that the UN impose sanctions against China for its attack. The news from the Russians had been revelatory. In a live broadcast by the Russian President himself, the President had shown to the world the US military-issue satnav device that had purportedly been found at the site of one of the attacks. Bellicose as ever, they too were demanding sanctions against the US for the attack on Russia's territory. The Russian Armed Forces had been placed on their highest alert level, and the Russian state media outlets were showing almost continuous footage of increased activity at both mobile and static strategic intercontinental ballistic missile sites. In the financial pages, she also noticed that the price of a barrel of Brent crude oil had reached an unprecedented high of one hundred and ninety dollars per barrel.

Over a rare lunch at the Al Abbasin house on the banks of the Tigris, just two kilometres from the University, Fatima began to explain to a reluctant Hamed that, even without a Russian counter-strike against the US, they had created the perfect conditions to begin the final phases of their grand plan.

"But Mother, the Americans are still strong; they could send their armies once more to the Middle East, and this would stop us dead in our tracks."

"My dear son, the Americans are far too pre-occupied with the Russians at the moment, not to mention the instability between China and Japan, to even conceive of getting involved in the Middle East again. Anyway, if we co-ordinate this correctly, not even the Americans have the economic and military power to intervene in uprisings across the entirety of the middle East."

"I suppose that, looking at it that way, it does sound more convincing."

Fatima pushed her plate to one side, and looked across the table to her son. "Very soon, my son, you will be the new Caliph. I have called a co-ordination meeting with Faisal ibn Abdullah from Jordan, the old Wahhabi Prince Suleiman from Saudi Arabia, and our Egyptian friend, Tariq Al Khazari. The meeting is to be after Friday midday prayers, here at our home."

"Here!" declared Hamed. "It's not safe!"

"It is safer than you think; all three guests are travelling incognito, and, anyway, everyone is too focused looking for attackers in Russia and China; no one will be monitoring a lowly university professor's house in Baghdad. Saying that, I still want to remain cautious; we are too close to our goal and you are the last of our line. Hamed, forgive me, but I want to send you away from here. Far away, until the revolutions have happened, and it is time to present the new Caliph to his people."

"What? you must be kidding, Mother!"

"I am deadly serious, my son. You are far too precious to risk being caught up in any violence. No, I insist you must be kept safe until the time comes."

"But where is safe, Mother?"

"Indonesia."

"Indonesia! Why there?"

"They have a huge Muslim population, and I have many contacts amongst those in the mosques and madrasas, people I know will keep you safe, especially when I tell them who you are. They will see it as their holy duty."

With lunch finished, an unhappy Hamed was left packing his bags to catch the 9.50 p.m. flight to Jakarta, Indonesia. Meanwhile, Fatima took a leisurely stroll back along the banks of the River Tigris to her faculty building at the University. She enjoyed the walk, and wondered how many more times she would be able to do it once Hamed became Caliph. When she entered her office, she found Ameera, the cleaning girl, carrying out bags of rubbish from her office.

Ameera was a relatively new cleaner, and had only started

working in Fatima's faculty over the last three months. Fatima had grown fond of the inquisitive young girl, who seemed much more fastidious than the other cleaners, and was always to be seen pottering around Fatima's corridor. "Ameera, how are you?"

Ameera looked up at Fatima, and, just for a moment, appeared startled. Recovering her composure quickly, she spoke.

"Oh, doctor, how good to see you. Will you be working this afternoon?"

"I am afraid so, Ameera, my child."

"Would you like me to make you some tea?"

"Not right now, my dear, but maybe in an hour or so."

"I am sorry, doctor. Today I must leave early; my cousin is visiting from Al Basra." Smiling graciously, Ameera excused herself, and left Fatima's office, carrying out the rubbish bins with her.

Ameera walked out of the University entrance, and, as she stepped on to the pavement, a dusty blue Toyota saloon car pulled up in front of her. "Get in," the man commanded in Farsi. Mahmoud was an Iranian Revolutionary Guard Corps agent who had been Ameera's agent handler ever since she had taken the job as a cleaner in Fatima's faculty. As they drove off, Mahmoud began to question Ameera. "What do you have? Do we have a date and location for the meeting?"

"I think so. She nearly caught me snooping today. She returned from lunch early, and caught me leaving her office."

"Don't worry; if you have the information, then today was your last day at the university. We will transfer you back to Tehran tonight. You have done good work, Ameera."

"As I say, I have some information. She has booked time off work on Friday after lunchtime prayers. This is highly unusual for her. I saw the entry in her desk diary, and, next to it, she has a shopping list; it looks like she will be holding a dinner party. She has ordered much food, to be delivered to her house at three p.m."

"Perfect," Mahmoud said, glancing in his rear-view mirror, and smiling at Ameera. "I will drop you at the safe house; then I must get this information to Tehran immediately."

"What will happen then?"

"I said; you will be sent back to Tehran and rewarded for your work."

"No, I mean what will happen to the doctor?"

"The doctor and her dinner party guests will receive a visit from our famous Quds Force Special Forces."

Ameera was startled by the news, but knew better than to continue asking questions. They drove on in silence to the safe house.

Latitude 1° 17' 28.8348'', Longitude 103° 47' 13.3296''. United Nations Centre for Technology and Culture Headquarters, Heng Mui Keng Terrace, Singapore - Wednesday 20 September 2017.
    Close Observation

Penny took the top secret message that had been passed via secure channels to her from MI6 in London, and placed it on Li's desk.

"Is this what I think it is?"

"Yes; our friend Donovan Utteridge, Head of Station in Baghdad, came through for us. The tech guys at GCHQ in Cheltenham managed to hack Fatima's work email account. It seems that she has been sending some rather interesting emails. It took the cryptanalysts some time to figure out what was happening."

Basically, from her terminal at the university, she has set up a ghost Virtual Private Network that is registered in Buenos Aires. Whenever she emails anyone from this ghost account, the messages are first encrypted then routed through upwards of four different servers, all located in different countries, before they arrive and are decrypted by the receiver. The receiving terminals all require special software to be able to decrypt the messages."

"My God," said Li. "What did they find out?"

"Invitations have been sent out to three target recipients, who we think, but are not sure, are based in Saudi Arabia, Jordan and Egypt. These three targets have been invited to a meeting at her house at some time this Friday."

"So soon?" said Li. "Dr Al Abbasin certainly doesn't waste any time."

"I believe it's called striking whilst the iron is hot," said Penny.

"OK," said Li. "Leave it with me; I will contact the Secretary-General to get the go-ahead for the mission. He will have to confer with the head of MI6 and the Director of Special Forces over there in the UK to get clearance."

"I know; please let me know as soon as you have authority and clearance. I am in constant contact with the SAS team commander in Baghdad through Donovan Utteridge, the MI6 contact."

"Good work, Penny. Tell the team to be ready to go at a moment's notice. If there is going to be a strike, I want Andrei and Maria on the team."

Barely two hours later, an excited Li ran over to Penny, and placed a secure fax on the desk in front of her. "We got the green light from London. Two SAS teams will lead a capture operation against Fatima's house once they are sure that the rest of her accomplices are in the house with her."

"Awesome," shrieked Penny.

"Now, then, just calm down a little." He turned to face Maria and Andrei, who were standing by Penny's desk waiting for the news. "I want to make it quite clear to you all that this is a capture and arrest operation, and not a kill operation!"

"Yes, sir," replied Maria and Andrei in unison.

The rest of that afternoon was spent preparing Maria and Andrei for the operation in Baghdad. The SAS team were alerted, and, although they were far from delighted at being joined by 'outsiders' on such a mission, they agreed to meet with Andrei and Maria in their secure compound in the Green Zone in Baghdad to go through the details of the plan.

Chapter Forty-Four

Latitude 33° 16' 6.7008'', Longitude 44° 23' 20.1408''.
The Al Abbasin Household, Baghdad, Iraq, former
Mesopotamia –Friday 22 September 2017.
Two Teams, One Target

For two days, since the message containing confirmation of the meeting had arrived at the IRGC HQ in Tehran, a group of twelve Quds Force Special Forces Operatives had been observing the Al Abbasin House and preparing for the attack. These highly skilled operatives had been operating within Iraq for many years, and were all fluent in Arabic and very familiar with the surroundings. The team consisted of seven men and five women.

Their orders were to observe the house. Only once they were sure that the whole group were inside were they to launch their attack. After observing the house and talking with Colonel Homayoon from IRGC counter-intelligence, Reza, the group's experienced commander, had received permission to carry out the attack. The colonel from counter-intelligence had made only one stipulation: that evidence of the dead bodies had to be sent to Tehran as quickly as possible.

Reza's team, who had been dressed in casual street clothes, and had been rotating through the task of observing the house, had kept a close log on the comings and goings within the house.

They knew from Ameera, the agent who had posed as the cleaning girl, that Fatima had eaten lunch with her son Hamed on the 20th, just two days previously. Although Hamed hadn't been seen leaving the house since then, it was presumed that he was still inside. It was not out of character for the Physics tutor to spend many days at a time at his computer terminal. Fatima had been seen entering and leaving the property regularly on her way to and from the university. The only other person present at the house was a cleaning lady, who generally arrived at nine a.m. and left the house by two p.m. Raza knew that Fatima was expected to hold the meeting on Friday afternoon, and that it was of vital importance that the three guests at the meeting were all killed in the attack.

"See that there?" The gloved hand of one of the SAS troopers pointed over the water to a large house built on the opposite bank of the river, set back in its own grounds. Handing the sniper scope to Andrei, the trooper began to describe all of the access routes that they would be covering from their sniper's hide, which had been set up nearly five hundred metres away, across the river Tigris, at the old oil refinery. "You see the access road, running along the river bank?" Andrei nodded. "If anyone tries to leave that house during the arrest operation in a vehicle, then it is up to you and me to immobilize the vehicle with a couple of .338 caliber rounds from our friend here, the L115A1."

The rifle the trooper was referring to was relatively new to the British Army. Balanced on a bipod, and equipped with day and night sights, the rifle was designed for first-round kill accuracy at six hundred metres, with an overall effective range of eleven hundred metres. The sniper hide that Andrei and the young Trooper occupied sat at five hundred and fifty metres from the target.

Maria was still back in the SAS secure compound in Baghdad's Green zone. She had been going over the plan with the SAS commander, Captain Steven Rowlings. Maria felt confident working with these men. They didn't display any of the 'hoohah' bullshit so common amongst so-called special forces soldiers. These men were quiet, almost introvert, she thought. Captain Rowlings was just finishing outlining the plan.

"So, once we get the green light from Sammy and Andrei at the sniper hide, we will jump into the helicopter, and drop in and pay the Al Abbasin household a little visit." Maria knew what that meant. For the last thirty-six hours, she had been practicing house entry and hostage rescue techniques with the two four-man SAS teams. Through their connections with the MI6 contact at the embassy, they had managed to secure the use of a very similar property in another part of the city. They had rehearsed every aspect of the assault, from the fast rope descent from the helicopter, to effecting a forced entry into the house and releasing stun grenades. All of this was practiced using only hand signals and whilst wearing respirators, to prevent any of the noxious gases from the grenades from affecting the troopers' breathing or vision.

Maria was familiar with house entry drills from her secret service training. She had never fast-roped from a helicopter before, but after a couple of practices, and some minor bruising and chafing to her thighs, she had quickly got the hang of it. "So we're set, then?" asked Maria of the tall SAS Captain.

"I think so, Maria. It's midday now. The call to prayer

should be heard any minute. After that, we just wait here until we get the signal from Sammy and Andrei. I suggest you relax a little. I know how hyped people get prior to such an operation, and it is quite draining having adrenalin pumping around your body for hours at a time. Try and chill for a while. Don't worry; we won't go without you." The captain smiled at Maria; she smiled back and went over to the rest of the team, who were playing cards, and asked to be dealt in.

After midday prayers, three of the IRGC Quds force operators took it in turn to tail Fatima back to her house. Once they were sure she was inside, they radioed Reza, the commander.

"The lady is inside," came the voice on the radio.

"OK, received. Remember, no one moves until I give the signal, OK?"

"Roger," replied the young Quds force operative, as he sat behind the wheel of the powerful Toyota pick-up truck, that had been parked out of site, about five hundred metres down the river bank, under the palm trees.

Reza had to rely on all of his experience and training now, if he wanted the attack to be successful. Farhad and Sara were both in the pick-up truck which had been packed with explosives. Mina and Zahid were both wearing suicide vests, and were waiting for his signal in a parked car two blocks away, behind Fatima's house. Reza didn't doubt the commitment of his Quds Force operatives to martyr themselves for the cause; however he realised that even well-trained and committed people had doubts, and wavered when they knew they were only minutes away from entering heaven. This is why he had arranged the two suicide bomber teams in pairs of the opposite sex. First of all, the men were less likely to back down in front of the women. As for the women, they would be keen to show that they were every bit as professional as their male counterparts. Reza just had to keep talking to the two teams now to keep their nerves cool and distract them from the thought of what was about to happen.

Yasser, who was the youngest, yet one of the most talented members of the team, had been given the task of confirming the arrival of the three guests. The Quds Force commandos didn't know the identity of the three guests, but knew that they would be Arabs, probably male, and not Iraqis. Yasser had two other team members working for him: Maryam, a pretty girl from Isfahan in the centre of Iran, and Mehdi, who came from the south, from a town called Bandar Abbas, that sat right on the Straits of Hormuz. This pair had been positioned along the street and were posing as date pickers. Both Yasser and Mehdi were perched high up in the date palms pretending to cut down the delicious juicy fruits. Maryam was stood beneath with a basket pretending to collect the dates from the two young men.

Captain Rowlings strode over to Maria and the troopers who were engrossed in a game of cards. "Guys, we have confirmation that Fatima has left the university and is walking home."

"How do we know?" queried Maria.

"The MI6 team out here managed to enter Fatima's office and smuggle a key stroke detector on to her work machine. I just received a message from the embassy, confirming that Fatima has logged off her computer for the day."

Impressive, thought Maria. "OK, what now?" she asked.

"We start to suit up, and then we sit and wait until Sammy

and Andrei give us confirmation that Fatima and the three other targets are definitely in the house."

It was now three p.m., and it was beginning to get really hot on the exposed roof of the oil refinery. Sammy had reported Fatima's return to the property almost an hour ago, but since then no movement had been detected. Andrei and Sammy were taking it in turns to monitor the target. Passing the sniper scope back to Sammy, Andrei said, "Check out the palm trees. Do you see movement?" Sammy was impressed that the Russian had noticed the movement at all. With the heat haze shimmering above the water, and the breeze blowing the palm fronds, it was difficult to see clearly.

"Yeah, I got that. I saw them about an hour ago. You see it all the time over here. Young kids picking dates." The young SAS Trooper had already spent several tours of duty in Iraq in his short career, and had witnessed people harvesting the dates from the trees that lined the streets and rivers many times before. "You see, the trees bear fruit several times a year. The skill is knowing when to pick them. If you pick too early, they won't be ripe. If you wait too long, some other bugger will come along and steal them." Andrei nodded his understanding, but couldn't stop thinking that something was wrong with the picture in front of him.

Just then, a dark brown American SUV drove slowly around the corner and entered Fatima's driveway. Using the rifle's powerful all weather scope, and the spotter's scope both Andrei and Sammy observed the older man, clad in the traditional dress of a Gulf Arab, a white *thawb*; the white square scarf covering his head, the *gutra*, was held in place by a black band, an *igal*.

"Aye up," said Sammy. "It seems our first guest has arrived."

"How do you know?" asked Andrei. "Look at his clothes. The *thawb* is very short; you can see the man's ankles. If you look up at his headdress, you will notice that it is pure white, and not multi-coloured. That isn't how they dress around here. They are the clothes of an ultra-conservative Gulf Arab. I would guess at Saudi."

Impressed at the young trooper's knowledge, Andrei radioed back to the team in the Green Zone to confirm the arrival of the first visitor. As he did so, still peering through his scope he noticed the pretty young girl standing at the bottom of the palm tree raise a black object to her head from the date basket. He dismissed it though. I mean, doesn't every young kid spend most of their day on the mobile phones nowadays? Why should the Arabs be any different?

The next car to arrive was an equally innocuous-looking taxi. The car pulled up outside Fatima's front door, and a tall, lean-looking man of about fifty stepped out of the vehicle, to be met by Fatima. He was wearing a dark grey business suit, and had no facial hair. His strong head of dark hair and aquiline features placed him as a middle-eastern man from a good family. He wasn't Iraqi, maybe Lebanese or Jordanian, thought Maryam, as she called Reza to report the latest arrival to him.

"Thank you, Maryam; be patient and let me know when the final guest is there." It was nearly time, Reza thought. He went over the plan one more time in his head. First, he would position the two attack teams. The vehicle-borne suicide bombers, whose vehicle had been packed with Iranian military-grade high explosive, would be driven into the building's exterior wall. After the explosion, the secondary team of suicide bombers would drive on to the scene in their saloon car, get out, and, after they had finished shooting anyone left alive, they would detonate their suicide vests, to ensure that nobody at the Al Abbasin house would be left alive.

It would fall to young Yasser and Mehdi to film the aftermath on their phones, and upload the video to the pre-arranged email accounts, before fleeing the scene in the boat containing the remaining team members. The River Tigris was a large, fast-flowing river, and a group of young Arabs with a cargo of dates would attract no undue attention from anyone on the water.

The final car arrived at Fatima's house. Out stepped a rather short, fat man. He seemed to be around forty thought Sammy, certainly not a Gulf Arab. By the look of his clothes and his complexion, Sammy placed him closer to the Mediterranean: Lebanese or maybe North African. Sammy had spent some time in Egypt improving his Arabic language skills, and he thought the man looked vaguely familiar. Had he seen him on TV? A politician, maybe? "Radio it in, Andrei. The mission is on," said Sammy.

Captain Rowlings was the last member of the eight-man SAS team to enter the Merlin helicopter. After looking over his black-clad troopers one more time, he reached for the helicopter's intercom, and told the pilot to take off. They were airborne in seconds, and would be over the target in less than fifteen minutes. They had chosen to approach the house in the helicopter from the South-East, using the river to camouflage their approach, then popping up at the last minute over the palm-tree-lined river bank, the team would be delivered to the target before anyone inside the house even knew they were there.

Chapter Forty-Five

Taken Out

Inside Fatima's house the three guests had finished drinking their first glass of coffee and were keen to start the meeting. Sitting around Fatima's large dining table, Fatima began to address her three accomplices.

"Before you start, Madame Al Abbasin," said the tall Jordanian. "Can I say, and I think I speak on behalf of all of us, that we are most impressed indeed by what you have managed to achieve so far. It is a pity that the Russians decided not to play our little game, and retaliate against America, but Allah only knows that your plan has already caused so much instability."

"And created so much more wealth for us from the increased oil sales," interjected the Saudi Prince.

"Yes," continued the Jordanian. "We were expecting to meet the new Caliph on this trip, though."

"Yes, I am sorry, but I am sure you can understand that, as the very last in our line, it is essential that he be kept safe until the transition is complete." Heads nodded in agreement around the table.

"So, gentlemen, shall we continue with the meeting? I am keen to hear your plans to seize control of your governments. Tell me…" Fatima could hear herself speaking, as if she was sitting outside her own body. Then, amidst a deafening roar, she felt the shock waves distorting her vision and tilting her chair backwards as she was blown backwards on to the floor. Her last image of the three men sitting at the table with her was the look of utter surprise frozen on to their faces, as the wall behind them was ripped apart and exploded inwards in a shower of masonry.

The blast wave was followed by a bright flame, then by thousands upon thousands of tiny shards of metal flying through the air like miniature darts with a devastating savagery. Fatima watched from the floor, her ears ringing and bleeding, as the head of the tall Jordanian was sliced clean off by a huge shard of metal. Next to him, she noticed the small pinprick-sized pools of blood starting to appear all over the crisp white *thawb* of the Saudi prince.

From their vantage point on top of the oil refinery, both Andrei and Sammy had been observing the house through their scopes when the explosion happened. Both men were temporarily blinded by the explosion. "Shit!" said Sammy. "What the fuck was that? I got to get in touch with the team. Mike Two Zero Alpha, this is Lima One Four, Contact Report."

"Mike Two Zero Alpha, send, over."

"Multiple explosions on the target. Possible vehicle-borne IED. I repeat. The target is being attacked by unknowns."

There was silence for a moment; then Captain Rowlings came back over the radio. "Lima One Four, keep observing, and intervene if you can. We will stay in a holding pattern until we receive an update from you."

"Roger that, Mike Two Zero Alpha. Out." Turning to Andrei, the young SAS Trooper, with several tours of Iraq under his belt, said, "It's you and me, Andrei. It is too dangerous to fly the helicopter into the target area. We are to observe, report and take action if we can." Andrei nodded his agreement, and, rubbing his eyes to try to clear his vision, placed the sniper's spotting scope once more to his right eye, and observed the scene of utter devastation in front of him.

As he did so, he saw more movement by the palm trees; the pretty girl who had been using the mobile phone had been joined by two young men. Moving his scope a little higher, he noticed another vehicle entering the Al Abbasin Compound. Nudging Sammy, he whispered. "Target, grey Nissan saloon entering the compound, range five hundred and seventy-five metres, wind four miles per hour east to west."

Sammy tightened the pressure of the sniper rifle against his shoulder, and began to slow his breathing. It was a difficult shot; the moist air shimmering off the river was obscuring his vision, and would certainly affect the trajectory of the round as it raced towards its target at over two thousand five hundred feet per second.

Two people stepped out of the vehicle and began to open fire with Kalashnikov rifles at the wreckage of the house in front of them. The two figures moved forward in a practiced movement, stepping over the rubble, and began to enter the house. After ensuring that the three Arab men were dead, the two Quds Force commandos turned their attention to Fatima, who had dragged herself into the kitchen and lay moaning on the floor. They had been given special instructions on how to deal with Fatima.

"Shoot, Sammy, shoot!" shouted Andrei. Slowly taking up pressure on the trigger, with a thin bead of sweat beginning to form over his right eye, Sammy took the shot. The person on the right dropped to the floor as if their legs had been cut away from beneath them. Pulling back firmly on the sniper rifle's cocking handle, Sammy ejected the spent cartridge case and forced another round into the chamber.

Andrei was on the radio to the helicopter. "Mike Two Zero Alpha, this is Lima One Four. Attack still in progress. One attacker neutralised, trying for the other. We suggest you approach the target area with extreme caution. Out."

Trying desperately to focus on the remaining attacker, Sammy was struggling to get a firm fix on the constantly moving shape. The figure paused, and Sammy managed to gain a good sight picture. As he was taking up the trigger pressure, the target erupted into a ball of flame. The bright flame seared through the rifle's powerful sight, and caused Sammy to drop the rifle and place his hands over his eyes in pain.

Andrei was still focused on the target and had noticed the three figures under the palm tree begin to move forward. As he did so he also heard the noise of engines. Was it the helicopter, he thought to himself. Shifting his position on the roof, he turned to look up the river. He couldn't see the helicopter, but he did notice a fast-moving boat heading straight for the shoreline where the attack was happening.

"Sammy, Sammy, are you OK?"

"Shit! I can't see clearly out of my right eye."

"Don't worry; give me the rifle," Andrei said. "Take the radio, and report what I tell you. We have an unknown speedboat closing in on the target, and three remaining suspects at the target. Sammy picked up the radio and relayed Andrei's message.

"Lima One Four, we are heading in low, down the river to your position. Be advised, we will be to your east and we will try to identify the boat you mentioned. Out."

Sammy relayed the message to Andrei. Andrei listened whilst he adjusted his position behind the rifle.

Sammy, we have three possible hostiles moving on to the target site. I am going to try to take them out. Placing his eye into the rubber socket of the sight, Andrei began to relax. He had trained for this hundreds of times. He had been trained to come into the kill at high speed on foot, then steady himself, lower his pulse, and make the shot. Entering a state of calmness, Andrei selected the middle of the three figures that were cautiously moving amongst the rubble of the Al Abbasid house. Just before he pulled the trigger, he imagined himself running up through snow high in the mountains in the Caucusas, with his team of specialist hunters known as the Wolf Pack. Slowly taking up pressure on the trigger, his body completely still, his heartbeat barely perceptible, Andrei Semynov, the forty-one-year-old elite FSB agent took the shot.

The body of the middle person dropped to the floor, and Andrei saw the other two people also crouch to the floor, desperately seeking shelter. Mariam, the pretty girl from Isfahan, lay dead. The high velocity round had entered the back of her head, and, as it left her body, it had ripped her face off. Yasser turned to Mehdi, his eyes filled with both rage and tears. "Those bastards will pay for this."

"Not now, Yasser. Now we just need to get out of here." As he spoke, another high-velocity round from the L115A1 rifle struck the floor, inches away from Yasser's head.

Mehdi reached for his phone and called Reza. "Reza, we are being shot at. Help!"

"Calm down, Mehdi. Do you have the pictures?"

"Yes, we have confirmation of four dead bodies. The pictures have been uploaded as you ordered," replied a terrified Mehdi.

"Good," said Reza. "We are in the boat right outside the house. Come to us now and we will get away." Mehdi relayed the message to Yasser, and the two young Quds Force commandos began to carefully make their way out of the shattered Al Abbasin compound, down to the water's edge.

"Mike Two Zero Alpha. Two targets making their way from the house towards the boat on the river."

"Roger that, Lima One Four. We will stop the boat." As Mehdi and Yasser appeared from under the date palms, and were trying to get into the boat, Andrei raised the rifle once more to his shoulder. He had predicted this shot, and was prepared. The sight picture was perfect. Waiting until the rear of the two men was about to step aboard, Andrei signaled to Sammy.

"Tell the helicopter team that only one man will be getting on to that boat." With that, Andrei closed his left eye, focused on the target that was desperately trying to scramble into the bobbing patrol boat, and took the shot. The bullet found its mark. Before Mehdi had even heard the sharp crack of the shot being fired, his bloody body was thrown backwards violently, and began to slide off the side of the boat and into the fast flowing River Tigris.

"Shit, let's go." Reza roared above the noise of the powerful outboard motors. The boat took off at speed, heading south, downriver. If Reza had been focusing properly on what was going on around him, he would have noticed the sleek fuselage of the RAF Merlin helicopter racing in low over from the south, with the sun directly behind them.

Captain Rowlings spoke once more to the sniper team on the roof of the oil refinery. "Lima One Four. Good work. Cease fire. I repeat cease fire. We are coming in fast from your three o'clock; we will take it from here."

"Roger that, Mike Two Zero Alpha," confirmed Sammy. Tapping Andrei on the shoulder, he said, "Stand down, Andrei. The boys have it covered."

As he spoke, both men felt the wash of the helicopter's downdraft as it sped overhead. The helicopter paused briefly in a hover, and turned, so that the rear door looked out on to the oncoming speed boat. The SAS sergeant, manning the .50 caliber machine gun, mounted in the rear of the helicopter, was an old hand at this. The gun erupted into short staccato bursts of fire. The whole airframe shook, and, despite her hearing protection, the noise of the pounding .50 caliber machine gun, firing carefully aimed powerful bursts of lead at the approaching speedboat, felt to Maria like being physically struck. She felt as if the gun would rip the aircraft apart, so violent were the vibrations that were shaking the airframe around her.

Then, as suddenly as it had started, it stopped. The peace returned, and the helicopter gracefully turned and dipped its nose, as it flew even lower to inspect the burning hulk of the speed boat. "Lima One Four. Boat destroyed. No survivors. We are going over to the Al Abbasin house to check on the situation over there. Please remain in overwatch until we are clear of the area."

"This is Lima One Four; we acknowledge. Out."

Seated so close to the rear door Maria was one of the first out of the aircraft. Six of the troopers fanned out and secured the perimeter. The remainder of the team carefully made their way through the smouldering remains to look for casualties. The stench was overpowering, and Maria felt like she was going to vomit. "My God, what is that smell?" she asked the trooper to her left.

"Burnt human flesh," he replied, in a dull, detached monotone voice.

Despite the devastation caused by the multiple explosive blasts, because of their knowledge of the house layout, the team could quickly find where the dining room was. Pointing to where the exterior wall used to be, one of the men shouted, "Over here, quickly." The group carefully picked their way over the rubble to the trooper. Looking down, they saw the dead body of an Arab male, dressed in a white *thawb*. The man lay pressed to the floor by one of the giant metal roof beams. His head and right leg lay twisted at awkward unnatural angles. His entire torso was a deep crimson red, and his once-crisp white *thawb* contained hundreds of tiny puncture wounds where the shrapnel and ball bearings from the vehicle bomb had torn through him.

Maria was transfixed by the sight. She was repulsed by what she saw, but at the same time could not look away. Slowly removing her camera from one of her pouches, she took three pictures of the dead man. It took another ten minutes of searching to find the decapitated Jordanian. The headless corpse lay in the fetal position, riddled with bullet holes, underneath the heavy dining room table. The remains of the fat Egyptian's lifeless body could be found scattered in the far corner of the room. It looked as of he had taken the full force of the suicide bomber's blast. His disfigured corpse had been forced against the exterior wall by the blast of the explosion, and the searing heat and shards of metal fragments had fused what little remained of his body to the wall. This sight was too much for Maria. Ripping off her respirator, she ran quickly to the edge of the room and vomited. After nearly five minutes of retching bile from her stomach, she slowly regained her composure. Returning to the burnt and disfigured corpse that was fused to the wall once more, she took out her camera and took more evidence photos.

The team searched for nearly half an hour before they found Fatima's body. It seemed that she had survived both the vehicle-borne IED and the suicide bomber. Gravely injured, she had crawled out of the dining room into the kitchen. Her body lay prostrate on the kitchen floor. It looked like the killers had taken their time in killing Fatima. The body had been mutilated and left in this position on purpose. Her eyes had been gouged out. Hollow black sockets stared back at Maria. Her throat had been slit and her hands cut off. She had been left to bleed to death. The attackers had definitely wanted to send a message to the Sunni Muslims with her death. Maria quickly took the final set of photos, and, trying to remove the image of Fatima's hollow black eye sockets from her memory, she walked back to the SAS team commander. "I think we are done here, Captain."

"I think so too. The local law enforcement will be arriving soon, and I would rather be a long way from here before those clowns arrive and start accusing us."

The team climbed aboard the Merlin once more, and flew

the short distance back to their secure compound. On the way, Captain Rowlings got back on the radio to the sniper pair. "Guys. Mission over, strip out and return to Base for a debrief. Let's try and work out how this fuck-up happened."

"Lima One Four, Roger Out," replied Sammy, as he and Andrei began to pack up their gear and climb down from the baking hot roof of the oil refinery.

Chapter Forty-Six

Latitude 40° 44' 54.8658'', Longitude -73° 58' 4.674''.
760 United Nations Plaza, Manhattan Island, New York –
Saturday 23 September 2017.
Breaking News

No rest for the wicked, thought Guilherme, as he put on his suit jacket and set off on his way to the UN headquarters in New York. After the events in Baghdad, he had called another extraordinary meeting of the Security Council. He had received the gruesome pictures attached to a complete report from Maria late on Friday night. He was repulsed when he saw the disfigured corpses in the photos, and a rage quickly grew inside him. It wasn't until he had finished the extraordinary report that he began to calm down. The report clearly outlined how the capture operation set up by the British team had been overtaken by the Iranian-backed kill operation. Seven Iranians had been killed, but, looking once more at the photos, Guilherme reminded himself that the Iranians would consider this to be a successful operation, as all of the targets had been eliminated. They were hardly going to admit that their own Quds Force Special Forces had been killed by another foreign force.

Arriving at the meeting, and settling down into his chair, the UN Secretary-General called the meeting to order. In addition to the usual Permanent Five members, the Japanese delegation were still in attendance, and Guilherme had invited the Iranian Ambassador to speak as well.

"Gentlemen, thank you all so much for giving up your time on this Saturday morning. I called this meeting to let you all know first-hand of a development that I am sure will greatly defuse the tensions between the member states." He had their attention. With the exception of the Iranian Ambassador, everyone in the room was listening with rapt attention to what Guilherme had to say.

"A newly formed sub-group of the United Nations, called the United Nations Centre for Technology and Culture (CTC) has been actively investigating the recent series of attacks around the world." The Chinese and Japanese Ambassadors were staring fixedly at each other and the Russian Ambassador was doing very little to hide his disdain for his American counterpart. "It was the CTC who developed many of the alternative energy technologies that you are now using in many of your cities and communities. It is the same international team that has carefully pieced together the puzzle of how exactly the world has been brought to the brink of all-out war and economic collapse." Guilherme paused briefly to let his words sink in and to take a sip of water.

Steeling himself for the next part of his speech, Guilherme began once more to address the assembled group of ambassadors. "In parallel to our own investigations it appears that the Iranian government had been conducting their own investigations. Both teams arrived at the same conclusions, albeit using different methods. At this point, I would like to allow the Iranian Ambassador to speak." It was difficult for Guilherme to give the

Iranians credit for stopping Fatima and her plan, but if he ever wanted to get the world order back to some sort of parity, then he would have to allow the Iranians publicly to take the credit for stopping Fatima. At least that way he wouldn't have to divulge the fact that he had been using the SAS on a similar operation.

"Mr Secretary-General, distinguished colleagues. I am honoured to be able to represent the Islamic Republic of Iran here today at the extraordinary meeting." The older Iranian man was articulate and spoke English with a very British accent. "I stress the word extraordinary, because the events that I am about to recount can only be described as extraordinary."

The Iranian Ambassador then spent the next hour outlining the history of Iran's surveillance of the Al Abbasin family. His precisely delivered speech culminated in the attack on the Al Abbasin household, and the death of Fatima and her three co-conspirators. "I am sure you agree, gentlemen, that it would have been impossible to allow these people, who posed an existential threat to all of us, to be allowed to live? In front of you I have placed a document which contains the evidence to support what I have just said. Communication between the conspirators, and with a group of Mongolian separatists, can be found within; also photos of the deceased and short biographies of each. I am sure you will find the evidence satisfactory." The Iranian Ambassador sat down to stunned silence.

He was no fool; he knew that the Iranians had only acted in their own self-interest, in their eternal struggle to stop the Muslim world from being completely dominated by the Sunnis, but diplomatic protocol obliged him, the erudite British Ambassador, Sir Richard Belmarsh, to stand and address the room. "On behalf of her Britannic Majesty, Queen Elizabeth the Second and her Government, I would like publicly to acknowledge the actions of the government of the Islamic Republic of Iran in bringing this dreadful situation to a swift conclusion. I recommend to this committee that all parties return to the *status quo ante* as soon as possible."

Next to stand was the Chinese Ambassador. Turning to his Japanese colleague, he bowed formally, and said, "The People's Republic of China regrets the attack on your oil storage site, Mr Ambassador, and is prepared to make financial reparations."

The Japanese Ambassador stood, and, bowing in return, acknowledged the statement by his Chinese counterpart, noting to himself that the wily old Chinese diplomat had stopped short of formally apologising for the attack.

Finally, the brash US Ambassador, Chuck Henderson, stood. Addressing the group, he said, "I think we have learned a lot from this recent crisis. My government hopes that we can return to normal diplomatic relations as soon as possible. I can confirm that, as soon as this meeting finishes, I will call for the US Seventh Fleet to be returned to harbour in Australia." Despite secretly knowing about the abortive Russian missile strike against the US, he turned to address the Russian Ambassador. "Mr Ambassador, your country showed great restraint in not attacking the US despite being presented with some pretty damning evidence as to our involvement in the attacks on your country. I suggest that we engage in formal discussions to de-escalate the alert state of our militaries."

Standing to accept the kind words from the US Ambassador, the Russian Ambassador was the last to speak. "Ambassador

Henderson, I will relay your request to begin the de-escalation of our Military readiness to my government immediately." Turning to address Sir Richard Belmarsh, he said, "Sir Richard, you can convey to your European colleagues that the Russian government will resume the pumping of oil through the 'Friendship' pipeline as soon as our pipeline network has been thoroughly cleaned. Our experts tell me that it will take at least another three weeks before we are ready to start pumping oil again. Of course," he added, with a wry smile. "The oil will be sold at the market value, wherever that may sit."

The meeting broke up, and the ambassadors went back to their respective offices to communicate the various messages to their respective governments. Later that same day, the Secretary-General held a brief press conference. His words were broadcast worldwide through all of the major international news outlets. Publicly acknowledging the part that the Iranian government had played in the affair, the Secretary-General confirmed that the attacks against China and Russia had been instigated by a group based in Baghdad, who were determined to do away with the many of the Middle East's governments, and form a new Caliphate.

He concluded his speech by stating that one good thing had arisen from the oil crisis. The world had begun a far more vigorous uptake in the use of non carbon-based power production. Currently, forty-six per cent of the world's energy was being produced without burning fossil fuels. This figure had risen significantly, from only twenty-eight per cent a little over six weeks previously. He hoped to see the continued growth in alternative energy production, and held out great hope that the world would finally meet its greenhouse gas emission targets.

Chapter Forty-Seven

Latitude 1° 17' 28.8348'', Longitude 103° 47' 13.3296''.
United Nations Centre for Technology and Culture
Headquarters, Heng Mui Keng Terrace, Singapore
– Monday 25 September 2017.
No Time to Relax

The team had been given the weekend off, following Maria and Andrei's return from Baghdad. Despite their mission being a failure, much praise had been lavished on Li and his team by the UN Secretary-General. They had all been sitting glued to their TV sets over the weekend, following the unfolding announcements about Russian and American strategic missile forces being stood down, and the return of the US Seventh Fleet to Australia.

The oil and currency markets had reacted well to the news of the decrease in tension between the major powers, and the Russian decision to resume pumping oil to Europe. The price of a barrel of Brent crude oil had dropped from nearly one hundred and ninety-eight dollars per barrel, to a slightly more respectable one hundred and ten dollars per barrel on the news. The price was still very high, and would probably remain so for several years, whilst Russia, China and the Europeans built up their respective reserves, thought Mathias.

Maria, Charu and Penny had organised a brunch for the team. They hadn't made the food themselves, but had got it delivered from a local deli that Maria said served the best bagels and coffee outside of Brooklyn. Li agreed about the bagels, but couldn't be persuaded to try the coffee, instead preferring to drink his own Chinese tea. The team were sitting around the round table in the briefing room, eating, drinking and chatting. After a while, Li stood, and, tapping his spoon against the side of his teacup, he eventually managed to get everyone's attention.

"I would like to say a few words, if I may, to you all. I am extremely proud of all of you. I can officially announce that the Secretary-General has confirmed that, as of today, the CTC ends its probation period and has been accepted as a fully integrated part of the United Nations organisation." Loud cheers erupted around the table.

Looking slightly more serious, Li continued to speak. "I know that this job has demanded a lot from all of us. It has tested our values, our commitment and our loyalty. I have decided to stay on as the head of the team for the foreseeable future. This comes at some personal cost, as it will preclude me and my family from ever returning to Beijing." The team were silent as they weighed Li's words.

Maria was next to speak. "I guess we have all grown up a little over the past few months. Working here really has put a lot of things in perspective. It is no secret that I had my doubts about you Li. All I can say is that I am sorry for doubting you, and I would be honoured to remain on the team and serve under you."

"OK, OK," interrupted Matthias. "This is all getting a little too emotional, don't you think?" A murmur of laughter rippled around the room. "Li, I think I speak on behalf of the whole room when I say that you have achieved the impossible. You have turned a group of disparate individuals into a cohesive team with a single purpose. I would like to make my own announcement. I can announce that, as of today, I have been sober for four months. I guess all this excitement and the long hours are helping. So, if you'll have me, I would be delighted to remain on the team. That is, as long as I don't have put up with those two love birds over their whispering in dark corners and enjoying stolen kisses every time they think my back is turned." Both Andrei and Maria, who were sitting next to each other, began to redden with embarrassment.

"I don't believe it," cut in Penny. "Our man of ice, the Russian super-agent, is capable of emotion!" The rest of the team laughed.

"So what's next?" asked Charu.

"Does she never stop thinking about work?" chuckled Philippe.

"Well, for starters," interrupted Li. "I want us to do some analysis, a sort of after-action review. I would like us to hypothesise how the world would look with a benign Caliphate in the Middle East."

"You're joking, right?" asked Penny.

"No, I am deadly serious. You see, this whole process started me thinking about what our core mission here is." Activating the LCD display behind him, Li flashed up the Mission Statement, which also served as a screen saver.

"To develop stable conditions for coexistence and development between different cultures and to support the

development of autonomous regions not subservient to a nation state through the supply and use of pertinent technologies."

"You see," Li continued. "I am not entirely sure that we were acting in the interests of our mission statement when we tried to stop this new benign Caliphate from being formed." Li looked at Maria and Andrei, who were still slightly flushed. "What was missing from the scene at the house in Baghdad?"

"I don't know," replied Maria.

"I do," said Li. "You see, you can't have a Caliphate without a Caliph. The body of the younger son, Hamed, was not found amongst the rubble, was it?"

"Er, no," replied Maria, annoyed at herself for overlooking such an obvious clue.

"Therefore, I conclude that somewhere out there is a Caliph without a Caliphate. Now, whether he tries himself to reform the Caliphate, or, maybe, just maybe, in the not-too-distant future, he is asked by the international community to do so, I think we should be prepared to offer our analysis and expertise. Don't you?

"So, if you ask me what's next, I would say a whole load of detailed research and analysis and a lot more Human Terrain Mapping. But first, I believe we have all deserved some leave. Now, I know leave can be taken at your own discretion, but I also have the authority to grant additional leave." The team looked excitedly from one to another. "I am granting you a long weekend from this Thursday evening until Tuesday morning." There were a few looks of mild disappointment around the table.

"You look disappointed, Philippe?" said Li, with a slight smile on his face.

"Well, it is just that, after rescuing the world from imminent Armageddon and economic ruin, I kind of expected more than Friday and Monday off."

Some of the other team members stifled laughs, unsure as to how Li would react.

"I know, I know; however, we need to provide an analysis paper to the Secretary-General before Thursday."

"Analysis of what?" asked Matthias.

"The India-Pakistan crisis."

"What India-Pakistan crisis?" cut in Charu.

"Well, it isn't a full blown crisis yet; but if someone doesn't intervene soon, it may well be. Whilst the attention of the world was focused on the superpower disputes, a series of eight seemingly related suicide bombings has happened in India's biggest cities. The Indian government is naturally pointing the finger at Pakistan. The population are becoming polarized, with the large Muslim majority blaming the ultra-nationalist Hindu prime minister for whipping up anti-Muslim sentiment in the country. The Indian armed forces have been mobilised, and their army is busy calling up reserves, and slowly massing on the India-Pakistan border.

"Bloody Hell!" said Philippe. "I guess we'd better get started."

At the end of another long day in the office, Maria and Andrei found themselves out on another long run around the parks and shallow rises that passed for hills surrounding Singapore. The twice weekly run had become a regular event, and, although Maria still struggled like hell to keep up with Andrei, she enjoyed the calming effect the runs had on her, and was even starting to be able to enter that state of inner calm that Andrei maintained when he ran. That was, of course, when she managed to keep her pulse below one hundred and eighty beats per minute.

"Andrei, I have something to tell you," began Maria, as they turned to head down past the port. "I am sorry for how I behaved the other day in the meeting before we went to Iraq. You see, you mentioned a name in the meeting that shocked me."

"What did I say?" asked Andrei, gradually increasing the pace as they left the port area and began to pick their way up through the parklands behind the CTC Headquarters.

"You mentioned the name of Dimitri Podoyenko. Who is he to you?"

"As I said, he is the just the boss of my old friend. I have only met him once, in a car park, as I told you. He seemed OK to me. He works in a different department to the one where I worked. I think he works in counter-narcotics."

Grabbing Andrei's arm, and forcing him to stop running, Maria said, "Look at me, Andrei. This Dimitri Podoyenko was one of the men on the botched drugs raid in Miami where my husband was killed. The whole affair was covered up by our State Department. Deemed 'not in the public interest'. But I know from my husband's former partner that he was shot by friendly fire, and the ballistics report confirmed that the shot came from a Russian pistol."

Andrei stared intently at Maria. "My God," he said, with real feeling and warmth in his voice. "I didn't know, I swear. I didn't know."

"I know that now, Andrei; I just needed to hear you say it. Andrei, I care a lot for you; but I will not rest until I find the man that killed my husband."

SACRED
SPACE
FOR LENT 2021

From the website www.sacredspace.ie

PRAYER FROM THE IRISH JESUITS

ISBN: 9781788122597

Weekly reflections are taken from books published by Messenger
Publications, or from *The Sacred Heart Messenger* magazine. For more
information go to www.messenger.ie

Designed by Messenger Publications Design Department
Typeset in Plantin and Bitter
Printed by Hussar Books
Cover Image: Nancy J Ondra / Shutterstock

Messenger Publications,
37 Leeson Place, Dublin D02 E5V0, Ireland
www.messenger.ie

Contents

Sacred Space Prayer

Bless all who worship you, almighty God,
from the rising of the sun to its setting:
from your goodness enrich us,
by your love inspire us,
by your Spirit guide us,
by your power protect us,
in your mercy receive us,
now and always.

How to Use This Booklet

During each week of Lent, begin by reading the 'Something to think and pray about each day this week'. Then go through the 'Presence of God', 'Freedom' and 'Consciousness' steps to help you prepare yourself to hear the Word of God speaking to you. In the next step, 'The Word', turn to the Scripture reading for each day of the week. Inspiration points are provided if you need them. Then return to the 'Conversation' and 'Conclusion' steps. Follow this process every day of Lent.

THE FIRST WEEK OF LENT
21–27 February 2021

Something to think and pray about each day this week:

'The Lord asks everything of us, and in return he offers us true life, the happiness for which we were created.' (*Gaudete et Exsultate*, 1)

Lent does not normally begin with happiness. We are more accustomed to hearing how hard it will be. The theme of conversion, which the season of Lent begins with, is often understood in terms of sacrifice, struggle and even suffering. An overly moralistic approach to Lent means, however, that Christians can sometimes look, in a line from the Pope's previous exhortation, *Evangelii Gaudium* (The Joy of the Gospel), 'like someone who has just come back from a funeral' (*EG*, 10). The challenge of the Gospel is to consider the call to repentance in the light of what we receive from God. This means holding the darkness of our lives up against the light of God's love, seeing the contrast between the sin of the world and the salvation offered in the kingdom of God.

Kevin O'Gorman, *Journeying in Joy and Gladness:*
Lent and Holy Week with Gaudete et Exsultate

The Presence of God
Lord, help me to be fully alive to your holy presence.
Enfold me in your love. Let my heart become one
with yours.
My soul longs for your presence, Lord. When I turn
my thoughts to you, I find peace and contentment.

Freedom
Your death on the cross has set me free. I can live
joyously and freely without fear of death. Your
mercy knows no bounds.

Consciousness
At this moment, Lord, I turn my thoughts to you.
I will leave aside my chores and preoccupations.
I will take rest and refreshment in your presence.

The Word
The word of God comes down to us through the
Scriptures.
May the Holy Spirit enlighten my mind and my
heart
to respond to the Gospel teachings:
to love my neighbour as myself,
to care for my sisters and brothers in Christ.
*(Please turn to the Scripture on the following pages.
Inspiration points are there, should you need them.
When you are ready, return here to continue.)*

Conversation

Begin to talk to Jesus about the Scripture you have just read. What part of it strikes a chord in you? Perhaps the words of a friend – or some story you have heard recently – will slowly rise to the surface of your consciousness. If so, does the story throw light on what the Scripture passage may be saying to you?

Conclusion

I thank God for these moments we have spent together and for any insights I have been given concerning the text.

Sunday 21 February
First Sunday of Lent
Mark 1:12–15

And the Spirit immediately drove him out into the wilderness. He was in the wilderness for forty days, tempted by Satan; and he was with the wild beasts; and the angels waited on him.

Now after John was arrested, Jesus came to Galilee, proclaiming the good news of God, and saying, 'The time is fulfilled, and the kingdom of God has come near; repent, and believe in the good news.'

- Only God could be so human as to endure temptation. Mark's Gospel depicts Jesus as divine but also deeply human. He enters the wilderness for one purpose only: to find God, to seek God and to belong to him totally. Only then does he come into Galilee and proclaim good news.

- Lord, come with me into my wilderness. Speak to my preoccupied heart. Reveal to me where addiction to power, possession and gratification choke my path. Only when I am free from these can I be good news to others. Only then do I become part of the solution to the world's problems.

Monday 22 February
St Peter's Chair
Matthew 16:13–19

Now when Jesus came into the district of Caesarea Philippi, he asked his disciples, 'Who do people say that the Son of Man is?' And they said, 'Some say John the Baptist, but others Elijah, and still others Jeremiah or one of the prophets.' He said to them, 'But who do you say that I am?' Simon Peter answered, 'You are the Messiah, the Son of the living God.' And Jesus answered him, 'Blessed are you, Simon son of Jonah! For flesh and blood has not revealed this to you, but my Father in heaven. And I tell you, you are Peter, and on this rock I will build my church, and the gates of Hades will not prevail against it. I will give you the keys of the kingdom of heaven, and whatever you bind on earth will be bound in heaven, and whatever you loose on earth will be loosed in heaven.'

- When Peter is moved to identify Jesus with the Messiah Jesus congratulates him, so to speak, on having allowed himself to be inspired in his answer by the heavenly Father: at last his thinking has been raised onto the properly spiritual plane.

- Jesus reveals that he is founding a church – a community of faith and worship – which the powers of hell will not be able to overcome. But community always needs leadership; and to Peter (whose name resembles the word for 'rock' – depending on the language being spoken) is entrusted the authority of binding and loosing – always associated with a people with whom the Lord has entered into a covenant bond.

Tuesday 23 February
Matthew 6:7–15

'When you are praying, do not heap up empty phrases as the Gentiles do; for they think that they will be heard because of their many words. Do not be like them, for your Father knows what you need before you ask him.

'Pray then in this way:
Our Father in heaven,
hallowed be your name.
Your kingdom come.
Your will be done,
on earth as it is in heaven.
Give us this day our daily bread.
And forgive us our debts,
as we also have forgiven our debtors.
And do not bring us to the time of trial,
but rescue us from the evil one.
For if you forgive others their trespasses, your heavenly Father will also forgive you; but if you

do not forgive others, neither will your Father forgive your trespasses.'

- The phrases of the Our Father may be very familiar to me. I might let just one of them offer itself now; I take time to let it sink in again and take it with me through the day.

- Debts, evil and trespasses are all brought before God and assume their proper place. I am drawn to God, being made holy, nourished and forgiven.

Wednesday 24 February
Luke 11:29–32

When the crowds were increasing, he began to say, 'This generation is an evil generation; it asks for a sign, but no sign will be given to it except the sign of Jonah. For just as Jonah became a sign to the people of Nineveh, so the Son of Man will be to this generation. The queen of the South will rise at the judgement with the people of this generation and condemn them, because she came from the ends of the earth to listen to the wisdom of Solomon, and see, something greater than Solomon is here! The people of Nineveh will rise up at the judgement with this generation and condemn it, because they repented at the proclamation of Jonah, and see, something greater than Jonah is here!

- Jonah converted the great city of Nineveh by his godliness and his preaching, not by miracles. Holiness is a greater marvel than special effects, but less easily recognised. The spectacular is what draws the crowds. Lord, your hand is more evident in saintliness than in extraordinary signs. Open my eyes to your work in my sisters and brothers.

Thursday 25 February
Matthew 7:7–12

'Ask, and it will be given to you; search, and you will find; knock, and the door will be opened for you. For everyone who asks receives, and everyone who searches finds, and for everyone who knocks, the door will be opened. Is there anyone among you who, if your child asks for bread, will give a stone? Or if the child asks for a fish, will give a snake? If you then, who are evil, know how to give good gifts to your children, how much more will your Father in heaven give good things to those who ask him!

'In everything do to others as you would have them do to you; for this is the law and the prophets.'

- Prayer is never wasted. Good things come in prayer, maybe not what someone asks for. Prayer opens the heart for good things from God. Be grateful at the end of prayer for time spent with the God of all goodness. Prayer time is always productive time in making us people of more love.

Friday 26 February
Matthew 5:20–26

'For I tell you, unless your righteousness exceeds that of the scribes and Pharisees, you will never enter the kingdom of heaven.

'You have heard that it was said to those of ancient times, "You shall not murder"; and "whoever murders shall be liable to judgement." But I say to you that if you are angry with a brother or sister, you will be liable to judgement; and if you insult a brother or sister, you will be liable to the council; and if you say, "You fool" you will be liable to the hell of fire. So when you are offering your gift at the altar, if you remember that your brother or sister has something against you, leave your gift there before the altar and go; first be reconciled to your brother or sister, and then come and offer your gift. Come to terms quickly with your accuser while you are on the way to court with him, or your accuser may hand you over to the judge, and the judge to the guard, and you will be thrown into prison. Truly I tell you, you will never get out until you have paid the last penny.'

- How challenging the Gospel is! I am called not only to do love but to think love! Can I invite Jesus into my heart to create that sort of loving, respectful heart for me?

- The Spirit is calling me to be changed, to become a more loving, kinder, more merciful and more just person, to be transformed. Do I notice the difference in me when I am loving and when I am unloving? Do I talk to Jesus about this?

Saturday 27 February
Matthew 5:43–48

'You have heard that it was said, "You shall love your neighbour and hate your enemy." But I say to you, Love your enemies and pray for those who persecute you, so that you may be children of your Father in heaven; for he makes his sun rise on the evil and on the good, and sends rain on the righteous and on the unrighteous. For if you love those who love you, what reward do you have? Do not even the tax-collectors do the same? And if you greet only your brothers and sisters, what more are you doing than others? Do not even the Gentiles do the same? Be perfect, therefore, as your heavenly Father is perfect.'

- There are times, Lord, when you lift us beyond what we thought possible. Here you ask me to be perfect: meaning that in my heart I should bless even those who hate me and wrong me. The love of God can be poured out in our hearts through the Holy Spirit who is given to us. Even when I feel far from blessed myself, even when old age makes me feel there is little I can do for others, I can still give my approval and blessing to those I meet; that will lift them.

- As I think of those whose love I return, I thank God for them and for the blessings we share.

- As I pray for those who bring blessings to me, I pray that I may include others in a widening circle of compassion.

THE SECOND WEEK OF LENT
28 February – 6 March 2021

Something to think and pray about each day this week:

Many years ago, when we were told about the hazards of alcoholism in secondary school, we were given the image of a timid, shy, person who had to consume alcohol to gain courage to socialise…

Conversations with students have made me realise that the addictions today are more subtle. Students tell me that they are more and more under pressure to project an image of themselves that is socially acceptable and, like the alcoholic, they often find themselves suppressing their real self.

…Over and over again in the Gospel, through His Son, the Father calls people from falsehood to truth. He's a lot easier on the real person who struggles; He finds oceans of forgiveness and understanding for them. … it's our deepest real and true self that matters and it is deeply loveable.

Our job is to love others without stopping to inquire whether or not they are worthy. – THOMAS MERTON

Alan Hilliard, *Dipping into Lent*

The Presence of God

I remind myself that, as I sit here now,
God is gazing on me with love and holding me in
   being.
I pause for a moment and think of this.

Freedom

'There are very few people who realise what God
would make of them if they abandoned themselves
into his hands, and let themselves be formed by
his grace' (St Ignatius). I ask for the grace to trust
myself totally to God's love.

Consciousness

Where do I sense hope, encouragement and growth
in my life? By looking back over the past few months,
I may be able to see which activities and occasions
have produced rich fruit. If I do notice such areas,
I will determine to give those areas both time and
space in the future.

The Word

Lord Jesus, you became human to communicate
   with me.
You walked and worked on this earth.
You endured the heat and struggled with the cold.
All your time on this earth was spent in
   caring for humanity.

You healed the sick, you raised the dead.
Most important of all, you saved me from death.
(Please turn to the Scripture on the following pages.
Inspiration points are there, should you need them.
When you are ready, return here to continue.)

Conversation

What is stirring in me as I pray? Am I consoled,
troubled, left cold? I imagine Jesus standing or
sitting at my side, and I share my feelings with him.

Conclusion

Glory be to the Father, and to the Son, and to the
  Holy Spirit,
As it was in the beginning, is now and ever shall be,
World without end. Amen.

Sunday 28 February
Second Sunday of Lent
Mark 9:2–10

Six days later, Jesus took with him Peter and James and John, and led them up a high mountain apart, by themselves. And he was transfigured before them, and his clothes became dazzling white, such as no one on earth could bleach them. And there appeared to them Elijah with Moses, who were talking with Jesus. Then Peter said to Jesus, 'Rabbi, it is good for us to be here; let us make three dwellings, one for you, one for Moses, and one for Elijah.' He did not know what to say, for they were terrified. Then a cloud overshadowed them, and from the cloud there came a voice, 'This is my Son, the Beloved; listen to him!' Suddenly when they looked around, they saw no one with them any more, but only Jesus.

As they were coming down the mountain, he ordered them to tell no one about what they had seen, until after the Son of Man had risen from the dead. So they kept the matter to themselves, questioning what this rising from the dead could mean.

- Peter cries out in delight and wonder, 'Master, it is good for us to be here!' This is how we are surely meant to experience the presence of God

– in wonder and delight, the created glorying in the Creator's presence. Too often, we glide along the surface of the spinning earth, never listening to its heartbeat. We look into the depths of the universe and never hear the singing of the stars.

- When did I last sing and make melody to the Lord with all my heart or clap my hands or shout for joy to him?

Monday 1 March

Luke 6:36–38

'Be merciful, just as your Father is merciful. Do not judge, and you will not be judged; do not condemn, and you will not be condemned. Forgive, and you will be forgiven; give, and it will be given to you. A good measure, pressed down, shaken together, running over, will be put into your lap; for the measure you give will be the measure you get back.'

- Jesus invites us to be as God is – nothing less! He does not intend to overwhelm us or cause us to feel frustrated by such an enormous invitation, but wants us to wonder at the immensity of God's capacity to love. In our humanity, we are not infinite, but we are called to great love and hope. The invitation reaches out to us as we are in our lives, calling us into the life of God.

- Judgement, condemnation and lack of forgiveness inhibit good and bind up the spirit. Lord help me to be generous, not by forcing anything from myself, but by sharing fully what you give to me.

Tuesday 2 March
Matthew 23:1–12

Then Jesus said to the crowds and to his disciples, 'The scribes and the Pharisees sit on Moses' seat; therefore, do whatever they teach you and follow it; but do not do as they do, for they do not practise what they teach. They tie up heavy burdens, hard to bear, and lay them on the shoulders of others; but they themselves are unwilling to lift a finger to move them. They do all their deeds to be seen by others; for they make their phylacteries broad and their fringes long. They love to have the place of honour at banquets and the best seats in the synagogues, and to be greeted with respect in the market-places, and to have people call them rabbi. But you are not to be called rabbi, for you have one teacher, and you are all students. And call no one your father on earth, for you have one Father – the one in heaven. Nor are you to be called instructors, for you have one instructor, the Messiah. The greatest among you will be your servant. All who exalt themselves will be humbled, and all who humble themselves will be exalted.'

- Although the content of this passage reflects conflicts in the early Church between the Christians and the Jews led by the Pharisees, there is no doubt the fierce denunciations of the Pharisees go back to Jesus. His denunciation is an indication that they were corrosive of true religion by not giving priority to the good and needs of the person.

- Jesus' disciples are not to make a big display of religion nor are they to seek honourable titles like 'father' and 'teacher' and 'rabbi'. Our teacher is God, and the true disciple learns only from God. I think of what it would be like for me to assume the lowest place, to really take to heart what Jesus says about humility. I begin my prayer by asking God for the help I need, humbly and sincerely.

Wednesday 3 March
Matthew 20:17–28

While Jesus was going up to Jerusalem, he took the twelve disciples aside by themselves, and said to them on the way, 'See, we are going up to Jerusalem, and the Son of Man will be handed over to the chief priests and scribes, and they will condemn him to death; then they will hand him over to the Gentiles to be mocked and flogged and crucified; and on the third day he will be raised.'

Then the mother of the sons of Zebedee came to him with her sons, and kneeling before him, she asked a favour of him. And he said to her, 'What do you want?' She said to him, 'Declare that these two sons of mine will sit, one at your right hand and one at your left, in your kingdom.' But Jesus answered, 'You do not know what you are asking. Are you able to drink the cup that I am about to drink?' They said to him, 'We are able.' He said to them, 'You will indeed drink my cup, but to sit at my right hand and at my left, this is not mine to grant, but it is for those for whom it has been prepared by my Father.'

When the ten heard it, they were angry with the two brothers. But Jesus called them to him and said, 'You know that the rulers of the Gentiles lord it over them, and their great ones are tyrants over them. It will not be so among you; but whoever wishes to be great among you must be your servant, and whoever wishes to be first among you must be your slave; just as the Son of Man came not to be served but to serve, and to give his life as a ransom for many.'

- Our prayer often finds us asking for what we want. As we grow in awareness of the presence of God we realise how God wants for us something greater. It may appear that we are asked to let go of our requests, but we soon realise that nothing we really want is lost in God.

- Jesus was clear about his relationship with God; he knew who he was and what was his to give. Lord, help me to know more clearly what is mine to do and what I might best leave to you.

Thursday 4 March
Luke 16:19–31

There was a rich man who was dressed in purple and fine linen and who feasted sumptuously every day. And at his gate lay a poor man named Lazarus, covered with sores, who longed to satisfy his hunger with what fell from the rich man's table; even the dogs would come and lick his sores. The poor man died and was carried away by the angels to be with Abraham. The rich man also died and was buried. In Hades, where he was being tormented, he looked up and saw Abraham far away with Lazarus by his side. He called out, 'Father Abraham, have mercy on me, and send Lazarus to dip the tip of his finger in water and cool my tongue; for I am in agony in these flames.' But Abraham said, 'Child, remember that during your lifetime you received your good things, and Lazarus in like manner evil things; but now he is comforted here, and you are in agony.

Besides all this, between you and us a great chasm has been fixed, so that those who might want to pass from here to you cannot do so, and no one can cross from there to us.' He said, 'Then, father, I beg you to send him to my father's house – for I have five brothers – that he may warn them, so that they will not also come into this place of torment.' Abraham replied, 'They have Moses and the prophets; they should listen to them.' He said, 'No, father Abraham; but if someone goes to them from the dead, they will repent.' He said to him, 'If they do not listen to Moses and the prophets, neither will they be convinced even if someone rises from the dead.'

- Jesus is asking his listeners to open their eyes to what is around them, and to open their ears to the simple command of the Gospel: love your neighbour.

- Praying on this story can challenge us into care for the needy in whatever way we can to improve the lives of poor people.

- All, whether rich or poor, must die. 'When we look at the wise, they die ... and leave their wealth to others' (Psalm 49:10). Death is inevitable for us all, and there is no escape from it. We prepare our future dwelling place now by charity and patient endurance.

Friday 5 March
Matthew 21:33–43.45–46

'Listen to another parable. There was a landowner who planted a vineyard, put a fence around it, dug a wine press in it, and built a watch-tower. Then he leased it to tenants and went to another country. When the harvest time had come, he sent his slaves to the tenants to collect his produce. But the tenants seized his slaves and beat one, killed another and stoned another. Again he sent other slaves, more than the first; and they treated them in the same way. Finally he sent his son to them, saying, "They will respect my son." But when the tenants saw the son, they said to themselves, "This is the heir; come, let us kill him and get his inheritance." So they seized him, threw him out of the vineyard, and killed him. Now when the owner of the vineyard comes, what will he do to those tenants?" They said to him, "He will put those wretches to a miserable death, and lease the vineyard to other tenants who will give him the produce at the harvest time."'

Jesus said to them, 'Have you never read in the scriptures:

'The stone that the builders rejected
has become the cornerstone;
this was the Lord's doing,
and it is amazing in our eyes'?

Therefore I tell you, the kingdom of God will be taken away from you and given to a people that produces the fruits of the kingdom.'

When the chief priests and the Pharisees heard his parables, they realised that he was speaking about them. They wanted to arrest him, but they feared the crowds, because they regarded him as a prophet.

- One of the saddest statements in the Gospels is this innocent comment of the father: 'They will respect my son.' I am frightened to think what would happen if Jesus came into our world today. His message about the kingdom of God would put him in direct opposition to so many other kingdoms. He would become an enemy to be got rid of.

- Jesus, you were thrown out and killed. But you took no revenge. Instead you excused your torturers and by your love you reconciled everyone with God. You showed what divine love is like. You love me totally, no matter what I do. May I always wish others well, and pray for them instead of taking revenge on them when they hurt me.

Saturday 6 March

Luke 15:1–3.11–32

Now all the tax-collectors and sinners were coming near to listen to him. And the Pharisees and the scribes were grumbling and saying, 'This fellow welcomes sinners and eats with them.'

So he told them this parable: 'There was a man who had two sons. The younger of them said to his father, "Father, give me the share of the property that will belong to me." So he divided his property between them. A few days later the younger son gathered all he had and travelled to a distant country, and there he squandered his property in dissolute living. When he had spent everything, a severe famine took place throughout that country, and he began to be in need. So he went and hired himself out to one of the citizens of that country, who sent him to his fields to feed the pigs. He would gladly have filled himself with the pods that the pigs were eating; and no one gave him anything. But when he came to himself he said, "How many of my father's hired hands have bread enough and to spare, but here I am dying of hunger! I will get up and go to my father, and I will say to him, 'Father, I have sinned against heaven and before you; I am no longer worthy to be called your son; treat me like one of your hired hands.'" So he set off and went to his father. But while he was still far off, his father saw him and was filled with compassion; he ran and put his arms around him and kissed him. Then the son said to him, "Father, I have sinned against heaven and before you; I am no longer worthy to be called your son." But the father said to his slaves, "Quickly, bring out a robe – the best one – and put it on him; put a ring on his finger and sandals on his feet. And get the fatted calf and kill it, and let us eat and celebrate; for this son of mine was dead and is alive again; he was lost and is found!" And they began to celebrate.

'Now his elder son was in the field; and when he came and approached the house, he heard music and dancing. He called one of the slaves and asked what was going on. He replied, "Your brother has come, and your father has killed the fatted calf, because he has got him back safe and sound." Then he became angry and refused to go in. His father came out and began to plead with him. But he answered his father, "Listen! For all these years I have been working like a slave for you, and I have never disobeyed your command; yet you have never given me even a young goat so that I might celebrate with my friends. But when this son of yours came back, who has devoured your property with prostitutes, you killed the fatted calf for him!" Then the father said to him, "Son, you are always with me, and all that is mine is yours. But we had to celebrate and rejoice, because this brother of yours was dead and has come to life; he was lost and has been found.'"

- The parable of the Prodigal Son gives me a picture of the steadfast love of God. There, Lord, you show how your heavenly father would appear in human form. When he welcomes back his lost son with tears of delight, kills the fatted calf, brings out the best robe, and throws a great party, it is not to please other people, but to give expression to his own overwhelming pleasure that his child has come home. You delight in me.

- Time and again and God promises me goodness. I pray that my eyes may be opened to appreciate where God is working in my life.

THE THIRD WEEK OF LENT
7–13 March 2021

Something to think and pray about each day this week:

The temptations of Jesus are not at all temptations
to this or that sin but, rather, fundamental options
that matter for the direction of his life. Jesus was
tempted in the course of his ministry to choose
other ways of being God's prophet, the Messiah
or anointed one. In a less obvious way, we too can
be attracted by choices that can shape the way our
life unfolds. We ask ourselves, what do I live on?
What's my true goal? Where is my nourishment?
The human, no less than the Kingdom, is more
than food and drink. Only the word of God truly
nourishes and illuminates.

Kieran J O'Mahony OSA, *Hearers of the Word: Praying
and Exploring the Readings for Lent & Holy Week, Year A*

The Presence of God

I remind myself that I am in the presence of God, who is my strength in times of weakness and my comforter in times of sorrow.

Freedom

St Ignatius thought that a thick and shapeless tree trunk would never believe that it could become a statue, admired as a miracle of sculpture, and would never submit itself to the chisel of the sculptor, who sees by her genius what she can make of it. I ask for the grace to let myself be shaped by my loving Creator.

Consciousness

Dear Lord, help me to remember that you gave me life. Teach me to slow down, to be still and enjoy the pleasures created for me, to be aware of the beauty that surrounds me: the marvel of mountains, the calmness of lakes, the fragility of a flower petal. I need to remember that all these things come from you.

The Word

In this expectant state of mind, please turn to the text for the day with confidence. Believe that the Holy Spirit is present and may reveal whatever the passage has to say to you. Read reflectively, listening with a third ear to what may be going on in your heart. *(Please turn to the Scripture on the following pages. Inspiration points are there, should you need them. When you are ready, return here to continue.)*

Conversation

What feelings are rising in me as I pray and reflect on God's word? I imagine Jesus himself sitting or standing near me, and I open my heart to him.

Conclusion

I thank God for these moments we have spent together and for any insights I have been given concerning the text.

Sunday 7 March
Third Sunday of Lent
John 2:13–25

The Passover of the Jews was near, and Jesus went up to Jerusalem. In the temple he found people selling cattle, sheep and doves, and the money-changers seated at their tables. Making a whip of cords, he drove all of them out of the temple, both the sheep and the cattle. He also poured out the coins of the money-changers and overturned their tables. He told those who were selling the doves, 'Take these things out of here! Stop making my Father's house a market-place!' His disciples remembered that it was written, 'Zeal for your house will consume me.' The Jews then said to him, 'What sign can you show us for doing this?' Jesus answered them, 'Destroy this temple, and in three days I will raise it up.' The Jews then said, 'This temple has been under construction for forty-six years, and will you raise it up in three days?' But he was speaking of the temple of his body. After he was raised from the dead, his disciples remembered that he had said this; and they believed the scripture and the word that Jesus had spoken.

When he was in Jerusalem during the Passover festival, many believed in his name because they saw the signs that he was doing. But Jesus on his part would not entrust himself to them, because he knew all people and needed no one to testify about anyone; for he himself knew what was in everyone.

- I imagine myself visiting the Temple when Jesus enters. I am accustomed to the money-changers, and to the hucksters who convenience worshippers by selling cattle, sheep and doves for the ritual sacrifices. The fury of Jesus startles and upsets me, makes me think. Surely these guys are making an honest few bob?

- But this is the house of God. When money creeps in, it tends to take over. Is there any of the Christian sacraments untouched by commercialism? Christening parties, First Communion money, Confirmation discos, wedding feasts ... They are meant to be the touch of God at key moments in our lives; but can God get a hearing amid the clatter of coins?

Monday 8 March
John 4:5–42

So he came to a Samaritan city called Sychar, near the plot of ground that Jacob had given to his son Joseph. Jacob's well was there, and Jesus, tired out by his journey, was sitting by the well. It was about noon.

A Samaritan woman came to draw water, and Jesus said to her, 'Give me a drink'. (His disciples had gone to the city to buy food.) The Samaritan woman said to him, 'How is it that you, a Jew, ask a drink of me, a woman of Samaria?' (Jews do not share things in common with Samaritans.) Jesus answered her, 'If you knew the gift of God, and who it is that is saying to you, 'Give me a drink', you would have asked him, and he would have given you living water.' The woman said to him, 'Sir, you have no bucket, and the well is deep. Where do you get that living water? Are you greater than our ancestor Jacob, who gave us the well, and with his sons and his flocks drank from it?' Jesus said to her, 'Everyone who drinks of this water will be thirsty again, but those who drink of the water that I will give them will never be thirsty. The water that I will give will become in them a spring of water gushing up to eternal life.' The woman said to him, 'Sir, give me this water, so that I may never be thirsty or have to keep coming here to draw water.'

Jesus said to her, 'Go, call your husband, and come back.' The woman answered him, 'I have no husband.' Jesus said to her, 'You are right in saying, "I have no husband"; for you have had five husbands, and the one you have now is not your husband. What you have said is true!' The woman said to him, 'Sir, I see that you are a prophet. Our ancestors worshipped on this mountain, but you say that the place where people must worship is in Jerusalem.' Jesus said to her, 'Woman, believe me, the hour is coming when you will worship the Father neither on this mountain nor in Jerusalem. You worship what you do not know; we worship what we know, for salvation is from the Jews. But the hour is coming, and is now here, when the true worshippers will worship the Father in spirit and truth, for the Father seeks such as these to worship him. God is spirit, and those who worship him must worship in spirit and truth.' The woman said to him, 'I know that the Messiah is coming' (who is called Christ). 'When he comes, he will proclaim all things to us.' Jesus said to her, 'I am he, the one who is speaking to you.'

Just then his disciples came. They were astonished that he was speaking with a woman, but no one said, 'What do you want?' or, 'Why are you speaking with her?' Then the woman left her water-jar and went back to the city. She said to the people, 'Come and see a man who told me everything I have ever done! He cannot be the Messiah, can he?' They left the city and were on their way to him.

Meanwhile the disciples were urging him, 'Rabbi, eat something.' But he said to them, 'I have food to eat that you do not know about.' So the disciples said to one another, 'Surely no one has brought him something to eat?' Jesus said to them, 'My food is to do the will of him who sent me and to complete his work. Do you not say, "Four months more, then comes the harvest"? But I tell you, look around you, and see how the fields are ripe for harvesting. The reaper is already receiving wages and is gathering fruit for eternal life, so that sower and reaper may rejoice together. For here the saying holds true, "One sows and another reaps." I sent you to reap that for which you did not labour. Others have laboured, and you have entered into their labour.'

Many Samaritans from that city believed in him because of the woman's testimony, 'He told me everything I have ever done.' So when the Samaritans came to him, they asked him to stay with them; and he stayed there for two days. And many more believed because of his word. They said to the woman, 'It is no longer because of what you said that we believe, for we have heard for ourselves, and we know that this is truly the Saviour of the world.'

- Lord, I am going about my business like the Samaritan woman, and am taken aback when you accost me at the well. You interrupt my business, my getting and spending, and the routines of my day. Let me savour this encounter, imagine you probing my desires, showing you know the waywardness of my heart. At the end, like her, I am moved with such joy at meeting you that I cannot keep it to myself. 'Lift up your eyes and see how the fields are already white for harvest.'

Tuesday 9 March
Matthew 18:21–35

Then Peter came and said to him, 'Lord, if another member of the church sins against me, how often should I forgive? As many as seven times?' Jesus said to him, 'Not seven times, but, I tell you, seventy-seven times.

'For this reason the kingdom of heaven may be compared to a king who wished to settle accounts with his slaves. When he began the reckoning, one who owed him ten thousand talents was brought to him; and, as he could not pay, his lord ordered him to be sold, together with his wife and children and all his possessions, and payment to be made. So the slave fell on his knees before him, saying, "Have patience with me, and I will pay you everything." And out of pity for him, the lord of that slave released him and forgave him the debt. But that same slave, as he went out, came upon one of his fellow-slaves who owed him a hundred denarii; and seizing him by the throat, he said, "Pay what you owe." Then his fellow-slave fell down and pleaded with him, "Have patience with me, and I will pay you." But he refused; then he went and threw him into prison until he should pay the debt. When his fellow-slaves saw what had happened, they were greatly distressed, and they went and reported to their lord all that had taken place. Then his lord summoned him and said to him, "You wicked slave! I forgave you all that debt because you pleaded with me. Should you not have had mercy on your fellow-slave, as I had mercy on you?" And in anger his lord handed him over to be tortured until he should pay his entire debt. So my heavenly Father will also do to every one of you, if you do not forgive your brother or sister from your heart.'

- Forgiveness is something very creative and goes beyond the existing facts. It recognises the deeper goodness in people, despite what they have done.

- As theologian Romano Guardini pointed out, there is no forgiveness if one wants punishment. Forgiveness means pardoning and letting go completely, creating and making the offender new again. It requires great grace to forgive.

- Justice can be the enemy of love. It indicates the normal legal way of proceeding. We often hear people say: 'We want justice done'. But mercy or forgiveness is far nobler and says, 'I want the person to be fully well and alive again'.

Wednesday 10 March
Matthew 5:17–19

'Do not think that I have come to abolish the law or the prophets; I have come not to abolish but to fulfil. For truly I tell you, until heaven and earth pass away, not one letter, not one stroke of a letter, will pass from the law until all is accomplished. Therefore, whoever breaks one of the least of these commandments, and teaches others to do the same, will be called least in the kingdom of heaven; but whoever does them and teaches them will be called great in the kingdom of heaven.'

- Jesus teaches by word and action, by saying and doing. His example of life is our guide and our encouragement. There is a link between what we say and what we do, and when this link is strong, we are strong in the kingdom of God. We are 'to walk it as we talk it'. Sincerity and integrity of life is what we are called to.

- I consider how my way of living influences others. I pray in thanksgiving for those places in my life in which I can imagine that I have a good influence. I ask God's help in the areas where my example and inspiration might be better.

Thursday 11 March

Luke 11:14–23

Now he was casting out a demon that was mute; when the demon had gone out, the one who had been mute spoke, and the crowds were amazed. But some of them said, 'He casts out demons by Beelzebul, the ruler of the demons.' Others, to test him, kept demanding from him a sign from heaven. But he knew what they were thinking and said to them, 'Every kingdom divided against itself becomes a desert, and house falls on house. If Satan also is divided against himself, how will his kingdom stand? – for you say that I cast out the demons by Beelzebul. Now if I cast out the demons by Beelzebul, by whom do your exorcists cast them out? Therefore they will be your judges. But if it is by the finger of God that I cast out the demons, then the kingdom of God has come to you. When a strong man, fully armed, guards his castle, his property is safe. But when one stronger than he attacks him and overpowers him, he takes away his armour in which he trusted and divides his plunder. Whoever is not with me is against me, and whoever does not gather with me scatters.

- When you have to speak in public, it helps if those listening are on your side, or at least give you a fair hearing. For Jesus it is often the opposite – men arguing against him, trying to catch him out. In today's scripture passage it is even worse. He is accused of being in league with Satan, the devil.

• How did he feel? Jesus, the Son of God, who willingly gave his life that we might have life. 'I came that they may have life and have it abundantly' (John 10:10).

• You know how painful it is if your motives are misunderstood, if a twisted interpretation is put on your good intentions. Such experiences help you identify with Jesus and feel with him. Be there with him; share your experiences with him.

Friday 12 March
Mark 12:28–34

One of the scribes came near and heard them disputing with one another, and seeing that he answered them well, he asked him, 'Which commandment is the first of all?' Jesus answered, 'The first is, "Hear, O Israel: the Lord our God, the Lord is one; you shall love the Lord your God with all your heart, and with all your soul, and with all your mind, and with all your strength." The second is this, "You shall love your neighbour as yourself." There is no other commandment greater than these.' Then the scribe said to him, 'You are right,

Teacher; you have truly said that "he is one, and besides him there is no other"; and "to love him with all the heart, and with all the understanding, and with all the strength", and "to love one's neighbour as oneself" – this is much more important than all whole burnt-offerings and sacrifices.' When Jesus saw that he answered wisely, he said to him, 'You are not far from the kingdom of God.' After that no one dared to ask him any question.

- Lord, why should I love you with all my heart? Because if a group of good people set up a beautiful house and gardens for me to live in, I would love them. If they worked against all that might hurt me, I would love them. If one of them were to die a horrible death to save me from disaster, I would love them. If they Lord, promised me eternal joy, I would love them.

- Lord, enlarge my heart. Make me more and more sensitive to the quality of your love, especially as Holy Week comes near. There you show me so dramatically how much you love me. Make me a grateful person.

Saturday 13 March
Luke 18:9–14

He also told this parable to some who trusted in themselves that they were righteous and regarded others with contempt: 'Two men went up to the temple to pray, one a Pharisee and the other a tax-collector. The Pharisee, standing by himself, was praying thus, "God, I thank you that I am not like other people: thieves, rogues, adulterers, or even like this tax-collector. I fast twice a week; I give a tenth of all my income." But the tax-collector, standing far off, would not even look up to heaven, but was beating his breast and saying, "God, be merciful to me, a sinner!" I tell you, this man went down to his home justified rather than the other; for all who exalt themselves will be humbled, but all who humble themselves will be exalted.'

- The Pharisee is not actually condemned by Jesus. In fact, many of the things he does are good. However, his prayer is less acceptable to God because he trusts in his own righteousness, whereas the tax collector throws himself wholly on God's mercy. One is centred on God; the other is centred on himself.

- The Pharisee derives his satisfaction from the fact that he does not commit the sins that other people do. But what matters is not avoiding this and doing that, but rather handing oneself over to God's mercy.

THE FOURTH WEEK OF LENT
14–20 March 2021

Something to think and pray about each day this week:

We are all pilgrims in the world and only passing through, but it is easy to get attached to things and believe the illusion of the material world. It goes without saying that you have to let go of a lot to be a pilgrim, walking the Camino de Santiago is the modern equivalent. As on the Camino and as in life, we have to travel light and adapt to whatever comes our way, whether it is the weather, health issues, unexpected obstacles or inner wounds or blocks. The point is that many of these things are beyond our control and leaving control aside and trusting in providence is the only way to really live. However, it's not so easy as it sounds as expectations get in the way like those for good food, rest, hygiene and luxury. Modern life presupposes control of our environment and lots of technology surrounds and cushions us. The liberation involved in letting go of comfort, ease and security is hard won.

Brendan McManus SJ
Contemplating the Camino: An Ignatian Guide

The Presence of God

I pause for a moment
and reflect on God's life-giving presence
in every part of my body,
in everything around me,
in the whole of my life.

Freedom

Many countries are at this moment suffering the
agonies of war. I bow my head in thanksgiving for
my freedom. I pray for all prisoners and captives.

Consciousness

Knowing that God loves me unconditionally, I
look honestly over the past day, its events and my
feelings. Do I have something to be grateful for?
Then I give thanks. Is there something I am sorry
for? Then I ask forgiveness.

The Word

Now I turn to the Scripture set out for me this day.
I read slowly over the words and see if any sentence
or sentiment appeals to me. *(Please turn to the
Scripture on the following pages. Inspiration points are
there, should you need them. When you are ready, return
here to continue.)*

Conversation

I know with certainty that there were times when you carried me, Lord. There were times when it was through your strength that I got through the dark times in my life.

Conclusion

Glory be to the Father, and to the Son, and to the
   Holy Spirit,
As it was in the beginning, is now and ever shall be,
World without end. Amen.

Sunday 14 March
Fourth Sunday of Lent
John 3:14–21

And just as Moses lifted up the serpent in the wilderness, so must the Son of Man be lifted up, that whoever believes in him may have eternal life.

'For God so loved the world that he gave his only Son, so that everyone who believes in him may not perish but may have eternal life.

'Indeed, God did not send the Son into the world to condemn the world, but in order that the world might be saved through him. Those who believe in him are not condemned; but those who do not believe are condemned already, because they have not believed in the name of the only Son of God. And this is the judgement, that the light has come into the world, and people loved darkness rather than light because their deeds were evil. For all who do evil hate the light and do not come to the light, so that their deeds may not be exposed. But those who do what is true come to the light, so that it may be clearly seen that their deeds have been done in God.'

- God loved the world. This is my faith, Lord. Sometimes it seems to go against the evidence, when floods, earthquakes, droughts and tsunamis devastate poor people. Central to my faith is the figure of Jesus, lifted on the Cross, knowing what it was to be devastated and a failure, but offering himself in love for us.

Monday 15 March
John 9:1–41

As he walked along, he saw a man blind from birth. His disciples asked him, 'Rabbi, who sinned, this man or his parents, that he was born blind?' Jesus answered, 'Neither this man nor his parents sinned; he was born blind so that God's works might be revealed in him. We must work the works of him who sent me while it is day; night is coming when no one can work. As long as I am in the world, I am the light of the world.' When he had said this, he spat on the ground and made mud with the saliva and spread the mud on the man's eyes, saying to him, 'Go, wash in the pool of Siloam' (which means Sent). Then he went and washed and came back able to see. The neighbours and those who had seen him before as a beggar began to ask, 'Is this not the man who used to sit and beg?' Some were saying, 'It is he.' Others were saying, 'No, but it is someone like him.' He kept saying, 'I am the man.' But they kept asking him, 'Then how were your eyes opened?' He answered, 'The man called Jesus made mud, spread it on my eyes, and said to me,

"Go to Siloam and wash." Then I went and washed and received my sight.' They said to him, 'Where is he?' He said, 'I do not know.'

They brought to the Pharisees the man who had formerly been blind. Now it was a sabbath day when Jesus made the mud and opened his eyes. Then the Pharisees also began to ask him how he had received his sight. He said to them, 'He put mud on my eyes. Then I washed, and now I see.' Some of the Pharisees said, 'This man is not from God, for he does not observe the sabbath.' But others said, 'How can a man who is a sinner perform such signs?' And they were divided. So they said again to the blind man, 'What do you say about him? It was your eyes he opened.' He said, 'He is a prophet.'

The Jews did not believe that he had been blind and had received his sight until they called the parents of the man who had received his sight and asked them, 'Is this your son, who you say was born blind? How then does he now see?' His parents answered, 'We know that this is our son, and that he was born blind; but we do not know how it is that now he sees, nor do we know who opened his eyes. Ask him; he is of age. He will speak for himself.' His parents said this because they were afraid of the Jews; for the Jews had already agreed that anyone who confessed Jesus to be the Messiah would be put out of the synagogue. Therefore his parents said, 'He is of age; ask him.'

So for the second time they called the man who had been blind, and they said to him, 'Give glory to God! We know that this man is a sinner.' He answered, 'I do not know whether he is a sinner. One thing I do know, that though I was blind, now I see.' They said to him, 'What did he do to you? How did he open your eyes?' He answered them, 'I have told you already, and you would not listen. Why do you want to hear it again? Do you also want to become his disciples?' Then they reviled him, saying, 'You are his disciple, but we are disciples of Moses. We know that God has spoken to Moses, but as for this man, we do not know where he comes from.' The man answered, 'Here is an astonishing thing! You do not know where he comes from, and yet he opened my eyes. We know that God does not listen to sinners, but he does listen to one who worships him and obeys his will. Never since the world began has it been heard that anyone opened the eyes of a person born blind. If this man were not from God, he could do nothing.' They answered him, 'You were born entirely in sin, and are you trying to teach us?' And they drove him out.

Jesus heard that they had driven him out, and when he found him, he said, 'Do you believe in the Son of Man?' He answered, 'And who is he, sir? Tell me, so that I may believe in him.' Jesus said to him, 'You have seen him, and the one speaking with you is he.' He said, 'Lord, I believe.' And he worshipped him. Jesus said, 'I came into this world for judgement so that those who do not see may see, and those who do see may become blind.' Some of the Pharisees near him heard this and said to him, 'Surely we are not blind, are we?' Jesus said to them, 'If you were blind, you would not have sin. But now that you say, "We see", your sin remains.'

- The blind man not only receives his sight, but the courage to acknowledge what Jesus has done for him. 'I am the man'. In the full story in John 9:1–38, when the Pharisees argue with him about how Jesus is a sinner breaking the law by healing on the Sabbath, he fearlessly replies, 'He is a prophet'. Finally when driven out of the temple and Jesus goes looking for him, we hear him say, 'Lord, I believe'. He now sees with the eyes of faith as well.

- Spend time thanking the Lord for what he has done for you. Thanking God and others opens our eyes!

Tuesday 16 March

John 5:1–16

After this there was a festival of the Jews, and Jesus went up to Jerusalem.

Now in Jerusalem by the Sheep Gate there is a pool, called in Hebrew Beth-zatha, which has five porticoes. In these lay many invalids – blind, lame and paralysed. One man was there who had been ill for thirty-eight years. When Jesus saw him lying there and knew that he had been there a long time, he said to him, 'Do you want to be made well?' The sick man answered him, 'Sir, I have no one to put me into the pool when the water is stirred up; and while I am making my way, someone else steps down ahead of me.' Jesus said to him, 'Stand up, take your mat and walk.' At once the man was made well, and he took up his mat and began to walk.

Now that day was a sabbath. So the Jews said to the man who had been cured, 'It is the sabbath; it is not lawful for you to carry your mat.' But he answered them, 'The man who made me well said to me, "Take up your mat and walk."' They asked him, 'Who is the man who said to you, "Take it up and walk"?' Now the man who had been healed did not know who it was, for Jesus had disappeared in the crowd that was there. Later Jesus found him in the temple and said to him, 'See, you have been made well! Do not sin any more, so that nothing worse happens to you.' The man went away and told the Jews that it was Jesus who had made him well. Therefore the Jews started persecuting Jesus, because he was doing such things on the sabbath.

- Jesus saw the man, who had been ill for many years, lying at the pool. He knew the longings that were deep in the sick man's heart. He took the initiative and said to him, 'Do you want to be made well?'

- This chronically ill person expected nothing new. There was no one to help him to get first into the water that cured. But God can always surprise us. There is no end to his creative ability.

- The three commands of Jesus changed his life completely: 'Stand up, take your mat and walk.' Or, in other words, become active again. Only when spoken by Jesus do these words have such force.

- If we allow Christ to speak these same words to us, we will achieve much.

Wednesday 17 March

St Patrick, Bishop and Patron of Ireland

John 5:17–30

But Jesus answered them, 'My Father is still working, and I also am working.' For this reason the Jews were seeking all the more to kill him, because he was not only breaking the sabbath, but was also calling God his own Father, thereby making himself equal to God. Jesus said to them, 'Very truly, I tell you, the Son can do nothing on his own, but only what he sees the Father doing; for whatever the Father does, the Son does likewise. The Father loves the Son and shows him all that he himself is doing; and he will show him greater works than these, so that you will be astonished. Indeed, just as the Father raises the dead and gives them life, so also the Son gives life to whomsoever he wishes. The Father judges no one but has given all judgement to the Son, so that all may honour the Son just as they honour the Father. Anyone who does not honour the Son does not honour the Father who sent him. Very truly, I tell you, anyone who hears my word and believes him who sent me has eternal life, and does not come under judgement, but has passed from death to life.

'Very truly, I tell you, the hour is coming, and is now here, when the dead will hear the voice of the Son of God, and those who hear will live. For just as the Father has life in himself, so he has granted the Son also to have life in himself; and he has given him authority to execute judgement, because he is the Son of Man. Do not be astonished at this; for the hour is coming when all who are in their graves will hear his voice and will come out – those who have done good, to the resurrection of life, and those who have done evil, to the resurrection of condemnation. 'I can do nothing on my own. As I hear, I judge; and my judgement is just, because I seek to do not my own will but the will of him who sent me.'

- It's not so easy to pray this gospel! Read it a few times, stopping wherever a phrase catches your attention. Talk it over to the Lord.

- 'My Father is still working, and I also am working.' St Ignatius Loyola used say that the Lord is ever labouring on our behalf: an unexpected outcome; you are in the right place at the right time. Signs of God's providence at work. Thank the Lord for these moments.

- 'My aim is to do not my own will, but the will of him who sent me.' We get a glimpse of Jesus' heart in unison with his Father. Jesus does nothing without praying to his Father. End by slowly praying 'Father' a number of times.

Thursday 18 March
John 5:31–47

'If I testify about myself, my testimony is not true. There is another who testifies on my behalf, and I know that his testimony to me is true. You sent messengers to John, and he testified to the truth. Not that I accept such human testimony, but I say these things so that you may be saved. He was a burning and shining lamp, and you were willing to rejoice for a while in his light. But I have a testimony greater than John's. The works that the Father has given me to complete, the very works that I am doing, testify on my behalf that the Father has sent me. And the Father who sent me has himself testified on my behalf. You have never heard his voice or seen his form, and you do not have his word abiding in you, because you do not believe him whom he has sent.

'You search the scriptures because you think that in them you have eternal life; and it is they that testify on my behalf. Yet you refuse to come to me to have life. I do not accept glory from human beings. But I know that you do not have the love of God in you. I have come in my Father's name, and you do not accept me; if another comes in his own name, you will accept him. How can you believe when you accept glory from one another and do not seek the glory that comes from the one who alone is God? Do not think that I will accuse you before the Father; your accuser is Moses, on whom you have set your hope. If you believed Moses, you would believe me, for he wrote about me. But if you do not believe what he wrote, how will you believe what I say?'

- The biblical rule of evidence required two witnesses. Jesus calls on John the Baptist and Moses to testify to his identity and his mission. What would a person of integrity say about me?

- John the Baptist fulfilled Isaiah's prophecy, that a voice would cry, 'In the wilderness prepare the way of the Lord; make straight in the desert a highway for our God'. As we make our Lenten journey, let us reflect on what we are doing to make our own crooked ways straight.

Friday 19 March
St Joseph, Spouse of the Blessed Virgin Mary
Luke 2:41–51a

Now every year his parents went to Jerusalem for the festival of the Passover. And when he was twelve years old, they went up as usual for the festival. When the festival was ended and they started to return, the boy Jesus stayed behind in Jerusalem, but his parents did not know it. Assuming that he was in the group of travellers, they went a day's journey. Then they started to look for him among their relatives and friends. When they did not find him, they returned to Jerusalem to search for him. After three days they found him in the temple, sitting among the teachers, listening to them and asking them questions. And all who heard him were amazed at his understanding and his answers. When his parents saw him they were astonished; and his mother said to him, 'Child, why have you treated us like this? Look, your father and I have been searching for you in great anxiety.' He said to them, 'Why were you searching for me? Did you not know that I must be in my Father's house?' But they did not understand what he said to them. Then he went down with them and came to Nazareth, and was obedient to them. His mother treasured all these things in her heart.

- The parents of Jesus were observant Jews. This vignette is the last we will hear of Jesus' early years. Jesus is coming of age. He is entering his teens. We see already the gradual, slow but steady growing into his sense of identity and mission.

- Lord, today I remember all the missing children of our world through slavery, bonded labour and trafficking. I pray for their distraught parents who frantically seek for the child entrusted to them.

Saturday 20 March
John 7: 40–53

When they heard these words, some in the crowd said, 'This is really the prophet.' Others said, 'This is the Messiah.' But some asked, 'Surely the Messiah does not come from Galilee, does he? Has not the scripture said that the Messiah is descended from David and comes from Bethlehem, the village where David lived?' So there was a division in the crowd because of him. Some of them wanted to arrest him, but no one laid hands on him.

Then the temple police went back to the chief priests and Pharisees, who asked them, 'Why did you not arrest him?' The police answered, 'Never has anyone spoken like this!' Then the Pharisees replied, 'Surely you have not been deceived too, have you? Has any one of the authorities or of the Pharisees believed in him? But this crowd, which does not know the law – they are accursed.' Nicodemus, who had gone to Jesus before, and who was one of them, asked, 'Our law does not judge people without first giving them a hearing to find out what they are doing, does it?' They replied, 'Surely you are not also from Galilee, are you? Search and you will see that no prophet is to arise from Galilee.'

- There is a wide range of views among the Jewish people as to who Jesus really is. Notice the constant appeal to the Old Testament. We may be more convinced by what the temple police report: 'Never has anyone spoken like this!' Jesus speaks with integrity, with wisdom and with authority. This impresses these unsophisticated men. They are able to recognise the goodness of Jesus, which was hidden from the religious leaders.

- Pope Francis teaches that we must listen to the poor and the marginalised because they have a special insight into the reality of the world and of God.

THE FIFTH WEEK OF LENT
21–27 March 2021

Something to think and pray about each day this week:

The angel made it clear that Joseph, the man to whom Mary was engaged, would have no part to play in the conception of this child. All Mary needed to do was give her assent, and then God's own creative power would bring this child into existence…

We are so familiar with the story of the Annunciation, that it can be easy to take Mary's faith for granted. It's easy to forget that that Gabriel's message opened up a vast new horizon for Mary. … Mary's focus was on God. She believed enough in God's power and love to accept the message that Gabriel communicated to her. She plunged wholeheartedly into the limitless ocean of God as she said: 'Behold the servant of the Lord, let it be done unto me according to your word' (Luke 1:38).

Thomas Casey SJ
Smile of Joy: Mary of Nazareth

The Presence of God
I pause for a moment and think of the love and the grace that God showers on me. I am created in the image and likeness of God; I am God's dwelling place.

Freedom
Lord, you granted me the great gift of freedom. In these times, O Lord, grant that I may be free from any form of racism or intolerance. Remind me that we are all equal in your loving eyes.

Consciousness
Knowing that God loves me unconditionally, I can afford to be honest about how I am.
How has the day been, and how do I feel now? I share my feelings openly with the Lord.

The Word
I take my time to read the word of God slowly, a few times, allowing myself to dwell on anything that strikes me. *(Please turn to the Scripture on the following pages. Inspiration points are there, should you need them. When you are ready, return here to continue.)*

Conversation
Sometimes I wonder what I might say if I were to meet you in person, Lord.

I think I might say, 'Thank you' because you are always there for me.

Conclusion
I thank God for these moments we have spent together and for any insights I have been given concerning the text.

Sunday 21 March
Fifth Sunday of Lent
John 12:20–33

Now among those who went up to worship at the festival were some Greeks. They came to Philip, who was from Bethsaida in Galilee, and said to him, 'Sir, we wish to see Jesus.' Philip went and told Andrew; then Andrew and Philip went and told Jesus. Jesus answered them, 'The hour has come for the Son of Man to be glorified. Very truly, I tell you, unless a grain of wheat falls into the earth and dies, it remains just a single grain; but if it dies, it bears much fruit. Those who love their life lose it, and those who hate their life in this world will keep it for eternal life. Whoever serves me must follow me, and where I am, there will my servant be also. Whoever serves me, the Father will honour.

'Now my soul is troubled. And what should I say – "Father, save me from this hour"? No, it is for this reason that I have come to this hour. Father, glorify your name.' Then a voice came from heaven, 'I have glorified it, and I will glorify it again.' The crowd standing there heard it and said that it was thunder. Others said, 'An angel has spoken to him.' Jesus answered, 'This voice has come for your sake, not for mine. Now is the judgement of this world; now the ruler of this world will be driven out. And

I, when I am lifted up from the earth, will draw all people to myself.' He said this to indicate the kind of death he was to die.

- In every death, there is life – this is the big message of Lent and of Easter. The grain of wheat will die and will through death nourish us with food. In the death of relationships, of health, of faith and all that may be dear to us there is always the invitation to deeper life. In our final death is the call to everlasting life.

Monday 22 March
John 11:1–45

Now a certain man was ill, Lazarus of Bethany, the village of Mary and her sister Martha. Mary was the one who anointed the Lord with perfume and wiped his feet with her hair; her brother Lazarus was ill. So the sisters sent a message to Jesus, 'Lord, he whom you love is ill.' But when Jesus heard it, he said, 'This illness does not lead to death; rather it is for God's glory, so that the Son of God may be glorified through it.' Accordingly, though Jesus loved Martha and her sister and Lazarus, after having heard that Lazarus was ill, he stayed two days longer in the place where he was.

Then after this he said to the disciples, 'Let us go to Judea again.' The disciples said to him, 'Rabbi, the

Jews were just now trying to stone you, and are you going there again?' Jesus answered, 'Are there not twelve hours of daylight? Those who walk during the day do not stumble, because they see the light of this world. But those who walk at night stumble, because the light is not in them.' After saying this, he told them, 'Our friend Lazarus has fallen asleep, but I am going there to awaken him.' The disciples said to him, 'Lord, if he has fallen asleep, he will be all right.' Jesus, however, had been speaking about his death, but they thought that he was referring merely to sleep. Then Jesus told them plainly, 'Lazarus is dead. For your sake I am glad I was not there, so that you may believe. But let us go to him.' Thomas, who was called the Twin, said to his fellow-disciples, 'Let us also go, that we may die with him.'

When Jesus arrived, he found that Lazarus had already been in the tomb for four days. Now Bethany was near Jerusalem, some two miles away, and many of the Jews had come to Martha and Mary to console them about their brother. When Martha heard that Jesus was coming, she went and met him, while Mary stayed at home. Martha said to Jesus, 'Lord, if you had been here, my brother would not have died. But even now I know that God will give you whatever you ask of him.' Jesus said to her, 'Your brother will rise again.' Martha said to him, 'I know that he will rise again in the resurrection on the last day.' Jesus said to her, 'I am the resurrection and the life. Those who believe in me, even though they die, will live, and everyone who lives and believes in me will never die. Do you believe this?' She said to him, 'Yes, Lord, I believe that you are the Messiah, the Son of God, the one coming into the world.'

When she had said this, she went back and called her sister Mary, and told her privately, 'The Teacher is here and is calling for you.' And when she heard it, she got up quickly and went to him. Now Jesus had not yet come to the village, but was still at the place where Martha had met him. The Jews who were with her in the house, consoling her, saw Mary get up quickly and go out. They followed her because they thought that she was going to the tomb to weep there. When Mary came where Jesus was and saw him, she knelt at his feet and said to him, 'Lord, if you had been here, my brother would not have died.' When Jesus saw her weeping, and the Jews who came with her also weeping, he was greatly disturbed in spirit and deeply moved. He said, 'Where have you laid him?' They said to him, 'Lord, come and see.' Jesus began to weep. So the Jews said, 'See how he loved him!' But some of them said, 'Could not he who opened the eyes of the blind man have kept this man from dying?'

Then Jesus, again greatly disturbed, came to the tomb. It was a cave, and a stone was lying against it. Jesus said, 'Take away the stone.' Martha, the sister of the dead man, said to him, 'Lord, already there is a stench because he has been dead for four days.' Jesus said to her, 'Did I not tell you that if you believed, you would see the glory of God?' So they took away the stone. And Jesus looked upwards and said, 'Father, I thank you for having heard me. I knew that you always hear me, but I have said this for the sake of the crowd standing here, so that they may believe that you sent me.' When he had said this, he cried with a loud voice, 'Lazarus, come out!' The dead man came out, his hands and feet bound with strips of cloth, and his face wrapped in a cloth. Jesus said to them, 'Unbind him, and let him go.'

Many of the Jews therefore, who had come with Mary and had seen what Jesus did, believed in him.

- I hear you asking me the same question, Lord: 'Do you believe that I am the resurrection and the life?' In the long run nothing is more important than my answer to this. I cannot grasp your words in my imagination, Lord, but I believe. Help my unbelief.

Tuesday 23 March
John 8:21–30

Again he said to them, 'I am going away, and you will search for me, but you will die in your sin. Where I am going, you cannot come.' Then the Jews said, 'Is he going to kill himself? Is that what he means by saying, "Where I am going, you cannot come"?' He said to them, 'You are from below, I am from above; you are of this world, I am not of this world. I told you that you would die in your sins, for you will die in your sins unless you believe that I am he.' They said to him, 'Who are you?' Jesus said to them, 'Why do I speak to you at all? I have much to say about you and much to condemn; but the one who sent me is true, and I declare to the world what I have heard from him.' They did not understand that he was speaking to them about the Father. So Jesus said, 'When you have lifted up the Son of Man, then you will realise that I am he, and that I do nothing on my own, but I speak these things as the Father instructed me. And the one who sent me is with me; he has not left me alone, for I always do what is pleasing to him.' As he was saying these things, many believed in him.

- St John wants the early Christians to realise that Jesus is totally unique: he belongs to the world of the divine. He reveals the mystery of what

God is like. When I knock on God's door, Jesus opens it and invites me in to meet his Father!

- 'I always do what is pleasing to the Father.' This reveals the heart of Jesus' spirituality. I pray that it may become the truth of my life too, because God is so good to me.

Wednesday 24 March
John 8:31–42

Then Jesus said to the Jews who had believed in him, 'If you continue in my word, you are truly my disciples; and you will know the truth, and the truth will make you free.' They answered him, 'We are descendants of Abraham and have never been slaves to anyone. What do you mean by saying, "You will be made free"?'

Jesus answered them, 'Very truly, I tell you, everyone who commits sin is a slave to sin. The slave does not have a permanent place in the household; the son has a place there for ever. So if the Son makes you free, you will be free indeed. I know that you are descendants of Abraham; yet you look for an opportunity to kill me, because there is no place in you for my word. I declare what I have seen in the Father's presence; as for you, you should do what you have heard from the Father.'

They answered him, 'Abraham is our father.' Jesus said to them, 'If you were Abraham's children, you would be doing what Abraham did, but now you are trying to kill me, a man who has told you the truth that I heard from God. This is not what Abraham did. You are indeed doing what your father does.' They said to him, 'We are not illegitimate children; we have one father, God himself.' Jesus said to them, 'If God were your Father, you would love me, for I came from God and now I am here. I did not come on my own, but he sent me.

- Jesus' promise is that the truth will make us free. Lord, I do want to be free, so let me listen to those who tell me the truth about myself. Let me listen also to your word, which tries to reach into my heart and liberate me. Let me start with the great truth of which you try to convince me: that I am endlessly loved by you.

- When in my life have I had an experience that made me truly see Jesus as the one sent by God?

Thursday 25 March
The Annunciation of the Lord
Luke 1:26–38

In the sixth month the angel Gabriel was sent by God to a town in Galilee called Nazareth, to a virgin engaged to a man whose name was Joseph, of the house of David. The virgin's name was Mary. And he came to her and said, 'Greetings, favoured one! The Lord is with you.' But she was much perplexed by his words and pondered what sort of greeting this might be. The angel said to her, 'Do not be afraid, Mary, for you have found favour with God. And now, you will conceive in your womb and bear a son, and you will name him Jesus. He will be great, and will be called the Son of the Most High, and the Lord God will give to him the throne of his ancestor David. He will reign over the house of Jacob for ever, and of his kingdom there will be no end.' Mary said to the angel, 'How can this be, since I am a virgin?' The angel said to her, 'The Holy Spirit will come upon you, and the power of the Most High will overshadow you; therefore the child to be born will be holy; he will be called Son of God. And now, your relative Elizabeth in her old age has also conceived a son; and this is the sixth month for her who was said to be barren. For nothing will be impossible with God.' Then Mary said, 'Here am I, the servant of the Lord; let it be with me according to your word.' Then the angel departed from her.

- For Mary the angel's message is a blessing; but very much a blessing in disguise. It is placing her in a very difficult position, socially, culturally, religiously, personally. She has to trust this interior movement in her heart and 'go with it'. And she does.

- In our lives too there are turning points where we may experience an invitation to embrace something difficult rather than discard it. Something which wrecks our dream for ourselves or for our loved ones. There's a need to discern the spirits.

- Is there release from something into another way of being more open, more generous, more humble, deeper in service of Christ Jesus?

- If it is disconcerting that does not mean that it is bad. What response would your better self give?

Friday 26 March
John 10:31–42

The Jews took up stones again to stone him. Jesus replied, 'I have shown you many good works from the Father. For which of these are you going to stone me?' The Jews answered, 'It is not for a good work that we are going to stone you, but for blasphemy, because you, though only a human being, are making yourself God.' Jesus answered, 'Is it not written in your law, "I said, you are gods"? If those to whom the word of God came were called "gods" – and the scripture cannot be annulled – can you say that the one whom the Father has sanctified and sent into the world is blaspheming because I said, "I am God's Son"? If I am not doing the works of my Father, then do not believe me. But if I do them, even though you do not believe me, believe the works, so that you may know and understand that the Father is in me and I am in the Father.' Then they tried to arrest him again, but he escaped from their hands.

He went away again across the Jordan to the place where John had been baptising earlier, and he remained there. Many came to him, and they were saying, 'John performed no sign, but everything that John said about this man was true.' And many believed in him there.

• The works of Jesus are the works of love. This is the love we know of him – love unto death. What we see in Jesus, we can see of the Father. What the Father sees in Jesus, he sees and loves in us. We pray that our hearts may be made like the heart of Jesus.

Saturday 27 March
John 11:45–56

Many of the Jews, therefore, who had come with Mary and had seen what Jesus did, believed in him. But some of them went to the Pharisees and told them what he had done. So the chief priests and the Pharisees called a meeting of the council, and said, 'What are we to do? This man is performing many signs. If we let him go on like this, everyone will believe in him, and the Romans will come and destroy both our holy place and our nation.' But one of them, Caiaphas, who was high priest that year, said to them, 'You know nothing at all! You do not understand that it is better for you to have one man die for the people than to have the whole nation destroyed.' He did not say this on his own, but being high priest that year he prophesied that Jesus was about to die for the nation, and not for the nation only, but to gather into one the dispersed children of God. So from that day on they planned to put him to death.

Jesus therefore no longer walked about openly among the Jews, but went from there to a town called Ephraim in the region near the wilderness; and he remained there with the disciples.

Now the Passover of the Jews was near, and many went up from the country to Jerusalem before the Passover to purify themselves. They were looking for Jesus and were asking one another as they stood in the temple, 'What do you think? Surely he will not come to the festival, will he?'

- The chief priests and the scribes – among the most learned people in Israel – did not recognise Jesus. Blinded by prejudice, they decided to put him to death. Do I ever harbour death wishes for another, even sub-consciously?

HOLY WEEK
28 March–3 April 2021

Something to think and pray about each day this week:

Is Holy Week a strange name for the week of Jesus' passion? It seems a week of torture, pain, imprisonment, denial and betrayal, ending in death for Jesus. It was a week of enormous crisis for the followers of Jesus, and a week of intense pain for Mary, his mother. Why call it holy? Why call Good Friday 'good' when it seems to be one of the worst days of human history?

For us Holy Week is not just a memory. It is a week to remember all that Jesus did to save us; a week to grow in holiness ourselves, and a week that leads into the joy of the resurrection, which is the beginning of the new life of Jesus.

Donal Neary SJ
The Sacred Heart Messenger, April 2020

The Presence of God

I pause for a moment and think of the love and the grace that God showers on me. I am created in the image and likeness of God; I am God's dwelling place.

Freedom

I am free. When I look at these words in writing, they seem to create in me a feeling of awe. Yes, a wonderful feeling of freedom. Thank you, God.

Consciousness

In the presence of my loving Creator, I look honestly at my feelings over the past day: the highs, the lows, and the level ground. Can I see where the Lord has been present?

The Word

I read the word of God slowly, a few times over, and I listen to what God is saying to me. *(Please turn to the Scripture on the following pages. Inspiration points are there, should you need them. When you are ready, return here to continue.)*

Conversation

Remembering that I am still in God's presence, I imagine Jesus standing or sitting beside me,

and I say whatever is on my mind, whatever is in
  my heart,
speaking as one friend to another.

Conclusion
Glory be to the Father, and to the Son, and to the
  Holy Spirit,
As it was in the beginning, is now and ever shall be,
World without end. Amen.

Sunday 28 March
Palm Sunday of the Passion of the Lord
Mark 14:1–15:47

It was two days before the Passover and the festival of Unleavened Bread. The chief priests and the scribes were looking for a way to arrest Jesus by stealth and kill him; for they said, 'Not during the festival, or there may be a riot among the people.'

While he was at Bethany in the house of Simon the leper, as he sat at the table, a woman came with an alabaster jar of very costly ointment of nard, and she broke open the jar and poured the ointment on his head. But some were there who said to one another in anger, 'Why was the ointment wasted in this way? For this ointment could have been sold for more than three hundred denarii, and the money given to the poor.' And they scolded her. But Jesus said, 'Let her alone; why do you trouble her? She has performed a good service for me. For you always have the poor with you, and you can show kindness to them whenever you wish; but you will not always have me. She has done what she could; she has anointed my body beforehand for its burial. Truly I tell you, wherever the good news is proclaimed in the whole world, what she has done will be told in remembrance of her.'

Then Judas Iscariot, who was one of the twelve,

went to the chief priests in order to betray him to them. When they heard it, they were greatly pleased, and promised to give him money. So he began to look for an opportunity to betray him.

On the first day of Unleavened Bread, when the Passover lamb is sacrificed, his disciples said to him, 'Where do you want us to go and make the preparations for you to eat the Passover?' So he sent two of his disciples, saying to them, 'Go into the city, and a man carrying a jar of water will meet you; follow him, and wherever he enters, say to the owner of the house, "The Teacher asks, Where is my guest room where I may eat the Passover with my disciples?" He will show you a large room upstairs, furnished and ready. Make preparations for us there.' So the disciples set out and went to the city, and found everything as he had told them; and they prepared the Passover meal.

When it was evening, he came with the twelve. And when they had taken their places and were eating, Jesus said, 'Truly I tell you, one of you will betray me, one who is eating with me.' They began to be distressed and to say to him one after another, 'Surely, not I?' He said to them, 'It is one of the twelve, one who is dipping bread into the bowl with me. For the Son of Man goes as it is written of him, but woe to that one by whom the Son of Man is betrayed! It would have been better for that one not to have been born.'

While they were eating, he took a loaf of bread, and after blessing it he broke it, gave it to them, and said, 'Take; this is my body.' Then he took a cup, and after giving thanks he gave it to them, and all of them drank from it. He said to them, 'This is my blood of the covenant, which is poured out for many. Truly I tell you, I will never again drink of the fruit of the vine until that day when I drink it new in the kingdom of God.'

When they had sung the hymn, they went out to the Mount of Olives. And Jesus said to them, 'You will all become deserters; for it is written,

"I will strike the shepherd,

 and the sheep will be scattered."

But after I am raised up, I will go before you to Galilee.' Peter said to him, 'Even though all become deserters, I will not.' Jesus said to him, 'Truly I tell you, this day, this very night, before the cock crows twice, you will deny me three times.' But he said vehemently, 'Even though I must die with you, I will not deny you.' And all of them said the same.

They went to a place called Gethsemane; and he said to his disciples, 'Sit here while I pray.' He took with him Peter and James and John, and began to be distressed and agitated. And he said to them, 'I am deeply grieved, even to death; remain here, and keep awake.' And going a little farther, he threw himself on the ground and prayed that, if it were possible, the hour might pass from him. He said, 'Abba, Father, for you all things are possible; remove this cup from me; yet, not what I want, but what you want.' He came and found them sleeping; and he said to Peter, 'Simon, are you asleep? Could you not keep awake one hour? Keep awake and pray that you may not come into the time of trial; the spirit indeed is willing, but the flesh is weak.' And again he went away and prayed, saying the same words. And once more he came and found them sleeping, for their eyes were very heavy; and they did not know what to say to him. He came a third time and said to them, 'Are you still sleeping and taking your rest? Enough! The hour has come; the Son of Man is betrayed into the hands of sinners. Get up, let us be going. See, my betrayer is at hand.'

Immediately, while he was still speaking, Judas, one of the twelve, arrived; and with him there was a crowd with swords and clubs, from the chief priests, the scribes, and the elders. Now the betrayer had given them a sign, saying, 'The one I will kiss is the man; arrest him and lead him away under guard.' So when he came, he went up to him at once and said, 'Rabbi!' and kissed him. Then they laid hands on him and arrested him. But one of those who stood near drew his sword and struck the slave of the high priest, cutting off his ear. Then Jesus said to them, 'Have you come out with swords and clubs to arrest me as though I were a bandit? Day after day I was with you in the temple teaching, and you did not arrest me. But let the scriptures be fulfilled.' All of them deserted him and fled.

A certain young man was following him, wearing nothing but a linen cloth. They caught hold of him, but he left the linen cloth and ran off naked.

They took Jesus to the high priest; and all the chief priests, the elders and the scribes were assembled. Peter had followed him at a distance, right into the courtyard of the high priest; and he was sitting with the guards, warming himself at the fire. Now the chief priests and the whole council were looking for testimony against Jesus to put him to death; but they found none. For many gave false testimony against him, and their testimony did not agree. Some stood up and gave false testimony against him, saying, 'We heard him say, "I will destroy this temple that is made with hands, and in three days I will build another, not made with hands".' But even on this point their testimony did not agree. Then the high priest stood up before them and asked Jesus, 'Have you no answer? What is it that they testify against you?' But he was silent and did not answer. Again the high priest asked him, 'Are you the Messiah, the Son of the Blessed One?' Jesus said, 'I am; and

> "you will see the Son of Man
> seated at the right hand of the Power",
> and "coming with the clouds of heaven."'

Then the high priest tore his clothes and said, 'Why do we still need witnesses? You have heard his blasphemy! What is your decision?' All of them condemned him as deserving death. Some began to spit on him, to blindfold him, and to strike him, saying to him, 'Prophesy!' The guards also took him over and beat him.

While Peter was below in the courtyard, one of the servant-girls of the high priest came by. When she saw Peter warming himself, she stared at him and said, 'You also were with Jesus, the man from Nazareth.' But he denied it, saying, 'I do not know or understand what you are talking about.' And he went out into the forecourt. Then the cock crowed. And the servant-girl, on seeing him, began again to say to the bystanders, 'This man is one of them.' But again he denied it. Then after a little while the bystanders again said to Peter, 'Certainly you are one of them; for you are a Galilean.' But he began to curse, and he swore an oath, 'I do not know this man you are talking about.' At that moment the cock crowed for the second time. Then Peter remembered that Jesus had said to him, 'Before the cock crows twice, you will deny me three times.' And he broke down and wept.

As soon as it was morning, the chief priests held a consultation with the elders and scribes and the whole council. They bound Jesus, led him away, and handed him over to Pilate. Pilate asked him, 'Are you the King of the Jews?' He answered him, 'You say so.' Then the chief priests accused him of many things. Pilate asked him again, 'Have you no answer? See how many charges they bring against you.' But Jesus made no further reply, so that Pilate was amazed.

Now at the festival he used to release a prisoner for them, anyone for whom they asked. Now a man called Barabbas was in prison with the rebels who had committed murder during the insurrection. So the crowd came and began to ask Pilate to do for them according to his custom. Then he answered them, 'Do you want me to release for you the King of the Jews?' For he realised that it was out of jealousy that the chief priests had handed him over. But the chief priests stirred up the crowd to have him release Barabbas for them instead. Pilate spoke to them again, 'Then what do you wish me to do with the man you call the King of the Jews? 'They shouted back, 'Crucify him!' Pilate asked them, 'Why, what evil has he done?' But they shouted all the more, 'Crucify him!' So Pilate, wishing to satisfy the crowd, released Barabbas for them; and after flogging Jesus, he handed him over to be crucified.

Then the soldiers led him into the courtyard of the palace (that is, the governor's headquarters); and they called together the whole cohort. And they clothed him in a purple cloak; and after twisting some thorns into a crown, they put it on him. And they began saluting him, 'Hail, King of the Jews!' They struck his head with a reed, spat upon him, and knelt down in homage to him. After mocking him, they stripped him of the purple cloak and put his own clothes on him. Then they led him out to crucify him.

They compelled a passer-by, who was coming in from the country, to carry his cross; it was Simon of Cyrene, the father of Alexander and Rufus. Then they brought Jesus to the place called Golgotha (which means the place of a skull). And they offered him wine mixed with myrrh; but he did not take it. And they crucified him, and divided his clothes among them, casting lots to decide what each should take.

It was nine o'clock in the morning when they crucified him. The inscription of the charge against him read, 'The King of the Jews'. And with him they crucified two bandits, one on his right and one on his left. Those who passed by derided him, shaking their heads and saying, 'Aha! You who would destroy the temple and build it in three days, save yourself, and come down from the cross!' In the same way the chief priests, along with the scribes, were also mocking him among themselves and saying, 'He saved others; he cannot save himself. Let the Messiah, the King of Israel, come down from the cross now, so that we may see and believe.' Those who were crucified with him also taunted him.

When it was noon, darkness came over the whole land until three in the afternoon. At three o'clock Jesus cried out with a loud voice, 'Eloi, Eloi, lama sabachthani?' which means, 'My God, my God, why have you forsaken me?' When some of the bystanders heard it, they said, 'Listen, he is calling for Elijah.' And someone ran, filled a sponge with sour wine, put it on a stick, and gave it to him to drink, saying, 'Wait, let us see whether Elijah will come to take him down.' Then Jesus gave a loud cry and breathed his last. And the curtain of the temple was torn in two, from top to bottom. Now when the centurion, who stood facing him, saw that in this way he breathed his last, he said, 'Truly this man was God's Son!'

There were also women looking on from a distance; among them were Mary Magdalene, and Mary the mother of James the younger and of Joses, and Salome. These used to follow him and provided for him when he was in Galilee; and there were many other women who had come up with him to Jerusalem.

When evening had come, and since it was the day of Preparation, that is, the day before the sabbath, Joseph of Arimathea, a respected member of the council, who was also himself waiting expectantly for the kingdom of God, went boldly to Pilate and asked for the body of Jesus. Then Pilate wondered if he were already dead; and summoning the centurion, he asked him whether he had been dead for some time. When he learned from the centurion that he was dead, he granted the body to Joseph. Then Joseph bought a linen cloth, and taking down the body, wrapped it in the linen cloth, and laid it in a tomb that had been hewn out of the rock. He then rolled a stone against the door of the tomb. Mary Magdalene and Mary the mother of Joses saw where the body was laid.

- As I read these seminal verses, I pray to have the faith of Peter, who was the rock on whom the early Christians leaned. I look at Jesus and seek words to express what he means to me, and open my heart to God's revelation.

- She came to comfort the man in danger. A woman who put her own reputation and safety on the line to comfort the one she loved in thanks for his compassion for her. Her action would be remembered forever, and the scent of her ointment is the scent of resurrection: this nard would soothe the spirits of those who would always miss Jesus.

- Part of our prayer is missing Jesus when he seems so absent, and prayerful feelings seem so distant. The scent of the Lord in our lives keeps us going.

Monday 29 March
Luke 4:16–21

When he came to Nazareth, where he had been brought up, he went to the synagogue on the sabbath day, as was his custom. He stood up to read, and the scroll of the prophet Isaiah was given to him. He unrolled the scroll and found the place where it was written:

'The Spirit of the Lord is upon me,
   because he has anointed me
   to bring good news to the poor.

He has sent me to proclaim release to the captives
and recovery of sight to the blind,
to let the oppressed go free,
to proclaim the year of the Lord's favour.'

And he rolled up the scroll, gave it back to the attendant, and sat down. The eyes of all in the synagogue were fixed on him. Then he began to say to them, 'Today this scripture has been fulfilled in your hearing.'

- Lord, this is a scene I would love to have witnessed. Let me unroll it slowly.

- Jesus' good news is that we are all loved unconditionally by God, no ifs, no buts. When I accept that, truly believe and live by it, I gain freedom of heart and mind and a new insight into the ways God works in our lives.

Tuesday 30 March
John 13:21–33.36–38

After saying this Jesus was troubled in spirit, and declared, 'Very truly, I tell you, one of you will betray me.' The disciples looked at one another, uncertain of whom he was speaking. One of his disciples – the one whom Jesus loved – was reclining next to him; Simon Peter therefore motioned to him to ask Jesus of whom he was speaking. So, while reclining next to Jesus, he asked him, 'Lord, who is it?' Jesus answered, 'It is the one to whom I give this piece of bread when I have dipped it in the dish.' So when he had dipped the piece of bread, he gave it to Judas son of Simon Iscariot. After he received the piece of bread, Satan entered into him. Jesus said to him, 'Do quickly what you are going to do.' Now no one at the table knew why he said this to him. Some thought that, because Judas had the common purse, Jesus was telling him, 'Buy what we need for the festival'; or, that he should give something to the poor. So, after receiving the piece of bread, he immediately went out. And it was night.

When he had gone out, Jesus said, 'Now the Son of Man has been glorified, and God has been glorified in him. If God has been glorified in him, God will also glorify him in himself and will glorify him at once. Little children, I am with you only a little longer. You will look for me; and as I said to the Jews so now I say to you, "Where I am going, you cannot come."'

Simon Peter said to him, 'Lord, where are you going?' Jesus answered, 'Where I am going, you cannot follow me now; but you will follow afterwards.' Peter said to him, 'Lord, why can I not follow you now? I will lay down my life for you.' Jesus answered, 'Will you lay down your life for me?

Very truly, I tell you, before the cock crows, you will have denied me three times.'

- Peter hit deep points of his life here. His sureness of following Jesus was challenged by Jesus himself. He would later find himself weak and failing in this following. But this would not be the last word; even when Peter said later that he didn't know Jesus, there would be time for taking it back and speaking it with his life. We oscillate in our following of the Lord; these days let us know in the certainty of Jesus' love that there is always another day, another chance, another joy in our following of Jesus.

Wednesday 31 March
Matthew 26:14–25

Then one of the twelve, who was called Judas Iscariot, went to the chief priests and said, 'What will you give me if I betray him to you?' They paid him thirty pieces of silver. And from that moment he began to look for an opportunity to betray him.

On the first day of Unleavened Bread the disciples came to Jesus, saying, 'Where do you want us to make the preparations for you to eat the Passover?' He said, 'Go into the city to a certain man, and say to him, "The Teacher says, My time is near; I will keep the Passover at your house with my disciples."'

So the disciples did as Jesus had directed them, and they prepared the Passover meal.

When it was evening, he took his place with the twelve; and while they were eating, he said, 'Truly I tell you, one of you will betray me.' And they became greatly distressed and began to say to him one after another, 'Surely not I, Lord?' He answered, 'The one who has dipped his hand into the bowl with me will betray me. The Son of Man goes as it is written of him, but woe to that one by whom the Son of Man is betrayed! It would have been better for that one not to have been born.' Judas, who betrayed him, said, 'Surely not I, Rabbi?' He replied, 'You have said so.'

- Holy Week is an invitation to walk closely with Jesus: we fix our gaze on him and accompany him in his suffering; we let him look closely at us and see us as we really are. We do not have to present a brave face to him, but can tell him about where we have been disappointed, let down – perhaps even betrayed. We avoid getting stuck in our own misfortune by seeing as he sees, by learning from his heart.

- Help me to see, Jesus, how you do not condemn. You invite each of us to recognise the truth of our own discipleship. You invite us to follow you willingly, freely, forgiven.

Thursday 1 April
Holy Thursday
John 13:1–15

Now before the festival of the Passover, Jesus knew that his hour had come to depart from this world and go to the Father. Having loved his own who were in the world, he loved them to the end. The devil had already put it into the heart of Judas son of Simon Iscariot to betray him. And during supper Jesus, knowing that the Father had given all things into his hands, and that he had come from God and was going to God, got up from the table, took off his outer robe, and tied a towel around himself. Then he poured water into a basin and began to wash the disciples' feet and to wipe them with the towel that was tied around him. He came to Simon Peter, who said to him, 'Lord, are you going to wash my feet?' Jesus answered, 'You do not know now what I am doing, but later you will understand.' Peter said to him, 'You will never wash my feet.' Jesus answered, 'Unless I wash you, you have no share with me.' Simon Peter said to him, 'Lord, not my feet only but also my hands and my head!' Jesus said to him, 'One who has bathed does not need to wash, except for the feet, but is entirely clean. And you are clean, though not all of you.' For he knew who was to betray him; for this reason he said, 'Not all of you are clean.'

After he had washed their feet, had put on his robe, and had returned to the table, he said to them, 'Do you know what I have done to you? You call me Teacher and Lord – and you are right, for that is what I am. So if I, your Lord and Teacher, have washed your feet, you also ought to wash one another's feet. For I have set you an example, that you also should do as I have done to you.

- It may be important for us to think of what we want to do for Jesus, to let him know and to seek his approval. Jesus smiles and invites us to listen first – to notice, to be. He asks if we can allow him to serve us. 'See what I do,' he seems to say. 'Accept who I am. Then be who you are!'

- Jesus says, 'Later you will understand.' Sometimes that's not enough for me! I want to understand now. Help me, Jesus, to live as you did even when I don't fully comprehend what you are asking of me.

Friday 2 April
Good Friday
John 18:1–19:42

After Jesus had spoken these words, he went out with his disciples across the Kidron valley to a place where there was a garden, which he and his disciples entered. Now Judas, who betrayed him, also knew the place, because Jesus often met there with his disciples. So Judas brought a detachment of soldiers together with police from the chief priests and the Pharisees, and they came there with lanterns and torches and weapons. Then Jesus, knowing all that was to happen to him, came forward and asked them, 'For whom are you looking?' They answered, 'Jesus of Nazareth.' Jesus replied, 'I am he.' Judas, who betrayed him, was standing with them. When Jesus said to them, 'I am he', they stepped back and fell to the ground. Again he asked them, 'For whom are you looking?' And they said, 'Jesus of Nazareth.' Jesus answered, 'I told you that I am he. So if you are looking for me, let these men go.' This was to fulfil the word that he had spoken, 'I did not lose a single one of those whom you gave me.' Then Simon Peter, who had a sword, drew it, struck the high priest's slave, and cut off his right ear. The slave's name was Malchus. Jesus said to Peter, 'Put your sword back into its sheath. Am I not to drink the cup that the Father has given me?'

So the soldiers, their officer, and the Jewish police arrested Jesus and bound him. First they took him to Annas, who was the father-in-law of Caiaphas, the high priest that year. Caiaphas was the one who had advised the Jews that it was better to have one person die for the people.

Simon Peter and another disciple followed Jesus. Since that disciple was known to the high priest, he went with Jesus into the courtyard of the high priest, but Peter was standing outside at the gate. So the other disciple, who was known to the high priest, went out, spoke to the woman who guarded the gate, and brought Peter in. The woman said to Peter, 'You are not also one of this man's disciples, are you?' He said, 'I am not.' Now the slaves and the police had made a charcoal fire because it was cold, and they were standing round it and warming themselves. Peter also was standing with them and warming himself.

Then the high priest questioned Jesus about his disciples and about his teaching. Jesus answered, 'I have spoken openly to the world; I have always taught in synagogues and in the temple, where all the Jews come together. I have said nothing in secret. Why do you ask me? Ask those who heard what I said to them; they know what I said.' When he had said this, one of the police standing nearby struck Jesus on the face, saying, 'Is that how you answer the high priest?' Jesus answered, 'If I have spoken wrongly, testify to the wrong. But if I have spoken rightly, why do you strike me?' Then Annas sent him bound to Caiaphas the high priest.

Now Simon Peter was standing and warming

himself. They asked him, 'You are not also one of his disciples, are you?' He denied it and said, 'I am not.' One of the slaves of the high priest, a relative of the man whose ear Peter had cut off, asked, 'Did I not see you in the garden with him?' Again Peter denied it, and at that moment the cock crowed.

Then they took Jesus from Caiaphas to Pilate's headquarters. It was early in the morning. They themselves did not enter the headquarters, so as to avoid ritual defilement and to be able to eat the Passover. So Pilate went out to them and said, 'What accusation do you bring against this man?' They answered, 'If this man were not a criminal, we would not have handed him over to you.' Pilate said to them, 'Take him yourselves and judge him according to your law.' The Jews replied, 'We are not permitted to put anyone to death.' (This was to fulfil what Jesus had said when he indicated the kind of death he was to die.)

Then Pilate entered the headquarters again, summoned Jesus, and asked him, 'Are you the King of the Jews?' Jesus answered, 'Do you ask this on your own, or did others tell you about me?' Pilate replied, 'I am not a Jew, am I? Your own nation and the chief priests have handed you over to me. What have you done?' Jesus answered, 'My kingdom is not from this world. If my kingdom were from this world, my followers would be fighting to keep me from being handed over to the Jews. But as it is, my kingdom is not from here.' Pilate asked him, 'So you are a king?' Jesus answered, 'You say that I am a king. For this I was born, and for this I came into the world, to testify to the truth. Everyone who belongs to the truth listens to my voice.' Pilate asked him, 'What is truth?'

After he had said this, he went out to the Jews again and told them, 'I find no case against him. But you have a custom that I release someone for you at the Passover. Do you want me to release for you the King of the Jews?' They shouted in reply, 'Not this man, but Barabbas!' Now Barabbas was a bandit.

Then Pilate took Jesus and had him flogged. And the soldiers wove a crown of thorns and put it on his head, and they dressed him in a purple robe. They kept coming up to him, saying, 'Hail, King of the Jews!' and striking him on the face. Pilate went out again and said to them, 'Look, I am bringing him out to you to let you know that I find no case against him.' So Jesus came out, wearing the crown of thorns and the purple robe. Pilate said to them, 'Here is the man!' When the chief priests and the police saw him, they shouted, 'Crucify him! Crucify him!' Pilate said to them, 'Take him yourselves and crucify him; I find no case against him.' The Jews answered him, 'We have a law, and according to that law he ought to die because he has claimed to be the Son of God.'

Now when Pilate heard this, he was more afraid than ever. He entered his headquarters again and asked Jesus, 'Where are you from?' But Jesus gave him no answer. Pilate therefore said to him, 'Do you refuse to speak to me? Do you not know that I have power to release you, and power to crucify you?' Jesus answered him, 'You would have no power over me unless it had been given you from above; therefore the one who handed me over to you is guilty of a greater sin.' From then on Pilate tried to release him, but the Jews cried out, 'If you release this man, you are no friend of the emperor. Everyone who claims to be a king sets himself against the emperor.'

When Pilate heard these words, he brought Jesus outside and sat on the judge's bench at a place called The Stone Pavement, or in Hebrew Gabbatha. Now it was the day of Preparation for the Passover; and it was about noon. He said to the Jews, 'Here is your King!' They cried out, 'Away with him! Away with him! Crucify him!' Pilate asked them, 'Shall I crucify your King?' The chief priests answered, 'We have no king but the emperor.' Then he handed him over to them to be crucified.

So they took Jesus; and carrying the cross by

himself, he went out to what is called The Place of the Skull, which in Hebrew is called Golgotha. There they crucified him, and with him two others, one on either side, with Jesus between them. Pilate also had an inscription written and put on the cross. It read, 'Jesus of Nazareth, the King of the Jews.' Many of the Jews read this inscription, because the place where Jesus was crucified was near the city; and it was written in Hebrew, in Latin, and in Greek. Then the chief priests of the Jews said to Pilate, 'Do not write, "The King of the Jews", but, "This man said, I am King of the Jews."' Pilate answered, "What I have written I have written." When the soldiers had crucified Jesus, they took his clothes and divided them into four parts, one for each soldier. They also took his tunic; now the tunic was seamless, woven in one piece from the top. So they said to one another, 'Let us not tear it, but cast lots for it to see who will get it.' This was to fulfil what the scripture says,

'They divided my clothes among themselves,
   and for my clothing they cast lots.'
And that is what the soldiers did.

Meanwhile, standing near the cross of Jesus were his mother, and his mother's sister, Mary the wife of Clopas, and Mary Magdalene. When Jesus saw his mother and the disciple whom he loved standing beside her, he said to his mother, 'Woman, here is your son.' Then he said to the disciple, 'Here is your mother.' And from that hour the disciple took her into his own home.

After this, when Jesus knew that all was now finished, he said (in order to fulfil the scripture), 'I am thirsty.' A jar full of sour wine was standing there. So they put a sponge full of the wine on a branch of hyssop and held it to his mouth. When Jesus had received the wine, he said, 'It is finished.' Then he bowed his head and gave up his spirit.

Since it was the day of Preparation, the Jews did not want the bodies left on the cross during the sabbath, especially because that sabbath was a day of great solemnity. So they asked Pilate to have the legs of the crucified men broken and the bodies removed. Then the soldiers came and broke the legs of the first and of the other who had been crucified with him. But when they came to Jesus and saw that he was already dead, they did not break his legs. Instead, one of the soldiers pierced his side with a spear, and at once blood and water came out. (He who saw this has testified so that you also may believe. His testimony is true, and he knows that he tells the truth.) These things occurred so that the scripture might be fulfilled, 'None of his bones shall be broken.' And again another passage of scripture says, 'They will look on the one whom they have pierced.'

After these things, Joseph of Arimathea, who was a disciple of Jesus, though a secret one because of his fear of the Jews, asked Pilate to let him take away the body of Jesus. Pilate gave him permission; so he came and removed his body. Nicodemus, who had at first come to Jesus by night, also came, bringing a mixture of myrrh and aloes, weighing about a hundred pounds. They took the body of Jesus and wrapped it with the spices in linen cloths, according to the burial custom of the Jews. Now there was a garden in the place where he was crucified, and in the garden there was a new tomb in which no one had ever been laid. And so, because it was the Jewish day of Preparation, and the tomb was nearby, they laid Jesus there.

- Who is really on trial in the exchange with Pilate? Who has the real authority? Jesus is the Truth, Pilate does not know what truth is. Am I a person of truth?

- I watch him subjected to disgraceful injustice and unspeakable torture and humiliation as he moves through his passion. He does not protest or cry out. How do I respond to injustice, ill-treatment, humiliation in my own life? What can I learn from him?

- 'I thirst.' Jesus once promised the Samaritan woman the water of eternal life with the Father, the life to which he is now going and for which he longs. He offers that water to us.

Saturday 3 April
Holy Saturday
Mark 16:1–7

When the sabbath was over, Mary Magdalene, and Mary the mother of James, and Salome bought spices, so that they might go and anoint him. And very early on the first day of the week, when the sun had risen, they went to the tomb. They had been saying to one another, 'Who will roll away the stone for us from the entrance to the tomb?' When they looked up, they saw that the stone, which was very large, had already been rolled back. As they entered the tomb, they saw a young man, dressed in a white robe, sitting on the right side; and they were alarmed. But he said to them, 'Do not be alarmed; you are looking for Jesus of Nazareth, who was crucified. He has been raised; he is not here. Look, there is the place they laid him. But go, tell his disciples and Peter that he is going ahead of you to Galilee; there you will see him, just as he told you.'

- The disciples are slow to believe in Jesus' resurrection. They are stubborn, mourning and weeping, stuck in a grey world. Perhaps I often feel that way? But Jesus does not despair of his followers. He gives them the extraordinary commission to bring good news to the whole of creation! Pope Francis echoes that call: every Christian is to be an evangeliser, to bring good news to those around them. This leaves no space for sulking or self-absorption or doubting!

Suscipe

Take, Lord, and receive all my liberty,
my memory, my understanding,
and my entire will,

all I have and call my own.
You have given all to me.

To you, Lord, I return it.
Everything is yours; do with it what you will.
Give me only your love and your grace;
that is enough for me.

— St Ignatius of Loyola

Prayer to Know God's Will

May it please the supreme and divine Goodness
to give us all abundant grace
ever to know his most holy will
and perfectly to fulfill it.

— St Ignatius of Loyola